I0634479

The Reality Shifters

Level one - The Desire to Become Aware

Table of Contents

Books by Nadine May
Awakening to the Ascension Series
Novel 1. The Reality Shifters – 2018 (Ingrids Journal – Romance)
Novel 2. Orphanage of Souls – 2019 (Richard's Journal – Romance)
Novel 3. Vanishing Worlds – 2020. (Annelies' Journal – Psychic awareness)
Novel 4. Parallel Realities – 2024 (Tulanda's walk-in Journal)
Novel 5. Riddles of the Prophet's Game – 2025 (POWAH – the Guide)
The Language of Light – workbook in Full colour 2021
The Language of Light – workbook in Grayscale 2021
Meditation on the Language of Light 2021 (Full colour) Seven. Doodle Symbology journals on the 7 Chakra channels in full colour or greyscale
The Body Codes of Light – workbook—(forthcoming)
The Self-Employed Housewife book 1 – 2018 (novel)
The Self-Employed Housewife book 2 – 2022 (novel)
The story of the Jaarsma Clan and their awakening was downloaded over a period of twenty years. *My love We are Going Home* was written in 1995 and published in 2001 this award-winning novel was twice updated.

Published by: The Power of Words – SA
Contact Details:
Website Author: https://nadinemay.company.site/
Author's blog: the End of Time https://nadinemay.com /
Novel Blog: https://allrealityshifters.wordpress.com
The Language of Light workbooks and journals: https://light-workerjournals.wordpress.com
ISBN – SKU: 9780796148971 print copy
978-0-796148-98-8 (e-book) Previously published by Kima Global Publishers. © Copyright Nadine May 2018
Cover Art by Author Nadine May

World rights by the Author. Except for small passages quoted for review purposes, no portion of this work may be reproduced, translated, adapted, stored in a retrieval system, or transmitted in any form or through any means, including electronic, mechanical, photocopying or otherwise, without the Author's permission.

Foreword / Dedication

After my dear soul mate of 22 years, Robin Beck, my publisher and the love of my life, passed away from this physical reality, I asked for guidance, especially to complete my soul purpose project, which involves writing about our awakening to our ascension through the genre of visionary fiction.

My years of research took me on several roller coasters with many different beliefs surrounding the questions: where we came from, who we are and why we choose to incarnate.

In 2001, I served as the book stylist and cover designer of Kima Global Publishers and travelled with Robin to many book fairs. During those years, we kept up our Spiritual science studies. Our motto was to make a difference in people's lives.

Robin was the kindest man alive. He passed over in January 2023, and it broke my heart. I thought the best was behind me, but as the staggering weight of despair and unforeseen circumstances descended, I knew I needed to regain control of my Soul's purpose, completing my visionary five-stage novels about the Jaarsma Clan. The duality of our lives and the power of perception gave me a chance to look back in wonderment and gratitude. It is that awareness that I try to bring with this novel, and at the same time, my grief lifted.

I have decided to release all my publications under 'The Power of Words', starting in April 2024, for humanity during the upcoming challenging years. Additionally, readers can access electronic and printed versions of my 'Awakening to Our Ascension' novels and workbooks.

I dedicate all my visionary fiction writings by acknowledging Robin Beck, who, during the month before his passing, started writing the first pages of the fifth novel in the Awakening to our Ascension series: The Prophet's Game.

Nadine May

Preface by Tulanda

No one knew me as Liesbeth, and only later, when I was about to write my journal, did my friends get to know me as Tulanda. My 'father,' one of the Galactic Superiors overseeing the Federation of the Twelve Planets, is in regular telepathic contact with my soul partner and me during our lives on Earth as Hans and Liesbeth.

My assignment as a walk-in will soon end; the reality of Time holds a different meaning for us both.

Many 'Reality Shifters' have already awakened into a new Earth by clearing and healing their karma and releasing their fear-based ego restrictions. By sharing their journey, the reader will still experience a tug-of-war between the light and the dark. People's awareness has shifted, but unfortunately, Outer Dark Forces have found a way of getting around this by getting a man on Earth to plunder Souls still asleep to their spiritual power!

I will share with the reader how we are all Divine beings participating physically by playing an Ascension Decoding Card Game titled *The Body Codes of Light* to encompass multiple spiritual dimensions while on the physical plane.

The incoming light frequency upgrades between 2012 and 2030 had not yet awakened everyone on Earth, so Ingrid's journal translation became my assignment. Many can now sustain fifth-dimensional consciousness while still existing in 3D/4D, and this journal will explain how this is possible. Ingrid's journal suggested that POWAH's Prologue, dated 1888–2019–2035, be omitted. The reason was to guide the reader through the story faster. They can be found under The Reality Shifters – Excerpt 1 https://allrealityshifters.wordpress.com/powah/the-[1]awakening-game-excerpt-1/[2]

Namasté

---

1. https://wordpress.com/page/allrealityshifters.wordpress.com/394

2. https://wordpress.com/page/allrealityshifters.wordpress.com/394

Liesbeth / Tulanda

Cast of Characters

The Jaarsma Clan represents a Soul group. The people of the Jaarsma Clan learn about the various density vibrational frequencies through the 22 excerpts about "Program Earth"(*published on the internet*) to prepare themselves for a new 5th-density level Earth reality realm.

- *Ingrid (Kitty) Barendse:* This is her story, translated into a novel, *The Reality Shifters,* by me (Tulanda)
- *POWAH*: A spiritual guide for the Jaarsma Clan from a higher frequency reality.
- *Sascia:* Ingrid's daughter, the photographer, is Jeroen's twin sister.
- *Jeroen:* Ingrid's son and twin brother of Sascia. He works for his grandfather's steel business.
- *Debbie:* Ingrid's younger daughter. She is a nurse in Utrecht.
- *Quincy:* Ingrid's younger sister who owns a health shop in Delft.
- *Jan:* Ingrid's late husband.
- *Ed:* Ingrid's late husband's brother is a good friend of Toon Haardens. He lives in Australia, where he is building a community.
- *Toon:* a philanthropist and a half-brother of Annelies who builds communities worldwide.
- *Roelof de Beer:* Contractor to Harry Brinks and husband of Tieneke, the art teacher.
- *Harry Brinks:* Ingrid's boss, owner of Pleasure Parks.
- *Tieneke:* Harry Brinks' daughter and artist who gives drawing and doodling workshops on the Language of Light.
- *Carla:* Ingrid's colleague at Pleasure Parks.

- *Piet:* Ingrid's colleague at Pleasure Parks.
- *Marijke:* Ingrid's colleague at Pleasure Parks.
- *Ula:* Ingrid's colleague at Pleasure Park.
- *Liesbeth:* Ingrid's magazine journalist friend rewrites the Awakening to Ascension diaries into novels. She becomes known as Tulanda, a walk-in hybrid and a Galectic Council Incarnated Member.

In the Crime scenes, you will also meet.

- *Nick du Toit:* a gambler, ex-husband of Jill, Otto's wife.
- *The Boss:* criminal.
- *Bruce:* criminal.
- *Iris:* criminal.
- *André:* a detective and colleague of Ben Jaarsma, Annelie's husband.

During the 12-week 'Reality Shifting' workshops, you get to know Annelies' friends and family.

- *Annelies Zwiegelaar: The Body Codes of Light workshop facilitator and part-owner* of the PrinseGracht Hotel in Apeldoorn. Her journal is titled *Vanishing Wolds*.
- *Fred Jaarsma:* Annelies' brother and owner of the bookshop "The Power of Words".
- *Ben:* Annelies' husband, who is an undercover agent for Interpol.
- *Hans:* Annelies' and Ben's adopted son, a walk-in and partner of Tulanda.
- *Otto:* Annelies' half-brother and civil engineer who is a good friend of Toon Haardens. He is the manager of "Buttercup Valley community" in Austria.
- *Jill:* Otto's wife, who is also a civil engineer. She manages all the cottages on the property.
- *Peter:* Otto's adopted son who manages the Half Way house in France.

- **Helen:** Peter's wife with their three children Timmy, Karin and baby Jenny.
- **Yolanda:** Annelies' niece works in the Power of Words bookshop.
She is the estranged wife of Piet, Ingrid's colleague at Pleasure Parks.
- **Connie:** Yolanda's daughter who helps her mother in the bookshop.
- **Gerrit:** Class participant and Artist.
- **Niels:** Class participant and computer technician.
- **Zola:** Class participant.
- **Wim:** Class participant.
- **Richard de Jong:** class participant, archaeologist, and manager of the Pannekoek. His journal is titled *Orphanage of Souls*.

Chapter 1
Mental Telepathy

Apeldoorn – Holland

"Are you awake?" The famous song of that title was playing on her car's internet radio. A sly smile dimpled her cheek as she recalled her mystical encounter of the previous night. The words softened her heart, reinstating her enthusiasm for life that crisp Tuesday morning. Strong, resolute hands holding the steering wheel started to drum with the beat. Ingrid's silk blouse, worn under her elegant suit, portrayed a graceful, sensual woman, mature yet still youthful. Her natural, curly, short auburn hair flattered her delicate, bone-structured face that a sculptor might have chiselled. Her large eyes with the same golden tone expressed her soft, feminine nature.

Apeldoorn's business centre hummed with activity. After parking her car, she noticed a big sign in a newly-opened bookshop called 'The Power of Words' advertising: The Body Codes of Light: workshops Starting Soon!

Good grief, how intriguing. The title of the workshop raised Ingrid's spirits. She dashed around the corner through the wide glass doors of Pleasure Parks' modern office building. The tall palms in the foyer half-hid the unoccupied receptionist's desk. The elevator door's infrared detector responded to her body heat, opening the doors, as her colleague CARLA, who looked like she'd just fallen out of bed, called out...

"Hi! Stunning suit! Trying to dazzle someone?"

Carla was a voluptuous, free-spirited, outspoken woman in her thirties. She was both clever and fun-loving with a good sense of humour. Her eyes teased, and her smile and glint all at the same time were pale blue, staring out of a soft, round face.

Ingrid loved her job. She oversaw the maintenance of twelve European holiday resorts, created artistic impressions for their new developments, and handled some PR work. All this kept her from being bored. The chief attractions of Pleasure Parks resorts were the exotic fantasy gardens with a wide range of bathing and sun tanning beaches combined with wave pools, gymnasiums, health clubs and shops galore. These extensive facilities are all housed under one large glass geodesic dome, which ensures a subtropical climate year-round.

She had been looking for the right job for some time. These were hectic times, with thousands of refugees relocated to Holland. Some who had received a residence permit in the Netherlands in the previous two years would like nothing better than to work for a living, so finding a job would be a miracle. Then, eighteen months earlier, this position became available, and her three grown-up children encouraged her to apply.

After her husband Jan's death, her move to the outskirts of the town of Apeldoorn had been challenging. Leaving the harbour city of Rotterdam, which she had shared with him for 26 years, closed a chapter in her life. They had been high school sweethearts and married when she was pregnant with the twins.

Ingrid glanced through the glass partition of her office. MARIJKE, her down-to-earth assistant, was late. She programmed and invoiced the holiday bookings from the ANWB VVV offices all over Holland into their database.

Marijke had lost her little boy, Kees, in a car accident four months previously, and she had great difficulty coming to terms with her loss.

Her grief still hung around her like glue. Her grave grey eyes, more vacant than ever, reflected the otherwise tailored suit that needed a wash. Thinking about Kees made Ingrid recall her grievous times after Jan's death, but her mystical encounter the previous night marked a turning point for her.

She was about to switch her computer on when suddenly she froze...

A message had appeared on her touch-screen monitor! The question was very bright and clear!

<Would you like to take part in the Body Codes of Light workshop?> How weird! Her computer! She had not yet switched it on! How was that possible? She sat for a moment like a statue. Nobody took any notice of her. Marijke popped her head around the door to apologise for being late. The words were still bold and straightforward, but her monitor was not on! She touched her screen, and then it went blank.

How weird! She first heard the song on the radio, 'Are you awake this morning'; then she saw the new bookshop that advertised a workshop on experiencing a Reality Shift, and now this. Were these coincidences? She had attended a creative doodling seminar titled the Language of Light, focusing on awakening her psychic strengths so that her awareness would go beyond her physical senses, but...was it happening?

The loud melody of her cordless desk phone jolted her back to the reality of the workplace. It was someone from the Tree Fern Landscapers Construction firm. Her thoughts were still somersaulting while she stared at her dark screen.

"To whom am I speaking?" she asked since a man's penetrating voice brought her back to the present.

TOON HAARDENS. This firm has changed hands. I see that we do a lot of business with your company." In a self-assured manner, he spoke to someone in the background who had just walked in.

When he handed her over to NEL, his receptionist, she picked up on his irritation with NEL. Her digital time display said nine twenty, so Ingrid felt the man was justified. After giving Nel the information Mr Haardens wanted, she was about to switch on her HP workstation when her screen lit up again like it did when a fatal error occurred. But the words!

<I ask you a question? Do you want to take part in the Body Codes of Light workshop?>

She jumped out of her chair as adrenaline surged through her bloodstream. Were the words meant for her? Slowly, she sat down again, staring at the large yellow letters on a blue screen.

Who are you?

With trembling fingers, she typed in response on her wireless keyboard, seeing to her amazement her italic text appearing underneath the question. Someone must be playing a trick on her, surely? Or her PC must be on!

<Nobody is playing a trick on you. I asked a question! And... I am you: a multidimensional spiritual being.>

That remark! With whom was she...? Everyone was working on their computers as if it were a typical day. Well, things were, but what was going on in her mind? Then, the text changed.

<I am your mind.>

That stunned her! Who was reading her mind?

Could you explain to me what you mean by my mind?

Her text showed up, so who was reading it?

<Your mind and the mind of the collective mind are all the same!>

Oh, sure! Meaning...what?

Her heart was pounding.

<You live in an intelligent and benevolent holographic universe. Have you forgotten?>

What did that mean, holographic? Yes, she knew all about her holographic artist's impressions for the new Pleasure Park; that was her job, but...who was this? Her heart began to pound, beating so hard she felt it would burst from pure astonishment.

< Truly, I speak because you are always asking questions and are entitled to the truth. Did you not ask to live this life to your full potential? The time is critical!>

She stared spellbound, wondering how on earth someone could know her thoughts. With shaking fingers, she typed...

Are you real? Let me know HOW you can express yourself on my computer when it is not on.

Marijke stuck her head around the office door.

"Ingrid, are you busy? Have you got a minute?"

"I've got myself into a muddle; I'll be with you soon." She repressed her tone in a soft, calm voice, but inside, she felt electrified with curiosity. Ingrid was good at viewing life objectively, but this was not.

<I am the wind, the ocean and the air; If you need to call me by a name, you may call me P–O–W–A–H.> appeared on her screen.

It was real! Her computer was off! ... There was no taskbar, no icons, just what looked like a test screen. Was she the only person seeing it? She was not in a trance. She could hear all the noises around her. Nobody had taken any notice of her. Was she experiencing a higher frequency of thought? Lately, she has listened to a constant high-pitched ringing sound with no external source. What was going on? Her bewilderment was once again interrupted by Marijke.

"Sorry, Ingrid, but I have a client on the line. She wants to book her holiday bungalow in Tilburg for July, but she wants to know if there are any Buttercups or Cup of Gold creepers growing at the new complex in Tilburg. She's very insistent. She read somewhere that those flowers are very poisonous, and she's worried about her small children." She would have to find that out from Nel, whom she had just spoken to and whose firm handled the landscaping.

"Marijke, tell the client you will look into it and call her back. That will keep her happy."

Ingrid peered at her now blank computer screen. The text stated that she had asked to live this life to her full potential. Now, who would know her private thoughts? She turned on her workstation, and her familiar taskbar and icons appeared after a moment. She resumed typing on her keypad to whoever it was while her blood was pulsating in her throat.

POWAH? Where are you from? You say you are me! Do you mean you are speaking into my mind?

This was so silly! What was she doing? Nothing happened! That felt even more unnerving. Was she texting to herself? Was this all happening in her imagination? While staring at the terminal, she recalled the extraordinary experience of the last evening.

How do you know what I want?

She typed again. She had fallen for it as if someone was playing a trick on her.

<Do you know what you want, Kitty?>

YES, I do! But...how did you know my nickname?

Her amazement increased...thinking about her reply.

<What exactly do you want to know, and why?> After that question, she just sat there transfixed. Why?

She wanted to know the absolute truth about life! She would then understand life better and why bad things happen to good people. Why are all the tragedies hitting many parts of the world? Her mind raced as new text jumped suddenly back onto her screen:

<Kitty, you have the right intention; that is everything in life. You want to experience things, to know something. From now on, we will have a working relationship. You will grow in awareness of the DNA 'coding system' we are working on together.

It's time to prepare you and others for your reality-shifting process.>

Love P–O–W–A–H

Her screen now reverted to the regular screen saver. Who was reading her mind? That was how it felt. What could have been meant by 'a DNA coding system'? What was she getting herself into now? Who was communicating with her on her computer? How? From where?

Ingrid wondered who POWAH was. Could the five letters be a name? Was it all happening in her mind? Had she become psychic? Her whole body was in turmoil. She struggled to concentrate on work for the rest of the day.

Ingrid kept things to herself and almost forgot to phone Nel about the Buttercup flower details Marijke had been waiting for. She looked it up on Google and dialled Nel's office before going home. "Tree Fern Landscaping." It was the same resonant voice she had spoken to earlier. Where was Nel? She cleared her throat as if...why was she so nervous?

"Hi, I'm Ingrid from Pleasure Parks. May I speak to someone about the type of plants you use in the landscaping of our resorts?" She had never heard of 'Buttercups' growing in Brabant's Heather fields, where a construction company had built another Pleasure Park holiday resort.

"I spoke to you this morning. What would you like to know? Perhaps I can help?"

"We have received a query from one of our clients. She asked if Buttercups or Cup of Gold creepers are growing in our new Tilburg complex. They are very poisonous. Do you have any idea?" She wondered if he knew anything about plants. There was a silence.... Did she hear...or feel...him chuckling?

"Ingrid, I doubt whether this firm has used either of these plants in the past, but I will investigate the matter. Shall I come back to you on this?" His masterful tone sounded amused. Ingrid was very receptive to emotional undertones in people's voices and picked up much more than most people with this man. She repressed a stirring feeling of...what?

Being naturally curious, she asked. "This Cup-of-Gold creeper, what plant is it? I have never heard of it."

"I am not surprised, Ingrid, some species of Buttercup flowers grow in the mountains. But the Cup-of-Gold creepers are subtropical and very spectacular, with yellow flowers in a cup-like shape. The big subtropical types could have narcotic properties. Your client is probably mixing it up with a large shrub called Angel Trumpets, which is poisonous," he voiced knowledgeably. Mr. Haardens was very informative and charming but somewhat imposing. They seemed to have an undercurrent mental connection. She thanked him for his enlightening chat about the flowers, asking him to phone back so that she could give the client an answer.

Something about his voice was almost familiar. But what was it? Why did he make her feel... what, interested?

"That I will, Ingrid," He replied. She was puzzled by his change of tone, which had become almost playful when she heard music playing in the background.

It was the same song she had heard on the radio that morning, titled: **Are You Awake?'**

Ingrid longed for the summer to arrive, but heavy clouds were building up. Her floor-to-ceiling office windows looked out over Apeldoorn's main shopping street. Many people huddled up in rain gear. She remembered that Beekbergen had a market on a Tuesday. On the way home, she would detour there to buy fresh groceries.

When she closed her office, an inner joy —a sense of rapture — was still with her, due to the rather baffling dialogue with POWAH.

She was the last to leave. When stepping out of the lift, ULA, a vibrant redhead receptionist of Pleasure Parks remarked on her cheerful ambience with a speculative glance, asking her if she had a date as she tidied her desk before going home herself. If only Ula knew! She did feel different. Wouldn't anyone, after what she had experienced today and last evening?

"Ingrid! You missed a creepy caller asking about you; he refused to give his name." Ula's frown showed discomfort. She didn't know anyone you would call creepy.

"I'm sure he'll phone back if it is important." Ula proudly showed off her ring, smiling again. She was going to meet her fiancé's mother for the first time. Ula's boyfriend was a detective like Marijke's husband.

***

She decided to visit the new bookshop, The Power of Words, to gather more information on the Buttercup flower and to inquire about the Body Codes of Light workshop.

A young blonde girl with sparkling blue eyes behind the counter excitedly informed her that it was their opening day. The shop had an extensive selection of books, including an esoteric section, and displayed vintage Anton Pieck posters at the door.

"I'm CONNIE. My mom went out momentarily, so I'm standing in for her. What can I do for you?" Connie looked as if she were expecting her.

"I would like to look up something in a plant book. And about this workshop you advertised, do you know anything about it?"

"Something to do with genetic decoding of your DNA blueprint through sound. Have you been asked to write the first journal?" Connie speculated.

"What journal are you referring to?" Ingrid's mind leapt in amazement.

"Oh, I overheard my aunt Annelies informing my mom. She said a lady in your description would ask about her workshops while browsing our bookshop today. This lady would write the first awakening journal."

"Who's Annelies? I have no idea...what..." Ingrid was perplexed.

More customers entered the shop, so Connie attended to them. She did not inquire any further, but would remember the name 'Annelies'!

***

As rain hurtled down relentlessly, it cut her vision to almost nil. The driveway of the Prinsengracht Hotel was upon her so fast that she did not see the Tesla sports car in time. To avoid it, she drove into a ditch. She rested her head on the steering wheel, her heart pounding. The knocking on the window broke her shock.

"Are you all right?" A towering figure asked as he stood there getting drenched. People from the hotel gathered around the car. She lowered her window to reassure him.

"I'm so sorry, I'm fine, please go inside. You will all get soaked."

"*What a beauty.*"

When the man asked where she was heading, she was tongue-tied. Had she honestly heard him telepathically? All she saw was his mouth.

She dismissed her thoughts and reassured him once again. His concern touched her.

"Yolanda." He called to his companion. "Go inside. I'll follow her to see if she is okay; you go on." His dynamic voice caused an uproar, jolting her back to today's phone call. What was going on with her?

He got back into his electric sports car and followed her. When she parked near the market and waved at him, he paused, looking at her as if he recalled something. Then he hooted and drove off.

At the food market in Beekbergen, the rain had stopped; the fish seller cried tunelessly, "Fresh herring." His voice lunged at the min-

gling crowd, hoping to attract a buyer. Ingrid reflected on all that
had happened the previous night.

***

While soaking in the bath the previous night, she had a strange
experience hearing a voice! She knew she was utterly alone in the
house. She grinned as she recalled looking everywhere after her
bath to satisfy herself that she was alone. The words: *"My beloved,
can't you remember me?"* It still rang in her ear. "Who are you?"
She had responded aloud, but of course, there was no answer. Hearing herself speaking to nobody made her grin to herself. Her father
used to tease her about it.

However, the voice was so authentic! Then she heard clearly, *"Kitty!
Wake up, be still and listen!"* Except that it was different! Both
phrases had been as precise as if someone else were speaking typi-
cally. That is, if one accepted conversing in verbal sounds as stan-
dard.

"Listen to whom?" she replied while her heart had skipped a beat,
speculating that if someone was in the bathroom with her, why had
she not seen anything?

Ingrid could still not explain what had happened to herself, but the
feeling of rapture, of being in love, as if she had never been alone,
was profound. Going to sleep after this most mysterious experience
had been challenging.

***

A sudden cloudburst switched her mind to the present just in time
to reach her car with her groceries. The traffic was heavy while driving home, and her Internet car radio was interrupted by a voice
saying...

"Good morning, you're listening to Apeldoorn radio, and I'm Rob. We have an important announcement to make. Due to a significant surge in the sun's electromagnetic X-ray flux, transmission disruptions may occur. We cannot rule out the possibility of power outages. But we have an expert in the studio who can shed some light on this. Mr. Haardens, would you please explain to our listeners what's happening? The broadcaster requested.

Ingrid was struck by the name 'Haardens'!

"There is no immediate cause for panic at all. This has been going on for a long time. The effects of climate change are starting to show. We know that our Earth's weather has been greatly affected for aeons by the increase in electromagnetic radiation," ...a deep, resonant tone replied.

That voice! Had she not just heard the same...?

The tall figure in the fancy Sports car was in a hurry. Why? To give an interview? The new owner of Nel's firm's name was Haardens. But how would a man who had just taken over a construction firm be connected to investigations into weather patterns?

"Was that the only reason for our hot weather, the global warming theory?" the announcer asked.

"We know that the Earth's magnetic field shifting is directly linked to this increased solar activity. The effect on bird, plant and marine life is profound in Australia and New Zealand, where the ozone hole is expanding." Mr. Haardens stated with conviction.

"You are saying that the sun is also affecting our weather?"

"Earth's magnetic field changes over time because it is generated by a motion of molten iron alloys in its outer core. The Earth's field reverses, and the North and South Magnetic Poles relatively abruptly switch places. Earth's magnetic field has flipped its polarity many times over the millennia. Earth's last magnetic reversal took place 786,000 years ago. It can happen very quickly and causes climate changes, but not necessarily due to global warming."

"You are implying that Global warming is not true?"

"The Great Global Warming scare during the last twenty years is the brainchild of a former vice president turned climate change activist. Funding and political factors influence his documentary film promoting an opinion on global warming."

"You are implying that global warming is not caused by pollution, which traps extra infrared radiation?"

"Correct. I do not believe that human CO_2 emissions cause global warming. All solar activity is driven by the solar magnetic field that is constantly shifting. The current state of extreme weather and warming is caused by the Sun, not by trace gas elements from our industries."

"So, we do not have to take the rising of tides seriously?"

"No, I did not say that. I suspect political elections are being won on promises to invest money to protect against flooding, like warnings from scientists about the rising sea levels. In the worst-case scenario, the rate of sea-level rise could reach a foot per decade by the 22nd century, about ten times faster than today, but nothing like some websites predict."

"So, you are saying we in Holland do not have to worry about the sea levels wiping us out?"

Mr. Haardens was silent for a while, and her intuition told her he was getting impatient with the interviewer.

"In response to your message, I want to clarify that the information circulating online about the rising tides caused by global warming is not entirely accurate. It's a ploy to create fear and confusion among people. A psychological battle is going on to influence how we perceive our planet and the universe around it, which can significantly impact all life forms and hinder the physical and spiritual growth of the human race.

"What you are implying is that great changes are coming that have to be taken seriously, but that the human population's perceptions are deceived? That goes beyond me."

"OK, so let's get back to our planet's changes in the ionosphere during geomagnetic storms. Strong electrical currents driven along the Earth's surface during auroral events can disrupt electric power grids all over our planet."

"Oh, you mean we might all be cut off from the internet due to no electricity?"

"Yes, that could be, so we need to start planning for alternative living strategies before facing blackout conditions, meaning no electricity."

Ingrid wondered whether this could be the same man. He seemed knowledgeable, but what connection would a construction guy have with Solar flares and the tipping of Earth's Magnetic Poles?

"That does sound alarming. Having no power. What preparations do people need to make without electricity, our network and internet technologies?"

The implications of what the interviewer called alarming made her sad. How many people listening would wonder what life would be like without the internet and computers?

"We have prepared a website on the Internet for anyone who wants to learn more, and further lectures on the effects of this solar activity will start soon."

"Was that the only reason for our hot weather, the global warming theory?" the announcer asked.

"Yes, and we know that the shifting of Earth's magnetic field is directly linked to this increased solar activity, "Mr. Haardens said with conviction.

"You are saying that the sun also affects our warm weather?"

"There are various changes currently taking place, and we need to assess their full impact on a global scale and look at what specific preparations are essential. Anyone who still doubts the onset of global warming needs only look at what's happening in the Arctic and Antarctic, where glaciers are retreating. Icebergs are calving at a scary rate."

"So, the rising of tides has to be taken seriously?"

"Yes, but even more so, we need to plan for alternative living strategies that might be necessary when facing blackout conditions, meaning no electricity soon."

Ingrid wondered whether this could be the same man. He seemed knowledgeable, but what connection would a construction guy have with global warming?

"That does sound alarming. Which comes first, flooding of major proportions or having no power? What preparations do people need to make when there is no electricity, not to mention the water levels?"

The implications of what the interviewer called alarming made her sad. How many people listening would wonder where to go if the sea levels rose, especially in a country where the sea levels were higher than the ground they all lived on?

"We have prepared a website on the Internet for anyone who wants to learn more, and further lectures on the effects of this solar activity will start soon."

Mr. Haardens continued in the same knowledgeable tone as the man who had described the Buttercup flower. The radio announcer thanked Mr. Haardens and told the listeners that a program would be scheduled later.

***

When Ingrid arrived at her driveway, she stretched her still, youthful, curved body full length. She was trying to regain her stability and recalled the music playing in the background when she spoke to Mr. Haardens. There was something about his... Was she suddenly seeing and hearing things? Gee, first the voices, then the message on the massive screen at work today! Could it all be in her imagination? She couldn't tell anyone because no one would take her seriously.

"Guess what, I am communicating out loud with a voice in my head," she mumbled while running through the rain, grabbing her groceries from the boot of her car. "Oh, really?" she mimicked, reaching for her front door, which was all wet.

"Yes, these texts are addressed to me through my computer when switched off!" She giggled, and she could read my mind! People would look at her as if she had suddenly lost her senses. Observing herself while scratching for her keys made her feel silly.

The next-door neighbour waved while she dumped unwanted goods at the curb for the garbage collection the following morning. She must be spring-cleaning. Ingrid waved back.

Fluffball, her ginger cat, was sitting at the window meowing. She sidestepped her mail as she opened her front door.

An impressive blue envelope stating **"Dear Kitty – Excerpt one"** fell out as she picked it up. The printing seemed familiar, and so did the symbols, but not the watermark.

Excerpt One[1]

Program Planet Earth

The Body Codes of Light preparation manual

After reading the manual, her hands were shaking. Sitting on the kitchen chair, Fluffball in her lap and her wet, dark curly hair dripping, she could hardly stop reading the contents repeatedly.

She read why planet Earth's Ether body frequency layer is fast-evolving and how important it is for people to focus primarily on love, forgiveness, peace, harmony, balance, acceptance, and oneness.

---

1. https://allrealityshifters.wordpress.com/powah/the-awakening-game-excerpt-1/

The name POWAH at the bottom of the printout must have been the same person she had encountered on her screen at the office. How could he have now sent her step one of a manual on paper?

It further read that changes happening at a galactic level will soon influence Earth's reality grid, and humanity's accustomed lifestyles may never be the same again.

In that new shop, the girl Connie had asked if she would write the first journal; had she not mentioned Annelies? Was she going to write about the twenty-two fragmented parts of what? Herself...mentioned in excerpt one. Yes, she understood very well that the people in her life were often reflective mirrors of herself. It's difficult to grasp how, but had she asked for this? Why the hidden parts? She knew she had an inner desire to attract individuals who felt as she did about the real meaning of being alive, but was this the result?

The pelting rain grew more insistent as Fluffball purred on her lap. Was she supposed to include this 'Program Planet Earth' manual in her journal? She noticed that the text 'Excepts One' was a hyperlink.

It was the first time she read of a frequency layer, whatever that was, but the promise that she would be welcomed into a parallel reality where a guide would reveal the 'Riddle' of The Prophet Game. Now that sounded very intriguing!

Ingrid's inner turmoil created a strong need for her to share her thoughts; she could hear Jan saying, "Ingrid, you are getting like your sister Quincy, "More up in the clouds than down on Earth!"

Had she imagined it all? Was it all just her fantasy? If only she could speak to her clairvoyant sister, Quincy, who was on a tour with people from a health centre in Delft. Quincy had her health shop there.

When the phone rang in the hallway, her friend Liesbeth's face sprang to mind. Ingrid had always been good at guessing who was on the other end of the line.

"So, you knew it was me?" Liesbeth laughed.

"Yes! How did you guess? How are you? When did you get back?" Liesbeth was a freelance literary agent who wrote articles for several scientific magazines. It had been a while since she'd seen her.

"Ingrid, can I meet you tomorrow after work at the Pannekoek, near you? A friend gave me a pamphlet about a workshop that is starting soon. I'm sure you'll be interested. It is all about how to deal with experiencing a reality shift." Her voice carried an excited tone.

"You're kidding? Do you mean these Body Codes of Light-related workshops? I've also seen it advertised in that new shop close to my office building. Gosh, what a coincidence."

She was tempted to share her experiences with Liesbeth there and then, but she kept quiet because she still couldn't believe it herself. Ingrid knew she could fantasise about people rather than dealing with real life. She also didn't cope well with spontaneous happenings.

After her shower and while she was brushing her natural curly auburn hair, she suddenly heard an inner voice again loud and clear saying:

"Kitty! Be still and listen to your heart to experience the magic of who you are!"

Chapter 2
The Body Codes of Light

An Introduction to a Game.

Returning to work was like taking on a new chapter in her life. Being disappointed made her angry with herself.

"Ingrid, I need the original aerial view photo. You have it stored on your external hard drive." Piet de Wit whined.

"Why?" She peered into the floor manager's shifty eyes. PIET made her skin crawl. His sallow complexion reflected his poor health, and he was very underweight for his height. Ingrid's burning gaze poured into his soul like boiling tar. Piet's mouth frothed with fury. His pestering about the drawings for the French complex started to annoy her. Ingrid could be very aloof.

"Never mind why! Have you got it?"

"No, not here in my office. Why the sudden interest?" Gosh, he was getting under her skin.

"I have my reasons! What did you do with your external hard drive?"

"Good grief, don't be so secretive! Remember you gave me the one I'm working on two weeks ago?" Her tone flew at him.

"So, what did you do with the original aerial photo?" he snapped.

"Bitch you know very well what I mean."

"Look for it yourself." She was startled by her sudden telepathic sensitivity.

"Piet, stop bothering me. His eyes were hot and bright, and moisture was across his upper lip. "Phone head office and ask for the original photo; I'm sure they saved it in Cloud storage." Her coolness disguised her rage.

"One day, you'll be sorry for how you talk to me." He yelled back and stormed out of her office.

Ingrid's blood was still boiling with anger after Piet's outburst when her phone rang. What was he insinuating? She answered in a professional but slightly abrupt manner.

"Still at the job, are you? I'm impressed. I promised to phone you back with the information on the buttercup flower. Are you always that quick and efficient?" Mr Haardens' masterful tone acted as a catalyst.

Good grief, she'd forgotten to call back and tell him it had been sorted with the client. She should have apologised, but felt flustered by his undertone.

"I think so. Aren't you?" she replied instead. It was out before she realised it. What had made her say that? She was usually not so abrupt.

After a short silence, she apologised for her rudeness, explaining that someone else had influenced her reaction. Somewhat annoyed at herself for being so irritable, she could almost feel his thoughts as if he were probing into her mind. *"It must be...?"* That's impossible! Was he questioning himself? Surely, that must have been her mind talking to itself? She didn't know this, Mr. Haardens. Could he be the same man who had spoken on the radio the day before?

"You have a lively mind, Ingrid. By the way, I'm glad you weren't reacting to me. I will speak to you again," he laughed as if he knew something she did not before he hung up. What did he mean by a lively mind? Oh, well, at least he was not offended by her manner.

He felt like a somewhat challenging personality who might not take 'no' for an answer. She speculated about his appearance. A powerful voice didn't always match the physical form.

***

As she passed the new shop on the way to the coffee house, a new big sign in the window read "Decoding Workshops / Starting Soon!

Connie, the salesgirl, waved at her to come inside. Ingrid hoped that Connie's mother would be there.

"I think your name is Ingrid, isn't it?" she said, biting her lower lip.

"Yes! How did you know?"

"My mother asked me to give you this." The girl handed her a blue envelope, making her shaky. She had never given Connie her name. Other customers were waiting for her, so she left.

***

The Pannekoek coffee shop was across the street. She spotted Liesbeth through the window, waiting for her at a corner table. As she was about to greet her friend, her mouth gaped in absolute astonishment at Liesbeth's appearance! She looked at least ten years younger than she had when she had last seen her four months earlier!

"What has happened to you? What artefacts did you find on that dig that you joined? A rejuvenating tonic?" Her voice leapt in amazement as she hugged her. She thought Liesbeth's appearance might be due to a new non-surgical and powerful anti-ageing treatment to counteract the decline in enzyme activity levels. Her sister Quincy's health shop was promoting it.

Liesbeth was five years younger, around 40, but now looked in her early thirties. She was tall with a delicately sculpted nose, bright, dark brown eyes, and satiny, suntanned skin surrounded by playful, shiny dark ringlets that gave her an almost aristocratic Egyptian look. Her smile expressed warmth that was difficult to describe without concern or vanity. She was the most compassionate woman Ingrid had ever known.

"Hi! Richard will join us, and I've ordered two cappuccinos."

"Who's Richard, a new boyfriend?" She admired Liesbeth's stunning, glowing expression as if...Something had happened, but what was it?

"Ingrid! I've heard all about you," a man in his late thirties, quite attractive in an intellectual way, remarked while serving them two steaming coffees, his lively eyes conveying an alert mind. A rubber band casually held back his longish, wavy, dark brown hair. His thoughtful dark brown eyes turned into a smile of amused friendliness and pleasure, which aroused feelings of warmth and something more.

"Well, you have me at a disadvantage, for I know nothing about you." Ingrid liked him on the spot. He was pretty charismatic but far too young for her.

"Ingrid, as you know, I joined a group of archaeologists in Egypt. They were investigating some very new, secret sites at Luxor. It was my job to write a report on their findings for the sponsors of this dig.

Richard was with this group of archaeologists."

Richard explained how he took over the expedition from his late brother, who had been the organiser. He knew about all the preparations his brother had processed two years in advance, mainly handling the authorities, meaning the red tape.

"Richard is a part-time lecturer at the University of Utrecht," Liesbeth voiced proudly.

"Oh! What subjects do you lecture in?" He looked very young to be a lecturer.

"Egyptian mythology, mainly on the translations of their Hiero-glyphic scripts, and lately I'm looking into another symbolic lan-guage used long ago'." The coffee shop became busy, so Richard ex-cused himself, saying he would join them later.

"Wow, what an interesting guy. I love his hairstyle; both creative and sophisticated all in one."

The Pannekoek was a famous coffee and snack bar. It advertised the many holiday attractions of Gelderland on the walls. Customers could write their remarks on a sizeable electronic keypad at the en-trance.

"Richard is managing this coffee shop for the owner." Liesbeth con-tinued. Ingrid raised her eyebrows speculatively, but Liesbeth ig-nored her glance.

"His aunt, who is visiting her children in South Africa, owns the coffee shop, and he needed the money. The passing of his brother Theo has been a financial as well as an emotional ordeal. You're wondering if he is my boyfriend, but he is not, so stop scheming. I can read your mind. He's just an excellent friend." Liesbeth pushed her playfully.

"Really?" Liesbeth ignored Ingrid's teasing undertone.

Liesbeth's pamphlet about the 'Decoding workshops' on the phone looked intriguing. It covered many creative class exercises where one would make one's deck of cards. The decoding of our genetic blueprint seemed to be translatable due to the 22 spacings occupied on the holographic grid.

Her heart was beating from astonishment. Had this POWAH not mentioned something about it? As she was reading, the coffee shop noises started to fade away. Making your own 22 individual cards promises to be a creative adventure. It is mentioned that by creating these cards, hidden potentials would be revealed, including memo-ries of the possibility of physical ascension. Ingrid recalled Connie telling her about this genetic decoding related to sound.

"Are you both interested? I know about Annelies through Theo, my deceased brother." Richard queried when he brought them their favourite snack, two extra-large vegetarian spring rolls known as loempias. Ingrid jerked when she heard the name Annelies! Richard shared what he knew about the decoding workshops while helping customers. Ingrid had difficulty not letting her inner turmoil get the better of her. She was so unprepared for all this synchronicity.

"Richard's deceased brother had known Annelies when she assembled the material for the workshops and the card game with the help of a 'guide.'" Liesbeth added, peering at her frowning.

"Really?" Ingrid's voice leapt in astonishment, thinking of POWAH and knowing her friend was probing her mind.

"Yes. That's how I reacted at first, doubtful." Richard leaned over to clear the table.

"Annelies is looking for participants willing to write a journal." He added.

"What for? Why?" she asked.

Richard shrugged his shoulders. "I guess it is writing a journal about our awakening while creating our cards. My brother often mentioned Annelies; that is why I'm curious, and I immediately thought of Liesbeth, who told me that you might be as well." They both waited for her response.

"I'm very keen to find out more about it," Ingrid swallowed her genuine bewilderment while her palms started to sweat, thinking about the envelope Connie had given her.

"Good, I'll phone her now."

Richard worked hard. The coffee shop was noisy because all eight tables were occupied. He looked like an attractive man, younger than her friend, but why had Liesbeth denied the boyfriend part? Richard returned to their table to tell them Annelies had been waiting for his call!

"She is looking forward to meeting us and asked if one of us is called Ingrid."

"Really?" Liesbeth arched her eyebrows.

She ignored her friend's nudge to speak up. She couldn't share her encounter yet because she wasn't ready to disclose the bizarre computer incident with POWAH. Even the excerpt she had mysteriously received held her back. Richard was unknown, and she was still somewhat wary about explaining something so airy-fairy to a stranger. Liesbeth was a friend, but lately, she felt she had to be cautious. Too many unexplained phenomena were happening.

All three would join the 'introductory class' the following evening. They arranged to meet again the next day at the Pannekoek after work. They would drive together to Annelies' home on the Veluwe, where she gave the workshops.

Ingrid was about to open her umbrella as she stepped out of the coffee shop into the rain when a tall, well-built man bumped into her. "Uh-huh. We are in a hurry." His voice triggered an immediate sensation. For a moment, their eyes connected, and for a split second, the depth of his glance overwhelmed her like a tidal wave.

**

The rain was pelting down when she arrived at her driveway. She felt shaky after that confrontation. His penetrating gaze had made her heart jump.

"Where have you been? I have missed my supper." After preparing cat food, she checked for telephone messages. One was from Debbie, her younger daughter, to say she would be coming home for the weekend.

Ingrid still missed her three children. She hoped by now to have heard something from the twins Jeroen or Sascia; her twenty-six-year-old twins were very independent.

Jeroen worked for the family's steel construction firm when her late husband was ill. After Jan died, Jeroen returned to complete his studies in Eindhoven. He then impulsively took his last semester off and went backpacking to 'find himself', as he called it. Ingrid realised that Jeroen had taken on the role of the man of the house very seriously when he knew his father was very ill. She wondered if he would have chosen to follow in the family business. Jan's dad, Dennis Barendse, who still ran his steel company, had been happy about Jeroen's decision to finish his studies.

The music from her audio system brought her back to the present while revitalising her energy field. What a shower or bath did for her physical body, music did for her whole being.

Ingrid was relieved that it had stopped raining. She opened the sliding door leading onto the veranda. Everything smelled fresh and ready for summer to arrive. Her thoughts went back to what the girl had said in the shop.

She settled down with a glass of wine on her outside table and Fluffball on her lap and opened the blue envelope from Connie. She held her breath in great anticipation.

Excerpt Two[1]

Program Planet Earth

The Dimensions and their Densities

She was spellbound. Excerpt two was also hyperlinked, but it was definitely for her. The five-card game levels, including descriptions of the body codes of light, made her wonder. Was it something to do with her DNA codes? If she wrote a journal about her desire to become aware, thinking of the diary beside her bed, how could she know the absolute truth? This decoding card game had a connection with the shop. Was everything already planned without her knowing about it?

---

1. https://allrealityshifters.wordpress.com/powah/the-awakening-game-excerpt-2/

Oh, she needed to talk to someone about all this. Why her, of all people? Now, she wished she had confided in Liesbeth about POWAH. Her fear of making a fool of herself had stopped her from sharing.

Throughout her marriage, she had tried that. The fear of being ridiculed was still genuine to her. She'd been on her own for over two years since Jan had died, and it still felt lonely at times. She would turn 45 this year, but dating did not interest her. Most of the interesting men were married anyway.

Ingrid had learned a lot about herself during their twenty-four-year marriage. Some friends had described their relationship as stormy. At least she'd become emotionally and mentally independent.

When Jan passed over, it felt as if she had lost a Soul mate who had been her best teacher, her best friend and, just before he got ill, her best lover. Those memories had blocked her from a new relationship. She liked being on her own. She did not anticipate meeting anyone when she joined Liesbeth at functions. Nobody stimulated her, and she hated idle chitchat.

She had met Liesbeth at a party that she had been persuaded to attend by her sister, Quincy, just after Jan had died. It was the first outside activity she had participated in, and she had fun after all. Liesbeth had approached them both because she needed to write about the health shop for a magazine. They clicked immediately.

Liesbeth owned her own house on the outskirts of Apeldoorn. When Ingrid told her of the job offer, her friend encouraged her. Together, they looked for a place for her to live. Meeting up with her again, Ingrid could still not get over the noticeable change in her. Not only did she look younger, but it was also something else she could not name. It was a change that took away the look of any age!

When the phone rang in the hallway, she knew it was Debbie, her youngest.

"Mom, my train arrives at 11:15 on Friday evening. I want to come directly after my late shift instead of Saturday morning. Will that be alright?

"Great! I'll be at the station," Ingrid bubbled. Her youngest, Debbie, was a fully qualified nurse at the Academic Hospital in Utrecht. It felt like life was taking a turn, so she decided to pamper herself with a detoxifying treatment.

***

After she had arranged everything around her bathtub, she settled languorously into the warm, soapy bubble bath, allowing all the tensions of the day to ease out. Her feet just reached the top while her head rested on a towel. Her short, curly, auburn, brown hair fell playfully about her oval face, creating an effect of agelessness. Her well-shaped, firm body had not lost its youthfulness, even after giving birth to three children. She revelled in having this time to herself and contemplated what POWAH had written.

She pondered on the five levels of the decoding game, starting with the first level. POWAH said that the decoding would awaken her to her Soul's full potential, or was it her oversoul? Not that she knew or understood what was meant by an over-soul. She should look it up on the internet. And what about the 'Riddle' of The Prophet's Game? Oh, how weird...was it all for real?

Back at the office

"Hello, Ingrid, what time is it?" Carla called out as they arrived simultaneously by car at the parking area near the office. The dull, overcast sky held the promise of rain again.

"It's 08:15, five minutes to browse in that new shop." Carla had to buy a present for her sister's birthday. Ingrid spotted Marijke sitting inside on her haunches, in the corner, engrossed in a book. They were both very aware of Marijke's silent despair.

Carla inquired what she was reading while Ingrid approached a very artistic-looking woman with long blond hair at the counter. When her blue eyes met hers, Ingrid recognised that she was a friend of Tieneke, the lady who gave mind drawing workshops. She recalled meeting her at Tieneke's Language of Light doodling classes a year ago. This creative workshop revealed a lot about herself. "You're Yolanda, aren't you?"

"Ingrid! I'm so glad to meet you again. Did Connie give the envelope yesterday?"

"Yes, she did, but I was surprised it was for me." Mother and daughter did look alike. Yolanda was about to explain when Carla and Marijke reminded her of the time. Yolanda said that she would see her at Annelies' place that evening.

***

Ingrid's office phone blared out its caller tune. The air was charged with tension as holiday bookings had begun. Before she could say anything, a familiar man's voice queried, "Ingrid, we spoke about Buttercups the other day." She tried to imagine what he would look like. His voice reminded her of the man she bumped into at the Pannekoek.

"Ingrid, can you arrange a meeting with your Director, Mr Brinks, in Amsterdam? This company I took over last week seems to do much business with your firm." He sounded as if he expected an immediate answer. She looked up the list of subcontractors on her computer.

Ingrid saw that the Tree Fern landscaping division did most of the maintenance. She was thinking of the new complex in France.

"Yes, that's correct. Most of the landscaping and maintenance of our complexes is handled by your firm. No meeting is scheduled for the subcontractors for the new site. Can I come back to you on this matter?" She asked while she felt her heart beating.

"I'll wait for your call." She noticed the chuckle in Mr. Haardens' voice; again, he reminded her of something. It was as if...No, that wasn't possible. She had better snap out of her sudden fantasy world. She was getting annoyed with herself. What was going on with her?

Annelies

After work, she met Liesbeth for dinner at the Pannekoek near the bookshop. The three of them would drive to Annelies' house. Connie had offered to run the coffee shop so Richard could join them. She never told them about POWAH; instead, she pondered over Mr. Haardens.

Annelies lived in a very affluent part of the outskirts of Apeldoorn, surrounded by needle and birch trees. They scrambled out of the car, running through the heavy rain to the front door. Others were arriving as well. A tall, dark-haired, striking woman in her late fifties, very flamboyantly dressed, greeted them with a big smile, her eyes sparkling.

"Welcome, I'm ANNELIES." She emanated an impressive aura.

Long, black hair with some grey-white streaks pulled tied up while playful ringlets bounced on her oval face, like Liesbeth's, except for the big earrings, which gave her a gipsy look.

"Come in this way", she indicated in her musical voice. Her energy reflected her strength. She appeared to be a woman who had seen it all. They hung their raincoats up before entering her classroom. On a door was written:

Introductory class

OUR BODY CODES OF LIGHT

Very unusual symbols and colourful, kaleidoscopic wall decorations were on the walls. All eight of them introduced themselves. Each of them had to describe in their own words how they were triggered by the phrase the body codes of Light. Hearing some of the comments broke the ice. The term parallel realities was mentioned, meaning the many-worlds interpretation of quantum physics. It was clear to Ingrid that they all had one thing in common: they were unwilling to allow mediocrity in their lives.

"The day you decide you are more interested in being aware of your thoughts than you are in the thoughts themselves — that is the day you will find your way out," Annelies remarked.

Ingrid's eyes wandered around the room. There were eight participants in the class: Richard, of course, and three other men, Niels, Wim, and Gerrit. The three other women were Liesbeth, Yolanda, and Zola. Zola and Wim were a couple in their late twenties.

"The purpose of my decoding workshops is to reclaim our power. This means to lift the veil that has kept our real multi-dimensional potential hidden for so long," Annelies' whole posture, accentuated by the colourful caftan, reminded her of gipsies.

"Annelies, do you believe physically shifting into a different parallel reality is possible?"

"Yes, Ingrid, we do it all the time, but are unaware of it. Ingrid, we've all chosen to incarnate at this significant time to spiritually wake up fully. Most people will encounter the doubt I hear in your voice because of many challenging 'thought programmed patterns' that reflect the fact that every living creature on Planet Earth has a cycle ending in death. This has been the biggest lie humanity has been subjected to for many centuries. I've chosen to fully wake up during this incarnation before my earthly cycle is completed."

"You mean you will not physically die?"

"WIM, nothing ever dies. However, the imaginary identity is what people are attached to, which must switch through being spiritually awake. That is my intent, but for now, you will all experience your reality shifts at the first level. When you have awakened to the third level, far more facts that have been concealed will be made known. That supports our theories."

"He's not taken it all in. He is resisting something."

For a moment, Ingrid's thought was recalling what POWAH had written in the first Excerpt about structured dematerialisation and materialisation, but at the same time...was she hearing Annelies' mind speak out loud? Wim's expression was indeed sceptical. His eyes were of the usual blue but remarkably cold. Otherwise, there was only an indefinable, faint expression on his lips, something unforthcoming but not a smile.

"Annelies, will these workshops assist us in that reality shift, as you call it? I mean, overcoming that doubt? By awakening our unimaginable potential, will that enable us to leave this third-dimensional reality physically?" Gerrit's eyebrows arched over his glasses. Gerrit must have been remarkably handsome in his youth and was still a very fine-looking man at sixty.

"If that is your intent, then yes. By accelerating our consciousness and spiritual energy, we can break free from the holographic consciousness of the brain and leave this physical dimension behind through our light body while taking our identity to a new perspective.

Nobody said a word. They were all pondering.

"Remember...as long as any of you believe it is impossible, you close your mind to understanding it." Annelies' voice sounded far away. Everyone was silent, taking in what Annelies had just said.

"Some call this shift a rebirth or resurrection. Many words are used to express enlightenment. I do not see enlightenment, Soul ascension, or awakening as having anything to do with 'religion' or even 'spirituality'. Our genetic decoding techniques, with the help of sound frequencies, will expose the incredible power of your real spiritual selves."

That comment and the symbols on Annelies' wall reminded her of the doodling mind-drawing workshop she had attended last year. The barking of a puppy dog in the hallway temporarily distracted her, but Annelies' further explanation brought her back.

"Every frequency resonates to a certain number, colour, and sound. The energy that forms patterns, numbers and geometric symbols is used to uncover the many personality masks we all wear on this level."

Annelies' musical voice was fascinating to listen to. Ingrid's eyes were drawn to the many unusual yet familiar symbols on the walls, and she wondered if this decoding was challenging.

"Annelies, if we gather and release all our fragmented parts, will this reconnect us to our Oversoul?"

She was amazed to hear the term Oversoul, which she had looked up on the internet last night.

"Liesbeth, I'm glad you asked that. The decoding will activate the memory stored in our DNA/RNA, reconnecting us with the cosmos. It will transform our minds, emotions and, ultimately, physical form. As we elevate our energy into the higher dimensions, our so-called "ascension" continually increases and sustains higher and higher energy frequencies. Our personality frequencies have kept us in this vibrational entrapment. We are still greatly influenced by the virus called "belief"."

Ingrid recalled that POWAH's excerpt had also mentioned Annelies' ascension process. He called it a Soul awakening.

"Each individual needs to attach to any belief, dogma or duality consciousness must be released to shift away from this reality."

Annelies' tone expressed her conviction. Ingrid now wondered about her age. Would this affect their ageing process? *"Oh yes, it will."* For a moment, Ingrid thought it was her mind answering.

"Our personality is the entrapment of our mind?" ZOLA, the youngest woman in the class, gasped. Her long, platinum-blond hair fell in loose waves past her shoulders. She wore a black mini dress and combat boots.

"Yes, Zola, the masks we wear for different occasions are the personality entities or aspects of the ego. These 'masks' resonate to wavelengths of various frequencies, depending on how we think and feel. This mind virus operates through consciousness and transmits through electromagnetic waves."

If not for the images on the wall, Annelies' replies would have been lost on her. She wondered who had created these graphics.

The image was titled The Human Design.

Annelies first explained the five levels of the decoding program, which reminded her of excerpt two from POWAH that Connie, Yolanda's girl, had given her the day before. So, it must have come from Annelies!

"Sound creates a form, which is vibration energy. You can say that we are born into existence first by thought and then by sound."

Annelies had everyone's attention.

"We all emanate a sound. We are energy expressions in a solid form. Decoding your 22 channels shown on the image on the wall and your energy field sheet will reveal your intentions and aspirations in this lifetime. These are your Genetic Body Codes of Light."

"You're saying that all life starts with a thought?"

"Yes, Ingrid, and thoughts create sounds and colour. In our decoding, we use numbers and letters because they represent sounds. We experience different vibrations on many frequencies by expressing them through our voices." Annelies glanced at each of them.

"You mean, we create our own lives because of the names we are given?"

"Yolanda, our daily thoughts create our everyday experiences. The sounds we have chosen to experience unconsciously reveal the genetic life blueprint. Each time your name is called, this sound, now more than ever, will activate the power the name reflects." This was not a new concept for Ingrid, but she had never given it much thought.

"I see. So, if we change our names, we use a different sound, which creates a change in our lives?"

"Yolanda, any change means a shift in vibration. We'll go into each card to understand the dynamics of sound and colour. You will all learn to react and respond to release what has held us back." Annelies squeezed Yolanda's shoulder. Ingrid intuitively picked up an inner mental communication between them. Yolanda is going through a divorce. How did she know that?

"On this first level, for the next five Friday evenings, we decode the 22 major spacings you all occupy on the board game. By playing this board game with your cards, you will all individually be shifting your perceptions and beliefs that do not serve you anymore." The idea of making cards and playing a board game became more intriguing.

"The human design project on the internet also influences my work. With your symbology, my decoding classes will awaken your genetic makeup, reflecting the real aspects and soul qualities you have chosen to embody during this lifetime." Annelies pointed at the image on the wall, which had been projected from her laptop. Ingrid could see crisscross lines that encased a human figure and a watermark behind with a three-dimensional grid pattern in blocks.

"We'll make the first five awakening cards on the next five Friday evenings. These five cards round off the first level of the decoding card game. The two weeks after that are set aside to integrate your process before we start the second level."

"Wow! What a lot of work!" Gerrit had the image of some artists, a bit eccentric but still distinguished; one of those people who seem to skip that middle-aged look.

"Except for Liesbeth and Wim, all of you have attended Tieneke's Language of Light workshops, haven't you?" That was it! The nodding of the others took her back to Tieneke's workshop, where she had found peace with Jan's death. Through her mind drawings, she released emotional memories to come to terms with all that had happened, but she had never met the others at that time.

"We all have to be drastically prepared and bio-energetically rewired to be outfitted with the translation devices necessary to communicate and read the Galactic levels of the Language of Light," Annelies added.

"So we commit ourselves for the first twelve weeks only?" Zola's pretty face was flustered as she looked up at Wim, who was staring into space, looking almost bored.

"Yes, you can, and Gerrit, the real work is processed by all of you during the following weeks. The Friday evenings are the fun times, believe me." Annelies observed Wim with more than just a glance, but then she carried on:

"In this first level, you creatively make your five Present Perceptual Consciousness Cards to reawaken your memories. They also ascertain how awake you are at this moment." That evoked a reaction from most of them. How awake was she? An immediate bond was established when they shared insights from Tieneke's Language of Light Symbolism courses. She had attended a weekend retreat on a whim, just after settling in Apeldoorn.

"Please note, I have a warning for you. Don't interpret any handouts you receive or download from our Internet site literally as an abstract truth, especially if your awareness is expressed linearly."

Someone must have arrived at the house because the young dog went berserk. Yolanda got up to take a look; then she heard her laughing.

"So be gentle on yourselves when you all begin to grasp that truth is often hidden by those whose arguments are false!"

"Yolanda, is that Toon?"

"You mean we all perceive truth differently?" Gerrit asked. For a split second, Ingrid was sidetracked. Did she hear that mental dialogue coming from Annelies? Did she hear a question?

"Yes, Gerrit, you're right. From a personal point of view, we can never agree on any intellectual information. Our external perceptions differ."

"Toon, can you take Otto's charts with you before you leave?" Ingrid was dumbstruck. Was Annelies talking to someone telepathically? Yolanda came back in again, nodding to Annelies.

"Your lives will become an adventure all over again. I hope to see you all tomorrow evening." Annelies concluded her introduction class by passing a form around.

"Annie, I'll see you on Monday. Be good." Ingrid's mind was racing. That mental voice! Then, the front door closed with a thump while a dog was still barking. Annelies smiled and asked if the three of them would stay behind.

"My guide has told me that the three of you will be approached in time to write about your experiences. Your journals will become an assignment of the reality-shifting process. Ingrid, have you not been approached to write about the first level?" Annelies' thoughtful glance had an intensity to it as if she knew what she was thinking! Ingrid was unprepared for this mind-probing. The guide she mentioned must be POWAH, but why? Then she heard, or thought she heard, the following sentence.

"When the student is ready, the teacher will appear."

"It is all new to you. I hope to see you all tomorrow evening." She said as she passed a blue envelope to her, like the one she had received before! The others were already in their cars, driving off, when Annelies took Liesbeth, Richard, and herself aside.

"Ingrid, carefully read the first awareness level from excerpt two, especially when writing your journal. Express your motivation so your reader can understand the intensity you need to wake up."

"But that is so personal! I'm not sure if I can do this," she almost beamed. Annelies emanated such warmth that she wanted to burst out about her encounters, but Richard interrupted her thoughts.

"Annelies, I think I speak for the three of us. I'm very excited about your workshops."

As they walked out into the mild spring evening, a young Labrador greeted them excitedly, coming from behind Liesbeth's car. Annelies cuddled the puppy, softly telling him his boss would return soon.

Ingrid wondered who his boss was.

A lift home.

On the way home, they were all occupied with their reflections. Ingrid picked up thoughts in Liesbeth's mind, but she hated to eavesdrop.

Both were impressed that she was asked to take on the first level of her assignment. She was far more shaken by this week's incidents and was still trying to come to terms with her telepathic ability, which seemed to be getting stronger by the day.

"Something happened to me a week ago that seems to be related. It's too incredible." Her voice trembled from sheer disbelief. They both wanted to hear her story at the Pannekoek the following evening. Liesbeth pointed at the envelope Annelies had given her.

"Who's Kitty?" Richard asked

"That's me... don't ask. Annelies says it's all about the five-card spaces we are decoding tomorrow evening. From now on, I must keep these excerpts for my journal."

"Yolanda told me during our coffee break that some of the concepts are published on her website," Richard shared.

Ingrid relaxed in the back seat, but her mental chattering, questioning if she would recognise a reality shift, kept her in turmoil.

Liesbeth dropped her off at the parking bay. She waved to both, feeling so jubilant inside that she drove past her house!

That realisation made her realise how distracted her mind had been while driving. Had she suddenly experienced a Reality Shift? When she turned the car around, an intuitive voice stated:

"Kitty, stay in the present, be more grounded."

Chapter 3
The Sound and Colour of Numbers

Pleasure Park Office

Ingrid always checked her e-mail before starting her workday, but ever since Tuesday, she has especially watched out for more of the exact text from POWAH on her large curved screen before switching it on, but it remained blank.

While reading an email from the Tree Fern Landscaping firm, Ingrid's attention was drawn to an intense argument outside her partition. The floor manager, Piet, stormed into her office during a row with Carla.

"Ingrid, about the meeting with this Mr. Haardens fellow and Mr. Brinks, this guy only wants to deal with you; he's very adamant about it," Piet's agitated tone flew at her.

"What do you mean? I don't have to be there!" Oh no! She had difficulty with her drawing. Her 3D modelling software program gave error messages when she wanted to use her 3D hologram projector. Why did she have this pressure? Piet was looking over her shoulder at her drafting proposal. His energy was so negative, and his whole presence emanated anger.

"Mr. Brinks wants you there with your plan. I spoke to him on his cellular phone, and he insisted on your presence."

"When is the meeting scheduled?"

"Next week on Thursday, two o'clock at the head office in Amsterdam," Piet snapped as he walked out. Gee, less than a week to get this lot right! Meeting this Mr. Haardens triggered feelings of caution since even his name aroused her emotions! For all she knew, he was tiny, short, fat and dull. Piet's hostility made her question what she would learn from it when suddenly her screen became very bright, and the familiar 3D text appeared! Her heart surged.

<Kitty, your job on Earth is not to learn because you already know but to remember who 'you' are and everyone else!>

Wow! Was it reading her mind? Piet had left her office, so she quickly typed back:

I want to ask so many questions, like: Who are we? Who are you? Are you Annelies' guide? You say my job is not to learn, but I always thought that life was a learning experience, like being in a classroom.

She was breaking out in a sweat...then the text appeared again:

<Kitty, life is not a school. You are here to reclaim your true self. The school is a place to learn about something you want to know. Life itself is an opportunity for you to know experientially what you already know conceptually. It would be best to learn nothing about what you already know; you merely need to re-remember and act on it. And yes, I am your guide, communicating as your Oversoul.>

Ingrid was staggered. How was this happening? Was she the only one seeing the text appearing on her computer screen?

Why do we not remember who we are? Is my higher self-aware? How do we know that we have to remember anything?

The running text instantly replied to her question.

<Your higher self already knows all there is to know all the time: nothing is hidden or unknown to your Oversoul. But your Soul seeks to experience Earth's reality so that a concept becomes an experience. It wants to share 'ITSELF' through a physical form.>

Which part of her was reading all this? Who was responsible for this...who was she typing to? Was this what a reality shift was like? She was about to ask a question when more text appeared.

<Your higher, authentic self is just an extension of your blueprint. It's your cellular memories that have now awakened. Whereas your lower self-embodies many fragmented parts that form your overall persona, these fragmented experiences from many lifetimes must be dealt with and released from your energy field for your Soul to complete its physical life cycle on this third-dimensional plane. Contemplate this

Love POWAH>

She recalled Liesbeth asking Annelies a question, using the word Oversoul! What was the question? Annelies replied that our Higher Soul Self is integral to the Oversoul cluster outside the time-space domain. She fully intended to live this life to her full Soul potential.

This POWAH made it impossible to focus on her work.

The workplace buzzing made her realise that she was still separating herself from...POWAH

She needed to drag her focus back to her drawing. Marijke would take her phone calls so that she could concentrate on her illustrations for the rest of the day. She was looking forward to their first decoding class that evening, wondering what her soul purpose card would reveal.

***

"Ingrid, Ula has the same man she told you about on the line again, insisting on talking to you. Do you want to take this call?" Marijke looked worried.

She had managed to do a fair amount of work but needed a break and nodded. She recalled that Ula had told her about a call she missed on Tuesday just before going home. Her mind was on her drawing of the dome position. She was not pleased with her work when an unpleasant squeaky voice interrupted her thoughts.

"Are you the woman who draws the artistic impressions of the Pleasure Park complexes?"

"Yes, that's correct. To whom am I speaking?"

"About the drawings of the dome position you are working on now, are you interested in doing a job for us?" Gosh, he sounded like an actual sleaze bag.

"Who's 'us'?" She regretted ever answering his call. The way he referred to the position of the dome gave her gooseflesh. The man's vibe was so off-putting, as if this person was evil.

"A group of businessmen would like to interest you in a lucrative business proposition." The man again ignored her request for his name.

What was going on with these drawings?

"I have no interest in conversing with anyone without a name. Whoever you are, please go through the proper channels and contact Mr Brinks. He is the owner of Pleasure Parks. The receptionist will give you the number. Good day to you," Ingrid cut him off. To say nothing of his tone, this man emitted an unpleasant vibration, which she intuitively knew conveyed a harmful intention. Had she caught on to his mental dialogue? He seemed false.

She phoned Ula and explained that if the same man called again, refer him to Mr. Brinks' office. She didn't think he would call back. She somehow felt the man knew Mr. Brinks.

***

The rest of the day went so quickly that she almost forgot to check and read her emails.

——- Original Message ——-

From: "T Haardens"

To: <Undisclosed-Recipient:;>

Sent: Friday, April-12, 2019 8:21 AM
Subject: Appointment
Our Landscaping division: THE BUTTERCUP
Dear Ingrid.
I have made an appointment with your Director, Mr. Brinks, for Wednesday, 24 April at two o'clock, and I have requested that you join us. I live temporarily in Apeldoorn. Would you like me to give you a lift to Amsterdam? I will be happy to do so.
Do you like the new name?
Yours
Toon Haardens.
He had changed the company's name, 'Tree Fern', to 'Buttercup.' How original! Ingrid was not interested in his lift idea. She was entranced by this unknown man, but decided to squash that feeling. He sounded very sure of himself. She didn't want to get involved with just anyone.
Monday would be early enough to reply. Ingrid was more intrigued by the following e-mail, which suddenly appeared with the title of 'Sound.'
<**Kitty, if you have the desire and the intent to awaken fully, then you were born to embody your authentic self, to re-learn how to think and know your thoughts. Remember, as you feel in your heart, it is with you.**>
Excerpt Three[1]
Program Planet Earth
Sound and Colour of Numbers
This third excerpt was in the same text format as the other two she had received through the regular email, as if somebody had typed it out for her, because it was also published online.
Ingrid was amazed at how well she intuitively understood the message.

---

1. https://allrealityshifters.wordpress.com/powah/the-reality-shifters-excerpt-3/

The howling wind outside her office triggered her thinking: Why was the human Soul imprisoned within this lower dimension? Annelies cautioned them against believing every article on the internet, including the one claiming that Earth was a prison planet.

The subject matter of the excerpt stimulated a deeper part of herself. Especially since colour and sound frequencies can help heal all viral diseases, including cancer, when they resonate with the higher harmonics of sacred geometry, this can stimulate regrowth and rejuvenation at the cellular level. Wow!

It still unnerved her that someone, or something, was communicating with her in this way, but for now, she would follow her intuition. The reference to the mental hologram full of deceptions started to give her hope. The world was in such a state of disarray. There was so much sadness.

Raging wars and threatening destruction created by humanity often clouded her day.

***

Her phone rang as she locked up in a happy mood for the week. Should she pick it up? They would decode the three soul cards tonight, so she had to hurry. She guessed intuitively who it could be, and it was a bit against her principles to let it ring.

"Pleasure..."

"Still on the job, are you? Did you get my e-mail?" Goodness, this man was direct.

"I have just read it, Mr. Haardens, but I must stay in Amsterdam. I have a daughter living there, so I'll organise my transport. Many thanks for the offer." She was very proud of herself, thinking quickly on her feet, and she wanted to find out how Sascia was doing.

"I would still like to meet you before the meeting. Are you free at all this weekend?" He persisted. She couldn't stop grinning, hoping it did not cross the line.

"Well, my younger daughter is arriving this evening from Utrecht for the weekend. This weekend is out." She held her breath as it sounded as if she was having him on.

"How many children do you have?" he chuckled. This man could very well respond to her evasiveness in the wrong way. Was she indifferent about seeing him...or was she? She reluctantly told him that she also had a son backpacking somewhere. There was a silence, and again, she could almost feel an intense mental energy probing her mind. Was she imagining this? To be polite, she asked him if he had recently moved to Apeldoorn since he had written that in his e-mail.

"Yes, I travel overseas a lot, and I've not settled in yet, so I'm staying with family until I decide where to live in Holland." *"It must be,"* Must what? She wanted to ask, but instead replied, "Oh, and you do landscape in other countries as well?" Ingrid was amazed. Something about this man was confusing, but what was it? Did she hear this man think?

"Mmm, yes, you could say that. Ingrid, may I ask what your surname is?" *What for! Why?*

"Barendse," she wanted to add, but didn't want to go into any detail with a man she had never met.

There was a long silence. She could almost instinctively hear him think, *"Well, well, bingo!"* She was about to ask why her name was so interesting when she realised it could be her overactive imagination.

"What about Monday evening? I'll tell you what. I'll drop by your office on Monday afternoon. Then, over dinner, we can go over the maintenance program. I want to get to know you before the meeting on Thursday. What time do you usually finish work?"

Ingrid felt as if she was being bulldozed into this arrangement. He was persistent, all right. Annoyingly, she had to admit, she was curious, thinking of the man Haardens, who had spoken on the radio.

"Mr. Haardens, may I suggest around five-thirty at my office on Monday?" She got that across in a very professional tone. Then he asked where to book a table. He certainly sounded very keen on the idea of dinner! She told him her dining preferences. It almost felt as if they were playing some sort of game! Who was going to have the last word?

"Ingrid, I'll meet you on Monday afternoon. Have a good weekend with your daughter." His tone implied victory. Well, was this a date or what? How had she got involved in this? And his mental prob-ing, as if he were trying to get into her mind while he was on the line! Then,

"Could it be just a coincidence?" jumped into her mind telepathical-ly.

Not that those words had any meaning for her, thinking back to the evening when she had heard a voice in her head for the first time. Had she listened to the same voice? "Oh, get hold of yourself, girl!" She said out loud as Carla walked past, frowning.

"Staying over this weekend, are you?"

"Oh, Carla, remember I gave you that external hard drive, the one holding the aerial photo of the French building site? Did you keep it in the safe? Is it still there?"

"What! You as well? Piet was after that this morning! He was quite nasty about it. I'll have a look." Carla rushed away while Ingrid mulled over her date on Monday.

"I've got it. Piet was so unpleasant this morning; I'll gladly give the external hard drive to you instead, but what is so special about it?"

"I have no idea, but I'm going to investigate. You go, and I'll lock up."

Carla was far tidier in her appearance than before. She always looked as if she had borrowed someone else's clothes that did not fit her. Now she was wearing something that made her far more appealing. She had told her she had a new boyfriend she was keen on, Niels. He certainly had a good influence.

Suddenly, a vision of Sascia, her elder twin daughter, entered her mind when the phone rang again.

"Hello, Mom, what are you doing this evening?" She told her that she planned to meet Liesbeth.

"I must have picked up your thoughts. Mom, I've met a fascinating guy, and we're attending a lecture on our sun's solar flares in connection with our weather patterns. Have you heard anything about them? I believe your friend, Liesbeth, is involved."

"Really? When did you meet this new man?"

"Oh, at a friend's party. Mom, you can't believe it; he's interested in everything we have discussed at home. Remember, only Daddy never got involved...sorry, Mom, I said that without thinking. We think about you a lot, you know!"

"Oh, darling, you're right. It did not capture his interest the way it did with us. At least he never condemned it either." That was not entirely true in the earlier years of their marriage, but why bring that up? Ingrid was getting a lump in her throat at Sascia's sadness. Yes, she did miss Jan. The last few months before he died had been difficult. He had lost the power of speech and needed much physical attention. She had taken time off work to be with him full-time in the last months when she practised mentally communicating with his higher self, making up all kinds of conversations. It had helped to focus her mind. Creating an affinity on an intimate mental level had fulfilled a desire she had longed for. Meeting people of like mind. She convinced Sascia that she was doing well in Apeldoorn and asked about her twin brother, Jeroen.

"No, I have no idea where he is. Mom, don't worry about him; Jeroen needs time to think about himself and whether his future is with Grandpa's steel business. Now that Dad has gone and Uncle Ed lives in Australia, he is the only one left."

"Yes, I know, and it is his own decision. We can't help him in that, can we? How's your new job?" Thinking about the career choices her children had to make.

"Mom, I hate to be a journalist for this paper in Amsterdam. I don't know how long I'm going to last. I want to pursue my photography work, making real photos, not just snapshots, for the daily propaganda news and writing about it. I would love to work freelance, but I need more experience," Sascia sighed.

"Sascia, visualise your desire as if it happens every time you do your work. If you do this, you will manifest it someday. But make sure it is what you want!" Ingrid hoped she didn't sound too preachy.

"I know what I want to do. Visit ancient places and take photos like I've seen on the internet, but for that, I need to travel, but who will pay me for that?"

"Sascia, where did you get the idea that you cannot get paid for the things you love doing?"

"I don't know. It's almost as if...I can easily accept getting paid for something I hate doing. Where did that come from, Mom?"

"Darling, we're all programmed in one way or another. Daddy and I were probably responsible for some of that. Or, our education system is partly to blame, that is, if you need to blame anything."

"Mom, how do you know whether the person you like would be right for you as a partner?"

Ingrid knew this would not be the man she had just met. She would have reacted differently. It was not for her to say, so she changed the subject.

"Mom, are you asking for something in your life right now?"

"Believe me. I'm working on it. I'm learning. I play it safe; I'm only asking to live and express myself to my fullest potential. If I fail in any way, I try to express my gratitude for the opportunity the next day."

Ingrid was chuckling at her own words of wisdom.

"Sascia, are you home on Wednesday next week in the afternoon and evening? I need to attend an afternoon meeting in Amsterdam on the 24th. Can I crash with you for the night?" Sascia loved the idea because it would allow her to introduce her to Vinny, the new boyfriend, and then she hung up. At the last minute, before closing her office, she took the external hard drive Piet had been bugging her about home with her. Something in that aerial photo started to nag her.

Annelies workshop
At the Pannekoek, Liesbeth had already ordered a light dinner before Richard was ready to leave for the classes.

"Ingrid, someone asked about you; a very tall, big fellow, charming but...I got the impression that he knew you." Richard's eyes looked her over.

"Who? Did he say his name?" She was trying to read Richard's thoughts.

"Yes, I think so...Toon...I can't recall his surname; he described you well, so he must know you!"

"Really?" Could it be? Richard described a tall man. Was this Toon the one she had bumped into? Where had she heard the name Toon before? Knowing in her heart, she hoped it was so.

When Liesbeth told her, she needed to prepare a lecture on environmental issues that weekend, Ingrid remembered the weather patterns Sascia had referred to and the radio incident. She asked her what she knew about the effects of the increased solar activity.

"I know the sun's solar flares affect our Earth's weather. They said on the radio that it's creating higher temperatures, combined with droughts and flooding. Are Planet Earth's electromagnetic fields changing? I didn't know you were interested in this topic."

Liesbeth tossed her shiny mane of jet-black hair and pouted, her full lower lip quivering, so she waited for her reply that didn't come.

"I heard something about it on the radio. I might even know the person who spoke on the possibility of our being without electricity.

What are your thoughts on that?" Ingrid pressed on.

"Well... this is still speculation, something to do with the null zone, but today, geologists, seismologists, and volcanologists are closely monitoring these changes and what this effect has on the human population because higher vibrations function solely on magnetic energy, and it is speculated that our whole solar system will shift to a new position." Liesbeth waved for Richard to come over to their table to take their dishes.

"Our Earth's global light body is changing to the triple magnetic circle pattern over time from now on. That is the start of the detoxifying of electrical energy."

"Liesbeth, how do you know all that?" Richard eyed her.

"One day, I'll share with you both how I know more about the history of our planet. Some of the symptoms are that our physical hearing will change."

"You mean that some of us hear non-physical voices?" she asked. Or as voices that are thought-like, she thought.

"All I hear is an inner ear clicking and or high-pitched ringing, no voices," Richard shared.

"I knew there would be a program on the radio sometime. I'll let you both know when, but let's go now, or we'll be late," Liesbeth urged while winking at her.

Class 1

"Decoding of the fifth level stands for Freedom in Unity."

was written on the classroom door. All eight of those who had been there the previous night were back. Each handed Annelies their information sheets with the dates of birth, full names at birth, and any later given names, plus their addresses.

She could only stare at a beautiful, colour holographic image of a moving body being re-patterned and rewoven through its multidimensional layers. At least, that was what the text underneath implied.

Annelies made copies of the forms and returned them because they needed them for their decoding exercises. Then, Annelies explained the method of decoding. She walked behind them to see if they had done it correctly.

"Your numeral sound melody is your highest vibrational score for that particular card you are working with. As we go along, I'll explain what is appropriate now." Annelies held up an attractive-looking card.

She wondered whose it was.

"You are going to experience so much all in a short period that you mustn't try to grasp all the information at once. Please do ask questions." Nobody said a word. The stillness electrified the energy in the room.

"Annelies, have you ever read about Planet Earth being a prison planet?"

"Gosh, that question was unexpected...coming from her." Ingrid heard clearly. She felt judged. But why?

"Some of the information you will know already and some material you must assimilate before accepting it. So be gentle with yourself. Ask always for the highest good in all you do." Annelies winked at her as if to say: *""We will address that over the coming weeks, but for now, let's take it slowly. "*

She was stunned. Had she honestly heard Annelies speaking to her inside her head?

"Annelies, how important are nicknames?" Gerrit asked. She was glad of his question, thinking about her nickname 'Kitty' and recalling the mind drawing course where she used it in her drawings.

Annelies strolled around the big oval table, now and then looking over someone's shoulder. Could she feel as if she was listening to her thoughts?

"They are important as a vibration within your card, Gerrit." She replied while her hand rested on her shoulder as if to say: *"Talk to me during the week."*

"The numerical vibe of a nickname shows which Soul Quality you have added to your frequencies. When we come to the making of your cards, you will use them." All were busy calculating and adding their names to the numbers in their exercise books.

"The vowel sounds are related to our outer awareness, while the consonant sounds relate to our inner awareness. The most important numerical tone is your Soul Purpose Card vibration. It's the highest sound vibration of accumulated experiences you have chosen to reincarnate with at birth."

"The channels on your human design chart will determine what personality type you all have chosen this time."

"Annelies, mine is number eight, which I know is a karmic number. Does that mean I have asked for the experience of my relationship?"

Ingrid eagerly awaited Annelies' reply to Yolanda because her Soul Purpose card was also an eight!

"This is the eighth octave of love in the Language of Light to assist the Soul and the form in remembering divine union. Divine union vibrations release those patterns that have caused the masculine and feminine within to conflict." Annelies responded to Yolanda's anxiety.

Ingrid wondered if her relationship with Jan had mirrored that conflict.

"Before one can experience this divine union within, the need for competition between men and women must cease on the outside. It also reveals a strong power that was given to you in another life.

Please visit our website and click on the Reality Shifters button link. Or click on our End of Times and look for my articles in this blog under Annelies's Articles."

Some were already on their cell phones, bookmarking all the pages. "Please read your extended decoding interpretations online after publication."

Yolanda, wearing a fascinating outfit that complemented her long blonde hair, reminded Ingrid of her sister Quincy. Could she do her decoding, she wondered?

"Annelies, I have the number one! How can that be a high score?" Zola's eyebrows arched.

"Believe me, Zola, that is a high score in a vibrational sense. It has the gift of determination. It makes sense to me already and will to you, too." Annelies' long black hair was held together in a twist with one long wooden pin, which enhanced her gipsy look.

"Annelies, I was brought up in an orphanage for the first five years of my life. Nobody knew the name given to me at birth, so my adoptive parents gave me the name 'Liesbeth'. Is that valid? And do I use a four or the twenty-two number for my card?" Ingrid suddenly observed how closely Liesbeth resembled Annelies! Liesbeth was a lot younger, but they could have been sisters.

"Well, well, let me see. Do you know your date of birth?"

"I was found bundled up during May, so my nickname became May. They guessed I was one year old, so one year was added to the day of my discovery."

"Ah! Use the name 'May' as a vibration within the card later. Use Liesbeth for now and use the date given to you. You are right to use number twenty-two for your soul purpose card."

"Interesting indeed."

"Really, why?" Ingrid was stunned! Did she hear a mental dialogue between them?

"Liesbeth, if that vibration of truth is your Soul purpose card, that means that you will inspire the awakening in others who have been seeded to awaken fully." Annelies squeezed Liesbeth's shoulder.

"We'll have to talk." Those words! Did she hear them?

As Annelies passed behind the participants, she suddenly exclaimed:

"I see now, to my amazement, that three of you have the same surnames.

Are you aware of that?" Her tone gave away that she knew something they didn't.

"Liesbeth, in which orphanage were you left behind?" Gerrit peeked over his glasses.

"The Jaarsma Orphanage. I was named after the Orphanage and was adopted when I was five years old, but I kept the surname."

Gerrit took his glasses off in response.

"Really? Well, so was I, but I lived there until my eighteenth birthday," all heard his surprise.

"My surname is Jaarsma because my mother was named after the same orphanage. I must ask her about it," Niels added cautiously.

"Annelies, are we connected in any way?"

"Gerrit, I will tell you about the connection with this orphanage later. It plays a significant part in our awakening journey. But let's go on.

The Soul's motivational vibration numbers reveal how others see you!"

Annelies was good at keeping their attention. The decoding was quite strenuous.

"Now that I would like to know! My girlfriend is preparing supper tonight. I wonder what she sees in me?" Niels voiced his thoughts.

Annelies stood behind him, looking at his numbers.

"Niels, your girlfriend sees your positive faith in your abilities. It could mean that that is what she needs to discover within herself."

"Really? You can see all that by just looking at this number?" Niels' astonishment made her grin. Ingrid suddenly had a mental picture of Carla in front of her eyes. Could it be? They would make an interesting couple. Niels had Indonesian ancestry. He was not very tall but had a strong, solid body. He probably tended to put on weight like Carla.

Annelies peered over her shoulder at the paper on which she was decoding. Her guide number was twenty-two.

"Ingrid, this number vibration reveals a mighty guide. How do you feel about that?" Annelies winked. Then, Ingrid heard simultaneously the following further thoughts very clearly:

"Is it POWAH or a muscular polarity closing in on her?" What did those impressions mean? Never had she heard someone else's thoughts so clearly.

"You are telepathic, aren't you? Yet you have not been aware of it before, have you?"

Was Annelies projecting her thoughts?

"No, I have not!" she thought without sound.

Liesbeth just smiled. Had she heard it, too?

None needed any coats because it was already warm weather for a spring evening. April used to be much colder in the past. Annelies reminded them to look on the Internet and read about the awareness of the power of words, and asked Ingrid to stay behind. When they all asked for the Internet address, Niels told them that he had found the website when he was searching using the words reality shifters.

"Ingrid, if ever you want to talk, call me during the week. I'll wait for you to make the first move."

I have a lot of questions," Ingrid murmured. Annelies seemed to know her difficulty in sharing her thoughts with others. Suddenly, her hand felt something wet and cold. She almost jumped when she looked down into the sparkling brown eyes of a young Labrador wagging his tail.

"And who might you be?" stroking his ears.

"Joris, good blood." Annelies chuckled. Ingrid wondered if Annelies had a husband.

***

Richard gave them a lift back to the Pannekoek. She and Richard were unsurprised when Liesbeth told them she would take on the fourth level as her assignment. Richard had been given the second level as his homework.

"Did she say who's writing the third level?" Ingrid was glad to be writing about the first level. The second level involved their personalities and the left and right hemispheres of the brain. Richard must have a flair for that! But the fourth!

"Annelies herself is writing the third level, which is the most difficult one. She's not even aware of who's writing the last level.

"Ingrid, can you hear my thoughts?"

"Yes, Yes, I do; what about Richard?"

"Mmm, no, not yet, I think." Richard was unaware of their telepathic dialogue.

"Ingrid, I remembered that later this evening, someone is speaking over the radio, Apeldoorn 87.9 FM, about the solar flares you asked me about. The speaker is an Egyptologist or a Meteorologist, but I forgot his name. Richard, you should listen. It's right up your alley."

"Thanks for telling us." Richard dropped them off at the parking area behind the coffee shop.

Driving home

Since Ingrid had some spare time before fetching Debbie from the station, she switched on her internet car radio. She was curious to learn whether she would hear Mr. Haardens' voice again when her cell phone rang, showing her that it was Debbie—her free weekend had been postponed. She had to take on a friend's shift who had lost her brother in a motor accident that afternoon. Debbie sounded very sad and disappointed.

"Mom, I can't even attend her brother's funeral, for I have taken over her theatre duty, but I want to do this. I hope the weather will still be nice next weekend. See you then!"

Well, that was it. She would be alone this weekend. She could have accepted Mr. Haardens' invitation after all.

On the way home, the radio announcer introduced a Mr. Trevor Zwiegelaar, Annelies's surname!

"Mr. Zwiegelaar is an Egyptologist and a Meteorologist." The interviewer commented.

"Mr. Zwiegelaar, what's your response to the letters and phone calls? We have received hundreds of calls after Mr. Haardens spoke on the possibility of an electricity blackout. People are starting to panic."

"Mr. Haardens may have sounded like an alarmist, which he is not, but to survive the global changes, we need to cooperate in unprecedented ways.

The radio interviewer asked if Mr. Haardens had spoken out of turn since he was not a scientist.

"His interest lies in building communities where people can be relocated to. Many must be readjusted to living without the technology we depend on." Mr. Zwiegelaar replied with an authoritative voice, which reminded her of Mr. Haardens.

"So, he is a modern Noah, preparing the people on our planet for drastic changes?" The interviewer gasped at his sudden insight.

"Yes, you could say that, and I can just see his face when he is called that, but why not?" Mr. Zwiegelaar replied with laughter.

"Are all the many predictions that started during the millennium years ago truly happening?"

"First of all, I would like to point out that I'm not predicting anything. Nor am I talking about the end of the world. The scientific data on our weather patterns happen to coincide with tales from the past. They all refer to events that we know today might have been the shifting of the Earth's polar caps, climate changes, or even alien invasions, which is a lie; it's all rubbish.

Our research team is busy translating pictographic scripts from ancient slates as I speak."

"By scripts, you mean myths?"

"Ancient knowledge has often been translated as a myth. A good example is the creative work of J.R. Tolkien author of "The Lord of the Rings."

He must have understood the science behind the role of evil in human evolution to translate it well. Newly discovered pictographic scripts, dating back to before Sumerian times, all mention that solar systems change and have happened to other civilisations. They left us with warnings because they were not well prepared."

"Are you talking about the ancient days of the Atlantean times?"

"It could be. We are preparing a Solar website with detailed information. It will mainly be about how to make some basic physical preparations," Mr. Zwiegelaar reminded the listeners.

"How are we as humans affected by these changes? Apart from having to do without electricity."

"There are many planes of reality; likewise, different people will be affected differently. There is even speculation that humanity is going through a cellular transmutation on a blood level...but so are the plant, animal and mineral kingdoms."

"You mean that our human body is changing?"

"Yes, just as creatures that have evolved before. This information can all be found on our website. These changes are nothing to be alarmed about; they prepare us for rebirth into another age. Many religious institutions have speculated differently about how it will come about. Some regretfully chose to spread fear about these natural phenomena as a form of control, but it's everyone's free choice to act according to their perceptions."

"Are you giving more lectures on these subjects? The telephones have not stopped ringing in our studio."

When Trevor replied by saying that there were plans for regular lectures scheduled in July, the interviewer concluded the interview with the words:

"We found it appropriate to play the popular song 'Are you Awake?' from the new album called 'The Awakening' I wish my listeners goodnight. I'm Roger from City Radio, Apeldoorn."

As the music washed over her, Ingrid felt that her life had started to take on an entirely new meaning when that voice said: *"Kitty! Be still and listen."* a few days before. She was surging with newfound energy.

Her mind was full of questions and thoughts crisscrossing like a traffic grid as she switched off the radio. She kept seeing those eyes of the man she had bumped into...

Chapter 4
Soul Connections

Toon Haardens

Ingrid, there's someone for you at the front desk!" Carla said with frantic hand signals from behind her glass partition. Ingrid covered the mouthpiece, trying to reorient herself to what Carla was trying to tell her.

"Who?" seeing Carla's warning expression. Ingrid's drawing table was covered with sketches and photos, and her cell phone hadn't stopped ringing since Monday. It had been one of those hectic, crazy days. Roelof de Beer, Mr. Brink's son-in-law and the building supplier for the new French complex, was on the line. The poor man was on the edge of a nervous breakdown. His large lorry that delivered the building materials for the complex in France had been involved in an accident. Everything was scattered on the freeway to Paris. He asked her for a new supply order before the day ended. It was already after five o'clock!

"This must be Ingrid's office?" A deep voice filled with an inner conviction of power that could be both ruthless and compassionate rang forth.

A tall man was standing at the door opening to her office. Her light brown eyes went slowly from astonishment to stillness, and she held her breath. She met a pair of brilliant, grey-blue, laughing eyes observing her as only a man can. For a timeless moment, a wave of joy overwhelmed her. He distracted her. His tall body frame made an immediate impression. He was carrying a floppy bunch of handpicked pink and yellow flowers! "Buttercups?" She immediately knew who he was.

"Mr. Haardens, please do take a seat. Something urgent has just happened that I have to attend to. Do you mind?" As she pointed to the only chair beside her desk, the tremor in her voice betrayed her confusion.

"Not at all." He turned to Carla in the doorway and handed her the flowers. Carla's puzzled expression made her look quite comical.

He casually slid down in her chair, extending his long legs under her desk. His black polo-necked sweater under his sports jacket conveyed a casualness of male elegance that only some men could get away with.

She pressed the back of her hand to her eyes, trying to regain her concentration. Her arm movement made the creamy silk fabric of her three-quarter sleeve slide away, exposing her bare arm and revealing the contours of her sensual body. As she leaned forward, her light golden-brown eyes showed concern for the person she spoke to.

The accident, according to Roelof, had been a conspiracy, and he was rattling on about being blackmailed. She had heard he was going through a divorce, which could account for his agitated behaviour.

She tried to reassure Roelof de Beer, but she sensed Mr. Haardens' eyes observing her with such intensity that she was almost unable to concentrate. She nevertheless asked, "Mr. Haardens, can you supply building materials?"

"Roelof, can you hold on for a moment? Just hold on, don't go away, stay on the phone," gesturing at Mr. Haardens. She held her hand over the receiver and explained the situation to him. He promptly reached out. When he took the phone from her, his posture transformed into that of a self-assured businessman.

"Roelof! Toon Haardens speaking. Can you explain what is needed? I may be able to accommodate you." He confidently drew out a pen from inside his jacket and listened attentively.

Carla came back with a vase that displayed the wildflowers to advantage. So, these were Buttercups? How original! She wondered where he had got them from.

"Who is he?" Carla whispered in her ear outside her office. Ingrid smiled, trying to settle her inner turmoil. The whole day had been a nightmare, and now his visit had an inexplicably electrifying effect on her. He was the same man who had played on her mind ever since she bumped into him. This had never happened to her before. What was so different about him?

"Mr. Haardens is one of the subcontractors. At this moment, he is trying to help Roelof de Beer; at least, I hope he can." She whispered, thinking what a striking man he was. Tall with tanned skin, tousled blonde hair and deep blue-grey eyes that seemed to indicate an outdoor man and a real charmer. She judged his age to be somewhere around fifty. He was probably married.

"Has everyone gone home already?" Carla nodded as she handed her the vase with the Buttercups.

"What has Piet left as well? I wanted them to meet."

"Piet was arguing over the phone earlier, and I heard him threaten someone. He ran out of his office and never came back. Are you all right, Ingrid?" Carla glanced towards Mr. Haardens. "Shall I wait? He is very intriguing. Wow, that voice!" she whispered.

"Yes, you go home; I'll talk to you tomorrow." Ingrid gestured to Carla, grinning at her inquisitive facial expression.

"You'd better!" Carla grabbed her handbag.

Mr. Haardens was looking over her sketches and the 3D ideas projected onto her screen.

"Do you draw the whole plan in holographic imagery?" his admiration rang out.

"Oh, no. I obtained the drawing plans from the architects. I used to do drafting, but now I create an artist's impression that appeals to the public using Pleasure Park's latest 3D software; my idea of a retreat would be very different." She regretted saying that when he looked questioningly at her.

"Ingrid, if you ever decide to quit this job, let me know."

"You'd give me a job?" while trying to hide her nervousness.

"Anytime," His eyes expressed absolute sincerity. Those two words— they created a timeless moment.

"Did you manage to help Roelof de Beer?" They were standing so close that she felt shaky at his intrusion into her private space.

"Yes, I can help with some of the building materials." Then, while looking at his watch, he continued. "Ingrid, I've left my laptop at the office. May I use your computer to send an email? I need to send the materials list to a business associate who may have some of the equipment in stock, which neither Roelof nor I can deliver." His flirting put her on her guard.

"What is the name of your business associate?" She didn't want him to take her job over completely. He kept looking at her as if he knew something she didn't.

"Dennis Barendse." His eyes... he knew she knew the family, but did he know they were her in-laws? Well, she was not going to inform him of that. Let him do his detective work.

"With luck, some of the materials can be loaded onto the truck tomorrow morning and be on the way by about eleven," he stated while typing the order on her computer.

"You certainly came in at the right moment. Thank you!" Ingrid was grateful for his assistance. As he got up from behind her desk, she could sense him standing behind her when she was clearing papers from her printer.

"She is a talented lady,"

Good grief, did she hear that?

"Ingrid, I've booked a table for two at the Prinsengracht Hotel. I hope that's all right with you?"

"Oh, yes, fine... Mr. Haardens, thank you for the flowers." She touched the hand-picked bouquet.

"What made you change the name of your landscaping branch to Buttercup?" He said nothing, just looked at her, then suddenly threw his head back and laughed. This man has an inner joy that is almost catching, she thought.

"One day, I'll tell you where they came from," he whispered while holding her in the circle of his arm and guiding her into the lift. His eyes rested on her with such a satisfied grin that it made her heart race.

Downstairs, he took her elbow, guiding her to a luxury Tesla electric sports model parked right in front of the office building where people were not supposed to park!

* * *

It had been quite a day, Ingrid reflected, while Toon was driving to The Prinsengracht Hotel. She knew it had been an old castle from the late seventeenth century. For many years, the building was used as an Orphanage. Now, it is beautiful inside after it was restored, and it was costly. If he was trying to impress her, it worked! Ingrid wondered if her camel-coloured outfit was appropriate for the place.

"Table for Mr. Haardens, please," the head waiter called out as they walked in. Toon was known!

"What is she worried about? She's the most striking woman here."

Wow! Were those his thoughts? It was nice to imagine that he liked her appearance. While Toon considered the wine list, she tried calming her nerves. As they were studying the blue menu, she saw something familiar about the menu–the cover. That number! She'd seen that 1888 number before.

After the waiter had taken their order, Toon's intense observation made her want to look away. It took all her concentration trying to ignore the butterflies in her stomach while holding his glance with absolute self-confidence as if she was used to being flirted with.

"Ingrid, explain your statement back to me in your office. You implied that your drawings would be very different if you had your way." His intense gaze expected an answer.

"Oh, I don't know how to explain that. I think my perception about withdrawing from everyday living is different." He looked at her in silence, waiting to hear more.

"Mmm... In an illusory way, the Pleasure Park complexes replace our modern living. It seems to work for many people, but my idea of a retreat is different. Mr. Haardens, please, you don't want to listen to me on that subject; it's very 'alternative'. It's difficult to explain, and I don't want to sound judgmental." Ingrid hoped he would change the topic.

"Explain a bit more, and please call me Toon." He poured her wine after indicating his approval to the waiter.

Ingrid was visualising what she had to express: holiday retreats that were somehow unspoiled and natural, more peaceful like sanctuaries, surrounded by several pyramids built under specific measurements she had read about. These were the places where people would prepare food and children would have classrooms — the places that only really existed in her dreams, like a different reality where the turbulence and criminal destruction of the physical world could not penetrate due to the higher frequencies of the people in this community. She was about to attempt to verbalise it when Toon spoke!

"Let me guess, you imagine a community living environment with a central building, like a large pyramid, where all the activities are held.

The people in this community live in many attractive cottages, blending into the beautiful, unspoiled natural scenery to enhance privacy as if they belong there."

"Yes, how did you guess?" She was speechless; he had just described her vision!

"By looking into those beautiful eyes of yours," he told her whimsically, thinking. *"I love the way her mind is playing with me."*

Was he flirting mentally? She was lost for words. If only he knew that she could read his thoughts! When the waiter arrived with their starter, she was determined to steer the conversation back into his corner.

"Tell me, you travel a lot, don't you? Now that intrigues me."

"Why does travel intrigue you?" His gaze remained on her. Good grief, this man was determined to get her to talk while he was watching her for his pleasure. She was not having it.

"You are in the landscaping business, and you seem to know all about the construction business, including building a pyramid! Then you tell me that you travel as well! Now it's your turn: why do you travel so much?" Peering into his eyes, meeting his challenge while beaming, "Checkmate", made her feel proud that she had gotten all that out. Was he aware of the battle she had, keeping him mentally 'off her'? She looked down at her food, took a bite and waited for him to respond.

The silence made her glance up again. He was still observing her. She was not going to open her mouth. She had difficulty looking into those eyes as it was. They created an overwhelming feeling of ...wanting to melt into them. It was almost erotic. She raised her eyebrows at him instead, trying to keep her calm while thinking. It's your turn, mate!

He looked away into his plate of food. She had won this round, but his grin infuriated her. She would keep quiet until he contributed to the conversation verbally. She wondered if he was married, guessing a man like him would not be alone. She hesitated to ask him if he was. It might give him the wrong idea. He seemed uninterested in the fact that she could be married. She could have a husband waiting at home! Toon suddenly roared with laughter.

"Oh, Ingrid... no, I've never been married. I've never really found the right partner. I've worked worldwide on large construction sites as a civil engineer. I have various businesses around the world that I visit regularly. I have a deep love for everything related to nature.

My absolute passion is building small communities where people can coexist harmoniously. I have studied other community projects done in Russia by Valery Uvarov. He and several other scientists have inspired me to use my income to finance communities where they can share their talents and skills to make our planet a better, more peaceful place," he exclaimed while gazing at her.

Goodness! Could he read her mind as well? Was he for real? He had completely taken her by surprise with his reply. He must be the same Mr. Haardens from the radio! She remembered that communities were mentioned. She wanted to get to know this man. Somewhere deep inside her, she knew exactly what she wanted to do with her life: get involved with her community! She had never known it until now!

Yes, that could be the new way of living, thinking about the incredible changes occurring on the planet.

She found that the rest of the evening raced by. They discussed, amongst other things, the meeting for the following Thursday. He drove her back to the parking bay and walked her to her car.

"Let me know if you change your mind about a lift to Amsterdam. I've so enjoyed being with you."

She trembled from his touch when he took her hand, holding it much longer than necessary.

She was so shaken up that she took the wrong road home. This was a fascinating man, but he had never asked her anything about herself. Was he not interested? How would he know if she was married or not? Would that make any difference to him? Or did he know that she was a widow? Oh, Ingrid, get real! Stop acting like a teenager! She reprimanded herself.

Amsterdam

After an inner battle, Ingrid drove to Amsterdam in her car on Thursday afternoon.

"Toon Haardens, I'm pleased to meet you," Mr. Brinks held out his hand when they entered his office. He was close to retirement age, short and stocky, and he had a look of wariness, which could change when he felt relaxed or happy, which was not often in these difficult days. It was an excellent chance to observe Toon. She could see that Mr. Brinks had taken Toon immediately. They seemed to have a lot in common. He knew of Toon's construction firm that he had taken over. Not only was he very self-assertive when talking about business, but he also knew what he wanted from it and was very open about it. Regarding the layouts of the French project, they included her.

"Mr. Brinks, about the aerial photo of that building site: I've studied it, and something intrigues me. Will you both please take a look?"

Ingrid connected the external hard drive to her laptop, and the 3D aerial photo was projected on her screen.

"This lady likes intriguing things, I have noticed, but you have my full attention, Ingrid." Toon winked at her as she studied the 3D model in silence. She knew that, apart from her appearance, they both liked and valued her for her work. She felt the thrill of being in the company of two exceptionally talented individuals at their jobs. Both men would always do their utmost to deliver their best work.

"I think I've got it!" Toon played with her Geomagic Freeform suite program on her laptop. She sensed that he had seen the symbol as well.

Mr. Brinks sat staring into the distance. Ingrid had a sudden feeling that he already knew what she had seen!

"It looks like a formation... a strange pattern in the shape of.... an eye! It reminds me of how the Egyptians drew their symbols," Toon remarked, looking at Ingrid in surprise. "Has this been investigated?"

Mr. Brinks looked absent-minded. She sensed that he had lots on his mind.

"Geologists have told me that significant electric abnormalities within the rock formations below, let's call it the eye socket, were found, compared to the crystalline structure in the surrounding environment.

It's beyond my grasp of what that means, but I've got scientists looking into it. There's nothing to see from the ground, and I've been rather occupied with the Tilburg complex, so I've left it for now."

"Mr. Brinks, I've been approached telephonically by a rather dubious character. He refused to tell me his name. He asked me about the new drawing showing the position of the dome of our new complex. He even offered me a proposal to do some private work for him. I thought you should know." Toon became concerned; his frown had a nurturing effect on her. Then she somehow picked up an abstract thought, more like an idea in the form of an image from Toon.

Someone else must have found the spiralling tunnels that seemed to have been produced by sizeable electromagnetic field emitters. Today, only CERN can shape conical tunnels, so who else is interested in this spot?

Was Toon aware of something she should be mindful of?

"Thank you for telling me, Ingrid; I'll investigate the matter." Mr. Brinks mumbled. His secretary reminded him of a function he had to attend. They concluded their meeting.

Ingrid showed Toon around the reception room, where all the photos of the Pleasure Parks complex were displayed. He was entertaining company and asked her many questions. She knew he was far more interested in her than in the work. She managed to stay impersonal, which he made very difficult.

"Ingrid, are you free this weekend?" He walked her to her car, and she could feel his hand resting slightly on her waist.

"Do you remember that I told you on the phone my daughter was visiting me?" Reluctantly, she had to remind him while he opened the car door.

"Debbie, the nurse, yes, I remember."

"Well, she couldn't make it, so she's visiting me this weekend, arriving tomorrow evening." Ingrid sat behind the steering wheel, while he leaned over, holding onto her car door.

"Where are you going now?" He was leaning down, looking serious. Ingrid knew she was very attracted to him, but she had to see Sascia in half an hour!

"Oh, now I remember. You were going to see the other daughter. Ingrid, I want to see you again. *I want to get to know her better!*" His eye contact aroused her again; could he read her feelings, too? She hoped he would ask her out again; she was smitten by him big time.

Suddenly, he held his hand under her chin; all she could do was gaze up into his eyes, which were now laughing. Then he bent down and kissed her.

"Have a great time with your daughter. I'll see you soon," he said gently, closing her car door and walking away. Ingrid felt electrified! Never had she felt so aroused by just a single kiss! She was furious with herself for being so captivated by him. And what was worse, he knew it! She would try to keep her distance. She was no piece of cake just to be gobbled up.

***

SASCIA was already home when Ingrid arrived at her one-bedroom hideaway on the top floor, which offered a breathtaking view over some of Amsterdam's many canals. The sound of a Dutch street organ reminded her of her childhood.

"Hi, Mom! Gee, you look smart! How did your meeting go?" Sascia blurted out while hugging her.

"Very interesting," she said, still savouring his kiss. Had she attracted this fascinating man with her thoughts? She had never asked for a new relationship! Which part of her was in control? Was it her personality with its many needs, or was the agenda of her higher self still unknown to her?

"Mom, where are you? Why are you far away? I'm trying out a new recipe; please taste it." Sascia chattered away with a spoon in her hand.

Ingrid lovingly observed her tall, willowy twin daughter. She saw herself in many ways. They were different but shared a preference for their own independence and private space. Her slender posture with the same flawless complexion as her mother, except for the freckles, was endearing. Her straight, boyishly cut hair fell haphazardly onto her brow, hiding the shapely, arched brows that framed her large, expressive eyes.

While she was wondering about this new boyfriend, VINNY, Sascia's phone rang. Ingrid looked around, recognising many things in the tiny place from her Rotterdam home. She had decided to start afresh in Apeldoorn with new furniture and style. Liesbeth helped her with the decorating, which was great fun. Sascia ended her telephone conversation looking deeply disappointed.

"Vinny can't make it tonight. His partner has a client who could only come after hours. He's on duty. Vinny is a bit like Debbie, always pleasing others," Sascia sighed.

"You say, clients. What is Vinny's line of work?" Now she was curious.

"He is a psychologist sharing a counselling bureau with two other social workers. They all started practising at the beginning of this year, so their counselling bureau has not yet been established.

Apeldoorn

She left Sascia's apartment very early the following day. She drove straight to work on the A1 in a sluggish stream of traffic. Ingrid was glad she didn't have to go to work in Apeldoorn like this.

Marijke was at home with the flu, but Ingrid managed to whip through her office work. Piet was his usual grumpy, unpleasant self again. Knowing he was divorced, she made a conscious effort to remain tolerant. She had also heard that he gambled. Because of his involvement in shady activities, he was blackmailed, so the rumours went. Ingrid hated gossip and tried to sympathise with the man, but it wasn't easy.

As she was tidying up her desk and finishing for the week, her cell phone rang...She got an image of Toon. She'd been thinking of him the whole day and was annoyed with herself about that. She knew what she wanted for herself. Any relationship with someone who did not have the same spiritual interests was not worth considering.

"Yes, Pleasure Park, may..." *"She knows! She knows it's me,"* How did he...?

"What are you doing before your daughter arrives later this evening?" His projections startled her. How did he know that Debbie was coming later?

"I have art classes from seven until ten," she replied almost regretfully. What could she say? It was true, and she wouldn't miss them for anything.

"This woman is challenging me," Gee, had she become telepathic? Of course, the first level of the awakening process was it! She'd better be careful, in case he could read her mind. Was something like this possible? Were they playing a telepathic game?

"If she is playing hard to get, she will lose," that last mental statement revealed his willpower. Was she playing hard to get? That was how he perceived it.

"Ingrid, what about next Saturday?" She was aware of his effect on her, but she had decided. After Jan died, she promised herself that her life from then on would be for one purpose only. She wanted to attract people into her life who were motivated by the same passion for a spiritual awakening. Or better still, the Ascension preparation. "I will let you know around Thursday."

"So, I do have some effect! She feels the same," Wow! If he could read her thoughts, did he feel the same?

"Have a good weekend, Ingrid, and enjoy your art classes. I'll see you next week."

As she locked her office for the weekend, she tried to put him out of her mind by focusing only on the evening ahead. She would show Richard the aerial photo of the site in France. Toon was right; it did look like the way the Egyptians drew their eye symbols.

When she arrived at Annelies' home, there was no parking until further down the street. A luxury metallic blue electric Tesla with a dog's head sticking out of the car window pulled away, so she parked there.

"Hi, Ingrid, we waited for you," Annelies greeted her while taking her coat.

Class 2

Decoding of the fourth level, which stands for INTEGRATION and complete self-acceptance, was written on the door. They would decode their three higher, subtle-dimensional body cards. They belonged to the fourth level of the reality shift card game.

"Are there any questions from last week?" Annelies asked, but nobody seemed to have any. She reminded them that to experience an interactive class, they should join her Facebook group on Ascension Topics.

"Your Emotional body card reflects your feelings and your right hemisphere of the brain. The Mental, Etheric body card reflects your logical intellect and the brain's left hemisphere. The Astral body card represents the creative/intuitive body card. On this level, your higher real self blends all the experiences of your higher mental and emotional intentions. It's associated with your thoughts."

"Annelies, how do you know which one is in control?"

"Do you mean your personalities or your higher self?"

"Yes, how do you know? Is this a dumb question?"

"No, not at all, Ingrid,"

"Our many personality entities or aspects within our holographic space will always feel they have to cover or protect feelings of unworthiness, like pain, hurt, sadness, anger, fear, grief, lust, or greed. It will attract addictions to feeling good until they are ready to surrender to the will of the Soul."

"You mean our...many...personalities! I thought we had one!"

Ingrid was glad that Richard asked about the many. Thinking about it is a rather discerning way of perceiving it. She could think of ways to put on a different mask for every occasion.

"Gosh, Annelies, remember that repulsive character called Smeagle in The Lord of the Rings? That creature was good at playing two different roles simultaneously."

Excellent, Ingrid, I do remember that movie. It reflects our present time in many respects, but in a clever, creative fantasy epic.

"Oh, I recall Smeagle. He appears in part two. It's pretty schizophrenic how he listens to the two voices in his head. Gerrit added. The young couple had never seen the movie because it was shown before their time.

"Annelies, if personality entities perceive those feelings as real, does our higher self attract a 'desire' to experience feelings? I mean for evolving?" Thinking of her powerful physical attraction to Toon, knowing he triggered just that.

"You've got the idea. Many unconscious thought forms will surface into your subconscious and consciousness to be released. Some are nice, and some are not; Smeagol is a good example".

"Be discerning when hearing inner dialogue, Ingrid."

"What do you mean?" She beamed back.

"As long as you know that you are all perfect already. There are no needs that you cannot fulfil. Your Higher Self probably guides you to feel attracted to these workshops."

"Some inner thoughts of others can become attached to yours!"

Ingrid still wondered which of her was in control. She had been happy within herself during the previous few months. She finally started to love her own company. But how could other people's thoughts become her own? Annelies fiddled with her laptop, and a 3D image appeared on the wall. Colour streams of vibrations surrounded a moving human figure; what looked like threads of different shapes, textures and sounds!

"I'm giving you my perceptual interpretation; always remember that. Some of you may have different insights. Humans are perceivers, and our perceptions offer far more possibilities than our minds can conceive. The board game aims to gather our Soul-quality energies to perceive different spiritual dimensions. The following interpretation of the three bodies is used to play the reality shift game with your cards." She changed the image, and the sound was gone.

"Annelies, when we play on the third level, have we awakened most of the fragmented parts of ourselves?" Zola had nudged Wim to ask questions.

"I think it is safe to say 'yes' and hopefully disperse our shadow side".

It is also the most challenging level to pass through. We must completely release hang-ups or dependencies, addictions, attachments, rituals and any personal needs to proceed onto the fourth level. So let's go on." Annelies pointed at a large 3D image on the wall.

"It's important that you all understand the explanation of the three bodies. Our physical body is a solid thought–– form we can all see." She clicked, and the human figure was highlighted.

"Now, not all thought forms are physical...your emotional body is where your feelings are stored. Then, your mental, intuitive, and creative bodies comprise your soul/astral body. We will call it the astral body, the familiar term."

"You talk about the aura that surrounds all living things?" Yolanda pointed at the next image that appeared. The moving, colourful vapours that swirled around the human figure stimulated everyone's visualising ability.

"Yes, it is, and it comes into form through the life energy force or your spirit spark or the kundalini energy that enters the baby at birth.

This force is like a fire that funnels upwards through the spinal cord within your physical body."

"Annelies, this life force, or kundalini energy, does it come gradually into its full maturity every seven years?" Gerrit was making interesting sketches.

"Yes, I perceive it the same way. Try to visualise this life force as a vibrational spinal cord parallel to the physical spine. See it travelling from the back and the front of the physical body through the seven chakra vortexes. They are related to the seven layers of the Astral body." They were all closing their eyes, trying to imagine this life force.

"Liesbeth, can you see their energy fields?"

"Only five of them."

"I want you all to visualise this divine life force like a furnace, forming vibrational waves–patterns of colours." Annelies clicked, and the next image on the wall clearly showed an electric spark, the life force. Now close your eyes and see this energy in your third eye."

"Now I can see more! They are visualising it!" Ingrid was in rapture, hearing the dialogue, although she could not see what Liesbeth saw.

"Annelies, these seven layers all have a different colour, and they mingle, not so, forming a colourful symphony that most people sense through feelings. Am I right?" Niels commented while reclining in his chair.

"Niels must be the sensitive one," she heard Annelies mentally.

"Yes, and a clairvoyant person sees this as the aura or astral body and a clear auditory person can hear the sound of this celestial body. Are you all with me so far?"

"Annelies, is this the body of our Soul? I mean, the astral body?" Gerrit looked up from his drawings.

"Yes, you can call it that. Our Soul is the accumulated experiences of all lifetimes in and out of embodiments. Spirit or life energy is always part of the power of One of all that is. Our spirit is like the drop of water that is still part of the ocean. It is the same." Ingrid suddenly realised the difference between Soul and Spirit.

"Annelies, is our etheric or mental body the cover around our aura, forming our Soul cover?" Looking at the image, it seemed to be kept within an oval space. Some said the etheric was the first layer next to the skin.

"Yes, but your etheric or mental body permeates your other bodies. It's like a kind of bluish-white light. It is in constant motion and is meant to become our light body in this lifetime."

"Ingrid, they see a light body, not the etheric level. There are no levels, just vibrations."

"So, we are inside this Soul body?" Yolanda's arms made a loop.

"Or are we just vibrations?" Yolanda projected, joining their mental conversation.

"Soul is everywhere, but its elaborate consciousness is mostly cut off from our form. It will not dwell where it is not invited. The soul only responds to our feelings, not just thoughts."

"What do you mean by not invited and cut off?" Niels replied.

"Your Soul will not dwell and express when personality entities are in charge. In our reality shifts, we must release all personality entities. We must create space for our Soul to express itself through our physical form." *"Ingrid, other people's thoughts can clutter up your space!"*

"Annelies, how do you know that your Soul is acting through you consciously and not the personalities?" Ingrid responded aloud.

"You are worried, aren't you? You will feel the difference. The rapture that suddenly floods from the chakra vortices is immeasurably joyful. Also, your intuitive, creative body must be activated for the Soul to start communicating. Some call these intuitive flashes channelling."

"I read that we have more than seven chakra points," Zola commented, showing off her knowledge.

"Yes, we do. Our mental, etheric body carries more chakras. We will deal with the seven that most express our daily behaviour for now." Ingrid observed that Annelies enjoyed the questions.

"Where is our memory situated? Is it in the etheric body?" Richard frowned.

"That's an interesting question. I'll try to answer that, but remember, it's only my perception. In the card game, we use this interpretation."

"Richard needs this analytical data, so let's humour him."

"During an incarnation, our memory is in our etheric, mental body.
"Our mental body shapes and directs our astral body, and in turn
shapes and directs the etheric body."

Annelies waited for everyone to grasp that while she fiddled with
her laptop.

"When, until now, our physical body dies, or let's say when our life
force abandons our physical form, it takes about three days for our
consciousness and memories to withdraw into the etheric body and
then to disengage and blend with the astral plane.

"Why three days?" Niels asked.

"Do remember that all our bodies are no more than miniature universes. All of this is nothing more than energy fields. The timeline
of three days for our consciousness and our memories to withdraw
into the etheric body and then to disengage and blend with the astral plane might be a presumption. Some Souls won't cross over fully – there are stages to the crossing over."

Ingrid's thoughts went to Jan's consciousness, which would have
merged with this astral layer. Annelies suggested that they look at
their previous mind drawings while she was fiddling with her Flash
presentation. Then, a new image on the wall clearly showed how
a blue–white substance separated from the human figure, and the
colours slowly evaporated.

"Oh, is that why we experience an interruption in our awareness
of our past life memories? Because we incarnate again through the
birth process?" Gerrit's whole body straightened up from his insight.

"Bingo!"

"Yes, that's why we all must maintain our connection with our
Higher Self during this lifetime. Only the Higher Self can create a
light body. This light body will awaken us into full consciousness
while in the physical form." Annelies continued.

"But Annie, when do you know you are working through your Higher Self?"

Annelies switched off the laptop

"Yolanda, ask out loud, please."

"So, if our personalities are in control, we're not connecting to the Higher Self?"

"That's better." "No, we're not, or that is how I perceive it. Each personality entity has to become subservient to the Higher Self, which is guided by the Soul's purpose. If not, they have to be released."

Ingrid's mind soared with Annelies' spiritual multi-dimensional teachings.

Annelies waited for everybody to assimilate it all, but when she added. "Some souls at the time of their death are at such a low vibration – such as fear, hatred or anger that they cannot cross over because they're afraid." They were all stunned into silence.

"Now I understand why fear, anger, and hate are such negative emotions. Then, indeed, today, Earth has become a prison planet." Liesbeth remarked

They all nodded in agreement.

"Wow, some Facebook posts from people who claim to have interactions with nonhuman beings say that the 'Cabal' or the Illuminati will do anything to keep the masses of our population in anger, fear or hopefulness," Niels remarked.

"Oh, please, more conspiracy theories. Rubbish," Wim commented with a rather arrogant tone. Niels looked up, raising his eyebrows. *"Well, well, I wonder why he is so anti..."*

Annelie's mental projection got Ingrid thinking about how Ed, Jan's brother, was convinced of the Cabal agenda, while Jan spent most of the time dodging questions and responding to questions of his own rather than providing any answers.

"It seems to me that they might be on to something after all," Gerrad replied. "From the Iraq war to Fifa to the banking crisis, the truth is not only out there, but it's more outlandish than anything we could have made up."

"I agree," Niels said. Richard nodded in agreement.

"Who is the Cabal?" Zola asked, staring at Annelies.

"Zola, please look it up on the internet. Later in the workshop, we will explore deeper into the mysteries of what is happening in our world." Annelies intended to bring the group into focus by showing images from her laptop on the wall.

"We first let the Higher Self be in control through meditation, breathing techniques, humour, and laughter. Then, through developing our inner mental imagery, true compassion and unconditional love, coming from within our heart, we create a bridge from our astral-creative-intuitive body to our etheric body, which becomes the light body."

The Graphics on the wall were a fantastic reflection of her words

"We will develop this bridge on five levels during your decoding workshops, preparing us for a new evolutionary shift." Annelies' voice rang out passionately while passing around fascinating symbol cards

"Can this be achieved during our dream time?"

"Yes, partly. Richard, when we make the three cards for the second level, we will learn to reawaken in the dream planes while still in a physical body." Annelies smiled. *"He's the dreamer!"*

"So, your physical body is inside non-physical bodies?'

"Yes, so you see, Zola, we're all much more than you see with the physical eye." Ingrid wondered how her mental body picked up Toon's thoughts. Had she always been this telepathic?

"Ingrid, did you want to ask something?" ... gee, she'd better be.

"Yes, I can sometimes sense what someone is thinking, and lately, I encountered someone mentally powerful. I understand we are all interconnecting with other minds through our mental bodies...but when do you know when telepathy occurs?" *"I know it with you all, but...I was not always this sensitive; why now?"*

"Ingrid, when you say 'strong', you mean that you hear mental dialogue? Or did you make a deeper connection? We have a mental energy link. But you can also have what I call a wavelength fusion." Annelies demonstrated this by fluttering her eyelashes. Ingrid wished she had not asked this, for everyone laughed.

"Well, I can almost hear words forming as if I am talking to myself. Unless it is wishful thinking," she grinned.

"But your feelings are receiving more than just dialogue?"

"Yes, they do! But...yes, with this one person, my feelings are different from...like...I have with you."

"I should hope so!" Annelies' naughty look made her blush. Gerrit peeked with a mischievous look over his glasses.

"Could you experience telepathy, or is it more than that? Is this person very close to you? Come out with it, dear; we are all listening!" Ingrid felt all three mentally probing.

"Oh. No. It's probably my imagination; sorry for bringing it up," realising that Annelies was fishing! She reminded her of Toon in some ways. Annelies was still staring, observing her with an unnerving intensity. Suddenly, Yolanda interrupted with a chuckle.

"Don't worry about it, Ingrid. I have the same experience with some people I know!" *"Stop snooping, Annie."* Liesbeth just smiled, saying nothing but beaming.

"Ingrid, would you mind stopping at the Pannekoek on your way home? I need to ask you something."

During their coffee break, Richard had asked her about the guide Annelies had mentioned to them all. She had held back from talking about it while the others were having a light conversation, because discussing such an intimate experience was not her style.

"Annie, is Toon back from Austria? Fred asked after him."

Yolanda's projection startled her; the name Toon! Who were they referring to? *"Yes, he is, but...I'll tell him."*

Richard was still looking at her...waiting. "Yes, I'll meet you; I want to show you something, so have my cappuccino ready."

Annelies gave her the familiar blue envelope with an imprint of 1888, after which they all parted. That was it! She'd seen it on the menu cover in the Prinsengracht hotel. Annelies' phone rang, which prevented her from asking about POWAH.

Debbie

When Debbie arrived by train, her youngest daughter's eyes smiled when she spotted her mother on the platform. They were warm blue, staring out of a soft, round face. She was the Blondie of the family, with a caring nature, so she was suitable for the nursing profession. They entered the coffee shop, where she introduced Debbie to Richard, who flirted with her. Debbie was impressed with her mom's much older friend. They both connected when she showed Richard the aerial photo on her laptop.

"It looks like the symbol of the Eye of Horus," Richard called out.

"Do you think it's of any importance?"

"I don't know. This is where we erect the large dome, but there are already complications."

"Mmm, Ingrid, I wonder why they do not cover the whole eye with the dome structure. Something about pyramid energy made me say that. I'll have to do some reading on the symbol, so I'll come back to you, shall I?" Richard never did ask her what he wanted to know or talk about. Instead, he asked Debbie out.

When she opened Annelies' dark blue envelope at home, the sheet of paper mentioned the three cards they had decoded within the letter from POWAH. Annelies had text her the link to read Excerpt Four online.

Excerpt Four[1]

---

1. https://allrealityshifters.wordpress.com/powah/the-reality-shifters-excerpt-4/

Program Planet Earth
The Symbol of Consciousness

She read that the All-Seeing Eye is also a symbol of consciousness. A symbolic language has emerged to make sense of yourselves concerning your reality. The eye symbol represents the rules of the human game. Richard said that the Seeing Eye and the pyramid with the eye date back to ancient times and are often associated with secret societies such as the Illuminati and the Freemasons. POWAH seemed to say that when we can see things as they are, we can start collecting valid information about them and build a good understanding of them.

So, the Reality Shifting process was connected, including the eye image she had seen in the aerial view photo. Richard had remarked about the Eye of Horus, and now she reads that the all-seeing eye is a symbolic representation of a stargate. Were they for real? Was that a spiritual inter-dimensional portal?

She tried to remember what Mr. Brink had said about the eye symbol. Is it related to the energies from the stone or rock formations? But...why the upheaval with the technical drawings of the construction in France?

Wow, she must share this with Richard. He was majoring in archaeology, after all. Oh, she had so many questions! Would they ever be answered entirely?

Chapter 5
The Keepers of the Evolution Game

Office at home

That Sunday afternoon, Ingrid started retyping her diary pages into a journal on her laptop. The rain had stopped, and the smell of summer was in the air. Debbie, who had gone out with Richard on Saturday, made friends quickly. Her youngest had difficulty saying 'no' but had a good sense of humour and an ability to relate to people. She was the same height as her mother, but there the resemblance ended as she was blonde with eyes the colour of deep blue lace agate.

Her laptop screen suddenly brightened. This was the first time that it had happened at home. How did someone publish a document on her screen for her to see without knowing she was there? What technology was used to get into her laptop? She was not aware that she had ever given consent for that. She had to ask Annelies to get to the bottom of this mystery. This hyperlink was active; she clicked on it, and it appeared. She loved the graphic under the title.

Excerpt Five[1]

Program Planet Earth

The Eye of Horus

The subject of the excerpt riveted Ingrid. POWAH had responded to her query about the motif in the aerial photo. Who was the keeper of the game? Did POWAH imply that he had put it there?

---

1. https://allrealityshifters.wordpress.com/powah/the-reality-shifters-excerpt-5/

Reading over Excerpts four and five, she was impressed with Richard's conclusion.

She had given him the flash drive to study further. The file on the USB stick Piet had given her had the same image, but the vague watermark impression that reminded her of crop circles wasn't on it. She wondered if she could type a question.

POWAH, what happens when we go through this acceleration process?

To her amazement, a lot of text appeared in reply.

<Kitty, your questioning mind has activated the knowledge in the unconscious. New ideas will shift into your subconscious. Prepare yourself for some disturbances. The brain must go through a time-acceleration process during your awakening. For the brain to accept new knowledge, a new bioengineering process is activated to correct retrogressive evolution. You are now entering this acceleration period, which will last between 2019 and 2025.

Gee, what was so special about the years between 2019 and 2025? If today's technology reaches more people, what happens after 2025?

<Kitty, Richard is on the right track. In your aerial photo, you see the symbol of the Eye of Horus. The difference in the design is that there is a white hole in the actual planetary eye. The aerial photo projects a black hole!>

What does that mean, negative energy?

<As you make the body codes of light cards, we will release more on the black hole. Kitty, your mission in this lifetime is to allow your Soul to learn to love spontaneously while remaining fully grounded in your form and to open your heart chakra. Listen to what your feelings tell you. You seem embarrassed by this challenge, are you not?

What would POWAH mean by loving spontaneously? Was it something to do with her fear of revealing her inner feelings? She was now truly curious...

POWAH, are you referring to my handling of a love relationship? She felt rather silly to type this intimate confession to an unknown individual, but how could one distinguish between a purely sexual attraction and genuine affection? She probably overthought her feelings and wondered if she could recognise the difference.

<Kitty, you will attract your true strengths and gifts once you begin to let go of old mental and emotional barriers through the releasing process.

>Your Soul-knowledge will awaken and invite a Soul partner to experience a divine union reflecting your inner communions. See it as a gift>

What did POWAH mean by her Soul partner? Ingrid knew she was on the edge of falling in love. But how did she know Toon would be compatible on a Soul level? She knew nothing about him! For all she knew, she would hear no more from him. Her relationship with Jan had certainly not been easy. She was not about to start one like that again, no matter how good it had been at the end. She truly felt as if...was she already experiencing a reality shift while communicating in this way?

Her screen still showed the last text message...Thinking about Piet and the creepy caller at work, she now wondered...

POWAH, is the symbol a warning as well?

Thinking about the black centre she'd taken to be a pupil within the eye symbol, she knew that black holes are created when stars die catastrophically in a supernova. Richard would be very interested in what POWAH had just written. She would print it out if she could.

< Kitty, dark forces that were left behind by previous spiritual beings are now being manipulated like a virus in a computer.

You are right; black holes reveal a warning! Speak to Liesbeth about it.

Wow, at that moment, her printer started working! Gosh, this was getting uncanny. Fluffball kept asking for her attention as she jumped up to see what, who or why her printer was suddenly working. YES, their conversations are captured on paper... How creepy. She now wondered if she needed to stay discerning...

POWAH, does my personality have a negative or fearful effect on my reasoning? She typed quickly to verbalise her thoughts while the printer was working. How will I know the difference? Are we humans being manipulated?

<Your ego personality does not always have your best interests at heart on this physical plane. It feels lost and threatened>

Who are the dark forces, aliens?

<No Kitty, on this awakening journey, feelings reflecting fear are within the human hologram that must be released. Your Earth philosophies have advised that you reject it by giving it a very negative value for you to stop questioning it.

That reply made her think of Wim, who had belittled Niels in the workshop about conspiracy theories.

<When your true self, by loving self-acceptance, is not nurtured, a negative false self that reflects unworthiness and self-criticism will draw the dark forces into you. Can you see that in Piet? Your personality also pretends to protect you from disappointment and a sense of failure.** She suddenly jolted when Fluffball jumped onto her lap and settled in. Cats do know how to be comfortable. Her purring went right through her.

Gosh, reading the name...POWAH mentioned Piet! She was staring at a blank screen... then the text reappeared while the printer continued.

<Through expressing fear, humanity is trapped by dark forces that cause all the upheavals you might experience. Be aware!

The dark forces seek to prevent humans like you, now close to their evolutionary shift, from fully awakening. This means that you cannot leave any negative thought form behind.>

That almost sounded like an impossibility. How could she stop having negative thoughts?

<Cosmic consciousness will awaken globally. Love yourself, for you deserve it. Kitty, be prepared to experience a different union on a soul level, which often takes a leap of faith. Love POWAH>

First, the mention of Piet and then, entrapment by dark forces! What was all this? Who typed this? Was POWAH an Alien? Liesbeth had mentioned that he came from a higher level in the spiritual realm. Why would something or someone want to prevent their evolution? She must talk to Annelies and find out what union POWAH was referring to. Suddenly, it felt like she was back in her study, as if nothing had happened, but the printed pages told her otherwise.

Pleasure Parks

The week was over before she knew it. The courier delivered her drawings that morning with a letter from Mr Brinks. He requested that she set up a meeting with Toon Haardens.

While dialling the Buttercup landscaping firm, she wondered where Toon was. She had not heard from him and was annoyed with herself for still thinking about him.

"The Buttercup, can I help you?" a young woman chirped. She wondered what had happened to his previous receptionist, Nel.

"May I please speak to Mr. Haardens? It's Ingrid Barendse from Pleasure Parks."

"Mrs. Barendse, I will phone Mr. Haardens for you."

"Oh, where is he?"

"In South Africa. He will be back next week, but was adamant that I must phone him when you phoned." Toon's new receptionist in-

troduced herself as Ellie and said she had her work and home numbers. She wished Ellie a good weekend, wondering if Nel had been
fired. She couldn't focus on her work, and her heart skipped when
the phone rang.

"Ingrid speak..."

"Hello, stranger, I've been missing you. My receptionist told me to
phone you directly because you are going out tonight." She had to
grin.

That's very good. Let him think I'm leading a busy social life. Then
she heard the sound of roaring surf and gulls in the background.

"Toon. I hear seagulls. Are you busy landscaping?" She wished she
was with him in far-off South Africa. All she had read about that
country was the Western Cape's critical drinking water situation.

*"What's this woman doing to me? I don't enjoy myself as I used to. I
keep thinking about her, wishing she was here with me,"* ...did she tap
into his mind...or was this her wishful thinking? She hoped not.

"Yes, you heard correctly. There are seagulls because I'm near the
beach and landscaping, building a community like the one we've
discussed. I could use some of your creative drawing skills.

Are you interested in the job, and what are you doing tonight?" he
asked in one sentence.

How interesting, but him as a boss?! No way, never! Sorry, mate,
but that is not on; she would ignore that question. *"She wants to
be a business partner?"* That's more in the right direction, smiling to
herself for sensing his thoughts and wondering what that would be
like.

"Toon, Mr Brinks asked for you. Can you contact him on his cell
phone? It's urgent."

"I will, but I want to know where you are going tonight." Gee, he is
persistent.

"Remember my art classes on a Friday? Toon, tell me all about your community when you come back. When are you coming back any-way?" She hoped she did not sound too eager.

"I am glad you asked. Hopefully, next week, I'll see you again soon. By the way, what do you need art classes for?" Someone was talking to him in the background. He promised to phone her again just for a chat...

Class 3

DETACHMENT was written on the door as they all filtered into the room. Every week, there were different 3D symbols projected on the wall and a large colour drawing of a human body. The millions of other coloured lines, swirls and funnels, all encapsulated in a grid around the human body, dominated the room.

Annelies told them that Liesbeth had been called away.

"I'm sorry to hear that. Will she miss the classes? I hope not."

"No, I'll make a plan, don't worry. I wouldn't allow her to miss our little group. Tonight, we're decoding your three Youth and three Health cards. They belong to the third level of the reality-shifting process. Are there any questions from last week's decoding?"

"Yes, Annelies, I just want to clear this Soul stuff in my mind. Is our unconscious mind the intelligence of the Soul?" Wim asked in his colourless tone. *"Well, well, he's warming up."*

"Yes, that's how I have chosen to see it now.

All the experiences of many lifetimes on Earth or elsewhere are stored in our soul, etheric, and astral bodies. See it like an energy library that holds all information ever experienced." Annelies winked at Zola, who looked at Wim with affection.

"I never connected our Soul with the astral holographic body. I thought Soul was everywhere, but it makes sense to me intellectu-ally,"

Wim nodded.

"Our Soul is everywhere. Don't compartmentalise Soul. We are all channels of Soul."

"Annelies, this means that our Soul can be separated from our physical body, yet still be connected to the Etheric body through which the mind, the intelligence of our Soul, is channelling?" Richard's notepad was as untidy as his car, Ingrid noticed.

"I wonder if he remembers his dreams?" Annelies pondered.

"Yes, your subconscious mind relates to your Soul, and your Spirit relates to your animating spiritual life force that we know as a living being. Some call it Chi or Prana."

"Annelies, if the etheric body through which the mind channels is the unconscious intelligence of our Soul, does the Soul know about all the other lifetimes?" Ingrid asked, thinking of the many past lives the Soul must know about.

"Not past lives, more like parallel lives, Ingrid."

"Well...yes, and no. The Etheric body imprints the memory of an incarnation in the Astral body, but...yes, Ingrid, your Soul holds all the experiences of many lives, whether in or out of a thought form vehicle.

The Soul is the real us, the I Am knows no time."

"You mean that our Soul is independent of our body and not in the physical body? I'm getting all muddled up now." Yolanda remarked.

"Annie, you confuse me with the thought 'time.'"

"Our Soul is seen to hover above our physical form in general, but again...yes, and by the way, when we are dreaming, we travel mentally with the Etheric or astral body." Richard looked at Annelies with anticipation.

"Annelies, when people say they have had an out-of-body experience, does that mean they consciously remember their dreams?"

"That's right," *"and you do, right?"* Annelies projected, but Richard didn't react at all.

"We all travel astrally while still living in the physical body, but the spirit spark, the life energy that some call the IAM, remains within the physical body during that time. *"Come on, Richard, start sharing!"* Annelies projected. Ingrid looked at Yolanda, who raised her eyebrows.

"Annelies, when we see the silver cord where our life force runs through in our dreams, disconnect, people depart, not so?" Richard's voice quivered.

"Yes, my boy. It's their choice to do so. For many reasons, when the Spirit or the I Am leaves our physical body permanently, the Soul sees no point in staying due to a lack of spiritual awareness, or the Soul energy wants to work on the lower astral planes."

"Richard, ask Theo why he left." Ingrid wondered why Annelies talked to Richard telepathically. She could see that Richard was distressed.

"And during waking hours?" She asked. Ingrid wanted to change the subject, and her sister had mentioned seeing this.

"A clairvoyant told me that she could see when the aura was lopsided, as she used to call it."

"She is probably seeing an ungrounded person or someone out of balance. That is why grounding practices are important during our awakening. *"Ingrid, it is important to be in the 'feeling'; that is more grounding!"* Ingrid realized that Annelies intentionally stirred Richard's emotions so he would feel and deal with his pain.

"You got it. His dreams are, at the moment, fantasies, but will change soon."

"We'll discuss the grounding skills in more detail later. I know it's a lot to take in, but it will become clearer when we make the cards. Let's go on with the decoding of our three Youth cards."

The young Labrador named Joris wanted to enter the room, and Annelies let him in. "Joris, you promised me to be good. Be quiet so your boss will be proud of you when he returns."
Ingrid wondered if dogs are telepathic.
"Annelies, these six spacings we are decoding tonight, will they reflect why we were born?" Niels asked in his easy-going manner. Joris went straight to Niels, who adopted him on the spot as he settled under his chair.
"Your three youth cards will activate your genetic and etheric blueprint. You have incarnated this geometric pattern to reveal at what level your frequency has been the most effective between zero and seven years."
"Is that not the time our personality was formed?" Ingrid always enjoyed seeing Yolanda, who was dressed in quite way-out clothes. She must ask her if she made them during their coffee break.
"Well, Yolanda, you could say that. It's when your personality develops that behaviour patterns are shaped." *That is why rebirthing is important for some; Connie will need this.*"
"What do you mean by 'shaped'?" Zola questioned, frowning.
Ingrid became aware of Yolanda's pain. What did Annelies mean about Connie?
"Zola, in these early years, we have all been affected or even traumatised by our surroundings, especially when our feelings were threatened or attacked in some way. When we are very young, the little neurons in our brain connect rapidly, so any perceptual observation is immediately established or formed forever."
"Ingrid, any disharmony around children is destructive." That hit home! What about her children?
"The letting go of this programming is the most difficult stage of the resurrection process. In later classes, we will explore the lies we all have been exposed to." Annelies explained more about the decoding and the 22 spacings.

***

During the coffee break, Yolanda asked Ingrid about her drafting skills, and she asked Yolanda if she designed her clothes. Yolanda's long blond hair was all held up very casually by a sizeable red clasp. "Yes, that's my hobby. I love to create wearable art. For you to have noticed it is a compliment, you know!" Yolanda laughed with pleasure.

"Wow, what makes you say that?"

"Do you have any idea how well you dress? You have a natural talent for throwing things together and still look like you've stepped out of some designer's boutique."

"Thank you, but no, I was not aware of it. I don't perceive that in myself, but it's nice to hear." She smiled, remembering when she and her sister were teenagers in Amsterdam. Her mother always had a strict rule about what was not aesthetically pleasing and what was. It must have paid off.

Niels asked Gerrit what living in an orphanage had been like. Joris had not left his side, and she wondered if his boss was Annelies' husband.

"Well, I don't know what it's like growing up in a nuclear family, so I feel I was very fortunate that we learned a lot of things that you don't learn otherwise," Gerrit replied casually. He was both a scientist and an artist.

"Like what?" Niels hinted curiously, and Gerrit laughed.

"The nuns were psychics who inspired us to develop our psychic abilities. Unusual, but there you are..."

Niels contemplated this when suddenly he appeared startled as Ingrid watched him. Annelies asked Gerrit whether he remembered a baby found at the orphanage while he lived there." Ingrid was aware of an incredible desolation coming from Annelies. Why was that, she wondered?

"I left the orphanage when I was eighteen and can't remember. It must have been long after I left. Are you thinking of Liesbeth?"

"Never mind. Ingrid, look at your email when you get home. There is something for you for your journal." Ingrid was acutely aware that Annelies had quickly changed the subject. All were aware that the atmosphere had changed, but why? Even Joris got up and licked Annelies' hand. Had he sensed it also?

***

Driving home past Palace 'Het Loo', she had to think about her father-in-law. He lived in a modern palace in Mijnsherenland. He had phoned her at work, asking when she would visit him. He was significantly involved in his steel company but felt like retiring. He had been a great support during Jan's illness and encouraged her to learn to draw with the latest program on the market. He told her that he'd asked Ed to come home. Jan's brother had not been on her mind for a while since she'd met Toon. Her father-in-law had been probing her about Ed...All she wished for was that Toon would phone soon.

Arriving at home

At home, she checked her email on her laptop in her tiny office, hoping to hear from Jeroen, when the familiar bright blue background suddenly appeared with the exact running text. Somebody must have seen that she was home. Fluffball knows. He was upset at being left alone.

<Kitty, the time is at hand to lay the foundations for the next quantum leap in humanity's spiritual evolution. By diligently clearing and releasing all past ego actions that have brought pain or guilt, you begin to recognise them for what they are. In 'cyberspace', you will read that detachment means letting go of the old thought forms that occupy the auric fields of most humans. The three youth cards represent your genetic blueprint

chosen this lifetime. The three health cards reflect what you think, feel and believe yourselves to be.>

<Combine what you have learned by decoding your spacings with your Human Design chart online>

A feeling of guilt suddenly overwhelmed her. Letting go of old thought forms made her aware of her own. Could she ever forgive herself? Could she ever let go of the pain? The silence in the house was bringing up some loneliness

<Kitty, a woman who carries a secret, is exhausted because it will drain your chi, remember that. The three health cards are challenging for most of you to confront. Be prepared for the release process to proceed to the fourth level of the reality-shifting game.

LOVE POWAH>

Her emotions were welling up in her throat while reading the text. How did he know that she carried a secret? Most people held secrets, even Annelies and Richard, who hid something. She hated to spoil her wonderful evening and could not bring herself to think about it. The phone rang, and her sister's face appeared, bringing her relief.

"Hi, Ingrid, I'm back!"

"Quincy! I knew it was you! How was your trip? When did you get home?"

"Oh, Ingrid ... a lot has happened. Oliver and I had a nasty fight when I came home; Kim moved out. She's staying with a girlfriend, or so she says. I'm so miserable." Her sister's voice broke down over the line. Ingrid didn't know what to say, for her sister had had a very stormy relationship with Oliver for as long as she could remember. She asked her what the fight was about this time because Oliver hated anything Quincy was interested in.

"Kim asked me for money, which she needed for some college function. I told her to go and ask Oliver. Well, did that spark some reaction? But I don't think it's the money or the trip. Oliver's been secretive lately, and I can see his aura has many brown flecks."

Ingrid had always envied her sister for being able to see auras. Their granny had always tried to awaken the psychic gifts she was convinced they both had. Her mother disliked her mother-in-law because of the old lady's interest in the occult. Her mother had judged any esoteric practices evil, and she had banned them after Gran died when she was nine. Ingrid recalled her parents' combative marriage, and she had often suspected her father of being unfaithful. He was always away a great deal. She had usually felt abandoned by him because of his sudden disappearance. She now wondered if that was why she had difficulty trusting men herself.

"Quincy, did the trip reveal anything to you? I mean, what to do about your relationship?"

"Yes, it did. I'm getting too tired to make it work. I'm aware of being discouraged and feeling that I am never good enough." She probably tried too hard to please, she speculated.

"I've never been appreciated for anything I do. Kim says I take things too seriously, and I am too tense. Ingrid, tell me, am I too anxious?"

Ingrid knew her sister to be an absolute perfectionist. She could be upset if she felt others did not try as hard as she did. She evaded the question and suggested instead that Quincy come and stay for a while.

"I was hoping you would say that. I would love to be out of this house, and I have a friend who has offered to take care of the shop for me." Her younger sister was on her mind for the rest of the evening.

Quincy Hartman

Ingrid slipped silently out of bed to avoid waking QUINCY in the other room. The birds were chirping, nesting and preparing for a new season. Quincy suspected Oliver was having an affair. Despite the emotionally charged atmosphere, having her sister stay for a while was a rare treat. She could now share about POWAH and the reality-shifting workshop classes.

That Thursday morning, while driving to work, Ingrid felt a sense of joy again. The previous week, she had experienced restlessness and a loss of composure, which she didn't enjoy at all. She knew it had to do with missing Toon far more than she wanted to admit. For some reason, Toon had disrupted her whole existence.

When Ingrid arrived at her office, she could see by Marijke's posture that she was trapped in her world of misery. Oh dear, what could she do?

"Ingrid, I feel depressed. When is it ever going to stop?" Her sad voice conveyed her grey despair. Ingrid was at a loss for words and wrapped her arms around her. Marijke cried on her shoulder. She whispered the usual words of comfort, knowing that they were useless. Marijke's heaviness of grief and emotional stress vibrations drained her instead.

"I'm sorry. I'm not handling it very well. Paul has been away on a case, and Hendrika, my little girl, is withdrawing more and more into herself.

My oldest boy, Peter, has had his marks dropped at school. He so misses his little brother." All she could do was stroke Marijke's otherwise stylised shoulder-length straight black hair that needed a trim.

"Thank you. I feel better." Ingrid knew intellectually that suffering was a significant part of being human. It seemed the only emotion that could create shifts in perception.

The rest of the day passed uneventfully until the phone rang again. Her heart leapt, which irritated her. She waited, and instead of greeting the caller, she remained silent, holding the phone. *"She's playing a game with me; she knows it's me,"* she perceived very clearly. She didn't want to give herself away, suspecting he could read her mind.

"Ingrid speaking, can" ...

"You are playing with me, aren't you?" Ingrid had difficulty stifling her giggles when hearing his amusement; her heart was thumping. What an effect this man had on her!

"Toon! Where are you phoning from? Are you back?'" The words spilt out.

"Yes, I'm on my way. I want to take you out tonight after seven."

"Oh, Toon... my sister is staying with me, she's leaving tomorrow. I can't leave her alone tonight; she's going through a difficult time. I am sorry."

"Tomorrow night, are you going to your art classes again?"

"Yes, Toon, I am," she whispered. If only he knew how she felt, it might be for the best.

"*Heavens, now she's confusing me! She wants to go out with me but is unprepared to drop her art classes. What can be so special about them?*" Wow, was this for real? This was getting nerve-wracking! Was she genuinely hearing what some people were thinking out loud? Why now? Why with some people and not with others? She was used to picking up the texts her kids typed on their cell phones before they appeared, but this?

"Toon, I'm free on Saturday," she voiced cautiously, knowing she wanted to be with him yet not lose her independence. Oh, did she know what she wanted? She knew nothing about this man!

"I have a meeting in London on Saturday at lunchtime. Why don't you come with me?" Ingrid was stunned. London! His casual proposal was somewhat unexpected.

"Toon, let me think about that one. You...How...Oh, never mind, will you phone me on Friday evening? I'll be home after ten." Her inner turmoil made her almost incoherent.

"Ingrid, I do want to spend some time with you."

Relationships

While driving home from work, she had difficulty getting Toon out of her mind just after she had begun to feel more together. Walking up the driveway created some disturbance inside the house. The front door opened.

"JEROEN!" Both Quincy and Jeroen laughed at her surprised look.

"You're home!" The joy of seeing him helped disperse the conflict in her mind. Hugging her twin son reminded her of Jan, for he was as tall as his father had been but much thinner. Her twins were not a look-alike pair. She found him an exceptionally handsome male with tall, long eyelashes and thick, light brown, wavy hair that he wore at shoulder length, which his father would have hated.

"Coffee is ready! We've been waiting for you," Quincy called out from the kitchen. Ingrid could smell the Nasi-Goreng.

"What a treat!" Savouring the aromas of the cooking and the coffee, she glanced at another blue envelope lying next to the phone. The blue envelope made her think of the menu of the Prinsengracht Hotel and Toon! Jeroen had many stories to tell, and during the evening, Sascia, his twin sister, phoned to chat with him.

Annelies phoned to invite her to dinner the following evening, before the class started. Ingrid knew Quincy would go home that same evening. At least it compensated for her disappointment after refusing Toon's invitation to dinner, so she accepted with pleasure.

Jeroen had some work to do on her study computer, so they both relaxed in the lounge while Ingrid put on some tranquil music.

"Ingrid, I've been hearing lately that one has to practice being in the present. What does it mean to you?" She's in a philosophical mood tonight.

"Mmm, we must focus on our activity and not drift off mentally into the past or future. When we practice being fully in the moment by staying focused on the task, we are in the NOW. That's my perception of it."

"Mentally drifting away? What's wrong with that? My thoughts are always wandering,"

"I know what you mean, but I realise we create a fantasy world that way. Thoughts are very creative. We could unknowingly manifest the same stuff of the past or fear it will manifest again in the future."

Was that what she was worried about? Starting a relationship that could end like this, before Debbie was born? The sounds of a computer game Jeroen was playing from her office penetrated the walls. "Oh, yes, I get it. While cooking the meal this evening, I was thinking about my argument with Oliver."

"To avoid creating things we don't want in our lives seems very difficult for me, too. When you just said you were disappointed with yourself, you suddenly gave me an insight. I have only lately truly been pleased with myself. Mind you, specks of feelings, needs, and expectations are still there. Annelies calls them personality entities."

"You mean that I'm creating my problems with Oliver by mentally focusing on them?"

"Yes, I gather we all do, Quincy." She hoped her sister could handle this reflection. Her wavy, long, dark blond hair was fastened into a high, loose French roll with shorter pieces of hair falling around her face. They were of the same height.

"Mmm...where are our thoughts? Is that our immediate future? I'm always worried about not being perfect. I guess I'm not! I must learn at least to live it...or visualise what I want." Quincy speculated while stroking Fluffball.

"Yes, I gather we must live it first, already pretending we have what we want before it becomes real. It's something like faking it before you make it. That sounds, I suppose, as if I mean that you must deny your feelings. I don't mean it that way, but it feels as if we have to let go of the pain of it." Ingrid wondered if she could do that herself.

"I have to accept the way Oliver is. You're saying that's all I can do?"

"Yes and no, ...Quincy, the pain and hurt we are reacting to is an opportunity to discover what we want out of life...or...we learn to give ourselves those needs without needing others. Not easy, is it?" She hugged her sister as she observed her loneliness.

"No, say that again. I can see how I repeat or at least seem to attract the things I don't want. I probably give those thoughts the most power, especially when my feelings are involved. Are you saying that those are needs that I must acknowledge and give to myself? But how?" The tears flowed down her cheeks.

"Do you feel entitled to them?"

"Yes, I suppose I do, and Oliver feels entitled to have his needs met. So, he has found someone else who will do just that." Her sister's reply was objective, but the emotional pain had reached the surface. Ingrid knew that energy cords between people are an attachment, positive or negative. Breaking this attachment because it creates an unhealthy dependency is difficult to do. People become addicted to their attachments for their personal needs. To give Quincy time to balance her emotions, she poured more coffee and offered a stroopwafel she had bought fresh at the market.

"Ingrid, if we imagine mentally what we want out of life, could we create it, do you think?" Ingrid only had to think about her focus. She had been asking what it would be like to experience a spiritual awakening. She had focused on a feeling almost like being in love with herself instead of just liking herself. That must have attracted the latest people in her life.

"Yes, I think so. It will come about if you act or feel you already have it, providing you know what you want." She smiled like a well-fed cat as she thought about Toon. Had she asked for a new love in her life without knowing it? Why, then, was she in fear of a new relationship?

What was Toon reflecting on her, she wondered?

"So, if I've been focusing on things I do not want, I've created them!

Wow. I must begin to learn this trick of positive thinking. Now I can understand how it can work!"

Ingrid wondered how a relationship would function if it were established without one needing anything from one's partner. Would each one in such a relationship complement the other completely? Would it be possible? Would Toon have any needs he would want her to meet? She knew the answer to that one: Oh yes, he would like a sexual relationship. That was very clear to her, and what about herself? She had to admit that she had started to miss that physical intimacy as well.

But then she knew it would not be enough. She recalled her loneliness within her relationship, even when the sex was good. There was still a space, a void, and she knew Jan had felt it too. Was wanting to be in each other's company a need? She had repressed that need, which was ignited by being with Toon. She could not explain it, but even talking with him evoked a feeling of a once-lost love. It must have to do with their telepathic communication. Would Toon be aware of that?

"Ingrid, I've been thinking about what you told me last evening. What is the goal of your decoding classes?"

"To physically become a reality shifter." Quincy's expression made her laugh. Man found her attractive but somewhat analytical.

"As long as the personality aspects are in control, we will never know who we are."

"What do you mean by 'personality aspects'?" Fluffball's purring made her think of the personalities of animals. Or did they take on people's characteristics?

"Annelies explained that our Soul, through the many incarnations in the illusion of the 3rd dimension, has become fragmented. Those fragmented pieces became personality aspects."

"Really! That's a thought. Let me get this right. Are we scattered into 22 pieces or aspects? And what do you mean by fragmented realities?"

Quincy pressed on. Ingrid had missed these talks. How would Toon react to all this? Oh, what if he were like Jan, not all that interested? What then?

"I mean, our human form is an illusion, but our Soul decides to participate in experiencing this illusion to awaken to full consciousness. Our Soul will not achieve its purpose by believing that the past, present, and future are real. Those are personality concepts because they only know time and space." At least, that was how she grasped it for now.

"But that does not explain what you mean by shifting our realities. My personality thinks everything has a beginning, a middle and an end. When we look at nature or even our bodies, we experience that everything has a beginning and an end, as in birth, life, and death."

Quincy's disbelief at what she had said was apparent.

"I know, but the moment we consciously invite our Soul to participate in awakening to the possibility that it mightn't be real, our personality feels threatened. Our world seems full of whatever we focus on, but that is not the case. It will tell us that everything around us is all there is."

She shared the idea she had come up with during class about the character Smeagol in the movie The Lord of the Rings. They both had seen the movie years ago. She poured a liqueur for both of them while Fluffball jumped off Quincy's lap.

"And so, it still is for me; this life is all genuine. I remember ten years ago when we studied A Course in Miracles. I had difficulty with that illusion concept." Quincy sighed. Quincy had always shared her clairvoyant tendencies when they were home sharing a bedroom, but lately, she has kept them to herself as she did about her telepathic skills?

"To understand our oneness with all life properly, we must change our perceptions of ourselves and discover who we are. Annelies said that our inner self-talk is a running dialogue with the universe, so we create our outer reality." Ingrid thought about her sudden telepathic abilities.

"Mmm....do you mean that if our personality controls our daily thoughts, we'll keep creating the same illusory patterns and going around in a circle?"

"Yes, we are going in a circle. We've created our physical manifestations around us. What has been in our subconscious and conscious thoughts will continue." It always amazed her when she had an insight. "That's the illusion! Of course!"

"You mean that the past is at the same time our future?"

"Yes, so our future has already happened in the past. Quincy, it suddenly makes sense to me: being in the NOW is closer to reality! Annelies told us in the introduction class that the reality-shifting card game is designed to help us become aware that we get what we ask for!" This sudden self-empowerment made her feel in control. Quincy's grey-blue eyes looked dreamy as if she recalled a more profound, more soul-searching memory.

"Quincy, I feel so lucky to have an inner desire to express my Soul's purpose. Her face beamed as she re-lived some of her experiences.

"If my Soul wants to ascend with this physical body, then I have to let go of anything that would not be in accordance with this intention."

Toon's face jumped to mind when she uttered those words, but she squashed the reason why immediately.

"Good grief, that is a tall order!"

"Mom, there is an email for you from Liesbeth," Jeroen called from her study.

"I'd better have a look." She left Quincy pondering in the lounge.

——- Original Message ——-

From: "Liesbeth "

To: <Ingrid Barendse:;>

Sent: Saturday, May-18, 2019 7:21 AM

Subject: United World Congress

Dear Ingrid>

How are you? I am writing this letter on my laptop in my hotel room. I received an assignment the evening after we returned from our decoding class. I was asked to speak on the effect of the sun's solar flare. I wish you were here, as some of the topics made me think of the classes and Annelies' decoding workshops.

Ingrid, guess what? One of the speakers, Hans Jaarsma, spoke on Mother Earth – The New Consciousness and Life-giving Water! He's jolly interesting.

He explained that there were physicists who worked at CERN and that he warned them, but they ignored him.

"Annelies will help me with my decoding, and I believe she's invited us both to dinner tomorrow night. See you then, and we'll make a date to have supper together. I still want to hear your story, remember! Have a great day.

Love Liesbeth

"Mom! You must invite her for dinner...but now I'm going to bed. I know you want to know my plans: I'll enrol in September for my last semester; I've already confirmed it."

"Jeroen! I'm so glad." smothering him with a hug. "Do phone Grandpa and tell him tomorrow, won't you? I'll talk briefly with Quincy as she's going home tomorrow."

"Is she going to divorce Oliver?" Jeroen whispered

"I don't know, love. It looks as if your uncle has found someone else whom he prefers to be with, so who knows what's going to happen." When she returned to the lounge, she remembered the blue envelope.

"Quincy, let's see what's in the envelope that arrived mysteriously." Ingrid waited for Quincy to finish reading.

How was it possible that only a while before, they had been talking about being in the present when this letter was already in the room with them! Another coincidence? This letter was not called an Excerpt.

Dear Kitty

< Your reality happens only in a moment. The Past, Present, and Future are perceptions that are encoded in stone. Time is also encoded in the language you speak, specifically in the use of tense: past, present, and future.

< Only when one releases one's expectations of the outcome that things must look a certain way are you in the moment. Only then can a shift in perception take place.

< Humanity needs to let go of all concepts containing limitations. By allowing the mind to be more receptive to the flooding of the memory of who you indeed are, this shift in perception will prepare you for your communion with your Soul. By consciously grounding yourself daily with your planet and allowing the wisdom of your loving soul to come through, you can enjoy and love being fully in each moment, living in the present!

< Being in the present means letting go of all the memories of pain or anything that has inflicted pain on you. This means breaking the attachment cords, which are personality entities. Then the memory of emotional pain, suffering and hurt will not be experienced anymore. The experience of joy and peace carries no sense of fear. Only in the sense of fear do you give meaning to time. In reality, nothing exists that has an opposite.

>Only in your illusory world do you experience duality. Like this channel, stick with the plan of acting awake! You are already awake!

Love POWAH>

"Kitty, this is very thought-provoking! How did you get this, and from whom?"

"It almost seems that the message I get is always related to whatever is in my mind or our minds in this case."

"That's right, we were talking about being in the present, and you certainly did not type this! It all sounds fascinating," Ingrid smiled at the words; 'You certainly did not type this.' Her sister was always very upfront about expressing her thoughts.

"You are telling me you don't know who delivered this letter? Was it just thrown through your letterbox with no return address?"

"The blue envelope was next to the phone in the hallway when I came in. You must have been home when it arrived. I presumed that it again came through the post."

"What do you mean... again."

"I received the first excerpt through the mail since it was lying on the floor in the hallway. The second excerpt was given to me by Connie, who works near the bookshop. She told me that it came from her aunt Annelies."

"She is the woman who gives these decoding workshops?"

"Yes, but I never met her until a few days later. The third excerpt came through my email at work, straight after my chat with POWAH over the internet. What is so weird is that I'm not using any chat programs. POWAH suddenly appears on my screen. That still has me baffled." Quincy never used a computer, so she was not clued up on the technical mastery.

"And the fourth excerpt?"

"Oh, that came directly from Annelies. She handed it to me in the same blue envelope, always with Kitty on it." Quincy looked tired.

She sensed that her attention span had dwindled. She tried to read her mind but couldn't.

"I have been deceiving myself. I now realise that staying in my relationship with Oliver has become destructive for both of us." Ingrid felt proud of her sister's acknowledgement as she hugged her.

"Ingrid, you have to go to work in the morning. Let's go to bed. I have to do some serious thinking. I'll ask for a sign, for I realise now that I've tried to be someone I'm not, just to please."

Ingrid wondered how life would be with a partner with the same intent. At least Toon was interested in community living, but...what about the reality-shifting process? Could he embrace that possibility...?

Or...was she being tested? ...

Chapter 6
The Balance of the Two Polarities

At the office

A large box with twelve red roses arrived at her office that morning, accompanied by a note. 'I will not give up; see you Saturday. T.' Ingrid's thoughts about joining Toon in London had wavered between her head and her heart. Her heart said, 'go for it,' but her mind fluttered, fearing getting hurt.

Driving home, the colourful garden arrangements and hanging baskets outside the shop windows showed her that summer had arrived. After arranging the roses in the lounge, she went upstairs to change into something casual that was still smart enough for that evening. She then joined Jeroen and Quincy, who were having cool drinks on the veranda.

"Mom, you look stunning. Whom are you meeting tonight?"

"Ingrid, is there someone in your class we should know about? Who are the roses from that you sneaked into the lounge just now?"

"Someone in connection with work, and don't ask." They exchanged glances when she indicated the subject was not open for discussion.

"Since I'm having dinner with Annelies, I'd better look different than usual. Am I too dressed up?"

"No, not at all, Mom, you look great. Shall we go?" Jeroen would give them both a lift to the station so he could use Ingrid's car.

Quincy's posture drooped from heaviness as they waited on the platform for the train. Jeroen stayed in the car.

"I'll give it another go, between Oliver and me. But I think my marriage could be beyond repair if you know what I mean." Ingrid knew that Quincy was still emotionally attached to Oliver.

Would she have been able to release her needling discontent for not being able to share her emotions? Yes, a large part of her had, but she never knew that. Now, for the first time, she felt released from the pain of Jan's death because of Toon. So, what did that mean? Was it hormonal, and would she fall for yet another attachment to someone who would not share her spiritual quest, not to mention her communication with POWAH and Annelies' decoding classes?

At the busy platform, the glances they received due to their elegance and magnetism worked as a tonic for Quincy. The lively glint in her eyes shortly returned. Despite the contrast in hair colour, build, and dress style, anyone looking would see they were sisters.

"Ingrid, let me know how the classes are going and when more baffling information arrives. It has been playing on my mind a lot."

"I will, and good luck at home!" Quincy looked sad when she embraced her.

Dinner party

Jeroen dropped her off at Annelies' house, and she reminded him that Liesbeth would give her a lift home.

Annelies and Joris warmly greeted her. It was a mild evening, and she followed them to the back of the house.

"Ingrid, I'm so glad you could make it a bit earlier to join us for a drink in my conservatory. I'll introduce you to two extraordinary people." Large tropical plants and the musical cadence of a waterfall greeted her.

"Liesbeth has been here since lunchtime, and Ingrid, this is my son HANS. He surprised me with a sudden visit." A tall young man with a very wise and striking face and a thick mop of almost white hair greeted her warmly. He appeared around six and a half feet tall; his hair was as white as that of a person with albinism, yet his face was a light tan, and his eyes a pale blue. His almost elfin quality made him look ageless. What an unusual-looking person Ingrid observed, attractive in a different way, with a very fit-looking body.

"Hi, I'm glad to see you, and thanks for your email," Ingrid whispered to Liesbeth, who looked glowing.

"Toon, meet Ingrid, who is the participant who will write about the first level of the decoding workshops." When she walked in, Annelies introduced her to a man obscured by a giant plant. Ingrid couldn't believe it when Toon got up from his chair. The laughter in his eyes as he took both hands while greeting her showed how he felt as if she were the only person in the room.

"Have you two met before?" *"Toon, what have you been hiding from me?"*

"Oh yes, I've met Ingrid several times," while he mentally teased, *"I've got you."* She could feel she was blushing.

"Anyone involved with Annelies' decoding project is of great interest to me," Toon said for everyone to hear, pointing at an empty chair next to him.

"When I learned all about you this afternoon from Liesbeth and realised that it was you, do you have any idea what I felt?" He had taken her hand close to his mouth when he spoke. Ingrid was caught off guard. She recalled that Toon had said he was staying with a family member.

"You've been staying with Annelies all the time, where I had the art classes?" Ingrid felt a tumultuous joy, and how he looked at her made her want to hold him. She knew everyone glanced at them, and Annelies' expression needed no interpretation. *"Well, well, have you ever?"* Her heartbeat had accelerated from the pure rapture of seeing him and from the fact that they might, after all, have something in common.

"Annelies, how did you know that I was approached to write about the first level of the decoding workshops?" she knew, her voice slightly shaky while Toon's eyes on her revealed his obvious adoration. It was clear who Joris's boss was. The dog sat practically on his feet.

"Have you not figured it out yet?"

"Annie, what does she mean?"

"Look at the time! Let's go to the dining room and have supper. Toon, will you please serve the drinks?" Annelies had ignored Toon's mental beam.

"Ingrid, you look stunning! I can't take my eyes off you." No sound had come out of his mouth, but his hypnotic look said it all. When his hand caressed her shoulder, it felt like an electric shock that ran down her spine. She wondered if he was aware of her reaction.

"By touching her, I feel my energy field blending with hers, and I know she's feeling it too. Could this be it?" He felt the same! How could she not fall hopelessly in love with him now?

Then she realised why she was asked to write about the first level. She had unconsciously asked for it!

"Ingrid, your thoughts are mighty!" Annelies winked.

"Annie, you are shielding me. Why?"

"You figure that out, that's your punishment for not...." Both Toon and Annelies were mentally challenging each other! Ingrid's mind somersaulted from pure rapture when Liesbeth's loving eyes flickered at her momentarily.

The table was already set, and the food was standing on a warmer on the side table. They helped themselves while Toon organised their drinks. He placed her wine glass on the table next to his.

"Where do you know each other from?" Liesbeth asked them both. Ingrid looked up and met his steady gaze.

"You tell them. I want to hear it from you," Toon beamed.

"Pleasure Parks uses landscapers and building contractors, and it is part of my job to organise the various subcontractors used for constructing the Parks around Europe. Toon is the new owner of one of our landscaping businesses."

"Mmm," Annelies looked at Toon. *"Now I understand your change of plans,"* Ingrid looked at Annelies, who pulled a face at Toon. *"Annie, don't you dare."*

Liesbeth and Hans were talking together, so Ingrid pretended to hear nothing.

"Don't worry, Toon, your secret is safe with me, but I think she's already able to join in." Ingrid was almost choking with discomfort, but kept pretending she had swallowed too much food. They communicated as if they were having an everyday conversation, but she could hear everything. This was the clearest telepathy she had ever experienced!

How would Toon...she'd better be careful!

"Ingrid, I know your boss, Harry Brinks, very well. Toon, do you remember Nick du Toit? He was the man who lost the bid on the Prinsengracht Hotel because of Harry Brinks. Harry made it possible for Fred and I to own the castle to turn it into the hotel we both wanted to do for so long."

"No, I didn't connect him with the hotel. Do you mean the real estate tycoon? Losing out to Harry Brinks must have been a nasty blow to Mr. du Toit's ego," Toon mocked.

"Oh, it was, and still is, I think. I haven't seen Harry Brinks since his wife's funeral five years ago."

Ingrid was amazed at the connections Annelies seemed to have. She wondered if Fred was her husband and why he was not there.

"Hans, how did Trevor and Otto do at Zurich's United World 2019 congress?" Annelies was a good hostess and made her feel very welcome.

"Mom, you know Trevor. It always amazes me how he manages to captivate his audience, and Liesbeth made quite an impression with her introduction on solar flares. Toon, you would have enjoyed hearing her." Hans was clearly in love, and Hans enchanted Liesbeth.

"Is that so? Liesbeth, you and I must share some ideas. How was Trevor's latest report on the Earth's weather received?"

"Toon, was that not your topic?"

"Very well, lots of questions about the possible blackouts. He told the audience about a new type of weather-reporting called 'space weather', which will monitor geomagnetic disturbances." Hans seemed to share an inner joke with Liesbeth, who carried on:

"Yes, because the dangers of solar flares to satellites and telecommunication will affect our radio and television transmissions."

Ingrid was amazed at the conversation topic and now knew that Toon had been the man on the radio.

"Grrr, the 'Elite' at the top of our societal pyramid have long been on the record saying that the world would be a much better place if six and a half billion 'inferior' people would just go away," Toon remarked after sipping his wine.

"We're going to experience some severe weather-related disasters, especially with the recent discovery that the sun's solar flares can create tornadoes and solar quakes," Toon confirmed her thoughts. Liesbeth looked at Toon with a speculative glance.

"Sadly, in the next 1–8 years, there would be so many cataclysmic earth changes that unless we all are specifically prepared for it, we would not survive."

"Are you referring to Planet X?"

"What do you know about it, Kitty?" Toon asked. They were all silent, waiting for her reply.

"My son, Jeroen, belongs to a Facebook group who have been following a planet called Nibiru or Planet X. They tell me that this planet is estimated to be 7 to 44 times bigger than the Earth. And its dramatic gravitational effects would cause apocalyptic disasters upon the Earth."

"Oh, Facebook. I'm sure many Nibiru conspiracy theorists believe that a group of ancient families ruled Planet X at the beginning of time and continues to pull the strings from behind the scenes." Annelies replied.

"So, it's all a Hoax?"

Both Annelies and Toon looked at Hans to see what his input would be.

"One of the weird features is that the Kuiper Belt – a circumstellar disc full of icy asteroids, comets, and dwarf planets that encompasses the solar system – orbits in the opposite direction to the planets within it. The existence of an unknown planet would explain this anomaly." Hans' mind was far away, as he replied as if he withheld something, but what?

"If this planet is there, could this explain why the solar system is slightly off balance?" Toon asked.

"The Babylonians and Sumerians told of a giant planet Nibiru that orbited the Sun every 3,600 years. So who knows where the truth lies?"

Ingrid was impressed with Annelies' cooking skills. There was a choice of fish and tuna, served with wild mushrooms and a spinach soufflé with Gouda cheese, asparagus, and dill. Even the sea vegetables were delicious.

"Toon, when the solar flares increase soil temperatures, if such high temperatures bake our crops in the fields, combined with drought in several places, including Cape Town and flooding conditions, what could the consequences be, do you think?"

"Liesbeth, that's hard to say; many adverse conditions occurring now are due to increased sun activity, and who knows, Planet X?" Toon was eating with relish.

"There will be a continued increase in satellite malfunctioning or failing. That will affect computers and telecommunications, including excessive static and poor transmission of RF and television signals.

Especially for daytime TV, AM and FM radio. Nevertheless, the website has been visited very regularly." Toon poured wine for everyone.

"Regarding these 'End Time' events people are all talking about, there are two camps on the matter," Hans commented.

They were all waiting to hear more.

"There are those with a strictly scientific background who acknowledge the existence of Planet X, yet quickly dismiss any scriptural reference to such a past occurrence or future prophetic fulfilment, and then there are those who are overly-religious, who disregard the scientific evidence that such a planet may have played in past secular or scriptural history, as well as future geological or biblically prophetic events."

"What are your perceptions, Hans?" she had to ask.

"I think the best perspective includes spiritual science and the scriptures."

"Toon, I'm surprised you weren't there. Did Otto take over your public lecture?" *Or has Ingrid got something to do with it? Why did you take over another construction firm? Don't you have enough around the world? I'm surprised you're not yet off to Australia?"* Ingrid was spellbound by verbal and mental conversation, but did not like hearing about Australia. Mr Zwiegelaar must have been the Trevor they were talking about.

"Toon, what would you have spoken about if you had been there?" Ingrid's heart pumped jerkily when asked, but she was genuinely interested.

"Mmm, I'm more interested in preparing people for the coming changes since the world is about to plunge into a new era of dwindling fossil fuels, and no one is prepared, and the pollution on our planet is getting alarming. Remember when the US economy went into recession at the end of 2016, early 2017, after the new United States president's inauguration." *"Woman, keep looking at me like that and..."*

"Toon, go slow, will you?" Toon watched her silently.

"Annie, I wonder how much she already knows?" She started to feel quite shaky about intruding mentally.

"More than you think. Have you told Ingrid about your communities?"

"Ingrid, what do you know about the photon belt theory?" Toon startled her with that question, and she recalled an article she'd read about that two months before.

"Oh, I did look it up on the internet... that about every 26.000 years, our Earth travels twice through this higher frequency band. As for the rest, nothing." Her heart was still beating rapidly while she kept eye contact.

"My love, I'm so interested in building communities. Specific preparations are essential, and we need to plan for being without electricity;" *"Are you going to join me?"* His look reflected a longing for a partner.

"Is this going to happen? There is no evidence of it as of yet." Her rapture of him as a partner in his community building gave her such... She'd better watch her thoughts!

"I think there is; look at the disasters related to fires; things explode quickly due to the light particles that are changing in the atmosphere."

"You mean... that climate change is a prime suspect in the rise of wildfires worldwide?"

"Oh dear, that's enough. If 10% of our human population calibrates above the conscious awareness level, the remaining 90% will automatically shift. Our decoding classes are being prepared so humanity will be ready for a planetary shift into a higher-dimensional reality. So, let's finish our dinner on a lighter note."

"Annelies, you are right. Although our weather has been behaving rather alarmingly, the Book of Revelation that Hans was referring to may be symbolic, it may also be literal, it may have been fulfilled in the first century, and it may also be re-fulfilled in the Last Days, all in every paragraph." Liesbeth added.

"Sorry, Mom", Hans replied. "But sadly, the biggest lies are the easiest ones to get away with because of their simplicity and the inability of the public to accept the audaciousness of their perpetrators."

Toon looked pensive... "Who knows, the next decades with oil wars, economic collapse, a shortfall of fresh drinking water and environmental catastrophe will be challenging. As a result, our global industrial civilisation is likely to collapse as others have in the past, but this time, the scale will be global – yet we are being cautious not to create mass panic."

Toon leaned over, whispering: "Ingrid, the photon-belt is of a higher frequency. I can already feel its energy, can't you?" His eyes glinted, but his flirting would not throw Ingrid off guard.

"Is that what you would have talked about, the photon belt? Does this higher frequency relate to the blackout you discussed over the radio?" Ingrid looked over her glass coyly. Toon's stare became so intense that she needed to look away.

"She heard my radio talk!" She almost gave herself away by responding.

His sudden, serious expression made her realise a different man was behind this flirting mode.

"Yes, I would have because times are changing rapidly now. We all choose to incarnate here on earth to experience a unique opportunity to evolve." His eyes accompanied the rest.

"That's why I'm so glad you have joined Annie's decoding class. She has practised it on me, you know." Ingrid had difficulty not exposing that she had heard all that.

"My love, in this life, we must remember our soul's purpose and connect with all our past lifetimes. Ingrid, you never told me that you heard that radio program?" He leaned over, stroking her chin. Ingrid had difficulty holding her cool while reaching for his hand, which took hold of hers for a split second.

"I didn't know who the speaker was at the time. I heard your surname and tried to connect your landscaping business and this electromagnetic field story but couldn't see any connection then." His eyes mesmerised her so powerfully that she felt pulled right into them. For a moment, she was only aware of Toon mentally making love to her.

"I can already feel my hands stroking your lovely breasts," she gasped for breath. Good grief, this man made her lose control. If her imagination whispered in her ear, her blush would give her away. Had he done that on purpose?

"The time is now to prepare on all levels: physically, emotionally, psychologically and spiritually. Toon is trying to prepare people socially, including creating and strengthening our community relationships, because life as we know it, with our accustomed lifestyles, may not be the same within a few years." Annelies took the lead in the conversation again as if nothing had happened! Hans and Annelies dominated the discussion by telling the others about Trevor's theories. The name was familiar, and the topic surrounding the planet's catastrophic events during the last three years made more sense than ever.

"Leo says this solar peak activity will extend from 2019 to 2025. Only those pure in heart and consciousness will survive this period of cosmic purification." Hans commented with some regret. Ingrid was amazed at that statement coming from such a young person, but what age would he be? He looked so ageless!

"Hans, too much information-gathering from the media about geological cataclysms could suck a lot of people into mass hypnosis and paralyse them with fear," Liesbeth's tone was both soft and wise.

"Yes, I know. We must rather develop a global awareness by using our social media." Hans playfully tickled Liesbeth's chin.

"Although there is a lot of disinformation deliberately published over the net ", Annelies responded.

She had never felt so at home with these people, as if she had always known them, but why?

"We have an opportunity if we apply ourselves to do the Soul work of many lifetimes during this period. This is why making some basic physical preparations now would be prudent. Are you going to assist me?" Toon whispered the last words. All she could do was gaze into his laughing eyes. Toon had an air of permanent, irresistible playfulness.

"Hans, Toon, I have to leave you men alone. My class starts in ten minutes, and I want to get ready." *"Toon, go slow on her"*, Annelies beamed. *"Annie, push off."*

Liesbeth and Hans were so engrossed in their private conversation that they hardly heard Annelies' words. Toon flirted, knowing she felt the same as him. Or was he teasing? He was not embarrassed or shy; all she could do was smile.

"Ingrid, I feel as if I knew you from long ago." Thank goodness the classes would start soon, for she was becoming increasingly unsettled, like a volcano about to erupt. The closeness between them stirred something.

Just now, she was about to reveal how infatuated she was. She so wanted to entice him just a little. Liesbeth was still in conversation with Hans when Toon suddenly wrapped his arm around her waist.

"Are you coming with me to London?" he whispered, his lips stroking her neck. Could he not feel her quivering when he did that?

Annelies greeted the others in the hallway while Toon held on to her.

"Ingrid, you know you want me as much as I want you. I can feel it," Oh, so he could read her feelings! Ingrid searched his face; with Toon to London for the weekend, he would only end up one way.

"Yes, I want to make love to you." Wow, he could read her thoughts! Part of her wanted to jump at the suggestion of London, while the other part was very nervous. Was she ready for that?

"I'll let you go now. We'll talk later." Her knees shook when she got up to join the others in the class.

"You have plenty to tell me; what did I miss?" Liesbeth's eyebrows said the rest.

"Meaning?"

"Shall we have a Cappuccino with Richard before I take you home tonight, or have you two made other plans?" Liesbeth teased.

"Oh, all right, gosh, I hope I can focus tonight," *And don't tell me Hans is just a boyfriend. This time, you are not fooling me!"* she beamed back while pretending she was sending her a text message from her cell. At least it was safe to try out her newly–discovered skills with Liesbeth. *"Ingrid, watch out, you are beaming all over. Annelies can hear you!"* She giggled out loud when she intuitively picked up op on Liesbeth's thoughts, if only to get her composure back when they were all looking at her as if...

Class 4

BECOMING AWARE OF BEING UNAWARE was written on the door.

"Tonight, we are decoding your three cards that play a major part in the fourth-dimensional realm. We play with these cards on the second level of the Ascension Decoding Card Game." At the same time, she raised her eyebrows to both of them. How much mental dialogue did she hear, Ingrid wondered?

"Annelies, when you say the fourth dimension, do you mean the etheric-astral level?" Richard was eager to learn all about the level he would write about. *"My boy, a lot will be revealed to you."*

"Yes, both the third and fourth simultaneously. These three spaces will reveal how you utilise your brain's left and right hemispheres and what soul character type you work through while in this incarnation."

Ingrid wondered what Annelies knew that they did not.

"You say we use these three cards only on the second level of the board game?"

"Why are you asking this, Ingrid?" She knew by asking a question, her mind would focus again.

"You are saying Soul has a character? I'm confused." To her, her Soul was more impersonal.

"On the second level, the personality card reflects what is a personal entity or fragmented part of the Soul and the main character of your Soul. I will give you a link to an excellent website on human design where each person can calculate their chart."

"I found that website, Annelies. All you need to do is fill in your date and time of birth, and then you will see a map that tells you what type you are." She shared. "My sister Quincy gave me the link on Facebook."

Ingrid was curious about who else had a profile on Facebook. She never got to it until a year ago, not with all the dramas of the year's past. Her two girls were.

"The second awakening level that we are playing with our cards is mainly an expression of an awareness level, like the first level."

Annelies showed various colourful cards with familiar symbols.

"Tieneke must have told you that your Language of Light quality cards are an energy currency during the decoding, not so?" She was baffled. She couldn't even remember what she had done with hers. Annelies asked if anyone could bring them along next week. Except for Wim, Zola and Liesbeth, all had attended Tieneke's mind-drawing workshop.

"You are only decoding the 'spacings' on your grid sheet for the second level tonight!" Annelies was eyeing her when she explained again how important it was to recall, on an energy level, why they all had an attraction for the shifting during their journey. She didn't know how the card game would help, but being in this group was already a reality shift.

"Our Soul has an individual characteristic pattern of its own, and when you make the individual cards in later sessions, you will learn much more about how and why we are all made up of light and dark vibrational personality thought forms or entities." Annelies continued, pointing to the holographic wall image that was also displayed on her laptop. Ingrid realised more and more how much intensive work was involved. She was to write about her personal experiences of how she experienced this reality shift on the first level through her five awakening cards.

"That means very personal, Ingrid. Are you up to it?" She heard. Gosh, was she? All she needed to do was keep a diary.

"Annelies, are we consciously trapped in our physical arena because we experience life through our five external senses?" Gerrit always asked good questions. Annelies was still for a moment. Gerrit was a man who never spoke unless he had something to say.

"Interesting observation" was her mental reply.

"Annelies, you mean that five-sensed human beings perceive the world by feeling, smelling, tasting, hearing and seeing? Zola held her hand out to Wim, who held his hands in his pockets.

"Yes, we experience our lives externally. The logic of the five senses of personality originated in the mind. They are the products of the intellect. Every vision or dream is already realised. The mind tricks you into thinking you must get from here to there. Zola, who do you think owns your mind?"

"Owns it? Me, who else?"

"Indeed, many of our technologies today are already controlling the minds of the masses. That is a good question, Annelies". Gerrit replied.

Wim whispered into Zola's ears, but she couldn't pick up what. She wondered if Annelies could.

"When we make each card, we will start to understand how we came to each perceptual experience that we call our reality." Suddenly, Annelies asked her.

"Ingrid, what is your personality card number spacing?" "Well, if I've calculated it correctly, a five!" *"Well, well, the introvert observer, that figures."*

"Mmm, can you be aloof at times? Do you see yourself as an observer?"

Annelies was tapping into her inner world, which was still very private. Exposing her thoughts to anyone was not easy. Jan had often complained that she could be withdrawn and aloof, which was true because she liked to observe things first before participating. She was about to respond when she mentally heard Annelies reading her thoughts.

"What a challenge that is going to be for Toon!"

Annelies, I was about to say 'yes'! I do like to be in control of my own life and usually don't follow others that easily." *"What did you mean by challenge?"*

"Well, now, Ingrid, you and I have to talk. *When are you letting that poor man know you are telepathic?"*

"It's all new to me. I will soon, but don't you tell Toon."

"Oh, I think he knows it already."

***

During the coffee break, she wondered if Toon was still around, but she would not look for him. That would give away how much she was captivated by him.

"Niels, is your girlfriend's name Carla by any chance?"

"Yes, how did you know?"

"A hunch, I guess, we work for the same firm. Carla spoke about making dinner for her boyfriend," Ingrid was again amazed how lately the people in her life seemed to be connected one way or another. She hoped Niels would be the man for Carla, who tended to be bossy. She hoped Niels could share his interest with her, apart from the fact that they both had to watch their weight!

The rest of the evening went fast. Annelies gave her a blue envelope again with the same number, 1888. She now understood why she had seen the same number on the menu of the Prinsengracht hotel. She owned it. Suddenly, Toon stood behind them in the hallway.

"Ingrid, can I give you a lift home?"

"Toon, why don't you join us for a Cappuccino at Richard's coffee bar?" Liesbeth interjected before Ingrid could say anything. She glanced at Toon sideways, sensing he was determined to be with her for as long as possible. She was still plagued by anxiety about the possibility of an affair. She knew herself far too well to think she could temporarily be casually intimate with someone. She wanted to be sure it was not just a sexual attraction, no matter how he seemed to think on the same wavelength as her. She accepted his offer, promising to do what was right for her.

The Pannekoek

As they drove to Apeldoorn's centre, Toon took her hand in his. What were his intentions, she wondered?

"This woman still has no idea how ecstatic I am about her." Gosh, when would he know she was telepathic? At the Pannekoek, she was about to get out when his arm slid around her, pulling her towards him.

"You must stop me when I go too fast... but be gentle." She almost burst out laughing from sheer nervousness. When they walked in, Connie was serving behind the counter.

"Hello! Have you all come from Aunt Annelies?" Ingrid had forgotten that Connie knew them both, but of course, they were her family members, Yolanda being her mother. Richard carried five Cappuccinos to their table.

"This is on the house," he chirped. Toon held her hand when he moved into the only long seat against the wall. His body pressed against hers when Liesbeth, Hans, and Richard joined them.

"Liesbeth, about your trip to Zurich: please tell us about it," Richard begged. Liesbeth looked at Hans, who explained that he had met Liesbeth in Zurich. Toon was enjoying himself. Liesbeth was a good storyteller, and her reflections on the expo were genuinely entertaining.

"Richard, Annelies told me you're giving a lecture on Egyptian hieroglyphic scripts?" Toon queried. Ingrid began to relax seeing Toon with the people she had much in common with. Somehow, she knew this would not have been Jan's choice. Ed, Jan's brother, would have been the same as Toon. Now, what made her suddenly think about him?

"Yes, I've studied ancient scriptures and learned much from my brother, Theo. Did you know him?" Richard asked Toon.

"No, I never met him, but Annelies and Ben often discussed him. I've lived abroad extensively, primarily in Australia and South Africa. Which of you three has been contacted by POWAH, Annelies' guide?"

"I have," she blurted out, reacting involuntarily to the unexpected question. They all looked at her for an explanation.

"Wow, Ingrid, what did you want to tell us a few weeks ago?" Liesbeth called out, realising it would put Ingrid in the spotlight, which she hated.

"Yes, it all happened about a month ago, and I still have to come to terms with it." She told them more or less what she had experienced, but Toon's eyes on her made it difficult.

"Gosh, Ingrid, I think I would react just the same as you did. I would also think someone was playing a trick on me. I will tell you all about my connection with POWAH one day." Richard's comment made her feel a lot better.

"Richard, remember I showed you the eye symbol on my laptop? I received more information from POWAH, and you were right about the Eye of Horus. Wait. I have it in my bag; I printed it out." Then she remembered her questions to POWAH, and his reply was... but it was too late. Toon would love her to question POWAH about her sexual feelings. How would she get out of that one?

While Liesbeth and Richard were reading, Toon gazed at her. *"What is she hiding from me on that printout?"* Oops, he had picked up her thoughts!

"Toon, he warns us about the outer or dark forces as he calls them. Fascinating reading! Is this coming via Trevor, I wonder?" Hans remarked. She sensed that both Hans and Liesbeth interacted with each other, but she couldn't translate what they were mentally saying to each other.

"Kitty, I don't want you to get worried about any dark forces; we will work through them. We know the conspiracies that only want to control the global population by fear." His gaze beamed total adoration.

"How did you know my nickname 'Kitty'?" She whispered. His eyes told her that she had given herself away. She quivered, holding her breath. He tightened his arm, drawing her towards him and only when Richard passed her printout did he take his eyes off her. He read it while still holding her close. She scanned his face for any expression when his eyebrows shot up. Then she knew that he had arrived at her dialogue with POWAH.

"So, Kitty, you are attracted to me on a sexual level. Yes, it gets better, and then he glowed. *"You're my soul's choice for a partner, Kitty, don't you know that?"* Ingrid blushed in consternation, unprepared for this exposure, while Liesbeth regarded her with great amusement.

Hans threw his head back and laughed just as Toon's arm slowly slid down her back and encircled her waist, pulling her to him.

"Toon, it looks as if you've found her at last. Both your souls are practically singing a symphony of joy. It's wonderful to see you two so deeply in love with each other. Now I know we are speeding up to a higher frequency." Richard must be the only one who could not hear Hans' telepathic remark when he said: "Ingrid, I hope to tell you soon what the hieroglyphs reveal. I have to prepare a lecture on the Sphinx, but I will look into it when I have time. May I keep the disk meanwhile?"

"I will speak to Trevor about the symbol, so may I keep this printout, Ingrid?" Toon added. *"He will want to meet you."* Ingrid lovingly gazed up at him but suddenly felt tired.

"It's getting late, so I'm going to take Ingrid home," Toon read her energy levels well and quickly moved her through the farewells to the car.

They were silent on the way to her home, each lost in thought.

***

"Ingrid, what did your husband die of?" while taking her hand, holding it on his lap. His sensitivity was very apparent. The intimacy he created while he focused on the road made her heart reach out to him. He must have been investigating her since he found out she was a widow!

"Jan was bedridden for three years before he died. The only conclusion the doctors could come up with was that he had suffered some poisoning that affected his nervous system."

After a break, she added, "They surmised that it was some neurological disorder. When they arrived at her house, he parked in her driveway. *"Go on, love, there must be more."* he leaned over to her, stroking her hair.

"We went all over Europe together looking for alternative cures when it started to affect him five years before he died. I would say the three years before his death were the hardest. His illness affected our whole family, as you can imagine." Ingrid was relieved by Jan's emotional battle with the fact that he was dying.

"My sister got involved in alternative healing, and Debbie, my youngest daughter, was inspired to go into nursing.

"That must have been difficult. Was it a good marriage?" She was quiet for a while, thinking about how it had been. Yes, she thought so; every marriage has problems, and they had survived many difficult times. She had never felt these intense feelings for Ed, but remembered many good times, too.

"How intense are they, Kitty?"

"Mmm, I think our marriage was good, and you, why have you never been married?" Ignoring his thoughts. How was it possible that this attractive man had managed to stay single?

"I never lived long enough anywhere to settle down or... met anyone I wanted to settle down with. I've always been too interested in Eastern philosophies to pursue having a family." Toon fingered her collar, which made her shake slightly.

"The women I was attracted to were not interested in any ...well, the few.... they were .... outlandish, out of balance and airy-fairy. I've had some intimate relationships, but they never ended in marriage."

His finger travelled slowly inside her blouse. Ingrid's nipples reacted, and Toon's breathing became more apparent. She was glad they were in the car with no lights on.

"I spent some years in India and Tibet, which must have been when you started a family. I've always known I would find my true Soul mate in this lifetime. That's why I could never settle down. Kitty, are you the one? It certainly feels that way to me." His voice trembled while pulling her towards him. Ingrid tried to control her breathing.

Was that why she felt like this? Did she believe that he was? He was a natural flirt, being aware of his hand that was very firmly encircling her waist while the other one stroked her breast.

"Toon, you are going too fast for me." Her voice trembled while she slid her arms around his shoulders.

"Ingrid...please, won't you come with me to London tomorrow? I want to get to know you again," she could see that he meant it.

"Just for the day?" while trying to take his hand away from her.

He reacted quickly by grabbing both her hands and pulling them behind her, making her lean against him, and he kissed her eagerly. For a moment, she allowed her sexual arousal to run free by responding to him. Toon was caressing her all over. His hands were so sensual. He had become far too intimate. She needed to pull away, knowing she was fearful of her reactions.

"Kitty, I want to make love to you."

"Toon, I can't... Jeroen is home... It's too fast, too soon!"

"Can I fetch you tomorrow morning at eight?" his lips sensuously explored her neck.

"Toon, please, I... all right, I'll come with you on one condition,"
"Oh, she wanted him too!"

"Oh, Ingrid, what possible conditions are you imposing on me? Can I not hold, kiss, or make love to you?"

"Toon, ... I'll go with you if you... Oh, Toon, please stop doing that" ...she moaned, shaking. He let her go reluctantly, and she knew it took all his self-control not to give in to his sexual arousal as it did with her. They were behaving like teenagers.

Ingrid left the car and walked to her front door, which Jeroen had already opened.

"Who brought you home, Mom?"

"Someone from the classes." She still felt shaky as she waved at Toon as he drove away. Jeroen walked back into the hallway, still wearing his overcoat.

"When did you come back then?" trying to act normal.

"Oh, only 15 minutes ago. Mom, who was he? Is he from your class?"

"No, he's a house guest of Annelies." All she wanted to do was look inside the envelope to read what POWAH had in store for her and sleep, dreaming about tomorrow. She carried the roses up to her bedroom to be near him.

Excerpt Six [1]

Program Planet Earth

The Balance of the Two Hemispheres

After reading POWAH excerpts from her laptop online, more questions are always stockpiled in the inbox file of her brain. Again, the eye of Horus was mentioned in connection with the pineal gland and how the two-hemisphere cards play a significant part in the awakening of consciousness that is not the body or the brain. Still, it manipulates to produce the human mind.

< **The duality of your universe has to be mastered. Duality is used to create an "us versus them" mentality. One is positive, and the other is passive.**

---

1. https://allrealityshifters.wordpress.com/powah/the-reality-shifters-excerpt-6/

< **"worse", which leads to an inflated ego or hating oneself. If you want peace in your life, It's recommended to let go of duality altogether.**>

Reading about the rewiring so that the right hemisphere would be heightened made her question. A divine union within the self can only occur when in balance. When the giant geodesic dome is positioned directly over the eye symbol, it will become a hemispheric synchronisation temple. She must keep writing in her diary, but now all she seemed to do was toss and turn from desire... trying to fall asleep...

Chapter 7

A Dream not Interpreted is a Letter not Read

Dreamtime

Ingrid's consciousness slowly drifted away, moving into the reflecting creations her thoughts had emanated from her immediate causal dream plane.

The familiar place made her drift towards the mountains, trailing up the steep, winding, gravel road. Her attention is drawn to an unusual rock formation next to which a man in casual cowboy gear observes her with a smile.

"Would you like to do this test?" he beamed as she noticed the sign: You already have eternal youth, health, beauty, and freedom in any physical expression you want. Come in and see for yourself.

"Why not? How long will it take?" It was an adventure game.

"For some, forever, for some, just a moment; for most, a lifetime", he replied, and instantly, she was in a large changing room with many other men and women. A loudspeaker on the wall broadcasts exquisite music, interrupted by a voice asking them to undress and place their palms on the glass panel next to the mirror. Their test would begin.

A couple did as request, stepped past the mirror and disappeared. Ingrid is very aware of how her nakedness plagues her as she undresses, but curiosity wins.

The mirror opens like a sliding door, and she walks across a wooden bridge.

Below her, in a colourful tropical garden, people are picnicking. Despite being naked, she's not cold. They wave to her, which makes her feel embarrassed.

Her perception of being overweight in places and all the things she dislikes about her body come rushing into her mind.

As she arrives at a tunnel lined with mirrors reflecting her body from all angles, voices as if many eyes are watching her cause her to tremble.

Then a white marble staircase comes into view where a man dressed as a doorman asks for her Present Physical Consciousness Card.

Instantly, she is aware of herself when he tells her to visualize wearing a garment. Her awkwardness as she walks towards a ballroom, where people are dancing and having fun, is overwhelming.

When the doorman announces her by name, everyone turns to greet her. She's standing naked, exposed for everyone to see! Her over-sensitivity to her physical faults overflows her mind, and she does not perceive herself wearing any gown! A voice within says:

"Create a temple for your Soul to stay grounded in." Ingrid knows she only intellectually invited her soul, not her heart, to take control. It's a jubilation experience dancing naked! Does her partner not see she's naked? He gazes at her, his eyes! She wants to disappear on the spot, recognizing those grey-blue eyes...

"It's your masculine side within that you see as a mirror. Kitty, embrace me lovingly," he whispers into her ear with a reassuring smile to be more relaxed. Her need for privacy is almost impossible to let go of when the man takes her to an elevator. When Ingrid steps in, he disappears. She knows that the mirrors in the lift reflect what hold thought forms have on the physical form. When the lift doors open, she's handed a dressing gown and a form and asked to sit in a room with raked seating.

Everyone is looking at a screen on which a naked woman is crossing a bridge, and you can see just how she feels! Naked!

A voice requests her to fill in the name and age while relating details about the naked woman's background. She is told to study the scoring from one to nine plus the more substantial master numbers on her form and to fill in any appropriate number she feels applies to the woman as she moves. At each of the digits, a word and a sentence reflect feelings expressed by the woman's body language.

1. Don't look at me! A fear of not being perfect! Self-focus is under pressure.

2. Tries to look for approval? Feel threatened and alone? Cautious, afraid to try something new?

3. A feeling of having no imagination? Still hangs onto old ideas about the self.

4. Afraid to venture forward? Are you bored and cut off? Lack of faith? Unwilling to do the test?

5. Experiences inner turmoil and acts very aloof, reclusive, and withdrawn.

6. Unwilling to cooperate? Oversensitive? Afraid of being rejected? Rigid. Full of self-pity?

7. Acts a bit irresponsibly, shows some very insecure feelings and is inclined to run away.

A Dream not Interpreted is a Letter not Read 107

8. Shows off, flashy, acts bored, expresses jealousy, needs to dominate, wants to be recognized.

9. Very emotional, moody, easily intimidated, shy, lack personal confidence, shows a martyr complex.

11. Domineering, or very critical, showing resentfulness and eccentricity, acting as if with head in the clouds.

22. Quick-tempered, boastful, self-pitying, aggressive, lacks sex appeal, unappreciative, held back by feelings of inferiority.

33. Clings is afraid to let go, argumentative, abrasive, cold, seeking seclusion, cautious, and ignoring consequences.

Ingrid gasped, knowing she must have been observed walking across the bridge. Then, an elderly, fit-looking man on the screen walks briskly across.

He even begins to look younger. He shows that he is unreserved and feels good about himself as he walks into the crowded ballroom.

She was searching for the familiar man she had danced with as she felt attracted to him. Some of the people around her are leaving, handing in their papers. Had she failed the test?

"Yes, for this moment. So now you know what you think about yourself, which is what others will see as real. They will reflect what is in your mind. Do you want to try again?"

Why not! She was hoping to meet the man who had encouraged her.

She handed in her paper and was suddenly in the dressing room again.

The difference is that now she feels less conspicuous, but when the voice over the intercom asks her again to disrobe, she is still trembling; from what? Where does this shyness come from? Children don't have it.

When it's her time to go, many people are on the bridge greeting her, but the mirrors everywhere only reflect her! Looking at her posture, she straightens up proudly.

This time, she observes her thoughts with confidence and gratitude.

Her inner guide, her authentic self, is awakening to experience itself in a human form.

Peering at her somewhat rounded body, her still firm breasts and her waist that still has the shape it always had and knowing she has good legs, the nerves in her stomach slowly relax. As she moves towards the marble steps, she visualises a deep-blue sealskin flowing fabric, clinging and figure-hugging, draping around her body, feeling her body moving as sinuous, firm and youthful towards the ballroom.

This is how she will see herself from now on, still wearing some covering, but of flimsy fabric that flatters her shape. Her whole body trembles with a desire for herself.

Instead of the doorman waiting to announce her, the very handsome man she had danced with before takes her into his arms while a dazzling smile appears on his face... Rrrrrrrr.

***

Just as the dream began to be intriguing, the radio alarm woke her up!

Her thoughts lingered like an aftertaste, knowing she quickly had to write down her dream. For the first time, she felt what it was really like to love oneself. This was what honour meant, to honour thyself...

For the first time, she missed having a sexual relationship. Oh, how was she ever going to be content again? Was that Toon in her dream?

Recalling the voice telling her to embrace her masculine side was quite revealing. Had her fantasy created an image of Toon?

"Get real, stop acting like a teenager," she scoffed when Toon's face appeared as her landline rang beside her bed.

"Kitty, did I wake you?"

"No, the alarm clock beat you to it. What's happened?" She knew something was wrong.

"Oh, love, when I arrived back at Annelies' house, we received a message from a relative. Otto, my half-brother, had a mild heart attack and both Annelies and I are on the way to him now, so I will not see you for a while, but I'll phone you soon.

"Kitty...you were in my dream last night." Ingrid could feel herself blushing, remembering her nakedness.

"You were in my dream, too."

Pleasure Parks Reception

"Ingrid, please come downstairs!" Ula pleaded over the internal speakers while everybody was busy entering data on the computers that Monday morning.

"What for, Ula? I'm busy." Piet had been hanging around, getting under her skin, nagging about the original aerial photo she used for her drawing. She knew he meant the one with the eye symbol.

She also read about CERN, a European Organisation for Nuclear Research, where physicists and engineers are probing the universe's fundamental structure. Was there a connection? Their laboratories are located deep underground, astride the Franco-Swiss border, but somehow, there was a connection with the Eye symbol visible from a great height.

Disappointment for not having spent the weekend with Toon had made her irritable.

"Ingrid, lots of roses have arrived for you. You won't believe it; someone must have placed an order with every local florist. Please come down; I can't leave my desk."

By now, everyone in the office building was alerted by the P.A system. When she got down to the foyer, an aroma of flowers greeted her. Several arrangements with the same message: "Before I found you, what I feel now only happened in my dreams. T." crowded Ula's counter.

Ingrid was flabbergasted. Why all these roses? One arrangement would have been sufficient. She phoned Toon's firm and got Ellie on the line. When she commented on the multiple arrangements, there was a long silence.

"Ingrid, how many did you...receive?"

"Let me see...eleven...no, twelve florists have each sent individual arrangements. Ellie, they are exquisite but a bit extravagant, I would say!" wondering what could have happened. She heard a little girl's voice in the background talking to Ellie.

"Mommy, I know how to send e-mails! I wanted to help you!"

"Ingrid, what can I say? It was my mistake! I should never have left Sammy on her own...I'm sure Mr. Haardens is going to be angry... What shall I do?"

Ula pointed to the glass doors through which she could see two more florist vans. Ingrid burst into laughter while wondering how Toon would react when he saw the bill! The office heard that every florist in Apeldoorn and its surroundings received the same order through email. Ingrid urged everyone to help themselves to roses. It made up for her disappointment.

***

While making dinner, she laughed as she recalled the roses incident, speculating what it mirrored in their relationship. Abundance, that's for sure. Everyone was guessing where the flowers came from at work.

The sound of the phone in the hall triggered her into the shakes.

Would he have heard already?

"Ingrid speaking", trying very hard not to giggle.

"I believe you got my message very loud and clear *"Now you know my feelings!"* "Kitty, I'm deeply in love with you; that's all I wanted to say. You sleep on it. I'll see you next week."

Apeldoorn

"Good morning, this is Rob from the news desk in Apeldoorn with an update on the news. The police are investigating an alleged holdup that resulted in the terrific accident last month on the M5, the motorway to Paris." Her car radio broadcast.

Was Rob referring to Roelof de Beer? His company's truck had been involved in an accident about a month ago.

"The company involved was not available for comment, but it is speculated that a prominent businessman is connected to a real estate scam. We hope to have details later."...

Ingrid switched off the radio. Roelof de Beer was not in real estate, so it was probably something else.

Her mind returned to the dream she had woken up with just before Toon phoned, wondering about its meaning. For the first time since Jan passed away, she contemplated having a sexual relationship again. Her sex life during the early seventies with Jan had been passionate; she'd become pregnant with the twins just before she turned 19. Then, after the twins were born, something changed; they drifted apart. When Ed, Jan's brother, was around, things were terrible. She knew Ed's feelings for her were more than brotherly love. Jan was seldom home; she even suspected that he was having an affair.

Then, one evening, she had just had a bath; the twins were asleep when someone came up the stairs in their apartment in Rotterdam. She had expected Jan and only wore her dressing gown when she opened the front door. Ed was standing there, looking at her but saying nothing.

Later, he told her that Jan had asked him to collect some papers and told her he would not be home that evening. She knew that she was just as guilty as he was for allowing their sexual arousal to get the better of them.

Three months after that episode, Ed left for Australia, telling her he could not stay around any longer without revealing to his brother what he felt for her. Ingrid knew the moment she had intercourse with Ed that she had conceived. It took all her effort to have sex with Jan after he came home.

Jan had been very surprised at her sudden romantic interest, and for the first time in her life, she play-acted out of fear.

It almost destroyed her self-worth. Jan never suspected it then, but she always knew Debbie was Ed's child. Thinking about it made her feel sad and remorseful, for the cost had been very high. In her despair, she closed off, became numb and lived as a zombie for years.

She only saw Ed again nineteen years later at Jan's funeral, but didn't want to be with him. She was too raw; her feelings of grief and her guilt for that one time that she had been unfaithful had ruled her life.

During her pregnancy with Debbie, she denied the possibility that Debbie could have been Ed's child, and the long periods of loneliness within her marriage often made her want to head for a divorce. Years later, when she learned that Jan had had an affair, they both started to talk, which was very heavy going in the beginning. Jan had difficulty forgiving his brother for many years. Ed must have known that he had found out. Only after Debbie was twelve did she have a miscarriage, and then things started to clear up. The loss of that unborn child shifted her whole outlook on life.

They had stayed together, and now she felt their marriage had improved considerably. Even during Jan's illness, the last years had been good, and they had become lovers and best friends again.

A sudden emotional release from the pain of Jan's death engulfed her whole being. Then the memories were left, and the feelings of love she thought came from Jan were now for her. Now she knew she was free again for the first time, to love again.

***

Holidaymakers overcrowded the already packed parking lots in the centre of Apeldoorn when she saw Marijke being dropped off in front of the Pannekoek. With the loss of Kees in mind, Ingrid asked Marijke how she was doing while they strolled past Yolanda's bookshop.

"They say time heals, but there is still that heavy, sad feeling. I suppose you know all about it, eh?" Marijke looked at her sideways.

She was attractive in a motherly way, and Ingrid wondered why she worked. Indeed, her husband, being a detective, earned an adequate salary to support his family.

"Losing a child must be hard," squeezing Marijke's shoulder. She understood that Marijke was referring to her loss of Jan, but was unsure if that was the same. The thought of losing any of her children was more inconceivable.

"I dream about the accident often, but I wasn't even there when it happened! The other day, I was looking for a dream book in the bookshop to see if anything in it made any sense." Her voice trailed an air of sadness.

"The resentment and pain I feel in my dreams leave me so drained in the morning. I have difficulty getting out of bed. Work helps, but I should be at home for my other two children in the afternoons. Last week, I applied for a morning–only position with the firm."

"What did they say?" Thinking that would not be a bad idea.

"I can start part-time from next month. It's a drop in salary, but Paul agrees it would be better. He's glad I made that decision, saying it had to come from me. I'm still worried about the time I'll have on my hands.

Work gives me a temporary release." Marijke's agonised voice made her realise that the job was a temporary excuse, a fantasy to escape the pain. What could she do to help?

Arriving at her office, another beautiful arrangement with a card stating: "Thoughts are like boomerangs! They always come back to you, and you know mine!" made her day.

She wondered how deeply he could tap into her mental dialogue.

Only when she was near him could she sense what he was thinking and even hear the words; she wondered if it was the same for him. She had to acknowledge that he had an almost erotic effect on her. She was about to check her email for the day when suddenly, without her doing anything, the plain blue screen filled with writing appeared!

<Kitty, you asked why you dream.>

Yes, she had it in the car this morning!

<The human mind is similar to a giant computer, which acts and reacts according to its programming. While your active programming started the day you were born, influences are imprinted on your subconscious and conscious minds long before birth.>

Did POWAH mean that not all dreams were like the one she had? That was more of a fantasy, surely, not anything real. Sometimes, you can almost dream about a different life, but...

POWAH, when we dream, is it always about things that trouble us? She punched away at her keyboard.

<Kitty, dreams can serve as your inner guidance system. It is similar to when problems occur on your computer, and the troubleshooting options are there>.

Gosh, like the many flashing boxes on her screen when she did something illegal on her workstation. Some indeed carry solutions on how to resolve the problems.

<You learn from computer troubleshooting, do you not? In that way, you learn from your dreams. Most dreams respond to the impressions stored in your rational mind. Your dreams can also help you get in touch with your Higher Self, making the connection to your inner core, your IAM's auric field, which holds all its collective memories of many lifetimes. All these impressions are stored in your unconscious, ready for exploration>

For a moment, her dream flashed by.

What can I do to help Marijke with her pain? She typed, Ingrid earnestly wished she could help her get on with her life with her other three children.

<Kitty, Marijke's dreams will help her out of her confusion and into a deeper relationship with herself. Her desire to see Kees is still firm, and she still longs for something she cannot. She could not prepare herself for his departure, although he had made his inner preparations long before he left. Soon, she will awaken to this inner knowing that all is well with him.> Ingrid wondered if she could suggest to her that she start a dream journal.
<Yes! In that way, she will change her thinking and look for the guidance she so badly needs now. Remember, you cannot do it for her! Just love her. Ingrid was astounded by how the answer seemed to appear as if it were part of her mind. Was that what it was? A warm feeling of oneness, the moment she read it, as if she already knew the answer, still spurred her to ask more questions. She was typing:

POWAH, what did my dream mean?

There she sat, staring at her screen, when the words that formed a sentence appeared as if someone was typing a reply.

<Kitty, nudity in your dream is your Higher Self's way of telling you to get used to a new sense of freedom, a revelation, a shedding of all affectation, a new feeling of honesty and openness. As you see it, the world is nothing more than a projection of a wish.>

Of course, not all the mirrors in her dream were accurate. They only projected her thoughts back!

<That is correct, and they have no lasting significance. Don't centre your dreams on something as ephemeral as the outside world. Your feelings of embarrassment, in the beginning, ex-

pressed your fear of exposing certain emotions and inner thoughts about your self–worth! Think about that.>

POWAH, my inner feelings for...Toon, are they real?

She felt a bit odd asking that. Just now...

<Kitty, in the end, you did feel good about yourself, did you not? Meeting up with people in your daily life in a dream helps you recognise the qualities of yourself that this person reflects to you.>

Ingrid wondered which of Toon's qualities represented her. She realised that he had activated a need for her to take action. Her own need for empowerment had become much stronger lately. She wondered if that was the masculine polarity within her. Gosh, who was tying this back to her? How come? This was honestly very personal. Was it her higher self that she was aware of in the form of running text on her screen?

<Kitty, look up the root number of your PCP card. Then, become aware of which Language of Light qualities are already available. I have many more dreams, especially now.>

Love POWAH

An exhilarating feeling of joy flooded her whole body. This could become quite addictive. Was she receiving this reply from her own mind? This was still a bit hard to swallow. She could surely not have come up with all those answers? ... Which qualities was POWAH referring to? Was she tapping into the universal mind, and was her mortal mind only translating it? Or was it coming from a separate intelligence?

Class 5

MOTIVATION: the desire to become aware was written on the door.

"Tonight, we are decoding the first five awakening card spacings for the first level of the Ascension Decoding card game, beginning with the present physical personality card," Annelies looked very exotic in her colourful kaftan, which she seemed to wear a lot. Perhaps it was one of Yolanda's creations. She told them one evening that she was a gymnastics addict; they were discussing addictions; that was why she looked so athletic but still feminine.

Only Yolanda and she used their married names in their decoding. Ingrid felt that to be almost a tribute to Jan, for he had been her best teacher and friend to find things she liked and disliked about herself.

"Annelies, will I see where I went wrong in the energy of my married name? Yolanda whispered.

"Why do you say that you went wrong? Do I detect a desire for punishment or guilt?" Yolanda looked up at Annelies, and Ingrid could feel her sadness.

"Darling, perceive it as a blessing; it helped you to be what you are now."

Liesbeth winked at her across the large table. Ingrid realised how lucky Toon was to have Annelies as a friend; she wondered what this woman had to endure to become what she was now.

"Annelies, will each new surname bring new and different challenges? How unfair that men stay with the same name!" Her need to uplift Yolanda's mood worked. It evoked a joking response from the others, especially the men, and everyone became less severe.

"Thank you," Annelies beamed when she walked past to check on their calculations.

"Who decides to change your name, Ingrid? *"Names can become radioactive ownership thought forms."*

"Well, it's the custom, but I suppose...we do...you don't have to...My mother kept hers and added my dad's name to hers. I never gave it any thought." *"What do you mean by radioactive?"*

"Annelies, is that why you never took on Ben's name?" Gerrit asked her in all seriousness.

"That, my dear, was pure rebellion on my part," she laughed.

Annelies never sat down. Instead, she hovered around, peering over each shoulder at their calculations.

"Jaarsma was far too common for me, and it infuriated Ben, spurring me even more to refuse his surname."

"Really? Also, Jaarsma?" Liesbeth exclaimed. "But Annelies, how come?"

"Ben had been brought up in the same orphanage as Gerrit."

"Really? Gerrit, do you know Ben?" Yolanda's mood had shifted. Instead, she showed great surprise at the coincidence.

"Oh, yes, did I ever. Trever called the terrible twins. Leo is the eccentric loner, completely the opposite of Ben, a man with an inexhaustible imagination. Both brothers have an immense capacity for hard work and the ability to inspire others. Annelies, you must miss him!" Gerrit looked pensively at Annelies.

Ingrid wondered where Ben was. She didn't get the feeling that he had died, but she didn't want to probe. As she glanced at Niels, he seemed far away in his world, and she sensed that he was not very happy. Picking up people's inner thoughts was not always an advantage. The more telepathic she became, the more she was aware of the intense emotions people harboured.

"It's good that you become aware of that, Ingrid. Magnetic, radioactive and electrical energies are all thought forms."

That was something new!

"Where do our thoughts fall under?" How would you separate the essence of a thought, she wondered...?

"Through becoming aware of feelings that thoughts trigger. We'll go into that later."

"After the coffee break, we'll decode our last two cards, which have to do with your past or future lives that all happen simultaneously." Annelies opened the door for Joris, who greeted everyone abundantly.

"Annelies, is it necessary to know or remember your past lives?"

"Richard, other life experiences will flood our memory during these times. Often, during dream states, people gather something that has a bearing on their life. These are deep suppressed memories within our Soul blueprint. Your physical life is a mirror of the content of our Souls library, which is a spiritual one. But please, don't take anything I say as gospel," she urged, raising her hands.

"Annelies, I had an amazing dream the other night," She volunteered bravely.

"Will you share it in your journal, Ingrid?" Annelies made sure everyone heard her. *"I want to read all about that one. Is Toon in it?"* Joris suddenly perked up his ears when he heard Annelies think of the name Toon. Gee, she wondered if all animals are telepathic.

"I suppose I have to, now that I have blabbered that out. Gosh, that is very personal." Caressing Joris at the same time.

"That's probably the reason for having the dream in the first place," Annelies grinned while peeping at her numeral spacing.

"Ingrid, your life opportunity card is mirrored in the vibration of the twenty-one representing the world! You will have some large projects reflected by this card for this lifetime. Mmm, interesting." Annelies stood behind her when she beamed. "Annelies, how's Otto, Toon's half-brother?"

"Otto's fine, but it was a warning to Toon that he must stop travelling so much. Thank goodness he seems motivated to shed some of his many commitments." Annelies squeezed her shoulder as she announced a tea break.

***

"Yolanda, if I were to give you a drawing of an evening gown, would you be able to make it?" she asked while Joris had adopted her during their coffee break. *"Missing your boss, aren't you?"* his puppy eyes flickered.

"I'd love to try. What did you have in mind?"

"I love drawing ideas, but I've always restricted myself to drawing an artist's impression of architectural and building plans, but why not clothing?"

"All right, why don't we give it a try? You draw an idea with the colours and texture, and I'll see if I can put it into shape and form. That could be fun!"

Annelies and Joris accompanied her to her car. The sunset is one hour later due to daylight saving.

"Ingrid, I'm still waiting for your many questions." Ingrid's mind raced. Did she ever! *I'll let you know if I hear from Toon, but I think he'll contact you before me,* Annelies beamed, waving...

***

When she heard the phone in the hallway as she parked her car, she hoped Toon would keep ringing.

"Toon, is" ...there was silence, except for the telepathic message.

I've been miserable; oh, Kitty, I miss you. Ingrid felt ecstatic and alive. She felt similar only when listening to good music.

"Hello, love; I needed to hear your voice." I've arranged to meet on Wednesday at your office with Harry Brinks and, I believe, some other subcontractors."

"Toon, are you phoning from somewhere in Holland? I've never known anybody who can be in so many different locations all in the space of two weeks!"

"Yes, love, I've created a lifestyle with a busy schedule with many booked appointments, but I'll have to make some drastic changes now that I want to be with you."

"Where are you now?"

"At Heathrow airport. My flight to New York was delayed, but they are calling me now. See you next week."

"I'll try to visit you in my dreams during the flight; wear something.
..."

She heard them calling Mr. Haardens over the PA system.

Ingrid was already longing for the following Wednesday to arrive.

She was about to check her email when excerpt seven appeared.

Excerpt Seven[1]

Program Planet Earth

Time-warps

Wow! POWAH clearly said that 'time' was created by sound frequencies.

Her studio displayed many books she had collected over the years, but she would rather Google what 'time-warps' could mean. One website said that a time structure could be an electromagnetic force orbiting around the planet at an ultrahigh frequency or a change in the space-time continuum! Professor S.W. Hawking wrote that today's science fiction is often tomorrow's science fact. One author mentions that experiencing reality warping is like mentally not being in control, so he rejected the concept altogether.

When she looked up information on the 'Language of Light' from Tieneke's notes, the description read that man in the past communicated with other planes of intelligence due to a magnetic force that resonated with nature. It was an instant communication with the infinite mind, using ideographic and pictographic cybernetics. The graphics Annelies used as Language of Light symbols also come from Tieneke.

Last week, she found her Language of Light cards from Tieneke's mind-drawing retreat. She was amazed at how her symbols from the previous year reflected her experiences. All the qualities the symbols stood for had become part of her. At the time, Tieneke's Light Body workshop had just distracted her. Annelies explained that their symbols with numeral interpretations are symbolic language. How the energies from figurative language seem to have an effect reminded her that Annelies had mentioned that the recent

---

1. https://allrealityshifters.wordpress.com/powah/the-reality-shifters-excerpt-7/

crop circles made similar patterns. The eye symbol on the aerial photo was a good example.

Somebody wrote: "We have linked crop circles to 'time warps' and space warps."

Suddenly, she had a flash as if recalling a memory as if she should know about this space-time warp. Something to do with a star map? Ingrid started to feel quite weird, as if...but the flash was gone when she heard Jeroen arriving in the driveway.

She made a late-night snack for them and spent time with him before bed. She would be working on her journal after reading over the seven transmissions from POWAH, hoping that one day these excerpts would make more sense...

Chapter 8
It's all in the Eye of the Observer

Jeroen Barendse

Mom, can I borrow your car?"

"Jeroen, I thought you could use Grandpa's company cars until yours is fixed?"

"I could, but Kim's boyfriend borrowed the car to take her home last night after he dropped me off." Jeroen's tall frame just fitted in the doorway of her study. His light brown, wavy hair covered half his face. Unlike his twin sister Sascia, who was organised and tidy, Jeroen was very casual and disorganised. His cousin Kim, Quincy's daughter, had suddenly arrived on her doorstep yesterday, escaping from her parents, Kim told them in an emotional state.

They both heard a car in the driveway, and Jeroen looked relieved when he peeped through the blinds. He knew he was not supposed to hand over a borrowed car! Even if Kim's boyfriend seemed to be a nice enough guy,

Ingrid had withdrawn to her office to start sorting out the Excerpts and the notes when she sensed someone standing beside her. The computer screen suddenly beamed the same brightness as at work, and the text appeared similarly.

<Kitty, any emotion that you express is a reflection of the state of mind that you are in at the moment. If it represents love, it will bring you peace. If it expresses chaos or upheaval, it will reflect that.> That made her think about Kim and her sister. She missed Toon, but why was she still apprehensive about starting a new relationship?

POWAH, why am I fearful of getting involved again?

She realised that she was getting very personal with whoever it was! **<If you're thinking process encompasses believing that you have a basis for being fearful and must protect yourself, your personality will engage in conflict. You will feel an urge or a need to drive defensively.>** Yes, that she knew. She was very hard on herself, for she wanted to follow her Soul's desire and not her personality's needs.

POWAH, when I would like to know more about a man I've only just met, surely it is not wrong to feel this way? How do I know if I'm influenced by my personality or the real me?

She wondered if she knew the answer already.

<Kitty, the value of any relationship is achieved in that relationship when you are allowing yourself to express only LOVE and applying it in any relationship, intimate or not. Then you know it is the real you. There is no greater value.>

Did that not imply that she was getting addicted to this form of communication? She had to ask the following question.

POWAH, is there such a thing as a "cosmic Soulmate" or a twin soul?

She waited with bated breath. The stillness in the house after Jeroen and Kim went out made her feel at one with the consciousness communicating through the text.

<You are all reflections of one another. Remember to plan carefully all the experiences you have. Should you both have chosen to have a cosmic mate, your plans have no limitations.>

She liked reading about having no limitations, knowing that each experience must first originate within her mind.

<Kitty, the purpose of any relationship with another is to share your completeness. Your own individual Soul's desire will cre-

ate an opportunity for personal growth. If your Soul is longing for union with its creator, and by attracting its opposite polarity toward itself, then you can call that your twin soul.>

Did POWAH mean that this desire that she felt lately is the Soul's desire and not just her hormones?

<Yes, bless every relationship, for everyone will give you information about who you are or who you now choose to be. The feminine aspect of your being is your authentic and enduring spiritual self. When you have embraced and balanced the masculine and feminine aspects within you, you are ready for a Soul marriage.>

Ingrid knew that asking to live to her full Soul potential could attract all kinds of experiences, so why not a higher form of partnership?

<Kitty, you and Toon have an opportunity to become a cosmic couple. You are entering into a new evolutionary spiral, which means you will draw to you a Soul-to-Soul union that is very profound. You communicate telepathically, do you not?>

She knew those answers came from a part of herself that seemed coherently linked to her higher self. But then, did they share a consciousness on that level?

POWAH, what stops me from fully awakening from this reality since it is an illusion?

She typed feverishly, wanting to feel that she was participating with someone in whatever way. Was POWAH her mind, her guide, her own... She was not sure what to make of it. How could POWAH be her mind if Annelies shared the same guide? When she communicated this way, her adrenaline rush was always high. She could feel her heart pounding in her chest and wondered if her energy levels were more conducive to this type of communication.

<Kitty, we all share in the universal mind. The binding force of all life is consciousness. Love is the key to the new frequency,

and it expands your awareness by seeing 'you' already fully awake at this very moment. Still, as soon as your thoughts express anything different, you will return to experiencing the shadow of the truth.>

Do you mean being meditative when practising, having a one-pointed focus and holding the feeling that goes with it?

She had been feeling very exuberant lately, but that must be because of Toon. Would she have felt like this without him? Subconsciously, she knew that she would have to think like this even without a lover. She had been far more at peace with herself since she started working for Pleasure Park. She had often played with ideas at home after a day's work. Mainly to do with designing and layouts. Through this job, her visions surrounding future living conditions in communities or eco-villages created a purpose and inner joy.

<Yes, you've got it! The more you attempt to hold on to this feeling of joy, the more you allow yourself to get immersed in your HIGHER SELF, and the more it will be made known to you in ways that require no questioning.

For the INDIVIDUAL SOUL, joy must be recognised and experienced.

Your DIVINE/OVERSOUL knows euphoria already. Kitty, you have the motivation and the desire. The interpretations of your 22 grid spacings will guide you through the awakening process. Contemplate your five sacred tonal vibration spaces with their interpretations.>

Her printer was coming on, and excerpt eight appeared. Someone must have typed this! When they were at the Pannekoek on Friday evening, Hans had asked Toon if Trevor was sending POWAH's message. But who was Trevor?

Excerpt Eight[1]

Program Planet Earth

---

1. https://allrealityshifters.wordpress.com/powah/the-reality-shifters-excerpt-8/

The 1st Level of the Ascension Decoding Card Game

Ingrid felt overwhelmed by the volume of work, especially regarding the Language of Light. Only now did the mind-drawing exercises with Tieneke make sense. Even when she drew the symbols then, it must have had an impact in terms of energy. Making the cards slowly revealed what POWAH was talking about in his excerpts. Looking at her own spaces on the chart, she saw they had become the inner journey the workshops had promised.

Suddenly, an awareness of Toon's presence swept so powerfully over her; it was most unsettling, particularly as she'd always thought that if one reached a certain age, one would not land on this emotional roller-coaster. She was wrong!

The phone in the hallway rang, *"Toon, is that you?"* She wondered if she could communicate telepathically without knowing his location.

"Kitty! Pick up the phone and say nothing, listen!" She lifted the receiver to her ear and silently projected, *"Toon, if it's you mentally speaking to me, how can we do this?"* She hoped he understood what she meant.

"My Kitty, Soul love is a magnetic solar energy, and we have a Soul-to-Soul connection. I never again want to be without this dynamic magnetism with you." His thoughts electrified her whole being.

"This is called cosmic fire, Kitty. I would love to experience this physically; how about it?" She knew her passion would lead her to his bed, realising too late that he could read her mind!

"I heard that, but when?"

"Toon, I need to get to know you better; I mean, your personality."

"Do you realise how difficult that will be, not to mention unhealthy?" Toon sighed. *"Kitty, there is such a thing as sympathetic, empathetic and compassionate telepathy,"* his mental pleadings were persuasive.

"Toon, do you communicate with others this way, I mean with women?"

"Kitty, I am not in love with anyone but you....... I'll see you on Wednesday and show it when I see you. No other woman ever turned me on the way you do."

Apeldoorn city centre

"Good morning to all my listeners around Gelderland. Mysterious developments have come to light concerning the real estate scam of a prominent businessman, Nick du Toit. When Mr Brinks of the Pleasure Parks holiday resorts purchased the large estate of the late Donald Jaarsma."

Just then, a van with blaring music drowned out her radio. She remembered the name duToit! She knew the name connected with the Prinsengracht hotel or something about Mr Brinks, but who was Donald Jaarsma? She must ask Toon when she sees him at the next boardroom meeting.

Ingrid looked forward to visiting her sister on Wednesday afternoon after the subcontractor meeting. It was Kim's birthday on Thursday.

Kim, her niece, told her and Jeroen that her parents had been fighting every day, and she would not be living at home much longer. Ingrid had been so preoccupied with her agenda that she had neglected to contact Quincy. She had given Kim an envelope with a gift voucher on Saturday evening, just before she went out with Jeroen. A traffic jam on the Arnhem road at the entrance to the children's farm 'Malkenschoten' meant she was running late for work. A van with boxes of oranges had overturned on the way to the market in Beekbergen. The angry-looking man from the truck seemed all right, but the motorbike he collided with was mangled. The orange man was shouting at everyone. Accidents always gave her shivers; the ambulance and police created an atmosphere of gloom.

She spied Carla across the road after she found a parking space at the back of the Pannekoek.

"Carla, can you still take me to the station at lunchtime tomorrow?

My sister is going through some rough times. I'll be back on Thursday afternoon." Carla's hair could do with a makeover; what happened to her? She told her she took up sculpture again in her spare time, but was that a reason for letting herself go untidy?

"Ingrid, I broke off with Niels. I was fond of him, but suddenly he became very distracted, as if I no longer existed. You know my sensitivity; I call it quits when a man shows that his interest in me is wearing off. I'm not getting hurt again!"

Carla's outburst revealed that she was miserable when they walked through the office building's glass doors.

That's why Niels was so quiet last Friday at Annelies' class; he had been just as miserable! Niels was single and had his computer shop. He had told them charmingly that he never had time for girlfriends because he wanted to establish a business first, and also enjoyed a partner who shared the same spiritual interests. Annelies had asked about Carla, and he had shared his sudden anxiety that Carla might not be interested in the awakening journey. Ingrid liked Niels, who had a way of making everyone feel special.

"Carla, I'm sorry, but something tells me you may be casting him off prematurely."

"What do you mean by 'casting him off'? What makes you say that?"

"Carla, Niels is in my Friday evening class. Did he tell you?' she confided while waiting for the lift to come down.

"Yes, he did, and he is secretive about those classes, too, as if he cannot share them with me."

"Niels did tell me that he was looking forward to your cooking one evening, and last Friday, he was miserable as well, so something else must have happened between both of you," Ingrid carefully responded while stepping into the lift.

"Well, he was exhausted when he came to me after his classes two weeks ago, and I was very disappointed. I was so looking forward to an interesting evening. I wanted to know about the classes, and all he wanted to do was...well, you know what I mean!" Carla looked at her as if she understood! What was she implying, sex? She had told her that she had met Niels in the past when she was very young, but Carla had been married twice before, so she must have had a lot of experience with men. Carla was about to press the top floor button when Piet joined them in the lift. Ingrid could see by her expression that he was the last person she wanted to see. It stopped their conversation. Ingrid took the opportunity to inform Piet that she would be out of the office on Wednesday afternoon and Thursday morning.

"You have a meeting on Wednesday morning with Mr Brinks and that friend of yours."

"Mr. Haardens? Yes, Piet, I have not forgotten; I hope you will be there." He looked haggard, as if he had not slept in two days. Had he been drinking? He was undoubtedly short-tempered.

There was plenty of work lying on her desk and more graphics to play with for an advert sent to the overseas clients invited to the opening of the new complex in Tilburg.

When she walked past Piet's office, she overheard him shouting to someone on the phone about the new French site that seemed to be giving problems: something to do with the soil. She wondered about all the blasting that was taking place to make room for the giant dome and what effect that was having on the eye symbol.

Toon mentioned CERN, the world's largest and most powerful particle accelerator. Some YouTube videos had warned the public about the dangerous implications they were meddling with. She now wondered if there was a connection.

There were many emails, one of which was from Sascia. She made a lunch date with Carla, to whom she had promised an explanation about the Ascension Decoding on the body codes of light workshops.

She could sense Piet had walked in and was looking over her shoulder.

"Ingrid, will you work longer today?"

"Yes, I have to finish this proof. What is happening in France? Are there any problems with the blasting and the soil?"

"Oh, don't worry your little head over that. It will be sorted out."

He stared resentfully at her, which infuriated her. He was getting so obnoxious that she had difficulty not reacting to him.

"Piet, you had better not keep something from me that I should know about."

"Well, ask your boyfriend; he will be there."

"I will ignore that statement." He walked away without replying.

She felt guilty because her thoughts were not very focused on the job. What was she doing? Did she need this job?

While Carla took the proof pamphlet on the Tilburg complex and the artist's impression of the French Pleasure Park off her for the meeting, she experienced a surge of joy and lightness at the thought of seeing Toon the next day.

Den Haag

Her presentation looked good that Wednesday morning. She had been gliding along on a wave of joy, sustained by the anticipation of seeing Toon.

While rearranging things and looking at the clock, she suddenly felt something prickling her neck ever so gently. When she turned, she saw Toon standing in the doorway, looking at her with an intensity that produced butterflies in her solar plexus. She wanted to run to him but strolled, smiling gaily...

"How long have you been standing in the doorway?" Matching the flicker in his eyes with a sparkle from her own. She still felt determined to overcome the formidable mental power he seemed to have over her.

"Toon, say something; otherwise, I will ignore you the whole morning," she beamed, aware that he was observing her whole body. His look suddenly changed to a gentle, loving gaze. They held each other's glances without speaking, which created a timeless moment. She knew that he was appraising her trembling figure.

"That wonderful blue suit you wear reveals a delectable body underneath. Do you know that?"

"Oh, really, can you see through me now?"

"Ingrid, it's so good to see you!" he greeted her warmly, holding her briefly before settling, stretching his long legs under the boardroom table.

Good grief! Was he a clairvoyant, too? She tried her best to ignore him and moved away to her drawing board as the meeting started with a discussion on the problem they were having with the blasting. Roelof de Beer a short, chubby man in his early sixties, looked haggard, and Toon sat staring into the distance as if he was not there. The other four men she had never met all talked indifferently about how to use the explosives. Ingrid felt a revulsion sweeping her as if they were doing something wrong! Were they destroying something meaningful with these explosives? Mr. Brinks was very quiet. He let everyone have a say. She knew him to be a very discerning man.

"You have to move the site of the dome," Toon remarked in his deep voice. The other subcontractors were all reacting negatively to his proposal. One man's angry body language was almost threatening.

"Toon, can you show us what you have in mind?" Mr Brinks asked while ignoring the others.

Toon got up, took Ingrid's drawing, winked at her and started to draw on the map that showed the aerial view of the French building site. She was spellbound. Where did he get the ideas from? He gave the whole project a new dimension.

She could see how it would work, thinking about how the island would cover the whole eye! Recalling POWAH's excerpt, Earth scientists operate entirely within this fake reality, as he called it. Something that Liesbeth's boyfriend, Hans, had said over dinner about antimatter that could help doctors visualise the functioning of the human body. That idea went right over her head, so she kept silent.

Suddenly having the urge to participate, she took her drawing and sketched in a few lines to make the centre pool cover the eye symbol entirely and the island in the middle directly over the black pupil of the eye. Not that it was noticeable in the plan; it was more in her head, as if someone had mentally shown her how it should be. Did Toon have the same vision? He glanced knowingly at her, holding up the drawing for all to see. Mr Brinks got up.

"I am satisfied, Toon. Can your firm handle the whole project from now on? Ingrid, take all your time; if you need assistance, get it. Toon, thank you for being here; I'll leave it to both of you." The other subcontractors were outraged, storming out of the room after Mr. Brinks, arguing with him about their deals.

Both were standing, looking at each other.

"I thought you were going to ignore me," Toon projected while flirting. Everyone had left, and she wished she had the boldness to hug him.

She was about to walk out of the boardroom when he seized her arm, pulled her inside and closed the door with his foot. His arm held her firmly, pressing her against him. When she felt the clinging pressure of his mouth again and again and the firmness of his body through the soft woollen fabric of her suit, she succumbed with passion while breathing in gasps. When he pressed the length of his body into hers, feeling his maleness, she blurted out.

"Toon, what are we doing?"

"I'm catching up on the devouring of you that I've wanted to do for a long time," he quivered. "I've missed you terribly."

"What...do you mean by a long... long time?" while moving away just in time as she saw the door opening and Carla looking at them.

"Ingrid, were you not going to take the train to Delft at two o'clock?"

Ingrid had forgotten that Carla was taking her to the station because Jeroen had borrowed her car again.

"No problem, I'll take her. What time do you have to be in Delft?" Toon interrupted.

"About four o'clock. Are you sure it's all right?" She had hardly any time to regain her composure and felt utterly bewildered at losing it so quickly.

"Carla, my apologies, you've missed your lunch. Is Piet back already?"

"No, I've not seen him." She looked quizzically at both of them.

"Toon, I must get my bag from the office and instruct Carla about Piet's work. It'll take me only five minutes." She smiled happily at him, giving her feelings away.

She decided to give Carla more of the work Piet usually did for her. Carla was happy about that as she enjoyed the change.

"Ingrid, he's a real dish, and you can see he adores you," Carla whispered. "Don't let him slip through your fingers", probably thinking that Toon wouldn't hear it, but Ingrid knew he did.

"Is that advice from a pro?"

"Absolutely!"

As they hurried towards Toon's electric sports car outside the office, Ingrid simultaneously felt pleased and excited yet somewhat overwhelmed. Could he take her over so quickly?

Toon's straight blonde hair gave him the look of a man who spent most of his time outdoors. He was not your average city man. He was almost wild-looking, as if he had been living off the land and working with his hands.

"Have I survived your test, Kitty? I know you have mine. Do you have any idea what you are doing to me?" Ingrid looked at him with amusement while he was edging into the traffic.

"How did you know my nickname was Kitty? Was it from that print-out?"

He glanced at her with a secretive smile. *"I gave you the name, Kitty, can't you remember?"*

"What do you mean, gave me that name?" Ingrid uttered, her thoughts whirling.

"Kitty, we've been together before. Do you know how long I've been looking for someone I could communicate with this way?" Toon's excitement in his voice reflected the immense joy one has when meeting someone dear again after a very long time.

"Yes, I do have some idea." *"You're travelling stimulates a memory, but I don't know why."* Ingrid felt a connection she had never felt before with anyone when she beamed her reply.

She looked sideways, observing his strong hands holding the steering wheel while he was concentrating on the road.

"Do you trust me?" Ingrid wondered if she had heard correctly. Those four words made her stomach wrench! She started to talk while pretending not to hear.

"As a child, I always knew that I could read people's minds, but I never knew that nobody else did, and when adults were saying things that they were not thinking, I was always so confused. That's how I lost trust in people."

"You are avoiding my question, dear."

"Kitty, do you trust me?" Toon repeated out loud, glancing at her. Ingrid was grinning, realising she would have to be mindful of her thoughts now. Toon's look was identical to when they first met at her office. His smile and laughter were like the sound of a laugh that had transcended pain, and his voice was soft and low yet strong and clear. Did she trust him? It was more likely that she could not trust herself.

Toon laughed at reading her mind, grabbed her hand from her lap, and kissed it passionately. He did not take his eyes off the road again.

Instead, he inserted a USB stick into the Bluetooth drive, and Ingrid let the music take over, revelling in what was playing. This man knew what music to play to make her disappear into another world.

"What music is this? It's beautiful!"

"Kitty, what do you like about it?"

"It's... I don't know, is it Irish?" What pipes did she hear playing?

"It brings back a memory. Is that possible?"

"Kitty, that was the idea, and it worked!"

After driving in silence for a while, letting the music take over her senses that suddenly sprang alive as if she was in a different realm, Toon brought her back to the same question:

"Do you trust me, Kitty?" She tried to close her mind to counteract the feeling of being drawn in by Toon's magnetism. He made her feel like

A young girl, beautiful and desirable, instead of an almost 45-year-old mother. Did she remember him in her dream from long ago? It was all so real. She seemed to recall now that she had been very young when she had known him. Was it in some other life? Her feelings were in disarray.

"I'm not sure," her tremendous newfound joy in her voice revealed a love for him that had always been there but was now a new experience.

He was exploring her face, cherishing it as if he wanted to commit every part of her to memory.

"All I know is that I lost you, and now I have you back."

"Do you remember any other lives?" she projected.

"Yes, I do; that's why I played that music to see if it brought back a memory like it did when I heard it for the first time. You must tell me what you remember."

A wave of such happiness surged through her that she almost lost her physical consciousness. Was Toon her soul partner or a twin soul? Had she known him before, in a different life?

"Where are we?" she whispered while peering out the car window through the torrential rain.

"Just before Delft. Where do you need to go? Do you have to be at your sister's at four o'clock?" Glancing at her watch, she saw it was only after three. She had made arrangements to be at her sister's shop at four. She decided to phone her on the cell phone and make it later, about six. She directed him to the shop, and he parked opposite a Douwe Egbert coffee bar. He switched off the engine and turned to her; she felt his thoughts shaped into words as he held her with his eyes.

"Since the first time I saw you, I have longed for nothing but your body, that mouth of yours, and how your eyes look at me, and I remembered you... if... The trust you once gave me, knowing I must have betrayed you, the only person I ever respected... the best partner I could have ever had! ... Do you know what it's like to want you now? When I'm lying awake at night...I am constantly imagining taking you, teaching you any pleasure you want, seeing you need it and seeing you asking me for it, seeing your wonderful spirit awakening and surrendering to your passionate need. To watch you now as you are and then to see you at my side, forever... to see you in my bed, submitting your whole body to me in absolute trust, is what I'm hoping for at this moment."...

She heard it all while struggling very hard not to give herself away to his hypnotic beam. She inhaled while she thought, if this was mental foreplay, she was experiencing it.

He took her hand, raised it to his lips and, with a sudden movement, pulled her forward and kissed her most intimately. Was her body her own? It felt as if she had lost all control. When she felt lightning shooting through her spine, she could not stop responding to him.

"Kitty, please come to London with me."

"Toon, please!" she cried in a shaking voice.

"Kitty, I knew it; you are just as passionate as I am! Oh, how I want you! I never want to lose you again." She recovered a trickle of her former control but only wanted to be with him. Gosh, was this normal?

"Could we have some lunch, please?" she trembled as she pointed at the coffee bar and reluctantly got out of the car. Toon clutched her hand when they walked inside. His face expressed his reluctance to let her go. They shakily selected a corner table and ordered something to eat.

"Toon, remember that eye symbol? You upset them today with your new suggestion. You must know something to be able to make such a quick change. Is it because it has to be covered for a reason? What do you know that I don't?"

"What's going around in that head of yours that I've missed? Love, what do you know about crop circles?" He asked while fingering the contours of her face.

"I seem to remember reading that they are thought to have been formed by microwaves and that high levels of magnetic energy have been found within the circles, which affect people in different ways. Some feel headaches or dizziness. But then Mr. Brinks said that...Toon, I can't concentrate when you do that! Please stop," she whispered, taking his hand and trying to be serious. All he did was laugh with his eyes.

"You do gather a lot of information, don't you? I'm impressed.

There are two types of crop circles. The primary ones are the 'genuine' ones, whose origins are unknown, and the secondary circles are manufactured. The primary circle-makers are of higher intelligence."

"You mean, not human?" Toon's face retained a constant humour as if he had fun all the time.

"I believe that a form of intelligence is creating these patterns in the fields for some form of communication. Who knows, we are the artists of the future? Annelies uses them in her card-making classes."

"You mean the Language of Light symbols? Toon, why do you think the crop circles are appearing?"

"Kitty, I want to be alone with you." The waiter brought their food, and she heard him.

"There is an obvious deliberate intention to get man's attention, like with the impression of the eye. I must contact Ben, Annelies's husband, on that eye symbol."

"Toon, where is her husband?" Ingrid observed with amusement how he gobbled his hamburger with relish.

"If I can't gobble you up, this is second best."

"He's an undercover agent for Interpol. He's with Leo, his twin brother, last I heard." Again, their eye contact had such an undercurrent. Would that ever go away, she wondered?

"Does that mean he is away from home?"

"Our eyes are our Soul's windows, love. I want to merge with you." She pointed her finger at him, beaming.

"Toon, you are flirting and very good at it." Ingrid smiled with joy, loving his company.

"Toon, what connection does the dome have? Why did you change the drawings?"

"Kitty, the eye symbol is connected with Annelies, but I don't know all the complexities. I'm concerned about the rumours that I hear. It is to do with what they are doing at CERN, but that is all. I believe there are more sinister things going on that I don't want to go into now, but the dome needs to cover the symbol. Something to do with the energies from the underground stone formations."

"Why do I feel that all the explosions going on to make a clearing are evil?" Toon grabbed both her hands in his.

"CERN has been meddling with a technology that seems to affect the dome position. I've been contacted about it, and so has Mr. Brinks. Some say that a stargate could revolutionise space travel deep below the dome's position and open the way for intergalactic exploration."

"Look, it's beyond me, but I'll investigate since it seems all you want from me." Toon was studying her hands with such concentration that she giggled.

"Toon, please, I have many questions...I wish... My kids have been chatting with online friends for the last few years while I listen."

"What Questions? Kitty, when can I spend some intimate time with you?"

"Gosh, I have to get used to all of this. Ever since I've been involved with these body codes of light workshops, my life has turned upside down and...inside out." Ingrid giggled at his attempt to stop her from looking at her watch.

"OK ...Toon...here we go...did we ever land on the moon? Are there cloning centres around the world? Is all media controlled? Is Fluorine in the water a poison? Are governments all about the New World Order?" she rattled off, counting on her fingers. Toon's lifted eyebrows expressed surprise.

"Am I crazy to ask these questions? I have much more to say. Why are you travelling so much?"

The silence created a null space, making her feel naked. Had she let on too much about herself?

"Catching up on that London appointment. I wish you would come with me," he sighed.

"Toon, my son says that most people cannot handle the truth, and many don't want to see the truth. What is your take?" ...Toon grabbed her hands, leaned forward and kissed her.

"Kitty, there is enough crazy in this world without making ourselves crazy trying to convince anyone else of the truth. Everything in this physical realm is like a dream... we start there and work backwards." They seemed to be the only ones left in the coffee bar.

"Oh gosh...I have to go, Toon, as it's almost closing time for the shop. Where are you going from here? How long are you away for?" I ignored his request to join him while getting up. Ingrid looked with pride at his tall, attractive frame as he settled the bill.

"You're very hard on me, you know," he whispered soulfully, holding her hand while he took her bag out of the boot.

"I'm not myself any more, Kitty. Enjoy the time with your sister. I'll be generous and let you go for now, but soon, I'll want to spend more time with you, a lot more." He kissed her amorously while a passerby whistled.

His eyes looked mournful as she walked towards the health centre where Quincy had her shop. Before she entered the building, she looked back, waving at him and beaming simultaneously, *"Toon, I do want to be with you, but she is expecting me!"* She felt his eyes and thoughts travelling over her. "You have the loveliest legs I've ever seen." Ingrid reluctantly stepped through the large revolving doors. *"I heard that"*, she beamed.

Looking at herself in Quincy's shop window, she felt a surge of youthful energy as if she had shed ten years.

Chapter 9
Nine Character Vibrations of the Individual Soul

Apeldoorn

Ingrid watched for Carla as she arrived at Apeldoorn's crowded railway station at midday. Her visit to Quincy had been emotionally draining. Her sister was battling a crisis, and her feelings were in turmoil for a different reason.

Tourists who visited the many sightseeing attractions, especially 'Het Loo' palace, crowded the platform. The perfumed lilac blossoms, creatively displayed by a flower vendor, cheered her up.

"How was your visit?" Carla called out as she came out of the station. Her colleague seemed to have put on weight, which might be due to the baggy clothes. In the car, she explained what had gone on in her sister's life. As they walked through the foyer of Pleasure Park, Ula handed her a long, graceful box with one rose, beautifully wrapped, with no card, nothing...The afternoon flew by, and Toon was on the phone just before closing. As she picked up the receiver...there was only silence...

"Oh, Kitty, I want to be with you; I miss you. I feel like a teenager! Completely overturned my whole world."

"Where are you phoning from? I heard that! Where are you?"

"Kitty, I'm on an oil rig, of all places, not where I want to be, but I'll return after the weekend. Take care, love; I'll see you soon." The connection broke, and she heard a lot of static. It was weird that his

thoughts were clearer when the line was terrible. What was he doing on an oil rig?

Annelies' Reality Shifting workshop

Liesbeth arrived at Annelies at the same time as Ingrid. She invited her to dinner, telling her Jeroen wanted to hear about the Zurich conference.

"And I want to hear all about Hans."

"You're on for next week. Hans and I leave for the United States tomorrow to attend a seminar."

"Really, what are you both up to?" Liesbeth's suntanned look made her feel pale.

"Hans is speaking on 'life-giving water.' It's not new...It has always been on the planet, but...oh, I'll explain when I'm back...I'm giving a

lecture on 'The consciousness of our planet'. Oh, Ingrid...you know, being in love..." Before she could reply, Hans opened the door. He had eyes only for Liesbeth.

Class 6

Annelies had turned her classroom into a studio. On the door, it said: THE PRESENT PHYSICAL CONSCIOUSNESS CARD. Beautiful mandala patterns in many colours decorated the room. On the opposite wall, a large painting that resembled a night sky looked familiar!

"Now the work is starting! This is the fun part."

"What is so familiar about the star cluster painting, Ingrid?" She still had to get used to Annelies picking up her thoughts.

"I don't know anything about constellations, but..." She again got a weird sensation, like déja vu.

"Ingrid déja vu is a time-warp or a memory flash." The room was totally rearranged. All of their fixed, comfortable seating places were gone! Ingrid had to stifle a laugh at their discomfort.

"Now you experience how, through a small thing like a change of seating arrangement, you can get thrown out of your comfort zone," Annelies responded.

Ingrid chose a seat next to Liesbeth. The word time warp made her stare into space...when her eyes were drawn back into the room, she felt that the Language of Light symbols on the wall created an atmosphere of peace.

"We will do lots of creative drawing exercises with some decoding to make your cards. You will get a feeling and understanding of the vibrations that affect your daily lives." The booklet that came with the cards would hold their interpretations. Annelies introduced them to the Genogram, as she called it and showed them how to use the mandala pattern each had chosen. Although most of them began to enjoy themselves, Yolanda looked pale and run-down.

"Annelies, I think the painting triggered a memory, but...why?" Annelies pulled up her shoulders.

"Annelies, do I have to use any colour on my cards?" That must have floored Annelies because she looked at Wim in puzzlement.

"Can I restrict myself to using only black, grey, and white?"

"They are your cards, like your body. You create them, so do with them what you like."

"*No colour at all, now I get it... a lack of...what?*" she heard Annelies mentally thinking. Liesbeth added her observation of Wim.

"*He seems to have a rare type of total colour blindness called Cone monochromacy. However, it is accompanied by a relatively normal vision.*"

Her first card was a master number eleven named 'world power'; vibration number two was also represented twice on her card.

"*Annie, do you think I have no intuitive body? That is what my interpretations are saying.*" Yolanda beamed in anguish while resting her head in her hand at the sizeable horseshoe-shaped table they all shared.

"Love you are discouraged; use this opportunity to uncover a dark personality aspect. Muscle test if it's yours or Piet's." None of the others were aware of their telepathic conversations.

Liesbeth's head leaned against Yolanda's for a moment.

"Take hold of your power, dear, read on," Liesbeth pointed at Yolanda's booklet.

"Please study your interpretations well at home, and if you like, share any revelations they unlock." The rest of the evening flew by. Ingrid loved the creative activity, like being a child again, playing with crayons. As usual, Annelies kept their attention riveted.

When she drove home, Ingrid realised that she needed to see people and go out more than she had for ages. Toon had created an unsettling feeling of longing in her that she couldn't understand. Would she ever get used to his travels? She mulled over the words he had beamed at her: *"Oh, Ingrid, you have no idea how long I have longed for someone I could communicate with in this way."*

A dinner guest

What was left of that week had flown, especially now that she had to attend to the French project more than ever. Carla was a great help, and Marijke liked working part-time. Piet came back but had a terrible fight with management. She was trying hard to see past his aggressive personality. If only he could see that he had created all that happened to him by his manner. His thoughts were so vindictive that she wondered how he still managed to stay alive. He had shouted at her for interfering with the drawing plans, which made no sense at all. She knew that one word from her could jeopardise his job, but she hated being the one to do it. Today, his hatred was directed towards her more than just about work. Why was Piet so worked up about the changes?

Did he know something about the eye symbol? What was going on? A feeling of significant discomfort invaded her space.

After work, she purchased fresh vegetables from the Beekbergen market; when she heard " fresh oranges from South Africa, two boxes
for the price of one, hurry while stocks last," she was tempted to buy them because Toon was building a community there. Still, the man's big purple face with leering eyes made her feel naked; he even looked familiar! ... She shivered and changed her mind.

***

Driving home past the Prinsengracht Hotel made her recall the accident she had almost been in during the pouring rain when...good grief, that was Toon! The man who had asked her if she was all right! Of course, that voice!
Why did she only now...? Then suddenly she remembered where she had seen that creepy man from the market before! He was the angry man with the upturned van with the oranges! Had her mind sped up faster? Were more impressions submerging into her conscious mind?
Ingrid felt a stirring within her when she was close to home, as if Toon could be near. She speculated whether she could communicate on a mental basis from a distance. Could she send a thought to him?
She was mentally seeing a light beam projecting from her to Toon with the words forming in her throat...
"Toon, can you hear me?"
"Loud and clear, I've been waiting for you to contact me," She had to hold onto her steering wheel so as not to drive into her neighbours' prized possession, a Citroën called an 'ugly duckling'.
Her heart was still pounding when she picked up a blue envelope with the monogram of the Prinsengracht hotel from inside the hallway. She knew they came from Annelies, but now wondered who delivered them.

Jeroen was not home yet, and her longing for Toon annoyed her. He seemed to take up her whole mind.

She felt deflated after listening to a message on the answering machine from Jeroen, who told her that he would be home for dinner. As she unpacked the groceries, her thoughts were: what would she make for supper? While chopping vegetables and some chicken for Jeroen, her mind drifted again...could she send Toon a message? She was eager to see him, but what could she project that would travel on a beam of light?

"Toon, where are you at this moment?" ...she was now really grinning at herself. Who was she kidding? But the feeling of joy as if he were almost standing beside her became stronger.

"I'm near you; can't you feel me?" Did she hear this thought transference, or was it in her imagination? She heard a car door slamming and someone walking to the front door, and her heart skipped a beat when she opened it and saw, with astonishment, Toon just standing there, grinning.

"I'm so glad that you finally responded to my signals." Ingrid felt uncomfortably exposed, realising that she was blushing.

"What signals?" She played for time, pretending ignorance while trying to keep a straight face.

"You responded to me. Who are you trying to fool?" His eyes challenged her as he took her hands in his. Ingrid knew she had asked for it and felt outmanoeuvred. When Fluffball came running up, he let go and gently picked up her cat.

"How come Fluffball knows you so well?" Her bewilderment and his nearness caused her to perspire as she entered the lounge. Fluffball was purring away in his arms while Toon looked around with approval.

"I knew it would look like this," she said, studying her photo gallery.

"My daughter, Sascia, is the family's photographer." She tried hard to watch him objectively like an observer, discarding any emotion, which was very difficult.

"Are you alone this evening?" He stood very close, gazing into her eyes with that intensity that made her feel he was observing her whole being.

"No, Jeroen is coming soon," She was almost relieved because this was getting far too intimate. She knew that he had heard that. *"Kitty, relax; what are you frightened of? I feel such pleasure being with you."*

She could not relax, and her stomach was quivering. She could think of nothing important except that having Toon in her home felt good.

He followed her to the kitchen and looked at her water purifier with the floating crystals, which gave her some breathing space. She missed him when he was not around; when he was nearby, she was frightened of her feelings!

"Kitty, what do you know about water?"

"I have a sister who is very much into all health projects. She told me crystals restore life. I've no idea if it works, but" ...Toon was very silent for a while, just watching her while getting closer. He let Fluffball out of the kitchen door.

"By the way, I was the messenger today. That's how I got acquainted with Fluffball!" he whispered in her ear while stroking her hair.

"It feels perfect being here in your home, too."

"Messenger? What do you mean?" She jumped away, not trusting herself. He felt too near for comfort, but she could see in his eyes that he knew how she felt.

"Have you not just retrieved a blue envelope?"

"Are you? Do you deliver the Excerpts?"

"No, this is the first one Annelies gave to me to hand over."

She offered him coffee and studied his face while he looked out at the garden. There were wrinkles of humour at the corners of his eyes. Only his slightly greying hair showed a sign of maturity, but his high forehead and the large grey/blue eyes held such an arresting intelligence that one could notice nothing else. He looked back, catching her observation, and a smile of amusement appeared.

"Have I met with your approval?"

Oh yes, he must know he had. Everything about him had her admiration—his enthusiasm for life, sense of humour, and approach to people.

"Madame, where would you like to go for dinner?" He beamed as he seated himself on the high stool at the counter, drinking his coffee and picking up the blue envelope.

"May I have a look?"

"Yes, go ahead. Toon, who is Trevor?"

"He's Annelies' uncle. Why, have you met him?"

"No, but Hans asked you if POWAH's excerpts came from Trevor. Remember, at the Pannekoek." Toon silently stared at her, but she couldn't read his mind.

Excerpt Nine[1]

Program Planet Earth

The Nine Character Vibrations of the Individual Soul

Toon was reading the letter with such attention that Ingrid wondered about the content.

"Very interesting! Have you read it already?" "Yes, but you have to click on the Hyperlink to read the rest of the excerpt online." Toon typed the link address in his cell phone and read the rest. She inclined her head, still wondering why she couldn't read his mind.

"To answer your question, yes, I know Trevor. He is a very unusual man. Apart from being an Egyptologist, he is also a spiritual science researcher. He is not a person who would have written this, but Kit-

---

1. **https://allrealityshifters.wordpress.com/powah/the-reality-shifters-excerpt-9/**

ty, I would love to read your journal." Toon stood up as he spoke. His tallness had always affected her.

"What does a spiritual science researcher do?"

Toon laughed when he passed the excerpt to her. Toon stood behind her while she tried hard to concentrate on reading POWAH's letter.

It said her personality card number was a five, an accumulator of knowledge. She wondered where Toon would fit into the scheme, probably between the seven or eight, as he had so many things on the go.

"I now recall that some time back, Trevor was experimenting with a brain-operated machine. Like a non-invasive brain-computer interface using electrodes that collect scalp measurements of brain activities."

"Not nano-technology, I hope? That is scary stuff." She was intensely aware of his seductive caresses as he whispered that information in her ear. "Yes indeed, kitty, that is why it is important to distinguish between a technology per se and how it might be put to ill use."

Then, suddenly, she heard him speaking telepathically again.

"You already know me well, don't you? Relax, Kitty, I want to hold you."

His hands were softly exploring her breast, which made it impossible for her to relax; all she wanted to do was respond. She dropped the excerpt and turned around, curling her arms around his neck while pressing against him, feeling his mouth kissing her neck. Her body trembled as she clung to him.

"Toon...Jeroen can come in at any moment...Please...we must stop."

"You must make me stop, Kitty. I can't." Toon was cuddling her most intimately while she was inwardly feeling her longing to love him overwhelm her in a torrent of hunger. His eyes observed her as if he

was mentally... penetrating her. *"Will you share your deepest secrets with me?"*

"Will you?" she repeated in a shaky voice, trying desperately to control herself.

"Oh, very soon," he kissed her while sensually running his fingers down her back, making her shiver all over. Then she heard Jeroen coming up the driveway.

"Toon, do you like stir-fry?" She glanced up at him, trying not to reveal how difficult it was to resist his arousing effect on her.

"Are you inviting me to dinner?" he gaily responded. She started to turn to wash the vegetables in the sink when she again felt his exploring hands while his mouth travelled down her neck.

"Oh, Toon, please," her legs almost gave in, knowing she'd given herself away.

"Toon! Jeroen has just arrived!"

"A taste of family life? What a treat!" he said, ignoring her plea.

"You are adorable, Kitty! Do you know what you do to me?"

"No, tell me", she beamed back while busying herself with her cooking.

"Watch out, Madame, I'm not ashamed to show my real feelings for you, even when Jeroen walks in on us." She knew he meant it but reluctantly let go of her, enjoying her battle to regain her composure.

"Mom, whose sports car is parked in our...? Oh, hello...Mom, I see you have a visitor!"

She introduced them to each other, and Jeroen played the perfect host, offering Toon beer and making her a drink. The cosiness in the kitchen as the men were unwinding at the breakfast corner heightened when Fluffball purred as he swirled around her feet for dinner.

When Jeroen told Toon what his studies were, he responded with the right kind of questions. He was an excellent listener, and she compared him to Jan. Jeroen, who had never really experienced a father he could talk to the way he did now with Toon. Jeroen was nineteen when Jan started to get fainting spells, and the children were often too much for him. She realised what Jeroen had missed in the previous six years.

Looking at them both sitting relaxed at the kitchen counter, talking, now and then including her in the conversation, she knew then that she had been in love with this man the moment she saw him for the first time. Jeroen was telling Toon about his grandfather's firm. She stopped listening and just observed Toon. He would have made a great dad, so why had he never married?

For one moment, as their eyes met, she wondered whether he had read her mind. She could see that he had, which made her blush. Jeroen suddenly broke her train of thought with his following remark:

"Mom, did you know Toon knows Uncle Ed in Australia?"

"No, I didn't!" Oh no, not Ed! That shook her.

"Yes, I know Ed very well. He told me a lot about your parents. I only realised who your mother was after I spoke to her over the phone when she told me she had three children: twins and a younger daughter. It had to be the same Ingrid Barendse Ed was always raving about.

Jeroen, did you know your Uncle Ed had a big crush on your mother?"

"Mom, did he?" Jeroen peered at her as he got up to answer the phone in her office.

"I can see why he had a crush on you." Ingrid was stunned at this revelation.

"I always wondered why you never asked me if I was married!" She beamed back.

"Why didn't you ever question me about that? Were you worried I would get the wrong idea?" His eyes held an amused glint. Had he read her mind all along?

"What idea do you mean?" She wanted to provoke him, but she saw that his expression had become serious.

"Kitty, I've got to go away for a while. I do wish you could come with me."

His mental plea disturbed her greatly. But what about her work? What business could he possibly have that included so much travelling? Oh, how much she would miss him, too.

"How long?"

"You two are very quiet", Jeroen remarked when he returned to the kitchen, offering Toon another beer. She had made a vegetable stir-fry with Hong Kong chicken extra for them both.

"Mom, that was Quincy. I told her we had a visitor, so she asked if you could phone her back later." Jeroen resumed their easy, comfortable conversation while Ingrid served the meal in the dining room with a heavy heart. Toon asked about her sister's name, Quincy, which was not a Dutch name. She told him a story that Gran had told them.

The rest of the evening went by far too quickly. Toon remained the perfect gentleman and did not openly reveal his feelings for her at any stage of the evening, but she was reluctant to see him go when she walked him to the door while Jeroen cleared the table.

"Kitty, thank you for a lovely dinner," he whispered in the hallway. *"I want to hold you, kiss you."* Watching her sadly.

"Where are you going, Toon, and for how long?"

"I have to go to Australia for a few weeks, but I'll be back as soon as possible; I should already have been there. I'm closing some of my holdings over there, and Ed will take care of the rest in the future." Ingrid looked shocked, and she knew he could read her feelings.

Toon pulled her outside, next to his car, in the dark, drawing her to him urgently, holding her as if he never wanted to let her go. He let her know what he had in mind with a kiss. Oh, she now wished that she had been more...she allowed her feelings to run freely. His response was so overwhelming that they had to stop. Both their breathing had become unstable.

"When I come back, I'll take you with me." She gazed into his eyes while stroking his face, loving his mouth, knowing what he meant.

Toon moaned softly, *"Kitty, this is going to be so difficult, being apart from you; this can't be normal! I feel so incomplete without you; now that I have found you, I want to be with you always."* His body trembled.

"Oh, Snooks, I'll miss you as well," She held him firmly while his hands explored her all over. Then, he reluctantly let her go.

She stood outside for a while, steadying her breath before going inside after Toon drove away. The thought of his being far away gave her an unexpected feeling of bleak desolation.

"Mom, he has the hots for you, all right."

"Jeroen! What do you mean?" He grinned and went to the lounge to watch a sports match on the TV.

Class 7

When she drove to Annelies' home, she felt a sense of emptiness. Toon had been gone for a few days, and she had already missed him. A large sign of the words: THE PRESENT EMOTIONAL CONSCIOUSNESS CARD was

written in big letters on the door. Seeing the night sky painting again made her wonder where she had seen it before. What was it supposed to be? Nothing was ever on the wall for any reason other than the reality-shifting workshops!

Liesbeth came in, and Hans winked at her while calling Joris, who had sneaked in to greet everyone like only Joris could.

"How was your trip to the United States?"

"Oh, Ingrid, I've lots to tell you when we are alone," Liesbeth said, frowning. "Why do you look so sad? I see a heaviness pushing into your energy field?"

All she could do was sigh. *"I'm missing Toon."*

"Tonight, I'll introduce you to the Enneagram with a difference," Annelies asked if anyone had anything to share about the past week.

Yolanda's eyes sparkled again, and she told them all she had learned from her interpretations. Yolanda's sharing of her translations through accessing her blockages was a significant contribution.

"Thank you for that journey mapping. Others will benefit and go through the same obstacle quickly." Liesbeth beamed. Ingrid realised the dynamics of sharing.

"Ingrid, how are your clothing designs getting on?"

"I'll show you later!" she beamed back at Yolanda.

After they had done their decoding, chosen the graphics to go with their numeral vibrations, and Annelies showed them what to do next, Tieneke's mind drawing came to mind.

"Place yourself in the centre of the paper I've given you, and now visualise and feel your emotional body surrounding you on your paper—colour in the attachment lines to the people of your choice. You can also write the names of people you emotionally connect with. Use positive and negative reactions at the end of each emotional attachment line!"

"Even your late husband, Ingrid, if you still have emotional ties with him."

"At this present moment, or from last year? How far do we go back?" Yolanda asked as she helped herself to water if anyone wanted some.

"Take it from this year; then it will make it five to almost six months."

"Or any emotional ties that still prevail now, Yolanda."

"But, Annie, I haven't seen him for ten months!" Ingrid noticed that Liesbeth seldom participated in their telepathic dialogue.

"Next to your symbol, you can write, or colour or however you would like to do it, the person or persons you feel are important to you. As you can see, I've already given you a plan to go by. This is to establish the emotional attachments and connections you currently have. You are drawing your shimmering hologram vibration by colouring them in colour."

"Annelies, do we add more if we have more people who have strong attachments to us?" Zola queried while Wim sat staring into space. Ingrid could not read any thoughts coming from him.

Ingrid's empathy for Wim was somehow challenging to express.

Being colourblind, perceiving everything in shades of grey must be horrible. While Wim was smoking his pipe outside, Zola had told them that there were special glasses that claimed to restore colour vision for the colourblind. Wim had tried several, but without luck. Now, he is waiting for the latest lens implant, and he has found a sponsor who will pay for the operation after he has done some research for them. Zola had clammed up when Wim joined them as if she had shared too much.

"Yes, you do, Zola," Annelies replied to her question. "Remember to include anyone to whom you are still reacting with pain and hurt, as well as the people who make you happy."

"Ingrid, telepathy is only possible on a magnetic frequency; Wim, his thoughts are very electric, that's why."

"Annelies, but this can change from one day to the next!" Richard called out as he dropped his pencil.

"I'm glad you noticed. The last three cards are constantly changing, and even the vibration within the three cards can move around in case of a marriage, a different job or a new relationship." Annelies explained, glancing at Ingrid while beaming, *"Think about that, Ingrid."*

Ingrid blushed at Annelies's insinuation. This was an emotional exercise, so she even had to put Piet in there, realising how much he still affected her and Toon well... she was inclined to make the colour very orange with specks of red, blue and yellow between them and between Piet and her almost grey-black. Between her children, she chose a soft blue shade, and between her sister, she chose a yellow colour. Wow. How very interesting! Ingrid had used Toon, Jeroen, Piet, her father-in-law, Quincy, Liesbeth, and Ed, knowing she still had an attachment to him.

"Annelies, when are thoughts electric?" That was a revelation. So, thoughts operated on different wavelengths?

"When lower personality entities are in control, dear." Annelies handed crayons around, and Ingrid observed again that she always stayed on her feet!

Joris was growing fast. He now had his basket but still preferred Niels' company by relaxing under his chair. Annelies told her that Joris was Toon's birthday gift.

"From today, I want you all to start a dream journal that will prepare you for the making of the two life cards in a few weeks."

"I never dream," Wim remarked, shrugging his shoulders. He doesn't remember them, Ingrid thought when Annelies glanced pensively at Wim.

"Wim, when we are asleep, we are in a trance state, so our unconscious is more dominant and fills our perceptual screens with reality-based images from our soul memory records." Ingrid wished she had POWAH's explanation in her head.

"Wim, are you computer literate?" Liesbeth asked.

"You mean, do I use a computer?" The conversation did not come quickly to him. Was it because of shyness, or was he generally not interested? In a way, he reminded her of Jan.

"Do you?" Liesbeth watched Wim with more than just a glance. What did she see that nobody else was able to detect?

"People who lose their creative/emotional body do not remember dreams. His hologram reveals that this is the reason he is avoiding colour! His creative /intuitive body is missing!"

Ingrid tried to visualise what Liesbeth was describing, but she became more aware of the perfume of the lilac blooms in Annelies' large glass vase.

Wim never replied, and Liesbeth didn't press him further.

"Wim, we all do dream. The most simplistic way to fathom how our physical world or dream world becomes a reality is as follows.

Our brain is like a mental recorder that translates our sound, smell, sight, taste and touch sensations into codes. These codes, like the codes

behind the images on our computer screen, form images. Therefore, this exercise will enhance and activate your psychic abilities in your conscious state by writing down the images from your dreams, the storyline or the impressions from a symbolic point of view." Liesbeth advised.

Annelies is a good example of a person greatly affected by our wireless technology. He seems to spend an average of twelve hours daily surrounded by electro-electromagnetic devices. His aura is showing signs of overexposure."

"Liesbeth, can you see who took his intuitive body?" Liesbeth's relaxed pose as she slumped in her chair did not give away how attentive she was.

"Not really, it's more to do with people connected to the Large Hadron Collider at CERN." Both Ingrid and Yolanda had followed their telepathic discussion with riveted attention. She did wonder what CERN, an underground establishment involved in colliding particles of the atom, had to do with an electromagnetic frequency overdose. She knew all about what WiFi, radio, and many other wireless technology devices from Quincy could do to human health. Her wireless modem at home was only switched on when she needed it. She never had any devices like cell phones in her bedroom.

"What is the aim of CERN?" Ingrid asked telepathically.

"It seems to many that the intent is to open the dimensions where the creator gods of this reality can travel through, back into their creation to take over humanity," Liesbeth replied on their mental wavelength.

"What does that mean?"

"It would mean that humanity will be mentally permanently enslaved if they do not wake up in time." Both Annelies and Yolanda nodded in agreement.

"You mean to stop believing that our physical reality is real?" She knew the answer but wanted it confirmed.

"Yes indeed. Any belief, be it a religious or a scientific conviction, will be like a computer program that holds the reality in place." Annelies mentally replied.

Their interaction reminded her of the building problems they were having in France.

"Annelies, I've heard that we learn and experience more in our dream state. Does that mean we can gain access to experiences that could speed up our spiritual, mental and emotional growth?" Richard asked.

"I'm sure he is picking up on our thoughts." Liesbeth nodded at her.

"Ingrid, they are opening dimensional portals above the ground where people are unaware of what has been happening; any building constructions could be dangerous. Ask Toon," Liesbeth beamed on a private channel.

Wow, she had read thoughts.

"Yes, Richard, our mind can filter brain information on an elevated level when operating on Alpha into Theta and Delta brain waves. Richard, that will be your main subject when you write the second level of our awakening journey. It will mostly be in the brain, our organic computer," Annelies replied with a grin as she took out a file displaying human brain drawings.

Ingrid tried to digest the two different conversations. Gosh, she had been dreaming a lot in the past two weeks. Having recorded her dreams for a long time, she was beginning to know the different levels of her dream journeys.

During their break, she showed Yolanda a drawing of an evening dress she had been working on every evening for the whole week. Her small sketchbook showed a vision that still lingered.

"What do you think? Could you make something like that?"

"Gosh, Ingrid, that's gorgeous! What fabric did you have in mind?"

"I don't know, something dark blue, silky, and soft, I leave that to you. You have to work with it."

"For what occasion did you want to wear this? It's brilliant."

"I don't know, I don't have any evening wear, and I saw it in a dream.

I'll leave it up to you. Let me know what it will cost, but don't let that stop you from experimenting."

"Ingrid, how are you doing with your journal?" Annelies asked her after the others were already outside. It was still full daylight for the time of the year. She loved summertime.

"I'll show it to you soon." Ingrid had no idea what Annelies was going to do with it. Liesbeth seemed involved in translating their journals into a story format, but she had no idea how.

I will explain why the journals by people like you, Richard and Annelies are to become a visionary fiction genre.

"Ingrid, have you heard from Toon?" Annelies asked when she was about to step into her driver's seat.

"Not directly, no. I've received flowers, but I don't know where he is. Do you?" Annelies must have been aware they were in contact outside of office hours. Her eyes were laughing at Ingrid as if she knew something.

"No, I've no idea, but knowing Toon, he'll appear suddenly, so be prepared," while giving her a pat on her cheek.

Other lifetime memories

Before turning off the light that Friday night, she pondered on the explanations Annelies shared during class when sleepiness took over, and she drifted off... into the higher-frequency delta pulse... Her body felt heavy... the vibrations felt so different... cold...

The wind was streaming past her, and she fumed with anger. She galloped on her horse faster and faster, trying to get rid of the pain and hurt that burned in her chest. She needed to make some decisions because her dreams were shattered.

Tears were running down her face, and she cried like never before. She felt betrayed and abandoned. When she had looked into Mc-Nealy's eyes that morning, she had read in them remorse as if he knew that he'd betrayed her!

It had hurt her so to see what he did to himself. Why did he need to explore the world? Those grey/blue eyes had always made her feel beautiful, challenged, probed, and almost undressed, making her feel like a real woman.

She had never been with a man yet, and he knew it.

He always made her feel he would one day take her as his, and she had waited for that moment.

This morning, his eyes had lost all that sparkle as if he was already gone forever, almost as if he had willingly made a sacrifice, but for what? He'd told her he had signed up to leave with the others from his village to start a new life.

He would sail away in an hour. What had happened to him to make that decision? She had asked him over and over again. He had told her he dreamed of having a place of his own, that staying in their village would mean he would always work for someone else.

He thought she would understand. She remembered hearing the pipes that someone was playing, practicing for the annual dance in three days, and she would have no partner! McNealy knew what she had been thinking, for they had always had this communication between them. He tried to joke that every boy in the village would want to make her his wife because she was the district's most desirable, strong-willed woman. After listening to his plans, she remembered blurting out that she would come along, but he had not reacted. Or had he pretended not to hear?

In all her 18 years, Sonya only remembered feeling a deep love and longing for McNealy.

She had been in love with him from the age of twelve. When she was old enough to join their riding team, she became closer to him than anyone. He was ten years older, and during the last year they had ridden together, he made her feel wanted as the woman who would become his. She knew that and had always taken it for granted that they would be married after the last timber had drifted down the river.

She had hoped that they would wed before the winter had set in, after which they would be snowed in for months.

She always dreamt of the time that they would live up in the log cabin he had built himself.

She knew her father would not have made it easy, but she had always got what she wanted from him, and McNealy was the centre of her life.

As the weather was cold and a storm was coming, she knew she had to return to the manor before it hit her. She slowed her galloping horse to a slow trot, patted Prince on his flank and looked over the valley.

In recent decades, the last shift of the land had closed off the valley, forming a shallow basin filled by the river, creating a small lake behind the natural dam.

The previous autumn, a mudslide had dammed the outlet channel again farther downstream, containing the raging floodwaters within the confines of the valley and causing a backlash.

Looking at the scene below, she felt welling up in her a profound sense of belonging. Never could she live anywhere else; this was where she wanted to raise her family. This place always gave her strength.

Months had rippled by, but she had lost interest in seeking a soul mate. All she felt was the inner need to be free from being so in love.

Never again would she be trapped like that. Sonya decided she would live how her father wanted her to, remembering McNealy's words that every boy in the village tried to make her his wife as if that made it all right to leave her! She would look for a mate who would give her strong, healthy children, someone she could depend on and trust, who would never leave her but with whom she would never fall in love.

Only then could she avoid being hurt like this again. Why? Why? The alarm woke her up.

Ingrid recalled the dream vividly. The sorrow that the dream left behind felt very real. It was like she had just come from...Toon! This McNealy was Toon! And he went away. Was that why Toon had asked her if she trusted him? Did he remember the same life? Ingrid had difficulty taking herself seriously, but the emotion of desolation made her feel drained even now. If only she could speak to him, telling him she remembered and would trust him! She knew he would come back this time.

While eating her breakfast that Wednesday morning, Ingrid pondered over the week that had raced by, even though she missed Toon greatly. He had phoned her three times. In the last call, he begged her if he could book a flight to Sydney for her. He was trying to talk her into joining him and sounded rather depressed, but she was not ready to walk out on her job. Toon wanted to phone Mr. Brinks, asking him to give her some time off. When she tried explaining their difficulties with the French complex, Toon had asked many questions. Ingrid knew he had been in contact with Mr. Brinks to find out what was going on.

Leaving her job now, just like that? How could she?

She was glad of the hectic time at work, and she planned to see Annelies before Friday night. They would make their Present Mental Personality card on Friday evening, and she wanted to ask Annelies many things! She checked the time and decided to phone her before driving to work.

"Hello, Ingrid, we were having breakfast when your face suddenly popped up. You phoned to make arrangements to see me?"

"Yes, would tomorrow evening be suitable? You can perhaps answer some of my questions?"

"Why don't you come for supper tomorrow at seven? I'm looking forward to reading your journal so far."

Why not? she thought. Maybe they'd heard from Toon. She accepted the invitation gladly. Jeroen must have been sleeping late as he had not come down for breakfast before she left for work.

The day was hectic, with many enquiries about the Tilburg complex's official opening. The park was already fully booked. Ingrid had always liked her job, but it was not as fulfilling anymore.

Piet was challenging and grumpy, constantly wanting to review the changes in the drawings of the French complex. Carla also complained that he was impossible to work with. Carla had overheard Piet talking to a person on his private cell phone about the technical part of the drawings.

Not that that influenced any of her work. She only did the creative sketches of the new holiday resort, but Carla seems to suspect something sinister was brewing with the tower construction.

She usually never listened to rumours of any kind, but why had that creepy man pestered her to draw work for them a few weeks ago?

While she had heard Carla, she knew the tower would be built right over the centre of the eye formation, which could only be seen from far away. Richard had not returned to her about the mysterious symbol, but perhaps she'd made too much of it.

All she could think of was what Liesbeth had said about CERN.

Was the eye formation a significant symbol, like a portal into other dimensions?

"Ingrid, Roelof de Beer, our sub-contractor and a man called Richard are on the line; which one do you want to take first?" Ula told her on the internal line.

"Put Richard through first, will you!" Gee, just as she was thinking about him.

"Ingrid, I've researched recorded crop formations in England during the late 19th Century. It has been speculated that many stones, especially stone slabs, were used to build temples. Like the pyramids, they were, or are, formed by past human civilisations with a technology that could activate the structural sectors in stone. Maybe that is how they stored their information, like we do today, on microchips, which are also crystal."

"But what do you think is the significance of the eye symbol?"

"Well, the 'all-seeing eye' is also the symbolism of the Illuminati. It needs to 'watch out' in any direction!"

"I know that something is unclear to me, Richard. Why are there so many problems with the building of the dome?"

"Mmm, I wonder. There are seven different hieroglyphs used to represent the eye. Still, it seems that past human civilisations were far more advanced in studying the Frequency Barrier on Earth and have lived with the knowledge that we are living when it will be lifted."

Richard was wondering what obstacles could cause such a hassle.

"Ingrid, all I can think of is that we are only aware of this Frequency Barrier now; the eye symbol must be some sort of a warning, as if there might be some sort of black hole."

Wow, that could be it. The spot where the dome will be placed could prevent something.

"It's the blasting that worries me somehow. I know that Toon is more aware of what is going on. I have to ask him when I see him. It has something to do with a Star Gate."

"That could be it. The Eye symbol is the Eye of Ra or the Eye of Horus. It might be due to the missing capstone carved out of a rare, super-hard stone called Luddite, not found on Earth."

"Gosh, I have no idea where that idea came from...how weird."

She could see a flickering light on her landline that someone was still waiting for her to reply...

"Some archaeologists, like my brother, used divining rods or even a pendulum to date the slates with engraved undeciphered scripts. The reason must be because of the energy that is encoded in stone."

"You mean that any stone can be seen as a memory chip?"

"Yes, sort of. The accelerator control room was probably under the pyramids."

"Gosh, what a thought! These huge stones attracted many people. No wonder."

"Yes, and what's more, these formations speak in universal languages of symbology, mathematics, and geometry."

Richard further told her that most researchers suspected that mummifying was not a religious ritual originally, but rather a form of...freezing...like we do today. Richard speculated it had to do with the pyramids being giant resonating boxes. The priests were already seeking a means to travel inter-dimensionally.

The hieroglyphs all reveal that they were experimenting with cloning techniques.

"You mean...like genetic engineering?"

"I think so, they were looking for the missing genetic code that controls the DNA/RNA grid template," Ingrid remembered reading that the eye held the blueprint of creation. Suddenly, the star-map painting in Annelies' classroom flashed in her mind again. Were there any connections? She was getting nowhere and reluctantly finished her call with Richard, realising Roelof was still waiting.

"Ingrid, please, can I see you personally? I'm in a situation, and I need your help."

"My help? What do you mean? Is it to do with work?" She picked up on Roelof's nervousness.

"The blasting has to stop; they threaten me if I carry on...Your drawings are..., then she only heard a dial tone. Goosebumps crawled down her back...

Chapter 10
Is the 3rd Dimension a Hologram?

Dinner at Annelies

When Ingrid arrived at Annelies' house, Hans and Liesbeth were also invited for supper. The two of them appeared to be very close. Annelies seemed pleased with their relationship. They were having an aperitif in the conservatory. As Ingrid observed them both, she became aware of something else when they walked hand in hand in the garden. It was almost as if they were more than just a couple. It was the maturity of their relationship that impressed her.

Hans was a very unusual person with spiritual wisdom, as if he had lived and remembered many lifetimes. Was that it? Could that be possible? Was that the reason why so many men never got near Liesbeth? Hans had a quality about him like Liesbeth! Why had she never seen that before?

"Annelies, how does POWAH reveal himself to you, may I ask?" she inquired courteously, sipping her cocktail.

"The first time, about nine years ago, I only heard a voice...that is how it starts. I understood that the voice came from my own...let's say Soul group or my own Higher Self."

"How did you know that? I mean that it was your own Higher Self?"

"The voice felt somehow familiar. I knew or understood that our efforts are just a mental projection of what we agree to, so I felt that a part of me had contacted me, but that is just for lack of a better word."

Her puzzled expression must have been unambiguous.

"Ingrid, if our conscious Soul being is the observer of the choices and expressions of our thoughts and emotions, then in that way, we experience what we think and feel in a kind of mental projection of those thoughts and emotions. I'm not sure we can use the word holographic. That sounds very science fiction," Annelies explained. She could hardly comprehend what seemed so easy for Annelies to understand.

"In this universe, our conscience, individual Soul-being is directed through our efforts, intent and the expressions of what we all wish to experience while we are in an embodiment," she added.

"But... I'm not aware of having a 'contract agreement'. You mean at birth, I had?"

"Yes, you belong to the same Group Soul."

"Yes, I understand, but... can you see POWAH?" Knowing that Annelies was clairvoyant.

"Today, he is as real as you are now sitting opposite me. There is a transparency about him, but...ever since nine years ago, POWAH mentally talks to me like we can all telepathically."

"And he helped you create the decoding workshops?"

"Most of it, yes! I received the information over several years in small parts at first. Initially, I had no idea what I was in for, and I had a lot of help from Leo, my husband's twin brother, Tieneke and Fred, my younger brother. You remember Tieneke?"

"Yes, from the drawing classes, but I feel there's more to it."

"Yes, there is. Let me show you." Annelies invited Ingrid to follow her into a guest bedroom with shutters that opened into a bathroom. A large drawing in a frame dominated the room.

"See that Geneagram outline? It represents the offspring of the children who grew up in the Jaarsma orphanage from 1888 until 1976.

Come and retake a look at the star cluster painting that represents the same ancestral lineage." She followed Annelies to their classroom. So that's what it was, a family tree, but nobody was related physically. It looked like a chart of constellations.

"Annelies, all I see is a map of stars with faint lines between them. Why a family tree?" She still had an uncanny feeling that she had seen it before.

"I know that most of us are the stars on this map. Each of you must trace your family history if you have a family member connected with the Jaarsma Orphanage. The decoding workshops are related to recalling our discordant gridwork from our ancestral lineage at the third level.

Tomorrow night with the others, I will explain more about it, but come, let's have our supper and let me see what you have written."

"Does it have the same date printed on the blue envelope? Where was this orphanage?"

"It was what is now the Prinsengracht Hotel. Didn't you know?"

"Oh! ... now I see the connection... the date on the menu: Toon took me there the first time."

"Yes, I know; he told me about you just before he left for Australia. You know he is deeply in love with you, right?" Annelies glanced with a piercing look as if to say, *"Don't you hurt him"*.

"Annelies, the attraction is very mutual. I've never been so...I don't know the right word for it... I was tempted to rush after him when he wanted me to fly to Sydney. He sounded very depressed, which has been worrying me. Have you heard from him?"

"No, but don't worry, Toon is not the type to stay depressed for long. He's very smitten with you and can't bear to be away! I'm delighted for both of you." Annelies reassured her as she gave her the file she had been working on. She added what feelings and impressions came to her daily, hoping that was the idea. While they all helped themselves to the many cold salads on the sideboard, Annelies was peering through her folder.

"I love how you've written your thoughts about your transmissions with POWAH. Has Toon seen it?"

"No...yes, one conversation with POWAH about the eye of Horus. I showed a print-out to Toon a few weeks ago." Ingrid explained the aerial photo and Richard's theory about the eye.

"Annelies, what do you know about the eye imprint?"

"Very little, really; some call this the age of Horus because it means a passage through different spiritual dimensions we are experiencing now."

Liesbeth and Hans joined them, and Joris followed with a ball in his mouth, begging to play. After dinner, she helped Annelies clear up before they joined Liesbeth and Hans, who were playing a game of chess in the lounge.

"Ingrid, you've written in your journal that the pictographic symbols we use in decoding our 22 spacings and the makings of our cards are thought forms of light; Tieneke will like that!" Hans explained that the symbols were a biochemical language that could trigger the hypothalamus in the human brain as he was moving his King.

"How?" This was beyond her grasp, and she felt relatively simple.

"Ingrid, stop judging yourself; you are not stupid. By harmonising our holographic aura field with colour and sound, our eye's receptor cone is activated to see objects on the many levels of space." Hans replied, and Annelies carried on. "Last year, when a burst of energy wave came over Earth, some of us became clairvoyant."

Was that what happened? She remembered it clearly as if it had happened yesterday. The sky had suddenly become multi-coloured, and she felt much lighter. Happier somehow. From that moment,

her life had somehow changed. Her old laptop had stopped working, and even her other electronic gadgets were affected.

"Was that when an individual Soul occupies more of the human
form?" she asked. That was how she experienced it. Annelies' living
room was decorated with collected treasures. The two couches and
a massive wall hanging were by the renowned leather artist Her-
mien Pool. The large sliding doors revealed an expansive view over
the heather fields.

"Yes, and when our I AM, or our Soul, is more than 10% merged
with the physical body, it also provides us with a new nervous system in the brain, which gives us the full ability to communicate
telepathically,"

Liesbeth added while moving her queen. Ingrid felt exhilarated at
being in the company of people who held this kind of discussion,
but she still did not quite grasp this biochemical language.

"Ask Toon because he's lived with my husband's brother Leo, the
genetic engineering scientist."

"Hans, do you know where Toon is?" Annelies winked at her as she
poured the coffee.

"Who is asking?" Hans looked up teasingly from the chess game.
Ingrid knew she was lovesick. Their telephone conversations and
emails had strengthened their bond.

"Toon was in Sydney two days ago; he's now visiting a community
near Brisbane and has to be in New York. After that, unless he has
an appointment in South Africa, he should be back." Ingrid saw
Liesbeth make a move with her queen.

"Checkmate!" Hans blamed his loss and her winning on being distracted by Ingrid's questions with a show of witty humour that
changed the mood of the evening.

"Liesbeth, remember you were going to tell me something that had
happened to you in Egypt."

"Shall I tell her?"

"Start with your father; I think small bits at a time will do," Hans replied reluctantly.

"Ingrid, how much can you accept about visitations, I mean, actual visitations by beings from a different galaxy or a planet?" Annelies got up to change the music.

"You mean about Extra-terrestrials. I can accept that life is on different planets or dimensions, so why not live in different universes and life forms? Yes, but there are so many online articles and videos about different aliens, but some are apparently very... evil?" She was not so sure what was real and what was not.

"Mmm...Liesbeth, why are you asking me this?"

Annelies settled back in her chair, reading her journal, while Hans relaxed on the sofa next to Liesbeth, staring ahead as if he were not in the room with them.

"Well, as you already know, I lived at the Jaarsma Orphanage for five years before I was adopted, so I never knew my biological parents."

"This Jaarsma orphanage, what is so important about it, Annelies?" Ingrid queried, looking puzzled.

"Liesbeth, tell her your story first," Annelies said while reading her file.

"One evening at the beginning of this year, while I was writing an article, my front doorbell rang. I was surprised as it was already after eleven. When I opened the door, a man in his fifties was holding my cat. When he projected, I was about to thank him and take Plume from his arms. *I believe you took on the name 'Liesbeth.'* Well, that took me by surprise. "You don't recognise me, do you?" he said, introducing himself as my father!"

"Really? But... you said you'd never met your biological father."

"That's what I said to the man," Liesbeth said earnestly. "While he was in the hallway, something changed. I don't know how to describe it, but he suddenly looked different. Part of me was still in my flat, and another part was seeing a different reality, almost as if I was seeing a movie and was in it simultaneously." Liesbeth's whole pose reflected grace.

"While you were still standing in your doorway?"

"Yes, part of me was, but...I observed myself as Tulanda! I somehow knew that was my real name. Mentally, I was resting in my favourite place, high up in the mountains, where the brilliance of planet Earth after its new cosmic birth emanated pure splendour." Liesbeth's dark brown eyes deepened to become pools.

As she listened, flashes of the TV series 'Fringe" came to mind.

"Wow, what did that look like?"

"Beautiful, all plant life was again in harmony with the law of ONE.

I was surrounded by the elemental beings that had always been my friends. There was a harmony beyond description. A tremendous transformation had taken place." Liesbeth's face expressed a glow that one only sees when somebody has experienced something beyond description. Hans' hand rested comfortably in her lap.

"So, you looked into the future?" Ingrid's astonishment showed.

"Probably, I'm not sure... then he was standing in front of me again," Liesbeth said with a glazed look.

"You mean the man in the hallway?"

"Yes, and I asked him how this transformation had come about. He replied that it had to happen as it happened and that, in the end, all tragedies brought about a greater good. Then, he urged me to undertake this last assignment. Writing the fourth level of the Awakening to our Ascension journey."

"Gee, I thought I had a miraculous encounter with POWAH, but you!"

"He promised me that I would return to my timeline soon. I, Tulanda, recalled a previous life on Earth as a nun! That memory was...Well, I emphasised to him what that felt like." Ingrid got a flash of children surrounded by a nun! ... Liesbeth sighed with heaviness.

"Then my father replied that he remembered only too well. I saw myself bending my head, feeling remorseful that I had ever doubted his compassion. He understood my reluctance to undergo another incarnation." Hans handed her coffee; his attentiveness to Liesbeth revealed his affection for her.

"I don't understand. Is your father the man in the hallway? I'm confused."

"Yes, he continued, saying that he had followed my training over the previous Earth years as a nun and that his elders had brought to his attention that my level of understanding made me eligible for the next assignment. The physical form my Soul would embody would be born to a woman who would greatly influence my later life." Liesbeth said in a whisper as if coming out of a trance.

"Now you lost me. Your father tells you what?"

"No, I've explained it poorly. When I say my father, I mean he was my father from a different realm in a parallel universe to our planet Earth. He told me about an incarnation I would undertake again on your planet Earth." Ingrid still couldn't comprehend what Liesbeth had told her. Who was her mother?

"Ingrid, I only embodied a human form when this little girl's Soul gave full consent." Now, she was stunned. What was Liesbeth implying?

"You are what they call...a walk-in?" She grabbed her knees and took a deep breath to release the tension in her back.

"I suppose you could say that. My father told me how difficult it is to monitor some of the traumatic DNA re-alignments; that's why I entered the world differently this time."

"You mean, not through birth?" She could hear her disbelief in her voice.

"Mmm, no, but..." Liesbeth looked sideways at Hans, who shook his head slightly.

"Ingrid, then my father was standing in front of me in his full glory, shimmering with the brilliance of a jewel, and light particles were shooting out from him like energies of the purest love, bathing me with love." Liesbeth's face took on an agelessness that was quite uncanny.

Ingrid's attention was riveted as she slowly allowed the possibility of her story to sink in.

"I heard myself replying to him that his request was impossible. I could feel my inner reluctance because it was like returning to a place I did not want to return to. The feeling was powerful, but my father kept reassuring me that this was what I had been prepared for."

"You mean you remember a different life, and where were you asked to return to...Earth?" Was Liesbeth telling her she was an alien? *"Our human organic body is from Earth, Ingrid."* Hans beamed.

"Yes, Ingrid, I remembered he used a radically different language! It was mental but almost musical at the same time. His language was so clear that I knew I could never refuse. I did have a choice, but deep down, I knew he was right." Liesbeth looked far away as if she were experiencing it all over again.

"Right about what?"

"About what I came here to do, which I didn't understand until a few months ago. I then remembered him as my father, but not from this life."

"From a past life?"

"No, it's not a past life: it is as if I lived a different life, almost simultaneously. When we were inside my flat, this man, my father, addressed me as Liesbeth." She looked at Hans, who nodded.

"My father promised that I would receive all the help I needed. Then I saw what our planet would look like after her transformation! While I was still in my flat, my father showed the picturesque scenery through my mind."

Ingrid was spellbound. Was Liesbeth implying that she came from another planet in another spiritual dimension?

"Ingrid, my planet is from another timeline. It is wonderful. There I was, wearing a magnificent gown made of a fabric I find difficult to describe, almost translucent, vibrational, and the sounds of birds and water trickling down as if a small waterfall reflected a tranquillity of pure bliss. I even saw organic foods displayed in shallow glass-like dishes on almost suspended shelves. They were... perfect!"

Ingrid tried to visualise what Liesbeth was describing.

"Close your eyes, Ingrid. I'll take you there." Hans took hold of her hands.

Nothing happened...then, for a moment...all she saw were colours mingling around her, singing! And it was not the music, but the fragrance that created a feeling of rapture, yet it looked nothing like...Earth! Or was it? She could perceive forms but...they were all part of her! Then, what came into her focus astounded her.

She was high up, zooming into a landscape where giant trees in the forest surrounded a mountain with a flat roof. A spectacular scenery unfolded below her as she skyrocketed closer, almost over a forest. The trees' widespread horizontal branches were used as walkways. She saw people in the most amazing, colourful clothes walking on them as if they were pedestrians coming and going, like they do in a city. Instead of skyscrapers, the houses or buildings seem to be fastened onto the solid cliff of the mountain. Everything that resembled a building appeared between the branches of the trees. The closer she zoomed in, the more flowers and plants of indescribable beauty and fragrance were harmoniously intertwined around the railings on all the walkways on many different levels.

Then, Hans seems to show her a different scene. The closest description was a crystal glass-shaped pyramidal dome supported by gigantic tropical-looking plants...Shoals of flying craft spun around an intricate column of crystals. No race on Earth could construct such a marvel.

A voice in her head explained that the star astral technologies were different.

"Some are equipped with atmospheric drives and cavorted along the same flight paths as tiny ground-to-orbit planes."

All of them were landing or taking off from a roof of crystal arched overhead. Tulanda was holding her arm when hundreds of different species walked, slid, and in several cases, flew along together in a multi-coloured river of life.

All her pent-up breath exhaled in a single overwhelming "Wow"!

She sniffed the air, which contained so many scents. All she could smell was something like dry spice.

"Where do they all come from?"

"Some are species that live in our galaxy. Different species come here to perform exchanges," Hans replied mentally. It was his voice signature, but..." Some have ideas to give, some require knowledge to make ideas work."

"That all sounds noble," she thought out loud.

"We have opened our worlds to this act of sharing for a long time.

"Some races we have known since the beginning of our human history; others are new. All are welcome." Tulanda explained.

Apart from Humans, she intuitively reacted.

"As you know now, humans are free to visit." Hans reminded her

"But nobody knows about your home world?" she said in reply.

Suddenly, some blueish, birdlike, slender bodies dressed in one-piece overalls glided past where they were standing. She could almost see through them. Then... Liesbeth's voice brought her back to the room.

"Gee, what happened? Hans, how did you do that?"

"I projected a magnetic thought image so you could... feel and see and experience a mental transmission of a different kind." Hans' big grin observed her wide-eyed bewilderment. Her whole body shook from the revelation.

"That was amazing, and I now get it; humans have to pass an initiation test... if you are light. Once the frequency is light enough, you can visit your world."

"Correct. Ingrid, our universe consists of different thinking layers; the level of thinking you tune into determines the reality you experience ... The Soul urges the human to translate its experiences of the sensory realm... We must be honest with ourselves to see things clearly and objectively to become reality shifters."

Just before Hans took hold of her hands, a popping sound together with a bright flash in the centre of her head had given her a shock.

"Ingrid, now you know how I could see myself simultaneously in my flat and that other place! I asked my father if I could see him again."

"Was he real? I mean, did you touch him at all?" Liesbeth was still staring abstractedly in front of her as if she were again back at the place she had just described.

"Ingrid, it was as real as all of us sitting together in this lounge, but he also had transparency. His reply to me when I asked him if I would receive any help was that assistance would be given when necessary, but he said I would understand all of it only when I had completed my assignment. Then he put my cat down, told me he would visit again and left." Liesbeth finished her story and looked at Hans, who nodded, so she continued.

"Hans provided the assistance I needed as he is from the same place I come from."

"Hans? That explains it! Do you remember your other lives then?"

"Ingrid, we all have only one life in spirit, although for now, I have chosen to live in a physical body in this period of existence with Tulanda. I've always known that this was what I came here for. I was instructed to wait until the time was right. It has been a long wait, and I'm glad it's over!" With a twinkle, Hans embraced her.

Ingrid now suddenly realised what she had been unable to explain before: why he looked very young and, at the same time, not old, but...

"Annelies, have you always known about this?" She noticed how quiet Annelies had been during their conversation. Her file lay next to her as she was curled up in her chair.

"Yes, from the day Ben and I brought Hans home from the orphanage, he told us exactly where he came from." She smiled. "I must admit, in the beginning, Ben and I just pretended that we knew, thinking he had a terrific imagination. We only realised something was abnormal when he jumped his classes in school and later universities, and many small incidents that revealed he was too... aware for his age."

Ingrid was so stunned by Liesbeth's story that she sat in silence, her mind battling to store the information in a logically acceptable manner. Was there any more information that would ultimately throw her organised reasoning powers into chaos?

"I'm getting stiff and ready for bed," Liesbeth announced while stretching. Hans took her hand when they were getting up from the sofa.

"I think Ingrid has to absorb it first. Let's go home," Ingrid said. She realised Hans must have moved in with her. Thinking back, she wondered whether Liesbeth's story was any more bizarre than her own. Not many people would have taken her dialogue with POWAH seriously.

"Thanks for sharing that with me, Liesbeth, or do I call you...

Tulanda? What an unusual name. Yes, I've to mull it over, but if I may ask, have you seen your father again since?"

"Yes, I have; I'll gradually tell you more about it, and. ...I'll stay Liesbeth for now", Liesbeth replied with her usual sparkle.

"Thank you, Ingrid. You needed to take me seriously, even if I know it all sounds rather bizarre for now. You are very dear to me and one of my attachments." Ingrid embraced her, feeling privileged to be part of this unusual group.

The Pannekoek

A fabulous big bouquet of wildflowers was already on her desk the following day at work. Could that mean Toon was back? The card said cryptically, "New beginnings are always stepping into the unknown." *I am very willing to take that step. Are you? T.* That note made her feel ecstatic. She knew that she wanted to get to know him far more intimately.

Ingrid invited Marijke and Carla for lunch at the Pannekoek, as they had worked hard the whole week. When Richard took their order, he asked after Toon, which made Marijke and Carla look at her with astonishment. She read their thoughts as they battled to work out how Ingrid knew him and how Richard knew Toon. They fired questions at her. Both were attracted by the glamour of Ingrid's social connections.

She told them that Richard was also doing the same Ascension Decoding workshops. They were now even more interested in what the course was all about, so she told them. They took in what they could fathom, and the rest would come at the right time.

"Ingrid, last year you talked about special art classes. Is this an extension of them?" Marijke thought Tieneke's Art-analogue Symbolism mind-drawing classes and her workshops with Annelies were similar.

"Well, they are, in a way. Would you be interested in a creative art course? I can give you the name of the lady who gives them." Marijke's serious expression while clutching her straw in her mouth made them all silent, waiting for her to open up.

"I feel I have to get over my depression and do something with my life." Marijke still sounded grieved. She would look up the information on the mind-drawing workshops and give her Tieneke's address.

She remembered that Tieneke gave evening classes. Carla was also interested and wanted to attend an evening class together. As it was time to return to work, she promised to show the first three cards she had made soon. Marijke went home now that she only worked part-time, and Carla joined her back at the office. The rest of the day dragged on. There was still no word from Toon, only flowers. She started to wonder what he did. However, whatever he did, she would not feel any different.

When she checked her inbox before closing up for the weekend, she was delighted to find an email from Toon, recognising his email address.

———- Original Message ——-

From: "T Haardens"
To: <Ingrid Barendse:;>
Sent: Sunday, June-16, 2019 7:21 PM
sub>Subject: Kitty
Dear Kitty
I'm resting next to a waterfall that mingles with a river further down in the valley below.
The music of the water current celebrates the fact that there is always a tomorrow.

Then I see it joining the ocean in a constantly moving torrent of flaming glory.

Even the waves clasping in a playful embrace of power tell the same story.

Every creature, even the beetles in the white sand below my feet, mingle.

Even they speak of a union that tells me nothing in the world is forever single.

I look up at the sky, where the clouds play hide and seek together, and I see the birds are free, flying with one another in all types of weather; I see the mountains reach up high to embrace heaven above, and all around me, the sweet perfumes of the flowers speak of love.

Kitty, in my lonely solitude from where I am viewing my world unhappily, looking inside my soul, I feel it only has one desire: for your company.

I miss you, my love, my dear beloved. You are in all my dreams, and I find that the image of your elegance and beauty is engraved in my mind.

Will you be my companion, lover, and partner and forever celebrate the awakening of our spirits with their longing to be merged as one?

Ingrid's tears welled up. How could she ever have doubted him? Why couldn't she have let go of her fears and just gone with him? She wanted to write back but couldn't find the right words. She could not put down her feelings as well as he could, but she needed to send him something.

Snooks!

I dream of you, too, but you know you left me once before, remember?

You asked me if I trusted you, and the memory of what had been swept away.

Now, my desire tells me that all I want to do is surrender.

Next time, I will go with you when you come back to stay.

During my day and going home, my thoughts are with us.

All day, I miss you, and at night, I do not want to keep you away;

So, my answer is, yes, I trust you, I do now forever.

I look out for you every morning, night and day.

Thank you for the flowers, my love.

They give me comfort because you are so far away.

Did she have the nerve to send this? All she needed to do was one click, and it was gone. As she hesitated about sending the clumsy beginner's attempt at a poem, she envisioned him sitting on a rock with his laptop on his knees, typing to her. Her attention was then caught by a new e-mail from POWAH, always with the heading Program Planet Earth, with the title "I AM".

Excerpt Ten[1]

Program Planet Earth

I AM that I AM

"Ingrid, you are far away. Are you dreaming of Toon? Are the flowers from him? Did you two fight?" Carla commented, peeping around the door of her office. Ingrid was about to react when she realised she must have been miles away for a while.

"Toon had to go to Australia on business." She clicked with one finger to send her e-mail. She would read the Excerpt at home. She closed the computer for the weekend and walked out with Carla.

"How are you both, Carla, you and Niels?"

"I visited Niels after work in his workshop for the first time last week. I realised I wanted this man, especially after you told me about the reality-shifting card game. I did something I have never done."

---

1. https://allrealityshifters.wordpress.com/powah/the-reality-shifters-excerpt-10/

"Now, you make me curious! If you have been married twice, what have you never done? Or is that too personal?" Grinning gaily. Carla looked, paused and then smiled with a glint in her eye.

"I've never seduced a man before. Have a great evening, and don't you tell him I said that."

"Carla! What do you take me for? But I think you were very wise! I'll see you on Monday."

Class 8

That evening, they would be making their PRESENT MENTAL CARD.

Ingrid's thoughts anticipated the class eagerly as she drove to Annelies' house. Happiness radiated from her face as her mind returned to her psychic communications with Toon. Would her mental card reveal things that would give her more understanding of herself and how they communicated telepathically? The aspects in the two previous cards did refer to the mind-drawings with Tieneke. Could it be that the energy or qualities from the Language of Light symbols, which were the aspects of the cards, created an energy cord with others on a mental level?

Yolanda greeted everyone at the door as they all arrived simultaneously.

"Hi, Ingrid! Annelies is on the phone, but I think it's for you." Yolanda looked puzzled.

"Toon, she has just walked in; let me get her for you! Hold on," Annelies spoke as she beckoned Ingrid to the phone in her lounge. Ingrid felt a joy rising within that propelled her to the phone as if she had no control over her movements.

"Kitty, I received your email... you... lifted my spirits as no woman has ever done. You made me so happy; I want to take the next plane out of here to be with you. I will never go away for so long without you; I want to take you in my arms, hold you, kiss you, make love to you... Kitty, is it normal to feel like this?" ... Say something! I want to hear your voice! Make love to me over the phone, I dare you!" Ingrid thought of Carla. It was not quite the same, but telepathically... she could do it... *"Snooks, I'm visualising your sparkling eyes going over my whole body, caressing me, holding me! I can feel your hands stroking me all over. I can feel my longing for you, reaching out to and embracing you."* ... She projected the rest in picture form, as it seemed somehow more manageable to be intimate that way.

"Kitty, you'd better stop; you are making it too real for me! You surprise me more and more. If you can do it like this, well...I suppose you have to go to your classes," she heard him sigh.

"Where are you phoning from? What time is it when you are?"

"It's early in the morning. I'm in a cottage outside of Brisbane, waiting for Ed. We're going out on a hike around the large estate he purchased a month ago. He has some great plans for the community on this property. I wish you were here; I want you by my side while doing what I do best. Kitty, I feel so... happy for myself but also unfortunate for Ed." ... he whispered the last few words.

"Snooks, Ed needs a friend like you, but come home to me soon; Annelies is calling me." She heard Annelies projecting, *"Toon, phone her back when she is at home!"*

"I heard that!" "I adore you, you know," he spoke softly, which made her giggle. Was he ever going to hang up?

"Oh, Snooks, I miss you as well." And she gently placed the receiver back in its cradle, her mind joined to his. *"I love you,"* she said while visualising her thoughts travelling over a light beam.

"Kitty! I heard that! I... Oh, my other half... I love you too" ...

When she walked back into the classroom, they were all smiling. Was she so transparent?

"Ingrid, I've never seen or experienced Toon being in love! It's quite something!" Annelies projected.

"Are you ready to come down to earth again and make your Present Mental card?" Liesbeth winked. "You people suffer being separated, don't you?"

"Ingrid, share with us the spacing of your physical card from last week," Gerrit asked her with a chuckle. They all laughed.

"All right, you can all gloat, it's eleven! Satisfied?" She glowed with embarrassment.

The previous week, she had been reading up on the inner vibrations of her physical card, so it was very appropriate. She would be confronted by heightened activity in her second sexual chakra. Wow!

Their classroom reminded her of Tieneke's drawing classes, colourful and cosy.

"Why are Tieneke's doodling courses called the Language of Light symbols?" That question had been sitting with her for weeks.

"That is a good question, Ingrid. It is the original light language of our ancient ancestors."

"Oh." Not grasping who these ancient ancestors were.

"I was told that many symbolic shapes that appear through doodling were the original first externally spoken language in our Universe, and it is the natural language of the Christos – Founders Race. I will explain more about them in my journal."

Annelies explained the procedure as to how they had to use colour and symbols and write the things they were good at and the people they had drawn into their lives that were inspiring them to pursue their inner growth.

"Annie, when you say good at, do you mean how Tieneke showed me the five creative drawing techniques?" Ingrid also remembered Tieneke's analogue drawing exercises that showed how their mental world could create many situations to bargain with and reveal unexpressed emotions. Ingrid knew that Yolanda had finished her divorce proceedings. The music in the background, as they were all working on their cards, stimulated their mental visions.

"Annelies, are there any religions that preach what you often call our Ascension journey? A friend visited your website and read many articles, but she is a devout Christian. She was looking for any references to your ideas that she could feel comfortable with." Niels asked.

"Did he or she read our interpretations on the first three Soul card vibrations?" Did any of you look it up? None of you has come with any questions so far."

"I must admit, I only visited that page last week, and many of my questions surrounding religious dogma have now been answered," Gerrit replied. The silence in the room was electrifying.

"Let's hear it," Ingrid thought of her mother, who had been a devout Christian. Any slightly esoteric ideas or practices were abolished, but she kept her faith in Jesus as her saviour.

"Well, the Christians 'hope of a heaven and a new earth, meaning a physical resurrection into more dimensions, that dovetails remarkably well with the new scientific worldview of today."

"You can't be serious. You mean after one dies, there will be a time when all 'believers' wake up from the grave. I found that so unbelievable; I could never get my mind around that one." Yolanda responded in dismay.

"There is no death when you talk about resurrection. We are all investigating immortality concepts, but not so. Reading some of Annelies' articles, I realised that Christ's force represents the child within us all. I love Annelies's explanation that Jesus was embracing the love of the sun and that each human child within must fully wake up to feel the kingdom of heaven through the sun." Gerrit explained.

"Of course. It's our personality that must become subservient to the child within. That's it. The child will see into different spiritual dimensions, what we often call fantasy worlds; why not?" Liesbeth expressed it with such joy she wondered what she'd missed.

"Yolanda, it's misunderstood what resurrection is really about. Many religious-driven people would rather hide behind their religious rules that are easy to follow instead of allowing an encounter with their persona on a shadow EGO level." Annelies said.

"You mean for us to ascend from this 3D dimension, spiritually or physically? It has been prophesied all along, but misunderstood?" Yolanda's whole energy was suddenly electrifying.

"Certainly, the human ego is a powerful force, especially regarding religious beliefs that have become dogmatic. It's as if a child has to be given up as a hostage to secure a peace treaty with an enemy. This gesture has historically divided humans into separate tribes. The story goes that whichever God we believe in, he gave his only son as a peace offering to grant every immortal soul a peace treaty that we often misunderstand. One way to free ourselves from earthly burdens is to awaken the "I Am" within us. However, not everyone is interested in doing so. It requires a desire to awaken, but it's not a complex idea to embrace once we have that desire."

"No, not if you put it that way." They all nodded. Annelies' explanation did make sense. But she wondered why she questioned, which God?

***

Yolanda told her she had been separated for two years during their coffee break. Yolanda was anxious about her husband's strong influence over Connie. Ingrid had been puzzled about that, for he was her father, but somehow, she did not know the whole story. She squeezed Yolanda's shoulder as she got up.

"Ingrid, the awareness of telepathic rapport will have to be recognised first, and that is why you were chosen to write the first level. Ask POWAH about telepathy," Annelies projected.

Ingrid glanced back at her with a warm glow of gratitude for having this woman as a friend. She realised that she loved this woman with all her heart. What had awoken in her was the ability to love others more deeply, honestly and openly than she had allowed before.

As they were strolling towards their car, she invited Liesbeth for supper the following evening. She somehow knew that things would change when Toon would be back. It might be the last time she could have her friend over alone.

"My friend, I'm so happy for you. Toon is a fantastic man. He deserves you! I'd love to come. Hans needs to go away this weekend; I believe it has something to do with Toon's many enterprises. I look forward to spending some time with you. It might not happen again." She was stunned to hear that Hans worked for Toon.

***

On the way home, her thoughts were with Toon, visualising him with Ed...As her thoughts whirled around, she lost concentration and almost did not see a car from her left swerving in front of her. All she could do was to step on her brakes.

Her heart was pumping so fast it was sickening. An annoyance welled up in her, directed towards the rude driver! They could both have been injured or even killed! Her whole mood had changed. She blamed the other driver when she drove into her driveway and blamed herself for not paying more attention.

She realised how scattered her mind had been. It would not have happened if she had focused on driving; she would have spotted the car.

At least she was safe, but it could have been worse. The incident had shaken her more than she wanted to admit. She had been daydreaming! Annelies always reminded them to stay grounded!

Jeroen was staying over with a friend, so she read POWAH's tenth Excerpt on I AM that I AM and then went straight to bed.

Her dream journal and pen were still lying next to her bed from the other night. After reading POWAH's Excerpt paragraph:

The arousing of this love ecstasy will be felt in the depths of your Soul now that you have found each other. Celebrate your union together in your dreams.

She recalled her last dream but wondered if it could be confirmed. Fluffball curled up next to her, and she felt herself drifting off...

Soul memories

First, the driver of the car came into her mind again... Then a sense of warmth overtook her... then her consciousness... from a different dream time took over... she suddenly felt cold....

The tall pine that had been struck by lightning was burning. The flames illuminated the general contours of the nearby landscape. Sonya stared into the valley's darkness as if spellbound by the scene she had seen below. Another lightning bolt flashed, and the sound of thunder died away. She loved standing in the soft rain at the edge of her land, daydreaming. She was always in awe of the energy that came from the heavens. She felt part of that incredible power. There was little shelter, so she began to make her way back to the log cabin up the hill. She was overtaken by the rain gushing down, drenching her already-soaked clothing, and finally extinguishing the struggling fire in the tree. When she was near the log cabin, she saw Josh standing in the doorway, looking out at her with a worried face.

"Hi, I needed that; it was beautiful up there. Lightning hit a tree, but the rain doused the flames."

"You are all soaked, Sonya. When will you ever learn to take care of yourself? Come in; the fire will warm you. Sonya looked into Josh's face, seeing his love for her, and she always felt guilty receiving it. Over the years of being married to him, she had grown very fond of and loved him, but not in the way she had loved Mc. Nealy.

They were blessed with four children, all of whom had grown up and left. Her contentment was genuine; she had a good life and had never regretted anything except for the one thing she had never experienced.

Josh had given her everything a wife should be grateful for, and she was. But always at the back of her mind was this inner longing, this simmering passion that never really caught fire, like that tree. When the flames had engulfed the tree, she felt the appetite of its desire that the fire expressed to take it all; then the hard rain came down, and it lost its strength; the embers of passion somehow died. When Josh brought her a cup of tea, she felt she should get up to prepare his pack for the next day, as he would be leaving for a week. Sonya felt a weird tiredness, almost like the embers of a fire making a last bid for life before dying out completely. She needed to hold Josh's hand, so she called him, took his hand and brought it to her mouth. Josh bent down and stroked her hair.

"Sonya, about tomorrow, I think I'm not going," she heard...but he was far away...she was getting further away from him.

Part of her felt sad, but then she felt that inner fire flaring up, making her suddenly float! She felt herself moving out of her body, looking down at herself sitting in her chair with Josh still hunched next to her, stroking her head. Then she heard him utter a deep, anguished cry of despair, and his grief poured over her.

What had happened? She tried to shake him and tell him she was all right, but he didn't notice her. She heard a sound in the distance...her body felt so light, as if...

.... She woke up startled by the sound that came from her alarm radio.

She remembered! In the dream! The man was Jan! She knew it. He looked like Jan, but only...the period, and where? She could still see the scenery that surrounded her. It could be a Canadian landscape. But Mc.Nealy, that was an Irish name? What was the dream revealing to her? Had she died... in her dream? She would look it up in her dream book tonight. Her thoughts turned to the hectic week ahead, but the yearning to hear from Toon remained in her mind. Oh, how she missed him.

Chapter 11
Releasing Addictive Attachments

Liesbeth's story

As the sound of her favourite CD, "Paradise," played on her stereo, Ingrid was preparing dinner for Jeroen and Liesbeth. Music was all that could replace the feelings of emptiness. Even their mental dialogue was not enough. She wanted to feel Toon physically. Never had she expected to be this deeply affected by his absence.

"Mom, don't you mind me going away right after supper?"

"Jeroen! Please, I would love to have Liesbeth to myself. Are you kidding!"

"Mom, what's wrong?"

"Why would something be wrong?"

"You've been very different. Mom... where is that man who was here a few weeks ago, Toon Haardens?" Ingrid felt guilty for not sharing how she felt.

"Toon is in Australia. He was with your uncle Ed the last time I heard from him." She saw Jeroen peering at her, trying to read her face.

"He is a cool dude, Mom. He knows all about the conspiracies and lies most people still believe in. Some of my friends do not want to speak to me anymore. I'm even scared to talk openly to Sascia and Debby if they think I'm losing it."

Usually, Jeroen would still be in his office suit and tie, his grandfather's steel company dress code. He keeps saying that he is too well-dressed to be a geek. Seeing him change into a long black T-shirt over a pair of torn, distressed jeans made him look much younger.

She was about to confide her feelings for Toon when they both heard the front doorbell. Ingrid heard Jeroen greeting Liesbeth, whispering to cheer her up.

Liesbeth beamed happily. *"Haven't you told him?"* as she walked in. Liesbeth looked radiant, which made her look ageless.

"What do I tell him that I suffer from? A love sickness?" When the phone rang, Jeroen answered, but she knew it was Toon.

"Mom! I think this should cheer you up." his laughter rang out as she gave him a push, and then the world was just a blur...

"Snooks, where are you now?" Hoping she would like his reply.

"Oh, Kitty, I needed to hear you in this way. I have withdrawal symptoms; I cannot concentrate on anything. I am in New York; I adore and miss you."

"You said it: thoughts and feelings are like boomerangs. You have made me the talking point in the office with your flowers, but thanks; it helps me to know you are suffering as well."

"Are you suffering?" Ingrid wanted to say all kinds of things but didn't in case the others were listening.

"Are you landscaping in New York?" His laughter was so unexpected that she almost dropped the receiver.

"Oh, love, you are so desirable; I'll be back as soon as possible. I never want to be apart from you like this if I can avoid it. How do you feel about that?"

"Snooks, I don't either." She pictured herself loving him.

"Kitty, I could not sleep; I want you next to me...I can feel your thigh against mine; I can feel your hips sliding over me; I can feel your breast in my hand." Ingrid burst out laughing. They both had a one-track mind.

"Absolutely, and I do like my nickname." ... *"I'll let you go now. See you soon."*

When she returned to the dining room, Jeroen was pouring the wine.

During their dinner, Liesbeth answered many questions they both asked concerning the Zurich conference, and when Jeroen went out, Liesbeth helped her clear the dinner table. She told her Hans had left for New York to handle some of Toon's legal affairs.

"Hans has a degree in corporate law, and Toon is his largest client." Ingrid reminded her how little she knew about Toon, but she also wanted to hear about Hans and his talk about life-giving water.

"Ingrid, I would first like you to understand why I'm suddenly so attracted to a man after all those years, even a younger man. He is a walk-in like me "

"Wow! Hans is unusual, and I've been thinking a lot about your story. I still struggle with it, but I can see Hans fitting into the scene." Her friend did look ageless. What had made her change?

"Liesbeth, I never asked, but how old are you?"

"You're going to get a shock, you know."

"What about your age? Well, try me. I always thought you were around the middle thirties or a bit older, but now you look late twenties?"

"My host body was born about - I don't know the exact date, but... I've taken the date to be 15 2 1968, at least written on my cup, which was anonymously inserted in the blanket left at the orphanage.

What is different about both of us is the lack of incarnations on this planet. I have had only one previously, and for Hans, this is his first time, but we know each other very well from where I come from."

"But... that would make you forty, only four years younger than I am!" She had difficulty taking this all in as Liesbeth looked ageless.

"I told you, I warned you, Hans, his host body was born in 1977; my physical body is nine calendar years older. When I saw him for the first time in Zurich, I suddenly knew who he was when he looked at me across a large room, carrying a drink. He took my drink, put it down, and embraced and kissed me, beaming: *"Well, it took you long enough! How are you, Tulanda?"* Liesbeth's great, big smile confirmed her story.

"He knew your name instantly?" Recalling Toon's explanation about her nickname, Kitty...

"Yes, and at that moment, I again experienced an inner transportation to a different scene where I'm Tulanda, and I'm standing next to a tall figure who is my 'twin flame' as we call it. The union we experience is somewhat different from what you have in a physical body! When we connected, greeted each other, talked, and made love, my memory returned in a flash. He awakened in me all that I was and always have been," Liesbeth shared with a radiant expression. Ingrid's excitement bubbled up from accepting her story.

"How long were the two of you spellbound with each other in that room? That must have been quite something." They were having coffee on her sunny patio, leading out from the dining room. The weather was getting summery.

"That's the wonderful part because it happens out of time! When we returned to the conference room, probably only one minute had passed."

Ingrid knew her friend well enough to know that she was speaking from her heart, even if it felt weird for her to suddenly be confronted with a phenomenon she had only read about. Even with her own experiences, she still thought it was all in her head. Was she living a mental life that was so vivid that it felt real?

"Tell me about this special water," while pouring the coffee. Fluff-ball was purring away on her lap and grunted when she moved. She was so disgusted that she jumped off and settled herself on Liesbeth's lap without any consent from her. Liesbeth stroked her and explained about the particular water.

"When Hans started to explain this 'living water', I knew he was referring to a natural substance of the world where we both come from.

At the same time, while giving his lecture, he told me telepathically that part of his assignment was to reactivate the water element in its original state and assist Gaia in restoring her original grid formations for her to ascend. I am to be his partner in that assignment as he is in mine," Liesbeth said. She emanated such joy that Ingrid began to relate to Liesbeth's feelings the more she thought of Toon and herself.

"You're talking about our drinking water, oceans, and rivers?"

"He took the audience on a mental tour through our galaxy."

"You mean he did to the audience what he did to me? Transporting me to a different world? ..."

"If the people concentrated on his visual guidance, yes. Pointing out that planet Earth's magnificent splendour is unique and different from all the other planets."

"How do you mean by different?"

"When you come down to the surface of this planet, the four different life-forms called kingdoms that live on it are composed almost totally of water," Liesbeth continued while sipping her coffee and stroking Fluffball. She knew Liesbeth meant humans, the plant, animal, and mineral kingdoms.

"Every living expression of consciousness is attracted to water in some form. If we move through the forest to a river, our hearts are pulled to the water because its life energy attracts us." That's so true, recalling Toon looking at her floating crystals in her purifying jar.

"Then Hans proceeded with the lecture in a more scientific direction so as not to bore the intellectual audience, and he kept everybody spellbound."

"Our water is very polluted. Even our rivers and our drinking water?" Her eagerness to hear more was overwhelming. Liesbeth appeared more and more mystical. She was very different from most people, and now she knew why.

"Yes, he called it unstructured water, explaining that every cell, no matter how healthy, will become diseased if it's surrounded by unstructured water. The difference in the water is the number of electrons in the outer orbits, and unstructured water is missing these outer electrons."

"Liesbeth! Which is the water that is so unhealthy?"

"All water that goes through pipes, lead pipes are the worst, even if it's just a few feet, is under pressure, so the water can't rotate how it wants to. It's forced to move in concentric rings that rip off the outer electrons and form unstructured water, and we drink out of high-pressure water pipes that predispose us to disease."

"What was the response to all this? Did Hans give any clue as to how to change this and to make the water structured again?"

"Oh, yes, that was the whole aim. There were many questions; people wanted to know more about what they could do. Dr Emoto's work has already contributed to a great shift in people's awareness levels. He captured how water responds to messages, emotions, and feelings through images, not just words. This applies to our thoughts, too, since our bodies consume a high percentage of water. Hans alerted his audience that water is alive and is greatly challenged by the way water is abused globally. It has been stripped of the sacredness that indigenous cultures worldwide have always attributed to water. He warned the audience that if something is not done to change this, we do not have many years left on this planet."

"Really!"

"All life will gradually disappear because it is related to the planet's oxygen levels, and that will decline to a point where organic life cannot be sustained," Liesbeth continued in a serious tone.

"Hans, is that about why you look so much younger? I mean, you were for a moment back into the world where you came from when you met Hans?"

"Yes, ageing can be attributed to oxidative stress and the toxins we're encountering increasingly throughout our lives here on Earth."

"Gosh, when so much hangs in the balance for humanity and the future of this world, what more can we do?"

"Waking up, that's all."

"Yes, if one awakens from their spiritual inertia, they add light to the global awakening process. The Soul awakening process Annelies' workshops are all about is already gathering speed with this planet's spiritual awakening towards higher dimensions."

"How come all one hears on the news is accomplished through destruction?

"Yes, we know, but Hans and I are here to prepare, through storytelling, how this infinitely complex and intricate universal field of multi-level experiencing will appear. That is why your journal will be translated into a novel."

"Now you startle me. I've only just started writing it. Are you referring to the future? Who is doing the storytelling? Not me."

"That's my assignment, which surprised me, but now I understand how it will be accomplished."

"Because you are an editor? But Hans is not a scientist. He studied Law, didn't he?"

"He is a scientist of the highest order in our world, but he needed to know the laws on this planet so that they could benefit Gaia. Many still fail to realize that, as Earth's planetary field of experience gradually ascends towards higher vibratory frequencies, all life forms will soon be vibrationally unfit and unable to maintain their very physical existence."

"That is still a puzzle to me. How is that ever going to happen?"

"The Earth is going through a massive geomagnetic transformation, which creates opportunities and vulnerabilities at this time."

The latest newspaper on the coffee table had the headline: "Severe weather warnings."

"Several factors can convert thunderstorms into severe weather ... Floods, hurricanes, tornadoes, and thunderstorms are the most destructive weather-related patterns." The thunderstorm and lashing rain outside emphasised what Liesbeth was sharing. Her neighbour, the poor woman, had moved into a nursing home. She was glad for her, so she was not all alone in this storm.

"Yes, we are seeing more people start to lose coherence, exhibit lunacy, or have their light bodies knocked out of their physical bodies. Some people describe this as a nervous breakdown."

"You can see that?"

While Liesbeth was replying to all her questions, Fluffball was fast asleep, very relaxed, with her head draped over her lap.

"Yes, due to the magnetic field around Earth and the huge magnetic storms that have already started to strike Earth last year, disrupting satellites, this affects the functions of our biology, mind, and consciousness."

She thought about the people at work and even in her neighbourhood. Were they at all unaware?

"Ingrid, Toon's communities worldwide are designed to cope with the changeover to a different style of living."

"I know, and I am so glad to become a small part of his ventures; the more I hear about Toon's enterprising spirit, the more I love this man."

"The population of this planet will go through major upheavals physically as well as emotionally, mentally and spiritually, and we need all the help we can get to survive the changeover."

"Wow, this is something close to my heart! Ingrid sighed, wondering that this highly evolved man with such advanced vision and enlightened ambitions could be in love with her. She knew that by asking to express her highest potential in this life, other people in her life would act as a mirror image of herself, depending on the need or the lesson. So, on a Soul level, this must be likewise.

"Ingrid, Toon is besotted with you. Toon's lack of focus made Hans leave for New York."

"Oh, why?"

"Some large corporations in this world are aware of the discovery of this living water. Because of many other activities they are involved in, they don't want to see changes happen."

"What activities?"

"Those who have vowed their allegiance to darkness are still doing their utmost to retain as many people as possible, through fear-based manipulations and sheer violence, in the lowest possible levels of awareness, in an ultimately vain effort to perpetuate their power and domination over this planet."

"You mean through the duality of good and evil?"

"Yes, there is still a lot of fear among many people that cannot let go of the good and evil concept, so they are more receptive to being brainwashed by their own radioactive lower levels of creations from other lower astral and sub-realms."

"Wow, now you scare me. You mean lower frequency realms here on Earth. Are they already in control? ... Or do you mean people who believe in a preordained destiny?"

"Yes, to both. Control is achieved through the banking world, political groups, pharmaceutical businesses, military outfits, and the food we have consumed daily for the last forty years. Some religious movements are also being used and controlled by beings that have evolved intellectually and have fantastic technology but lack the compassion and love that is so essential to the evolution of the human species."

"But how is this achieved?'

"Their lack of compassion will keep people in a fantasy reality. They are like Mr. Smith in the Matrix movies."
She was still trying to comprehend that their reality was an illusion.
"Toon needed Hans to be at his side to oversee some major changeovers that will have a great effect on the stock exchange and ultimately the whole economy of the planet," Liesbeth got up from her chair, and Fluffball was highly offended by her move.
"Gosh, I feel guilty, wishing him to come home as I'm beginning to realise his commitments are enormous. I have to get used to going into a relationship with someone that I must share in many other ways, time-wise."
"Well, Annelies seemed to think you are very suitable for this position because of your need for independence, so you have a great supporter in her."
What Liesbeth told her made her ponder the Excerpt Ten I AM that I AM had mentioned: The "Soul catchers" here can easily catch the worm but have problems seeing the elusive butterflies. Were the people who are awakening the butterflies?

Pleasure Park Office
She felt at peace since Liesbeth's visit, her story about Hans, and her connection with Toon. She missed Toon, but knowing about his commitments, it was hard to believe he got involved in the landscaping firm and the Paris project. Surely this man could not divide himself amongst so many different enterprises?
At her office, she drastically revised her new drawings for the site in Paris and copied the huge files onto three Flash drives because she had no spare hard drive. Carla still had them on order. That weekend, she would take one flash drive home to work on the 'centre file'. She placed the other two into the back of her drawer. She checked her e-mail and downloaded one message...
Ingrid, they are blackmailing me because of you! ...

That message hit her solar plexus. No address unless you call de-sponded@wxs.nl. An address. It had to have come from Roelof; who else? As she deleted it, a bright screen with text appeared.

<Hello, Kitty. You know by now that there is no separation between your world and the many dimensions around you, only the awareness of the individual consciousness through the human mind and brain.>

Her back went rigid! Piet suddenly stood behind her! She thought everybody had already gone! ...

The screen still showed POWAH's writing, yet Piet did not comment. He just looked at her screen.

"Ingrid, I must look in your address book; I'm offline at the moment," The annoyance his body language revealed nauseated her.

Why not look at his computer again if he was angry with her? Or was he looking for something she might be hiding on her computer? Piet was approaching fifty but looked older. He had a small, thin-lipped, sulky mouth and wispy hair clinging to a bald forehead. The flesh of his face was washed out and soft. His eyes were hooded, expressing a chronic resentment towards the world. She wondered whether he saw the words at all.

POWAH's bright, radiant text flashed in a sort of brilliance, yet he did not remark on it! He took her mouse while leaning over to look up a name in her address book when she saw him glaring at the last e-mail message. He mumbled something rude while the screen was responding normally. Suddenly, the screen turned back with more of POWAH's writing, but he did not react to it; he walked away!

<Kitty, every man is the living expression of the consciousness at any given moment. Humans are luminous, spirit–beings; you must never forget that.> Trillions of questions were cramming her mind.

POWAH, how can I see your writing clearly, yet Piet does not acknowledge it?

Was she abnormal? The text with the blue background was always clear to her.

<Kitty, the mentally divided mind of man's 'personality' is the real problem. People in your physical world are told what to think. A.I. hive mind consciousness controls them. Only comparatively few – you are one of them – can think for themselves and will gain freedom from this illusory make-believe world.>

Her heart still raced as she saw the text appear, as if she were in some thought wave, or was this also a result of mental programming?

<Kitty, remember that everything on planet Earth is like a biological hologram, and your galaxy is a projection by humanity's united consciousness. Piet will only see, hear, smell, touch and sense what his mortal mind can comprehend, and only that will be real. Most of you cannot see the truth because you are all caught up in it. Kitty, use your intuition with Piet; he is an unconscious being living in the effect of his experience, which is why he is in trouble. Your conscious living means that you invite the cause of your living. You walk in the awareness of it.>

Part of it made sense, registering what POWAH was talking about, but what trouble was he referring to?

POWAH, are you telling me that because I believe in you talking to me, I can see your text, and he cannot?

Somehow, she already knew the answer, but wondered if POWAH knew that.

<Yes, Kitty, you are beginning to understand that whatever is in the mortal mind is dead; it is not reality but an illusion that has its foundation in a "lie" – a belief –. The words you see are also not real, but your mind has created them to be so. Consciousness and energy are interrelated.> Ingrid was stunned. The words were not actual! POWAH was rereading her mind, but she would

not have put it the same way. How could her mind be dead? She felt as if she were an open book to him.

< **That you are a spherical luminous mass of countless, static yet vibrant energy fields. The faster your energy field can shift, the quicker you can change the perception of a different universe.**>

She desperately wanted him to know what she knew and understood, but the screen returned to the screen saver. Toon had mentioned that Trevor, Annelies's uncle, was an archaeologist and spiritual scientist. Had electronic technology already so far advanced that it was possible to read the mind of someone who sat behind a computer? She knew one's tone of voice can be measured, but one's thoughts? However, her telepathic skills had recently undergone a significant enhancement. Was that a sign Liesbeth was referring to? Ingrid could still not quite understand who POWAH was. He said he was in her mind, but was she creating all this? She wanted some answers when suddenly, as if he heard her or could read her mind, the screen went bright again.

Excerpt Eleven[1]
Program Planet Earth
Acknowledging the One Source of All That Is
Rule one *of the Ascension Decoding Card Game.*

Wow, once again, she received an immediate reply to her thoughts. Now she understood it! The personality she was 'known' by at this time was Ingrid or Kitty. Her brain was just the computer that her mortal mind used. She was the operator of her bio-computer. When she quietened her conscious mind and only focused on one thought, she would connect with her higher self, her subconscious mind, which once more would remember all the experiences she had had in her unconscious Soul-mind. A vision of an advert came into her mind: an old advert with a woman standing displaying a tin on a tray.

---

1. https://allrealityshifters.wordpress.com/powah/the-reality-shifters-excerpt-11/

The can, which was the product she was advertising, had the advert on it, and the same image went over again, the one within the other... one hologram within the other...one consciousness level within the other... Ingrid knew that she was busy creating another attachment to Toon!

She wondered how that was going to affect her intent to ascend.

<Kitty, releasing the many addictive attachments is to be replaced by service. Contemplate this.>

POWAH, where are you about all this mind stuff?

She was still unsure if the text she saw was only her mind, and she had difficulty perceiving any entity without form.

<You and I are part of the whole! The greatest tragedy is the story of the fall. Humanity has been "hypnotised" from birth. Freedom only comes if humankind can escape from the prison of its mind. Kitty, all appearances in the mind have no reality, so don't fear them. Remember those words; don't fear them.>

How could you possibly escape from your mind? What was there if there were no thoughts?

<Through the workshops, you will discover the "real self" that exists beyond the mind. In this pool of silence, in which the eternal your IAM will unite with all there is.>

Ingrid realised that to be free from the conditioning POWAH talked about, she would have to understand the process of her mind, for nobody could do that for her. She almost grasped that she had to discover what was beyond the mind.

<Kitty, I am to guide you and others on bringing the supramental powers of the divine consciousness into the unaware mind, transforming the mind and body, thereby creating a godly life in matter.> Gosh, it all somehow made sense to her. From now on, she would not question how she had received these excerpts. When more text spontaneously appeared as if she was chatting with someone, it seemed to flicker.

<Do not accept what is written down as pure truth because it may become another belief. Until you make an inner choice to become an earnest expression of love and affection, you will not know what universal truth is all there is.>

She knew then that one had to experience truth before one knew it, and one could not push the truth down unwilling throats either. Everybody had gone home, and the silence in the office outside her glass partition became a blur.

POWAH, what has happened between Toon and me? Did we live another life together, and are my memories coming back? Is it because we operate on the same thought wave that allows us to communicate as we seem to do?

She typed with a pounding heart. Was this happening to many others as well? She knew only of Liesbeth, and that did not count.

<Kitty, when you communicate and make plans with those within this incarnate state, do you think there would be some unique way of being unable to communicate when you were in a discarnate state? Your mind is not within your body until you have chosen to have a body.> That did not tell her why they had this connection between them.

The text appeared again as if someone had been thinking and then replied.

<Your relationship with Toon can be an exceptional one of total acceptance, with both of you having open, expanded minds. When you release your personality's wants and attachments to accommodate another's growth, you attune yourself to that person's Soul. Remember, in the mind of All That Is, everything happens at the same time.> Could she be utterly open with Toon? They were different in personality, but that did not matter anymore. She realised that everything was perhaps still part of a divine plan, including her feelings. Even her feelings of the need to be with him were acceptable as long as she had no attachment or judg-

ment about them. She felt as if she had given herself an answer! It was the judgment that was so toxic!

<You have!>

POWAH, do you also communicate with others in this way?

She knew the answer to that question already, but what she meant was the computer.

<**Yes! As the years draw close, those at peace within themselves will find their lives increasingly aligned with others through any media. The computer is a powerful communication system until telepathy takes over to strengthen the thought fields of many individual Souls who have awakened to their I AM.**>

Ingrid had this vision of the Internet or cyberspace, an energy force you could tap into.

<**Magnetic love and light are two forms of the same essence. When love is honoured, light is understood. Spirit makes love with matter through light and sound and the human form. Divine love is now interfacing with physical matter, flowing through the human focus into a responsive substance, much like cyberspace, for this is the creation process.**> She now questioned if POWAH was a thought transmission from a parallel universe.

<**Kitty, the age of planetary awakening will pass, bringing your world with a biological system into a new world where all its inhabitants can interstellar travel through love and grace. There is no time, and no space; we are inseparable. Kitty, surrender to your inner feelings, whatever they may be, because they will be your closest link to the being of yourself.**> Ingrid felt very humbled at having access to this communication. Was POWAH on the consciousness level of an oversoul? Not that she fully understood that theory.

POWAH, how can I hear Toon's thoughts clearly but not others? With them, I seem to get a stronger sense.

There was a difference because lately, she could hear Annelies and Liesbeth similarly, but Toon was the clearest.

<Kitty, there are several types of telepathy. Instinctual telepathy is what you feel when others think based on the energies they project. **<Etheric telepathy is mainly sensed from all living bodies' etheric substance.**

Yes, she could understand that Piet must be very electric; she picked up on his mental action through her solar plexus, but not in dialogue, like with Annelies, Liesbeth, Toon, and Yolanda.

< Telepathy is mainly a throat-central activity, and there can sometimes be a little heart activity and a measure of a solar plexus reaction. Can you recall that? This is more of an electro-magnetic force.> That was the feeling she had with Toon. Was that the way she felt her heart pumping? Was that due to feeling very attracted to him?

<Then you have intuitive telepathy, which happens when you are in true meditation and a connection is made with beings not necessarily in a physical embodiment, but possibly from higher frequency sources. This is a pure magnetic force. Kitty, contemplate all the information you have received so far.>

POWAH signing off

Ingrid felt she had been suspended in space while communicating with POWAH. It always amazed her that hardly any time had passed. Was this intuitive telepathy that she had with POWAH?

She had been at her computer the whole of Friday, working on the program of the various maintenance subcontractors that looked after the Tilburg project scheduled to open this weekend. Her phone went off when she wanted to go on her lunch break.

"Ingrid, Harry Brinks. Do you have any commitments for Saturday and Sunday?" Ingrid was surprised to hear from her boss, but needed time to think.

If Toon were back, she would not be free, but he had given no indi-
cation when he would be back when he had phoned her last night
from Johannesburg. He must have the constitution of an ox, the
way he flew around the globe. All he had told her was something
about the Eastern Cape Province and how beautiful the coastline
was. "Mr Brinks, would it be for the whole weekend?"

"Yes, Ingrid, can you act as my hostess for the opening of the
Tilburg complex? My daughter has come down with the flu; she
suggested you." Ingrid was amazed at the thought. What would be
required of her as a hostess? The man must be desperate.

"Mr Brinks, the opening is tomorrow evening! I'll be honoured to
help out, but under one condition."

"And what might that be?"

"I'd like to meet your daughter tomorrow morning, even if she has
the flu, to learn what is required of me because I've no idea at all,"
she uttered with as much conviction as she could bring to her voice.

"Ingrid, that I'll arrange gladly. Tieneke will surely be able to convince you that you will make a perfect hostess. Otherwise, she
would never have suggested you."

"Mr Brinks,... you said Tieneke?" The only Tieneke she knew was
the mind-drawing facilitator, and her surname was... de Beer, not
Brinks?

Unless...Tieneke was married to Roelof de Beer, a subcontractor
for their firm! She would never have connected the two. She was
amazed at how things were all coming together, how lately the people with whom she came into contact seemed to be connected in
one way or another.

"Ingrid, can I arrange a car at five o'clock tomorrow afternoon?
You'll stay over at the park and be brought home after lunch on
Sunday, and oh, yes, if you can get hold of Toon Haardens, please
invite him. I spoke to him recently, and asking if he would be in the
country slipped my mind.

"Toon was on his way to South Africa the last I heard; I can send him an invitation by e-mail."

"Yes, do that. Thank goodness that's arranged. You have no idea how these social functions drain me, but I seem unable to avoid them."

The rest of the day flew by. She organised an invitation to the opening for Toon. She knew that he would join her if possible.

So Tieneke was Mr. Brinks's daughter, and Roelof de Beer was probably her husband. Would Tieneke know about her husband's problems?

Class 9

THE OPPORTUNITY CARD was displayed in big letters on the door when she joined the others.

"I believe you're going to have a busy weekend," Annelies remarked on her arrival.

"How did you know?"

"Ingrid, you'd better get used to it; you've been adopted into the Jaarsma Clan. Annelies arranged it all with Tieneke. I've got your evening dress ready. You might want to wear it." Yolanda's enthusiasm indicated she wanted to include herself in the Jaarsma Clan.

"Well, thank you, that's great!" she replied out loud. "I'll see Tieneke tomorrow morning. I've no idea what is expected of me at the opening, and I am nervous." The idea of exposure to any limelight gave her cramps in her stomach.

"You know how appropriate it is that you're doing your obstacle card next week! Ingrid, our talents are usually revealed by the things we fear the most, so you will have to tell us next week what it was like!"

All of the events of the last month came flooding in, and now Tieneke.

"Tonight, we will make the opportunity card, and it seems your opportunity is happening. Ingrid, this card is close to my heart. It's the one that helps us see our capability to develop communication on a different level. Liesbeth, will you do some explaining about telepathy?"

Everyone looked surprised. Ingrid realised that Liesbeth would probably be far more aware of many psychic gifts, an everyday occurrence where she came from.

"Are you a telepathic, Liesbeth?"

"Yes, Wim and there are three more here who are, and I suspect one more person is, but he's not aware of it yet. The rest of you have other psychic abilities that have not yet activated."

Wim's reaction to that was somewhat disturbing, but she could not fathom why that was so. *"He is scared that we can read his mind"* Annelies beamed. *"Can we? I can't read him at all, can you?"* Somehow, she knew the answer to her question. His thoughts were not on their wavelength. But why was he here? It must have been Zola who begged him to join her in these workshops. Would Annelies not be aware of his lack of... what... awareness?

"Yes, we are, but Zola must learn to recognise the difference. He is her best teacher." Liesbeth joined in.

"Liesbeth, how do you know the difference between hearing someone's thoughts or your own thoughts?"

"Richard, people adept at psychic hearing assume very often that they are merely thinking out loud themselves because they're so used to this psychic echo that it becomes second nature to them. Can you relate to that?"

"Yes, I suppose so; I always talk a lot to myself. I often find myself thinking, 'Those are my hunches.' But are they not just my mental judgments? Based on what I already know or understand?" *"He would see it that way."* Annelies winked at her.

"Richard, you are very analytical, aren't you?"

"Yes, I think I am. I want to understand things, and think what I hear is often a coincidence."

"Ingrid, I want to experiment on him. You hold Debbie in your mind while I ask him to pick up my thoughts," Liesbeth projected.

"Richard, I'll send you a message. Try to sense what I'm thinking," *"Debbie is working night shifts,"* Liesbeth beamed while Ingrid held the image of Debbie in her mind.

"No, I don't get it. All I'm hearing is myself talking again."

"Well, humour me! What were you thinking?" Richard grinned widely.

"I spoke to Ingrid's daughter, Debbie, on the phone; she told me she had night shifts."

"Did you speak to her? I mean to Debbie?"

"No, I did not; I spoke to her... a few days ago, but the thought must have jumped into my mind." Richard did show a somewhat surprised expression when he replied.

"And if I told you that the message I was beaming at you was... Debbie is working night shifts." What would you say to that? Liesbeth's smile was catching.

"I would say it was a pure coincidence." Richard chuckled, crossing his arms behind his head and stretching his long, lean body.

"You see, that's what happens to most people. They've been hearing their thinking for so long that they take it for granted, not realising that it can be a major source of psychic information."

"You're saying I did pick up your message, only I don't believe it myself?" Richard's frown spelt disbelief.

"That's right, Richard. It would be best if you stopped trying to talk yourself out of it and started learning to develop your natural telepathic skills," Annelies said with the firm voice of a teacher. With the help of colourful, musical, moving images from Annelies' laptop, the vibrations accompanying each Language of Light symbol started to feel familiar.

When they had to colour the symbols of their favourite music, or songs and place them around the head symbol plus the Language of Light vibrations, Ingrid's thoughts returned to the Celtic music from her dream and the music Toon had played in his car. It was music that had triggered her memories.

"Sound can shed light on an experience, not so?; You remembered the harmonic overtones." She looked at Liesbeth, whose eyebrows raised ever so slightly.

"Yes, I did, but...it was more of a feeling at first."

"Can I get the attention of you two, please?" Annelies grimaced at both of them.

"I want you all to practice two exercises during the week, visualising that you are wearing headphones, and when you see people talking in the distance, with only their mouths moving, pretend that you can hear what they are saying."

Niels told them of having a headphone sale in his computer shop.

The following exercise is: every morning, before you do anything, think up a mental mantra for the day, like a short phrase. "I'm the god/goddess in human form." Or "I intend to awaken in this lifetime fully." Create your mantra. Hold to that short mantra throughout your day. Bring this mantra back into focus while going about your daily chores."

The rest of the evening went very quickly. Wim joined them after he had smoked his pipe outside, which had become a routine, like Joris's, who had become a constant companion between Niels, Annelies, and herself. Her thoughts drifted to tomorrow, especially on Roelof de Beer's e-mail.

"What is troubling you, Ingrid?" Annelies beamed as they were clearing the room.

"Tieneke's husband, do you know him?" Annelies frowned.

"He's in bad company; that's all I know. Practice holding on to your boundaries, my dear.

"Ingrid, have a great time tomorrow. I know you will charm everyone, and Harry will be proud to have you next to him. I know Toon will be jealous." She gave Ingrid a great big hug. Annelies could draw out the feelings that she had buried for a long time:" ...

Chapter 12
Releasing Co-dependencies

Tilburg

Ingrid laid various garments out on her bed. She would wear Yolanda's stunning deep-blue evening dress for the opening function. It fitted her like a second skin. When she looked at herself in the mirror, the fabric looked like sealskin; the texture and sheen made it almost impossible not to stroke it. Yolanda had seen it at a fabric exhibition in Utrecht.

She looked forward to discussing a business enterprise together next week. Designing clothes had taken hold in her mind, and Yolanda had already devised some ideas. The blue three-piece suit would do very well for the following day's breakfast and lunch.

Her mind flipped back to the time she had spent with Tieneke that morning. She could hardly recognise the same woman who had facilitated the Language of Light workshops a year ago. From an elegant, sophisticated, well-dressed woman in her forties, not only did she look ill, but her anorexic look and bags under her eyes spoke of being in trauma. Roelof, her husband, had gambling debts that were forcing him into bankruptcy. That was also one of the reasons why Tieneke didn't want to be involved with the opening of her father's complex.

Roelof was not there, and she was relieved about that. Tieneke also spoke about her daughter Hennie, with misgivings, believing that she was in the wrong company. Annelies felt Roelof was also associated with the bad company, so she wondered which one that was, or were they both involved? Tieneke never mentioned any criminal involvement her husband might have, like being blackmailed, so she kept quiet.

"Mom, you look stunning!" Jeroen peeped around her bedroom door.

"Turn around, Mom. You look very cool. I mean, will that Toon fellow be there?"

"No, he will not, and I will miss him, but he's in South Africa at the moment, so..." his face flashed in her mind's eye as the phone in the hallway interrupted them. Jeroen answered.

"Okay, eat your heart out. My mom is wearing a silky dress with a very long split on the side that reveals her leg just enough to... okay ... and one shoulder is naked... very sexy." ... Jeroen was beaming a cheerful grin as he handed the phone to her.

"Go away, I want some privacy. Push off," she giggled gleefully.

"I got your e-mail, Kitty, and I would give anything to be there tonight,

The thought of someone else touching you, however slightly, makes me feel possessive." "I know my ego is having a go at me! I never knew I had it in me to feel so possessive suddenly. Kitty, what I most despised in others was the need to have a partner they wanted to control."

She already knew that she would miss him.

"Now I know what it feels like to need to have someone completely for oneself. Kitty, I'm ashamed of my mirror."

"Oh, Snooks, I wish you could be there. I know that I need to be independent in every way. To be my person, and yet, you make me want to give that all up! She whispered, standing in the hallway, *"But it's not you; my personality wants to be submissive, but not to my Higher Self. Oh no, to a male instead!"*

"Oh, Kitty, that is why I want to share my life with you; you are self-aware, fun and intelligent, compassionate and giving."

"Snooks, for the first time, I realise what I'm capable of, and now the real me is yearning to be independent, but simultaneously, to stay co-dependent; my personality manipulates you on a physical level. It is a lesson, I'm sure." She beamed with a whispering mouth movement.

"My love, you are so much more endearing by demonstrating your vulnerability. *Your femininity is so nurturing, so beautiful. Love, my thoughts will be there with you, and my spirit will soon be in union with you.*" Ingrid could feel his powerful energy triggering her sexual needs.

"Snooks, I'm very aware of that power within me to get you into my clutches, but..." "I want to love you without any conditions attached," she whispered.

"You already have me in your clutches in all senses of the word. Oh, Kitty, I know so well what you're telling me. I'm glad you realise your power and ability to see beyond your needs. I will be with you soon; my ego has to suffer a bit longer! ... Jeroen called her to say the driver had arrived to take her to Tilburg.

***

Mr. Brinks greeted her with an approval that was very apparent in his expression, and he offered her his arm. Like his daughter Tieneke, she could not ignore his tired, grey-looking complexion even if he was smartly dressed for the occasion. He introduced her to some people she needed to address later that evening. Ingrid then remembered her naked dream in a flash, recalling how she felt the second time she walked over that bridge. That was the feeling she would hold in her solar plexus to help her to control her nerves. "Mrs. Barendse, there's something that has been delivered to your suite that you will need before the official opening," the complex

manager told her. Relieved because of the break, she followed him
to the suite that had been booked for her.

As she walked in, a most unusual flower arrangement greeted her.
Huge yellow blooms were displayed together with smaller yellow
and pink flowers on a piece of bark as if they had seeded themselves
for the pure pleasure of her company.

She suddenly recognised them. They were CUPS OF GOLD
AND >BUTTERCUP flowers! How had Toon gotten hold of
those? It reminded her that it was through the Tilburg complex
that their relationship had started. Then she spotted a blue box
with the familiar 1888 date attached to the arrangement. Her heart
began to pulse while opening it, and a typed printout read:

To the one and only woman I want to be with forever, I give this
piece of jewellery that belonged to my mother. Please, will you wear
it? This gift will express our union through time, and only faithful
twin souls can celebrate the divine. The music piece on the sculpture is my vibration of love. The two figures holding our planet
above prove that our souls were born to be forever, helping to trans-
mit our world together...Yours forever!... Snooks.

With trembling fingers, she lifted the velvet cover, and a breathtak-
ingly beautiful silver and gold sculpted brooch appeared. The artist
must have worked for hours to create a detailed impression of the
two figures reaching out to each other, with one holding a violin
and the other holding together the old clock face that was visible
from the top. Two delicate dangling chains came from the back of
the brooch to the front, held up by a playful dolphin embracing the
planet. Small cog wheels accompanied the sculpture, which she had
only seen in ancient watches. It vaguely reminded her of a neo-Vic-
torian look.

Never had she seen anything quite so exquisite. She pinned it on
the shoulder of her dress, and it fitted into its place as if it had been
made for it. She wore no other jewellery.

Ingrid stood silently in her suite, knowing that this gift gave her the confidence she needed to be the best she could be, and silently thanking the only power for the love that she so abundantly received, knowing it had always been there.

**

When she joined Mr Brinks, he noticed her brooch because he raised his eyebrows. When it was her turn to thank the staff who built the complex, she looked into the video camera recording the opening for one moment.

She saw Toon's face flashing as if he were there, but she knew that was impossible. "Ingrid, stay focused," she mumbled to herself. Holding the microphone, she turned to the audience. She was observing herself to be entirely at ease, making everyone laugh. At that moment, she felt surrounded by love and feelings of rapture; she knew the people could also feel this nurturing energy. For the first time, she realised the incredible power of this healing force of LOVE that had awakened and would free her. The opening was a resounding success.

Summer rain

The relentless rain cascaded down, drowning the linden trees that were heavy with foliage as she drove past them to work. Ingrid turned on the radio just in time to hear:

"Good morning to all my listeners on this wet morning. This is your host, Roger, speaking with the news bulletin. The opening of Pleasure Park Holiday Resort in Tilburg got off to a good start. Still, there is nevertheless a cloud hanging over the resorts due to a rumour that the new complex near Paris is troubled with many unexpected setbacks. There is some speculation from a knowledgeable source that the area on the estate where they are building the dome is supposed to be riddled with underground tunnels. It is even speculated that many treasures stolen during the Second World War could still be buried there. There is a real estate dispute and an accusation that the owner, Mr. Brinks, never legally purchased the land, and it is being investigated!"

She turned the radio off when she spotted a parking spot near the Pannekoek, shaken at hearing the rumour that Mr. Brinks could be involved in something illegal. When she arrived at the office, Ula waved the newspaper.

"Hi, you are famous, look!" Ula pointed at a photo of her standing to hold the microphone. On the social page, the report, located underneath the headline, stated: ...

The opening of Pleasure Park in Tilburg will bring many overseas tourists to our country. Its success was guaranteed, especially after Mrs. Barendse charmed the stockholders, staff, and guests into exploring the many available attractions. Mrs. Barendse is the daughter-in-law of Mr. D Barendse, owner of the steel construction firm that supplies the large structures for the domes which maintain the constant sub-tropical climate all year round at the resorts. Mrs. Barendse was wearing a sleek, deep-blue evening gown created especially for her by Yolanda de Wit.

"Hi there. Ingrid, I never knew you were related to this large steel company." Marijke called out as she and Carla came through the glass doors together.

"Ingrid! Did you see the paper? Have you all heard the news?

Mr. Brinks had a burglary early this morning. My husband was called out to investigate."

"Oh, no, at his home?" Ingrid asked with concern as they all walked to the lift. They both asked many questions about the opening.

"Oh, Ingrid, you haven't heard yet because you left early, but Piet got fired late on Friday," Carla told her. Then she spotted the brooch.

They both drooled over it, speculating on the giver but Ingrid was too stunned at the news to respond.

"Who fired Piet? I was wondering how long he would last. Something was not right about that man." Ingrid realised that she was glad that he was gone. She knew that a part of him belonged to the same wholeness as her, but she had always struggled to grapple with the destructive part of his nature.

The bright blue screen flashed while her PC was booting up, and the familiar text appeared.

< Kitty, those who are awakening must be willing to pool gifts and talents and share knowledge. Piet is holding back information out of fear and greed, which makes him co-dependent on others. Look at your attachments.> Love POWAH

At the same time, her inbox downloaded a letter with the title Releasing Co-dependencies.

Excerpt Twelve[1]

Program Planet Earth

Releasing Co-dependencies

Rule Two *of the Ascension Decoding Card Game.*

Eagerly, she read rule two, knowing she needed to start her work.

Those who are addicted to the need to be loved, which is based on anyone's definition of themselves, create a co-dependency. Those people are already lovable just because of who they are.

Releasing co-dependence on another is to be replaced by bravery. Her screen suddenly changed as she read that paragraph in this Excerpt.

< Kitty, many personality entities that are not all your own have run the human drama on Earth for over 10,000 years. Your ego force is the fractured soul part that creates and reflects your willpower, as it still holds the power that your blueprint expresses.>

---

1. https://allrealityshifters.wordpress.com/powah/the-reality-shifters-excerpt-12/

Ingrid recalled decoding their three cards on the second level that Richard would write about. She wondered what he would share about the human drama, as POWAH calls it.

<Kitty, it's important to understand that the many aspects, personalities, or masks that you carry as an individual create a sense of duality that is unique to you. Unfortunately, many people on this planet feel guilty and ashamed for believing they caused the fall of man. However, this guilt is misplaced, as the story behind the fall has been lost and greatly misunderstood.> Would she ever be completely free from the masks she created for different situations and the guilt complexes associated with certain things?

POWAH, do we have to release all the addictions to qualify for the first level of Annelies' game?

She sat back and wondered what more needed to be released.

<Kitty, it is a good start, as attachments can be seen energetically as lines of energy connecting one individual to another individual or the animal kingdom or with material objects in one's life. The level of attachment to the third dimension can be seen as a thick spider web with cords.> That made sense, recalling Annelies' drawing of the holographic grid patterns around a human body.

<Yes, between these grid patterns are third-dimensional thought–forms that distort your thoughts when they emotionally express the personality as a need. The area between these cords can be so dense that there are very few spaces between the webbing through which energy and information can flow. That is why it has been difficult for your spirit spark (the I AM) to activate the embodiment of the Soul through this physical vehicle.> Ingrid wondered about Piet's Soul. Who controlled his destiny?

<He does, Kitty; humans must confront and address all soul-related experiences to fully ascend the physical plane. This initiation process is necessary.>
Love POWAH

Wow! The mind-reading was unnerving. Ingrid wondered if that was possible, ascending physically to a higher frequency. Imagining emotional energy lines like webbing was helpful. She composed flimsy viscose material in her mind and could understand that the thicker the webbing, as in fabric, the harder it would be for the person to be soft, flexible, receptive and floating. So, the spaces between the emotional webbing would be the channels through which one received inspiration. It was, again, information to think about.

The rest of the day passed uneventfully. She received several phone calls from people she had not heard from for a long time, and both Sascia and Debbie phoned. Sascia said that her boss at the newspaper had yelled at her for not being in Tilburg to take photos.

Passing the bookshop that morning, Yolanda, in considerable excitement, had invited her for supper as she wanted to discuss something. Ingrid loved summer with its extended daylight that ran into long, mild evenings enhanced by the buzzing of bees, insects, and birds, which created an atmosphere of peacefulness.

She followed Yolanda's directions to drive around the back of the Prinsengracht Hotel, where she and Connie lived. Yolanda was already on the lookout.

"Hi, I'm so glad you came," Yolanda walked ahead through a park-like setting towards a pergola with a patio from the olden days.

"This is Annelies' favourite spot. She told me that Ben proposed to her here at least four times."

Ingrid admired the view from the circularly arranged tables on the patio, adorned with a beautiful arrangement of flowers and vines, suggesting an expert garden service.

"Yes, Toon, Annelies' half-brother's landscaping firm, has taken over the maintenance of the grounds, which has made a big difference."

Ingrid realised that she also could read her mind, so she would have to be on guard with her thoughts in this family!

"Yolanda, have you always been telepathic?"

"Yes, I think so, and Annelies encouraged it. Toon is very good at it, and so is Ben and Leo. Her brother Fred is a clairvoyant but never reveals what he sees. He's very secretive about it except when someone is out of balance." Suddenly, a waiter arrived with drinks and the menu.

"Thanks, Jimmy. Please, will you tell Mr. Zwiegelaar we have our drinks here?"

"Well, I see that living at the back of a hotel has its compensations." Admiring the prompt service.

"Yes, I know; Connie must have told them you'd arrived, but let me show you this letter from the fabric expo where I purchased the material for your dress." She read they had invited Yolanda to exhibit her summer collection for next year in November on their annual fashion show, using their fabrics."

"Have they seen your designs?"

"Well... I'm registered as having my studio under the name of Yolanda. They have connected your evening dress at the Tilburg opening with me." Yolanda's excitement was infectious.

"Wow, that's quite a tall order; that's in three months!"

"Yes, I know, I want you to design some of the collection. Would you be interested?'

"So, this is the lady Toon has fallen in love with," a robust musical voice called out before the person appeared behind the greenery.

"Really? Gee, Ingrid, I was suspicious when he phoned you at Annelies' house." Yolanda turned to a man in a business suit.

"Ingrid, this is Fred, Annelies' younger brother. Ingrid, how did you all keep that away from me?" She shook hands with a very distinguished man in his fifties, with wavy streaks of white mixed with black, shiny hair hanging down almost to his shoulders. His dark–brown eyes were observing her with a gaze that made her feel entirely exposed.

"Don't worry, you've already passed the test." Yolanda beamed with a grin.

"I must have been the first person Toon confided in when he made the booking for dinner. Was it at the end of April?"

"Yes, the 26th"

"I saw you both arriving; Toon phoned me the same evening, asking me what I thought about you. I laughed because whatever I would have said would not have made any difference. Ingrid, I am so glad for that man. Toon has been searching for you for years, you know," Fred commented in a quiet, soft-spoken tone, but she immediately sensed that when he walked into a room, he had an air about him, and everyone listened, admiring his casual sports jacket. Fred joined them for a drink before the waiter brought their dinner.

After taking a sip, he casually remarked that the flavour reminded him of a specific wine he had tasted ten years before. They discussed Annelies' card-making workshop, and Fred knew a lot more about all the lies that were promoted on the internet. He and Jeroen would get on very well.

"Probably the hardest thing I have ever had to understand about Annelies' thoughts on transcending this lower reality we are all trapped in is how to accept that we have been thoroughly lied to and deceived here by the rulers of this world," Fred remarked.

"My son Jeroen reads a lot about topics you have mentioned lately, especially about cloning, but I cannot get my head around that one."

Fred nodded..." Humans have fought many wars against each other and murdered each other for many different reasons. A dozen countries, excluding the United States, have banned germ-line engineering, and scientific societies have unanimously concluded that it would be too risky. It's easy to be against genetic engineering today when it is in its infancy and still has not delivered the goods." Fred replied while finishing his dinner.

Somehow, she meant cloning a whole human being, or had she misunderstood that?

"No, I think cloning raises real concerns, Ingrid. The prospect of manufactured humans is a whole new stage in our times." Yolanda beamed while Fred looked at both of them somewhat as if...

"We are complex living creatures, made up of cells and chemical processes. Words like "spirit" and "soul" are metaphors for many, but we are ultimately both spiritual and physical beings. Fred added.

"I'm sure that Toon will soon introduce you to Leo and Annelies's husband, Ben," he added while zipping his wine.

"It seems like both of them are well-informed about what's happening. I heard that Leo leads a movement that teaches about the beginning of life on Earth, how it was formless and empty, and how darkness covered it for millions of epochs. Some refer to this period as the Elohim."

"I didn't know that," Yolanda replied.

Fred had to handle a customer issue at the reception, but he smiled as he left, saying...

"Ingrid, the controversies and debates about cloning and manipulating what could have been a child into reproducible tissue for manipulation and research are abhorrent. Tell your son to investigate the science of embryonic stem cell research."

Over dessert, they discussed the details of the fashion show. Meanwhile, Ingrid would start on some drawings. It was a stimulating evening, and she was glad to tumble into bed when she got home.

The Reality Shifting workshops

Going regularly to Annelie's comforted her. She felt closer to Toon there than anywhere else. He had phoned her at work and in the evenings, telling her he had made significant schedule changes. He pleaded with her to prepare Mr. Brinks for the possibility of her leaving her job.

She held back because of all the troubles and obstacles with the French complex. Mr. Brinks, whom she had got to know much better in the past two weeks, shared that he would not mind selling the whole company.

While driving to Annelies' house, she contemplated the power of music as she listened to the CD Toon had played for her before, the one that had triggered so many memories. Music profoundly affected her, and this piece made her feel even closer to him.

The previous week, Annelies had explained the Jaarsma Orphanage's role in the reality-shifting workshops. Annelies had told them they discovered documents behind the star painting that disclosed a genetic ancestral family tree. They were to do some research on their family history. They would make their last awakening card that evening and use some of their dream symbols for this card.

Niels arrived at the same time as she did and greeted her cheerfully. Ever since Carla had told her about her seducing him, Ingrid had to smile at the way Niels looked. He had changed from a serious, silent person to a more open and loving person. He seemed to be more in touch with his feelings.

Class 10

THE LIFE OBSTACLE CARD was written on the door. Yolanda winked at her, projecting, "I need to talk to you about the fashion show."

"Remember, as I've explained before, the last five awakening cards change if you have altered a name, a business, or, in the woman's case, if you've got married, moved to a different address, or switched your telephone number."

"You're saying that the three mental, physical and emotional cards take on a different tonal influence?" Yolanda radiated much more self-worth, and her long blonde hair created a romantic effect.

"Yes, or the inside of your card can be different vibrational. So, you see, you can always manipulate your opportunities and obstacles!"

"Somehow, I'm glad for that; at least I have some say." Yolanda's face took on a speculating look.

"We've always had dear; we can create any experience."

"Annelies, if I want to experience something, how do I attract that?"

"Yolanda, first make sure that's what you want. Then, if it is for the good of all and will benefit you, in your case, the awakening process, then start seeing that this is already happening in every detail. When backed up by a feeling of rapture, your visualisation will manifest, have no doubt." Yolanda pulled up her eyebrows.

"Really? What has stopped me from materialising a loving partner?" Annelies' expression beamed a glow of understanding.

"My dear, some things are so far hidden; exploring our subconscious is necessary for discovering hidden truths!" Their mental discussion riveted Ingrid; she knew that her longing for a Soul companion had always been there, but she had not been aware of it before!

"If one's aura has energies from the Language of Light, those qualities become like a magnet, attracting and mirroring experience through those qualities. If you want a partner to reflect on yourself, then you will. Anything is possible in life."

"Ingrid, we all want to know about your opening. I believe you were a tremendous success!" Zola remarked warmly. Ingrid knew that image was important to her. Her tight-fitting purple dress and matching earrings looked good on her slender body, but the heavy makeup had spoiled the effect.

"What makes you say that I was a success? It was terrifying at first and must have shown, but something gave me the courage to do it anyway, so it was not so bad. I even started to enjoy it."

"Ingrid, what gave you the courage." Yolanda's serious tone warranted her honesty, but that was a personal thing which her nature resisted discussing.

"That is part of your fear, my dear," Annelies projected.

"So, it is, thanks." When they were all drawing, pasting, and colouring, Annelies reminded her to share about courage.

"When I asked to go to my suite because I needed something delivered before my speech, I had no idea what it could be. I was grateful to escape for a moment. However, when I walked into my room, I saw the most exquisite arrangement on the dresser. It was more than just an arrangement; it was a reminder of someone special I got to know through the flowers in the arrangement and then a little box with a letter... Anyway...I'll show you what was in the box." Her voice became soft and warm when she showed them the partly hidden brooch pinned to her scarf.

Everyone was mesmerised by the intricacy of the brooch, and Annelies gazed at her. *"That's Toon's most valued possession from the mother he never knew."* *"Yes, I know, and that gave me the courage, knowing he loved me before I gave the speech. What could I lose? He loved me before I gained my inner power. Annelies, my feelings of self-worth were not all that great."*

"So, your talent might be to speak in public?"

"Speak in public? Annelies! I found anything that has to do with verbal communication difficult. Give me a drawing and planning job, and let me work on it independently. Now that is where my talent comes in handy, surely?"

"Ingrid, that's just it, that's what your personality tells you because it is comfortable and your inner knowing is good at it; so, for obvious reasons, it will convince you that that's where your talent lies! Don't be fooled by that; it's not always true."

Ingrid was stunned; she had never thought about it that way, but had always secretly admired people who were good at expressing themselves in public. She used to secretly stand in front of the mirror when she was small, pretending she was standing on a podium speaking.

"Ingrid, the number two vibration within your card reflects the need to have an image, and it also represents the priestess, meaning the overcoming of your obstacles! You have to do just that!" Annelies stated kindly but with firmness. That comment 'image' made her realise that Zola had mirrored the same addiction because she recognised it in her!

"Annelies, you know me well. Now, I always thought that creating wearable art and helping people in the bookshop was where my talents lay."

"Yolanda, let me see your obstacle card spacing and the vibrations inside, dear."

"Number fourteen." Yolanda's whole posture conveyed her viewpoint.

"Your Soul character is very...earthy and has an affinity to the animal kingdom." Annelies must know that some could read her thoughts. *"Meaning what!"*

"Mmm... Abundance, but true wealth is within. Yolanda, since you asked me tonight, you will share what you secretly fancied doing or working with the group, but it scared you."

"What do you mean by scared me?"

"You admire people who can do whatever you feel very uncomfortable doing. Think about it." Annelies dealt out sheets of paper with a Mandela in the centre with five partitions left open for them to work in. Zola tried encouraging Wim to join in as he excused himself again to smoke his pipe on Annelies' backyard porch outside.

Annelies instructed them how to express, through colour and symbols, feelings attached to their inner fears, lack of self-esteem, or harboured ambitions. Ingrid remembered her inner drive at school activities when she had to lead her group into action.

"Well, Yolanda, what did you get? Now, be open about it, let's have it." Annelies put her on the spot and wondered what Yolanda's challenge would be.

"I always admire people who ride horses and work in stables. Also, gardening is not one of my hobbies because you get your hands dirty, but I admire people who can. Are you telling me that is what I should do? To oppose or challenge my personality?" Yolanda looked proudly up at Annelies, who burst out laughing.

"*Your unconscious has just spoken! I must admit I can't picture you.*"

"You'd better read your interpretations. *"I have a feeling, a sort of precognition, that you will soon face an opportunity. Take some time to sit with it, dear."* Annelies' eyes were gleaming mischievously. Ingrid wondered what she knew. Liesbeth just gave her a wink. *"She might be right."*

While they were busy decoding their cards and choosing their appropriate graphic symbols, Ingrid wondered what her opportunities were and how they would be revealed to her. Joris let out an ecstatic whimper under Niels's chair; he was dreaming.

"Annelies, if our talents are not in things and activities that we feel comfortable doing because those are our persona's comfort zone activities that we are nourishing instead, how do we recognise our opportunities?" She asked, adding:

"Which is stronger, our unconscious or conscious willpower?"

"Ingrid, once we are aware of the real purpose that our Soul wants to experience, and once we are awakened to our real talents, we are in a conscious position to make use of the abilities that come our way and use them." She hoped that she would genuinely discover her true Soul purpose, hoping it was something to do with Toon's community projects.

The rain was pouring outside, and far in the distance, the rumbling of thunder affected by lightning created a cosy atmosphere in Annelies's classroom. Ingrid observed that Wim, who had joined them again, was very frigid; was he bored? She noticed that Zola kept whispering to him.

"This is not Wim's path to walk just now, and Zola must learn to let him go. He has a different agenda, but I can't get to it." Hearing Annelies' thoughts for Zola saddened her.

"How do we recognise our Soul purpose?"

"Richard, when we truly experience the real inner passion, the driving force and the joy of living for each moment in what we do, your IAM is awakened within. That's the reward most people look for and never find." Ingrid pondered, thinking back to how she had felt when she had to be the hostess. It had felt exhilarating. Somehow, she felt alive for having experienced it more than with every other activity.

As if she knew she had become her heroine. She had overcome her greatest fear of failing, but mostly, the fear of ridicule.

"Is it in those moments when you recognise your real talents and dare to test them that your Higher Self takes control? So only then can we expect excellence in whatever we do?" Gerrit asked in a slow, reflective tone. Most of the crayons were piled in front of him.

"Well stated! You've got it!" Annelies' smile was catching.

"When you were good at something, you loved doing it. I always thought that must be your special talent!" Zola commented slowly. Wim excused himself again for a loo call while they had a coffee and tea break.

"Well, in some cases, perhaps, but I've discovered that it can result in some people losing it because there is no challenge for the Soul. The personalities of these people can very often become dull!"

"You mean, those people do not grow... or?" Zola's posture gave away disappointment.

"Zola, if your personality's needs for comfort and being patted on the back are constantly being granted, like spoiling a child for the wrong reason, that is truly an act of destruction of your real self."

"How come I thought those people were content?"

"Errrr. ...Zola, most content people are dead people!" Annelies's whole body expressed what she had just stated, making everyone laugh.

"These people whose personalities have become their masters have huge egos and go around bragging about how good they have been, but deep inside, they feel a failure because they cannot fool themselves. They just played it safe."

"But surely, there is nothing wrong with being content?" Ingrid battled with that one. There had been moments when she had been content.

"Those were fantasy realities, my dear; one day, you will know the difference between being content or truly at peace with oneself."

"Is that why you very often hear of very successful people who commit suicide when things go wrong rather than face the challenge? Are they afraid to confront their failure?"

"Yolanda, people who are threatening suicide most often don't do it. Their Souls are just crying for help, to be given one more opportunity, and that's the hardest road to take."

"Annelies, but if people overcome that, then they are the stronger for it, not so?"

"Gerrit I... do not recommend it... For the Soul to travel through the fear zone is the most painful journey, and many lose themselves by going through with a suicide mission. But like any obstacle course, if we survive it, we will truly never be in bondage again. Then we know what freedom means," Annelies stated this with such conviction that they all knew she spoke from experience. Gerrit just nodded.

"You don't have to go to such lengths to experience this freedom, do you?" Richard appealed, throwing his hands in the air. Wim had chosen just the right moment to join them again.

"You don't have to do anything at all! That is the other end of the scale. If you do nothing and let your inner spirit, your Higher Self, your IAM, whatever you feel comfortable with, do it for you, freedom is also guaranteed." Annelies said joyfully, but when she saw all of them looking so serious, she explained how the Ascension Decoding card game came into being. That made everyone relax as she winked at Ingrid. After their coffee break, she explained the outlines and challenges on the first level of the card game.

"The following four obstacles prevent people from awakening to their full potential. The first two are releasing all relationships based on attachment, and the releasing of co-dependence addictions." That reminded Ingrid immediately of the last Excerpt from POWAH.

"Releasing all attachments? That's a big one because surely every relationship has some form of attachment?" Niels voiced apprehensively. Ingrid could relate to his worry.

"Yes, from the human perspective, but you must understand, attachments are usually there because of a need the person has. Then it becomes an attachment; we all make energy cords with one another."

Everyone was quiet. When the person needs to feel good, that becomes an attachment, Ingrid realised.

"What you're saying is when the person's needs are involved, the situation or circumstances are an attachment?"

"An attachment can be seen energetically as a line of energy connecting individuals to another individual or object within their lives."

"Now I understand that you are better off without material goods or assets because we have to release attachments to objects. If you need to possess it, it becomes an attachment, but if you release the fear of not needing it, you can still enjoy it to its fullest, but it does not own you!

Wow! That's not easy, Annelies." Zola replied. She loved her jewellery, especially her Purple earrings that banged against her cheeks, not to mention the orange hairstreaks.

"Excellent, Zola; think of it in this way: you can have everything you feel you need at the present moment to live this life to the fullest potential if it is for the good of all."

"That is such a powerful statement." Gerrit agreed when he tidied his rucksack. Lately, he had arrived on a Harley-Davidson motorbike with a sidecar. All the men had drooled over his bike, and Annelies kept teasing him to find someone for his sidecar.

"Thank you, Gerrit. By expressing this awareness, people experience no limitations. It's only the person who needs to own it or to be co-dependent with others. Your Soul says you can have it all, so long as you are not under its influence."

"When do you know that your need for something is gone?"

"Richard, any feelings of fear, sadness, pain, anger, unworthiness, guilt, blame, and the need for external additions or entertainment to escape these feelings are fantasy manifestations of your personality."

"Gosh, then I'm often in fantasy", Ingrid heard Richard's thoughts.

"You mean that if you escape in a novel or a movie and create a space to hide emotionally, you are in a fantasy?"

"Yes, Zola. If reading a novel or seeing a movie is a way to kill time, then your real-world needs tending. But, if you ask your Soul to

take control, answers will arrive with a clear message from within, even while reading fantasy novels. Then you will experience an inner joy that's real." *"But what happens if you don't get an answer?"*
They all helped Annelies tidy up, knowing where she stored her tools and electronics.
"Yolanda, for your Soul to communicate, you have to be grounded, be in the present in your body."
"Read your interpretations and the exercises you can do at home." Annelies looked at them with compassion. Ingrid realised that only through a daily focus on intending to reach self-realisation could the reprogramming occur on a cellular level.
"That's all you need to do!" Yolanda beamed in reply. Annelies nodded.
"There are two more obstacles to release: fear-based thought forms and the imbalance of narcissism (Introverted/extroverted). Releasing the above four obstacles is the aim of the first level of the card game." Annelies added
Joris' sudden bark made everyone jump in their seats. Ingrid's heart jumped momentarily, thinking it was Toon, but it was Hans, and Liesbeth left the room.
"Observe yourselves during the following two weeks on the four obstacles. Be aware of them."
"Annelies, the fear for survival and co-dependence comes from not having the information necessary to survive, not so?"
"Yes, I wish everyone could see that." Gerrit was polishing his glasses, waiting for Annelies' reply. Wim was looking at his watch, which made Zola somewhat nervous.
"Gerrit, yes, I think that within our civilisations, there are people who have no information on physical survival and no education; they end up being poor, homeless and abandoned. The willingness to share all knowledge will heal all nations." Annelies and Gerrit

seemed to have a particular regard for each other, and Ingrid noticed.

"Mmm, I'm looking forward to your card game because I'm curious how you have translated all the obstacles through playing a card game."

"Believe me, it still haunts me when I was shown, in a vision, how we lose our energy from moment to moment. The Ascension Decoding card game aims to shift our perceptions to learn or travel the different spiritual dimensions while fully conscious. We need lots of energy for that. Any change, no matter in what way, emotionally, mentally or physically, takes lots of energy."

"So, what you are saying is that our perception of reality absorbs energy, like holding an illusion of our reality in thought?"

"Yes, Ingrid, lots of it. That's why meditating is so important."

Everyone was silently pondering. Deep from within, she suddenly realised what type of energy Annelies meant. Some people feel larger, energy-wise.

"Yes, some people have chosen a personality type that can harvest more energy than others, but their mind drains that energy."

"Annelies, what you are implying is that... let's say manufactured factors may increase global warming, but gloom and doom hysteria based on conflicting data does nothing to address the problem.? It just depletes people's mental energy." It was the first time that Wim asked a question. They were all somewhat surprised.

"Mmm... The only thing necessary for the triumph of evil is for good men to do nothing. That is quite true, Wim, but of course, if the sea level is rising, we will need quite a lot of extra energy to adjust to the dykes, and our change of lifestyles, but... Wim, what is your part in all this?"

"What do you mean?"

"Humans do not cause global warming; we are contributing to a naturally occurring change in climate, but somehow I get a feeling that you. *" What is he hiding from us?"* Wim just shook his shoulders, saying...

"The question of survival has become more than a casual topic of conversation. It is not only cities that will die but the biological life in them. We have only a few years, not ten years but less, to do something; that's why I asked."

"Is that what you believe? Where did that conclusion come from?" Annelies asked.

They were all so surprised that Wim, who had never said much, suddenly shared this doom and gloom in so many words. *"Sometimes the very doom and gloom ideas are being spread to spread fear."*

Wim never replied to Annelies but walked to his car without saying goodbye. Zola tried to apologise, but Annelies stopped her. "Don't worry, he is who he is."

"Annelies, is the name of this card game ', The Eye of the Observer', significant?" Gerrit inquired in his normal, happy-go-lucky voice, plainly to disperse the gloomy energy that had crept into the hallway. The rain had stopped, and cloud shadows were racing across Annelie's wet driveway.

"Oh yes, Gerrit, you will discover how the card game works. I hope to see you all individually during the following weeks. Have any of you discovered any connection with the Jaarsma Orphanage?"

"Wim is involved, or hooked, into dark energy; that's all I get." Liesbeth beamed back at Annelies when she arrived in the hallway to say goodbye.

"My mother's not very eager to talk about her past, but I can't find out why. My brother never even knew about the orphanage. I explained the classes to him, and he became very interested. I'll ask my mother again. Niels replied.

Chapter 13
Fear-based Thought Forms

Ed Barendse

That Tuesday morning, when the phone rang in her office, she knew it wasn't Toon.

"Pleasure Parks, Ingrid speaking, may I help you?"

"Hello, lovely stranger. I finally got the courage to phone you." That voice! She had not heard from him for two and a half years! Her heart fluttered. It was so unexpected.

"Ed! It's so nice to hear your voice! Where are you?"

"I arrived in Amsterdam last night and heard from Dad how you captivated the audience at the Tilburg Pleasure Park opening; I'm very proud of my sister-in-law." She could detect admiration.

"Ed, what made you come back? I saw Dad two weeks ago, and he was fine," she said. She knew she was playing for time.

"Dad has asked me to come back to take over the directorship; when he saw you a few weeks ago, he convinced me to come back." She knew what her father-in-law was trying to do. When she visited him, he was very curious about her personal life, knowing that Toon was pursuing her. He liked Toon but didn't think he was the man for her, and he said so openly. She had tried steering away from his probing questions, but Dad had been forthright. She loved the man, but he was very domineering and went after things as vigorously as Toon and Ed, for that matter.

Oh, Ed, deep down, she felt sad for him. How would she be towards him if she could not give him the one thing he wanted from her?

"Ingrid, I know you are seeing Toon, but I need to see you before... you... make up your mind." When she had laid eyes on Toon for the first time, she had known there would be no one else for her, but she had not fully realised that until now.

"Ed, I'm deeply in love with Toon; nothing will change that."

"Ingrid, please, I need to see you. Can I take you out to dinner? I'll pick you up at seven-thirty?" His persistence was so strong that she found it hard not to yield, so she accepted the invitation.

When Ed phoned, her mind began to swim, and private schemes were tumbling about in her head for the rest of the day. She was unsure if playing Cupid was her style, but she wanted to see Ed happy with someone if only to make herself feel better! All she could think of was how Yolanda would connect with him. Should she follow up on her hunch now that Yolanda's divorce was final? ... She had been separated for two years so why not? Why did she get this strong feeling that those two needed to meet? ... Liesbeth! She would ask her! She dialled Liesbeth's cell phone, but her voicemail answered, so she left a message.

"Ingrid, what's wrong?" Wow! She was impressed. They didn't even need cell phones anymore!

"I need to speak to you about a dear friend of mine. Please can you come to the Pannekoek at lunch?" she projected.

"I'll be there after one; see you!" Gosh, that was easy! She'd never realised that her friend's telepathic skill was so powerful. Hers wasn't that good.

Directing her mind back to the drawings for the French complex was impossible. Her uncomfortable hunches, triggered by all the rumours floating around, were beginning to affect her, although Piet had gone. The police were looking for Piet concerning the burglary at Mr. Brinkis's house. Investigators were looking into all of their records, but the reason for the investigation was unknown to anyone.

When the e-mail icon on her toolbar began flashing, Excerpt 13 appeared on her screen. However, she quickly realised it was not sent to her as an email. Upon checking, she noticed that her screen was void of any background programs or the usual browsers she would usually see while browsing the internet.

Excerpt Thirteen[1]

Program Planet Earth

Releasing Fear-Based Thought Forms

Rule Three *of the Ascension Decoding Card Game.* Gosh, she was pretty intimidated by this Excerpt, knowing her own beliefs, when Piet's emotions of fear came to mind. Feelings of love and compassion were not the thoughts that came into her mind.

The flickering of her computer screen changed into a message.

<Kitty, we of the cosmic galactic council anticipated that it would be difficult for many participants to complete this releasing process, especially in relationships based on attachment rather than Soul agreements. We also know that those who stick with this process and follow their soul's desire above all else will experience a greater degree of joy, love, and freedom than they may have ever thought possible in human form.> She was relieved to read POWAH's response to her thoughts. Her soul's desire was strong, but plenty of 'karma' had to be stored. Her eyes were riveted on her screen in suspense whilst typing her next question.

POWAH, when do we know we have released our attachments, co-dependence, and negative thought patterns? Do we achieve that by overcoming personal fear and through service in one way or another?

---

1. https://allrealityshifters.wordpress.com/powah/the-reality-shifters-excerpt-13/

She wondered what service she could give at this moment.

<Kitty, if you were free from the emotional, mental and worldly attachments cunningly devised by the personality entities to enslave you, you would automatically serve.>

<If you are detached from your petty worries, you will serve.

<You would serve if you enjoyed better health by taking in only nourishing foods.

<If you prepared yourself for a new world, free from war, greed, hunger and poverty and free from the illusory addictions you feel you have a need of, like smoking, excessive drinking and eating, and harmful sexual activities, you would serve.

<If you could live freely in the moment without limitations again, you would serve. What is service but love in practical action?>

Did POWAH mean that her willingness to awaken fully was a service? Was that all one needed to aspire to?

POWAH about co-dependence, are we not all dependent on one another?

She knew that she wanted to please Toon and herself. The text jumped into action.

<Kitty, when a Soul unites with another Soul while both are incarnated and allows the experience of love and expansion to flow without judgment or preference between Souls, this communion will not create a co-dependency. That support only occurs when judgment or preference is present within one's field. The communities you, Toon, and many others are building around your planet are a service.>

Well, that was a relief, but... no judgments? Mmm, she still had preferences, especially around work. Looking up through the glass panel, her colleague Carla attacked the coffee percolator. Lately, many alarming threats to water scarcity around the world, especially in South Africa, where Toon was building a community, have been circulating through social media. Also, the refugees from war-riddled countries were creating a tremendous upheaval in Europe.

<Kitty, there will always be a variety of talents, gifts, and skills amongst all humans. Still, everyone will contribute equally to the smooth running of your communities, preparing people for the changes coming soon.> She wondered what changes would spur people to share their talents and know-how freely. Would Carla see the words...and if she did, would she want to share her conversations with POWAH?

The buzz outside her office was all about people speculating about the activities surrounding the large dome. The Facebook group shared conspiracy theories and video clips about CERN in Switzerland.

Jeroen remarked that many people online suggested that the Large Hadron Collider could create a black hole in the Earth. She tried to remember what POWAH had said about black holes. Something like that, planet Earth is a Looking Glass illusion where black is white and white is black. Jeroen claimed that something was happening there that would allow people to access new forms of power used against the Earth.

Niels and Gerrad said during a coffee break that the work might open a portal to another spiritual dimension. Somebody had sent her a Pinterest link with pictures of CERN and asked people to look up information on the Mandela effect. She was not supposed to visit social media sites during work hours, so she waited to see if POWAH would reply.

YES!

<Kitty, the Mandela effect refers to a phenomenon in which many people share false memories of past events caused by parallel universes spilling into their own.>

While she had been updating all her drawings, the interruption by a Facebook notification about a Pinterest link at the bottom of her screen, along with POWAH's text, which was again replying to her wishful thinking, baffled her.

Have we indeed been shifting into a parallel universe? I'm thinking about Hans and Liesbeth claiming to come from a parallel universe

<Yes, some individuals have experienced moving between different versions of reality, which may explain why they remember events that have not occurred in their current timeline. When there is a lack of information necessary for survival or personal development, individuals may rely on external sources such as governing bodies to survive. In such situations, fragmented aspects of one's soul may become dependent on others. <Being brave is crucial in all aspects of life, mainly when dependence is rooted in fear. However, gather the courage to overcome your fears, which is a paradoxical situation. You will take a significant step towards personal growth and evolution by bringing together the pieces of your fragmented soul on the ladder of progress.>

Wow, the fear of being ridiculed was still there, but she gasped with joy that she would become part of Toon's mission to create communities, as she could do the creative planning and whatever else was necessary.

<Kitty, lack of creativity and passion can also play itself out amongst individuals on Earth. The lack of creativity and passion causes people to lose the information necessary to manifest a vision within their lives, or they lack the chi or energy necessary to sustain a creation that has already come to fruition.>

Ingrid immediately thought of her fashion-design adventure and Yolanda's enthusiasm. Ingrid held her breath as she waited for POWAH's reply...

<Restoring one's creative potential revives lifelong aspirations and liberates from fear-based thoughts.>

Love POWAH

Her screen returned to her drawing program just before Carla entered her office. The rest of the morning flew by, but her thoughts kept turning to her meeting with Ed.

***

"Well, well, you are famous," Richard greeted her with a cheery grin. She joined Liesbeth while Richard served them coffee. Connie waved at her, and she spotted Ula in a deep discussion with an interesting-looking Indonesian man at the corner table.

"Liesbeth, look at the man Ula is talking to; who do you remind him of?"

"Mmm, Niels, but younger... and slimmer. Yes, he could be his brother. Niels did mention having a brother." They both summoned Richard, who was behind the counter. Asking him if he knew more about Niels' background, Ula and her partner stood up and left the Pannekoek. Ula never saw her, being so close to the entrance.

Richard went back to behind the coffee bar counter when Ingrid told Liesbeth about Ed, what had happened between them years before, his phone call and what Toon had told her, including his anguish because Ed was a good friend of his, her date for the following evening, and finally, her hunch. Liesbeth was a good listener who never once interrupted. "Ingrid, what are your feelings for him? You are certainly going to some lengths to make him happy, and you know very well that is impossible! Playing Cupid is all right as long as your motives are clear."

"Liesbeth, I love Toon and Ed but very differently. As for that one time, well, I probably unintentionally used Ed. I don't know, I was feeling very rejected then, and one thing led to another." Her regret was sincere, realising the truth only now that she had met Toon.

Nothing and nobody could make her feel the way he made her feel, as if he were a part of her.

"Yolanda. Mmm. ...What makes you think that they are suited to each other?" Ingrid had to smile at her reasoning. She could see Ed's face next to Yolanda's.

"I think Yolanda's talents could very well complement Ed's! I know I am not making any sense, but I visualise Yolanda working and living on a large estate in Australia, running a community. Ed is a very enterprising fellow, very different from Jan, who was steadier and more dependable. Ed is a businessman like his father. I know it's preposterous, but I can see it all somehow."

Liesbeth erupted in laughter, thereby attracting Richard and Connie to their table. As Ingrid looked up at Connie, she felt a strange sensation, as if she were spinning.

All she was aware of was... Connie! Was with... no, she was not sure... but... in her mind, she had a vision of seeing Yolanda together with Ed? ... they had... children! But where did Jeroen come into all this? She saw open spaces around Yolanda and horses! Yolanda was riding a horse with Ed riding next to her. They were looking at scenery that was very open with sparse vegetation. She saw it all in a flash, as if her mind had spun a movie script before her inner eye. Was this where Ed lived with Yolanda? Connie was also on the scene, and for some reason, she saw Jeroen running her father-in-law's business. What was he doing there where Ed lived? Had she had a vision of the future? Was that possible? And where was she in all of this? "Ingrid! Are you all right?" Richard asked her with concern.

"What? Yes, I'm fine, thanks. Wow, how strange. I was somewhere else!" Liesbeth's sparkle in her eyes told her that she knew what had happened to her. Richard looked worried but shrugged as he walked away to attend to other customers.

"Liesbeth, did I have some kind of precognition?" Liesbeth asked Connie for the menu, ignoring her mental question but still grinning.

"Ingrid, are you all right?" Connie anxiously asked.

"Yes, love. I'm fine." Ingrid reassured her, and as Connie walked away, she looked at Liesbeth, who still had a smirk on her face.

"Liesbeth, now I know what you were talking about the other evening when you said you could be in two places simultaneously!"

"All right, what happened to you was that your psychic mind, which can travel to any place in the past, present and future, visited the causal plane, usually five to six years ahead."

"You mean I saw into the future?" Her mind was stalling in disbelief.

"Yes, Ingrid, I created a space where you could project your unconscious thoughts. However, it's important to remember that what you saw was not set in stone and could still be changed. Furthermore, you mustn't disclose this to anyone. Premature suggestion can be a form of brainwashing, which goes against universal law." Liesbeth agreed to the plan but looked intently into Ingrid's face with a serious expression, adding: "But no meddling afterwards! We do this once only, and after that, well, nature must take its course, you understand?"

"What are we going to do? Do you have a plan?" The buzzing voices around them enhanced their conspiracy.

"All you have to do is let Ed take you to dinner at the Prinsengracht Hotel this evening and leave the rest to me."

"That is where Toon took me the first time, so it's rather special to me."

"Yes, Ingrid, there. I'll organise the rest, but we tell no one about this," Liesbeth impressed upon her.

"Never? Not even to Toon?"

"I didn't say 'never'! However, don't you say anything about this to Yolanda. Don't even consider it! Can you manage that?" Liesbeth looked serious.

**

Jeroen was making himself an omelette while Ingrid was waiting for Ed. To see Ed again was still nerve-wracking. Toon's brooch on her jacket gave her some form of support.

"Mom, why is Uncle Ed taking you out to dinner? What is going on?" Ingrid could hear in his voice that he was wondering about her feelings.

"Uncle Ed wants to hear from me how I feel about Toon. I've told him over the phone, but he wants to hear it directly from me."

"What did you tell him? May I know?"

"I am very much in love with Toon, sweetie, and I want to spend the rest of my life with him."

"Gosh! Really? I have to get used to that idea but... I'm glad for you," Jeroen swept her off the floor into his affectionate embrace, which he often did when he wanted to express his feelings to her about something.

"So, Toon was right; he still has a crush on you! Is Toon aware that you're going out with Uncle Ed tonight?"

"No! At least, I don't think so." They both heard the front doorbell. Jeroen put her down and went to greet him. She was glad that he was at home. She heard Ed cheering Jeroen with a very open and friendly note of approval. Ed was a very flamboyant and extroverted personality, similar to Toon. She greeted him immediately.

"You look very tanned and fit", hugging him. Ed's short, sun-bleached hair, a black short-sleeved shirt with a horseshoe pendant around his neck, and dark blue pants, like those of a western cowboy, made him look like Toon, an outdoor man. He looked at her, searching for a sign, but all she could give him was a soft smile expressing the same genuine love she had for her sister. His eyes were surveying her, but she felt no butterflies.

She could feel him watching her while they drove silently to the Hotel. When they arrived, Ed parked the car and turned to her.

"Ingrid, if I had known before that Toon would meet you, I would have tried to prevent it. I knew he would fall for you, so he did in a big way. I want you to tell me now, what are your feelings for him?" His direct manner, typical of the men she seemed to attract, was still nerve-racking.

"I fell in love with Toon the moment we met. Although I've not seen him for almost four weeks, which has been hard, I want to spend whatever time there is on this planet with him," she declared with the absolute sincerity Ed deserved. He just looked at her silently... The hotel's parking bay was filling up with guests.

"He is the luckiest person I know and a good friend, but I needed to hear from you. I am not surprised, not after spending time with him, listening endlessly to him expressing his feelings for you."

"Toon knows that you are here? Does he know you were going to ask me?"

"You bet he knows," Ed projected, his eyes gave away that he was telepathic.

"If you can read my mind, you know my feelings for him!" she beamed in astonishment.

"Yes, I do now, but I needed to be sure, Ingrid. I'm hungry! Come, let's have dinner, and you can tell me all about the children," Ed, over-cheerful, put on an act. A great relief flooded over her simultaneously, amazed at his ability to mind-read. Toon hadn't told her that he could.

As Ingrid recalled her arrangement with Liesbeth, she knew she had to warn her about Ed's ability to pick up thought waves.

"Mr. Barendse, we have a table for you waiting with the compliments of Mr. Haardens."

Ingrid was so flabbergasted that she glanced at Ed's face to see if he knew. All he did was throw his head back and laugh. The dinner table was thoughtfully set for seven esteemed guests, creating an ambience of warmth and friendliness that welcomed each individual to a special evening of shared company and delightful cuisine.

"Did Mr. Haardens order a table for seven guests?" Ed directly asked the waiter.

"Yes, sir, and I must give this to the lady. The head waiter took a white linen package from his side trolley and put it on a plate with her name. Ed took out her chair and sat down next to her. She was opening the white linen cloth slowly when suddenly, the sounds of music that reminded her of Toon filled the whole dining room. She looked up to see where it had come from, but it was being relayed over the speakers. Looking back to see what was inside the white cloth, she saw a beautiful little corsage made up of small miniature roses with a small card with little musical notes sprinkled on it! All it said was:

This delicate, haunting melody reminds you that you belong to me!
Then she heard the Uilean pipes! After the board meeting, Toon played it in his car when he drove her to Quincy! She fingered the delicate roses carefully, searching for the clasp at the back when Ed offered to pin it on her dress.

"I must hand it to him; Toon knows how to be present without being here." Ingrid started to feel more at ease, looking at his grinning face.

"Hello there! Great music, is it Irish?" Liesbeth and Hans suddenly appeared, followed by Yolanda and Annelies.

"So, this is Toon's friend he always talked about, Ed Barendse, I believe? Ed was a tall, typical Dutch-looking man who towered over most people like Toon. Annelies introduced herself and the others.

Ed was not letting on that he was surprised, and he greeted Hans, showing that they already knew each other.

"I must thank Toon for this unexpected welcome; I'm sure he would love to be here." Then he took Yolanda's hands in his. Ingrid observed that he was silent, just looking, while Yolanda was quite flustered. Her eyes became larger. *"Ingrid, who is this gorgeous man? Your brother-in-law?"*

"Ingrid could feel in her solar plexus that they had made a connection, and Annelies and Liesbeth were aware of it, too. Was it the same feeling she'd had with Toon, that immediate recognition and inexplicable attraction?

"Let me guess. Are you Yolanda? I've lost track of what part of the family you are, but Toon has always been very good at describing people." Ed's voice carried an amused tone as he held her hands close to his lips. Yolanda giggled.

"Well, his description of you was not far off the mark either. I can tell you that now."

"Ingrid, what game is this man playing? He is a real charmer, and he seems to know me." Ingrid knew Ed could mentally hear her, but he did not let on that he did. However, he looked at Yolanda with more than a polite glance. She could see that he was smitten with her!

"Ingrid! Say something! He makes me incredibly nervous! Is he married?"

Ed pulled out the chair next to him on his other side and asked Yolanda to sit beside him when Fred arrived at their table.

"Ingrid, I believe you have not met my brother Fred." Ingrid looked into Fred's dark-brown eyes as Annelies introduced him.

"I met Ingrid at the beginning of the week. I see that Toon has excellent taste in many things besides music, don't you think?" This was directed at Ed, especially while he was shaking his hand.

"I remember now! You're in the hotel business, and this is your place. To answer your other question, Ingrid is very special to me, and I'm glad to meet Toon's family for her sake. The next time I see him...I'll ask him how he organised this little family gathering." Ed had an amused smile. The party was enjoyable, but Ingrid's heart ached for Toon. Liesbeth winked at her, distracting her from her thoughts and drawing her attention to Yolanda. The waiter brought the main course. The hotel was known for its cuisine.

"Ed, how much did Toon tell you about us?" Ingrid knew Annelies was trying to get into his mind.

Ingrid, your brother-in-law's mind is a closed book, which is unusual. Is the man telepathic, yet he's purposely put on a mental barrier?

"Annelies, Toon usually talked at the local bar when he had a few drinks, and I seem to remember him describing the artists in the Zwiegelaar family," Ed answered while keeping his eyes on Yolanda.

Annelies, the man is making that up. Toon doesn't drink, at least not in the way he implies. Why do you think he said that? Ingrid, why are you silent? He's a big flirt! Do you think he's telepathic? Liesbeth and Hans were conversing, pretending not to be aware of what was happening, and Fred was ordering another bottle of wine from the waiter. Somehow, Ingrid wanted to warn Yolanda, but Liesbeth suddenly beamed:

Ingrid, remember what you promised at the Pannekoek. No meddling!

Gee, Liesbeth was entirely on cue. How did she do that... blocking the others...

"What meddling is she implying, Ingrid?" Ed mumbled softly, leaning over. So he heard! She had difficulty not giving herself away.

"I've no idea, Ed; why don't you ask them?" She softly whispered.

Annelies was looking at Ed very observantly. Surely, Liesbeth must know that Ed suspected a conspiracy. He seemed to want to keep his telepathic skills from them, so she'd better watch her thoughts. How carefully one had to watch one's thoughts while in the company of telepathic people! She wondered how Ed managed to block out the others mentally. Whether her plan between Yolanda and Ed would lead to anything remained to be seen. She would have to keep her promise to Liesbeth and not interfere.

Connie and Yolanda de Wit

Ingrid stretched her body, revelling in a glow of happiness that bathed her like warm sunlight. Somehow, she knew Toon would be home that weekend. It looked like a gardening day outside, hearing the busy chirping of birds. What a pity that she had to go to work! She heard Jeroen downstairs in the kitchen making breakfast. He was up early! When she joined him, her toast was already on her plate.

"What a treat. What's going on? Wow, are you going in for work, looking at your smart suit?" Jeroen's transformation from a casual hippy type into an executive businessman was uncanny.

"Grandpa asked last night if I could be at the factory early this morning for a board meeting. Uncle Ed has requested me to attend. You know, Grandpa is old school. I wonder if Uncle Ed is wearing a suit."

"Oh, wow, what's my uncle been up to?"

"You should know! You went out with him on Tuesday evening. I tried to phone him yesterday, but nobody knows where he is. How was it, Mom, the evening, I mean?"

"We had a perfect time, and Toon knew about Uncle Ed's plan to take me out, so we had dinner with five others. Ed now knows how I feel about Toon. I know what he's been up to, but I must run. Jeroen, are you home tonight?"

"No, I'll be back on Saturday. Will you be all right? When is Toon coming back, do you know?"

"I have a feeling this weekend, but that must not stop you from do-ing your thing. I'm glad that Ed needs you at the office as you'll be partly running the company, maybe." She suddenly realised how easy it was to start predicting the future, but remembered what Liesbeth had told her.

"You think so?" Jeroen sounded surprised.

"Would you want that?"

"Yes, I would, together with Uncle Ed, but I also want to see Aus-tralia. I would love to see what Uncle Ed's place looks like." As she focused on Jeroen's serious expression, she longed to tell him what she had experienced, but knew that was not allowed, realising what a responsibility it was to know certain things but not reveal them. When can you impart a vision of the future to someone?

"But mom, more so than ever, I want to explore... what solutions are for us with the coming land shortages and clean drinking wa-ter?"

"What do you mean?"

"Well, during my last semester, I joined a group of engineering and architecture students working on pilot projects to build whole cities at sea with desalination equipment."

"You're kidding. I never knew that." For the first time, she saw Jeroen in a state of... what, excitement.

"Yes, we all have to find innovative solutions in the coming years." I have been speaking to Ed, who has excellent ideas. He said that our traditional way of fighting the sea with dikes has to give way to alternatives, like going with the water."

I'm so glad you found your passion, or at least a direction. I must ask Toon his ideas on creating a community that coexists on water; that might be a very sustainable solution." She hugged him and sent her love to his grandfather.

When she arrived at her office, she knew it was Toon on the other end of the ringing line, so she closed her door before she picked up the receiver, glowing with happy anticipation.

"My dear Kitty, I will soon hold you, love you, kiss you, be with you," she heard in the silence.

"When is soon?"

"At the weekend, I promise. I have to create a completely different hologram with you in it permanently," Toon voiced his longing.

"Toon, do you think we live in a mental hologram?"

"Kitty, only the woman I love would ask that question. My love, if consciousness is an awareness of the "light" that reflects All That Is, and we perceive objects either because they emit or reflect light as it arrives at our eyes, then this invisible, undetectable field holds all of 'reality' together. Yes, we could very well be in our hologram."

"You mean that All That Is, is this field? Then this light, or field, when it enters our eyes as it does through the camera that is reflected on any physical object, see... matter?"

"Yes, we look at a three-dimensional world, and the camera detects it two-dimensionally."

"Good grief! Let me get this right: When we take a picture, we catch a light-sensitive view that arrives through the camera's lens. So, the total information recorded on a photographic film is the intensity of light caught in the film?"

"Yes, and Kitty, without getting into the science of photography, the question then becomes, what more is there to record than just the intensity of light at each point?"

"Now you've lost me. What do you mean?"

"I know, I'm racing ahead of myself, but the prospect of virtual reality can be very awesome because it appears real, but it is much less scary than real life because virtual reality technology is designed to put you in the scene. Kitty, I heard that the Pleasure Park complex in France will have a hologram island inside it."

"Now you've floored me! You mean a hologram deck?" Thinking of the movie Star Trek.

"The word hologram "merely records two-dimensional thought forms of three–dimensional reality. Yes, that's what they're planning. I heard this only last week, and I don't completely understand it, but the symbol has something to do with it. I must introduce you to Trevor; he's an uncle of Annelies. Kitty, they're calling me. Remember, I love you very much."

Ingrid was still savouring his last words when suddenly she became aware that someone was knocking at her office door. Carla was looking questioningly because she had never closed her door, asking if she was all right.

"Yes, I'm fine, thanks. I just spoke to Toon. Thank goodness. He's coming home soon!"

"Oh, good!" Carla's arms were hailed in gratitude.

The rest of the day flew by. Ingrid decided to have her evening meal at the coffee shop as nobody was home that night. Connie was helping Richard as a waitress now that the holiday season was in full swing.

"Ingrid, my mom has just phoned to ask if you would mind popping in?"

"Where's your mom now? Is she still at the shop?"

"No, she's already home. Could you come past the hotel before you go home?"

"All right, I will. When are you finished here, or are you working the whole evening?" Ingrid thought she'd better get to know this girl.

"No, I'm going in a few minutes. Richard said he will stay on longer."

"I can give you a lift unless you have a car."

While driving to the Prinsengracht hotel, Connie chatted away next to her. Ingrid liked the enthusiasm this girl had for life.

"So you're interested in the hotel business like your aunt Annelies?" Connie had told her she had enrolled in the hotel school to start in September because she would love to run the hotel one day.

"Uncle Fred wants me to learn the catering side first. I believe you're going into business with my mom?" Ingrid smiled, as she would not have put it quite like that, but if drawing a summer collection was going into business, why not?

"Does your uncle Fred own the bookshop?" she asked. She could not see Yolanda staying there long.

"Yes, when my parents separated, we lived with Uncle Fred; he always wanted to own a bookshop. He's quite a bookworm and likes collecting old manuscripts, but the hotel keeps him busy. Aunt Annelies has been very occupied with the decoding workshops, so Mom offered to run the bookshop as she needed a job." Ingrid always felt sad for children whose parents went through difficult times. Even her three children had experienced heavy arguments between Jan and her when they were small.

"Do you still see your father, Connie?"

"Not really. My Dad gambles a lot, and I dislike the friends he hangs out with. I wish he'd never got involved with them. Mom has tried, but I'm glad they're not together anymore. I love my Dad, but he's gone off the rails. I hope my Mom will meet someone else; I'd love to see her taken care of." Good grief, another one that wants to see Yolanda with someone, just as she did! As Liesbeth had said, nobody can make someone else happy, but she liked Connie's concern nevertheless.

When they arrived at the Prinsengracht hotel, they took the side entrance as they lived in a side building that used to be the stables and later the orphanage dormitories; Yolanda had told her she'd been there the previous time. Yolanda appeared from a side door and invited her in.

Connie would change her clothes to see some friends in town, so she left them to themselves.

"Oh, Ingrid, I'm so confused. Come, let's sit here; I badly need to ask you about your brother-in-law."

"What do you want to know about him, and why?"

"I don't know what to do. For the first time in my life, I've come across someone who understands me completely without needing me to explain anything. Ed said he felt the same about me. Ingrid, I only saw Ed Tuesday evening and the whole of yesterday. I feel as if I've known him all my life!"

Now Ingrid knew why nobody could find him. He'd spent Wednesday with Yolanda!

"So, what's your problem? It looks as if you've found each other. I'm happy for you both," she said. She was so happy that her hunch had paid off.

"Ingrid, he asked me to go to Ireland with him for a week, and I would love to go, but you know, I know myself! I'll sleep with him; don't you think that's far too quick?" Yolanda's anxious mind needed reassurance. Ingrid could feel what she was going through and realised again how much she longed for Toon. Ed had no intention of waiting; she wondered where he was staying.

"He's at the hotel tonight, waiting for me to make a decision," Yolanda responded to her thoughts.

"Yolanda, follow your heart. You're free, aren't you? I mean, from your ex emotionally?"

"Oh, yes, I only feel sad for how Piet's life worked out. I do not know where he is, but I am free. Ed told me that he finally understood how Toon felt when he was in Australia and that he had no intention of being on his own anymore. He said that he knew I was the one he wanted to be with the moment he laid eyes on me. Can you believe that? So quick, Ingrid! Do you believe in falling in love instantly?"

"I do believe me."

"Ed is so glad you found Toon, and he also told me to thank you for meddling. I don't know what he meant by that, and he wouldn't tell me." Yolanda's blue eyes were probing. She was not allowed to tell her but wondered if Ed had already revealed his telepathic skills.

"Yolanda, can you read his mind?"

"Oh, yes, I think he can read mine as well. What do you think? Did he ever let on that he could mind-read? Annelies thinks he is very telepathic and that he's testing me," *"Ingrid, don't let on that, you know. She has to discover that for herself,"* Liesbeth beamed while screening it from Yolanda! Her friend had given her a jolt, so she got up to leave to avoid giving herself away.

"Yolanda, follow your heart and do what feels right for you. Ed is a terrific man, but he stands his ground. I'm thrilled for you both. Allow yourself to have a great time. I must go! I'm tired!" She hugged her and left.

When she drove home and was reflecting on the many things that had happened, the music on her car radio was interrupted by the announcer:

"More conspiracy theories are coming to light concerning the Pleasure Park estate in France. There is speculation by a geologist that a substantial gold deposit was discovered on the site when the blasting for the Great Dome caused a collapse of the rocky ground near the river that runs past the French estate. The local population and the Greenpeace movement are voicing great objections to the blasting. When Mr. Harry Brinks was approached for a comment, he told our news reporters that a team of people from different sources had begun investigating the many allegations, and a statement would soon be released to the press."

Ingrid switched off the radio. Would her boss know far more than he let on? Fluffball greeted her with a rub when she walked into the hallway, and she mentally saw Toon dialling her on his cell phone.

Would it work? Would he phone her if she focused long enough on her mental vision? Thinking of Toon made her want to send a message to him because she needed to talk to him about so many things, wherever he was. When the phone rang, she almost jumped. Had it worked? *"Yes, love, I knew you wanted me to phone you. I'm coming home to take you with me this weekend."*

"Toon, how did you know I'd just arrived home?"

"I was wondering where you were. Kitty, can you take a leave from work? Please, love, I want to spend some time with you." There was an excitement in his voice she had not heard before. She recognised the sounds of an airport in the background.

"Snooks, I'll arrange some time off with Mr. Brinks. Will I see you tomorrow?" She wished she knew what airport he was at now.

"I'm in Johannesburg, hoping to get a seat, but the planes are full. I'll try to get on any flight now that I have finished what I need to do to spend time with you. Then she heard his name being announced over the PA system.

Chapter 14
The Imbalance of Narcissism

Richard de Jong

A massive display of exotic foliage with dashing blooms all snuggled around a magical waterfall greeted Ingrid in the foyer. The sound of trickling water enhanced the arrangement.

"Hi, Ingrid. Gee, Toon certainly goes to great lengths to express his love." Ula's wide grin as she handed a closed envelope made her heart leap while beaming: "Toon! I want you in person, no substitutes."

She marched to the lift while ripping the envelope, hoping his wording would soothe her longing.

This is the last display of my bewitchment for you at this address! I want to take you away forever! Your colleagues have to admire the plants instead of you. Love Snooks. **XX.**

She laughed in the lift. So that was why the arrangement was so enormous! Everyone would admire it when they walked through the foyer!

She and Carla were having lunch at the Pannekoek when Carla told her that on Monday, Ula had quite a nasty caller who insisted on speaking to Ingrid while she was gone to Mr. Brinks's estate in Utrecht.

When his house had been ransacked from top to bottom, Mr. Brinks established that the original aerial photos of the French site were gone, so he had asked her to come over that day.

"Gosh, why did you not tell me that before? Did Ula get his name?"

Connie served them two delicious whole-wheat bread rolls with many different kinds of Dutch cheese.

"I'm sorry, Ingrid, but I've forgotten with all the investigations going on. By the way, Ula's fiancé is the detective searching for Piet."

Ingrid suddenly recalled recognising this André when he arrived at Mr. Brinks' house. She'd seen him with Ula at the Pannekoek. Niels had Indonesian ancestry, and so had Detective Andre, but she never linked them together. He was not very tall but had a lean, fit-looking body, fitter and younger. Mr. Brinks had confided that a geologist had measured unusual readings at the French site that could delay the construction. She wanted to ask Mr. Brinks about the symbol when Detective André Jaarsma arrived.

"Ingrid, Piet phoned me at my flat one evening, grilling me if I had the USB I gave to you, but I brushed him off... Just before the burglary."

Ingrid remembered with a jolt that she must speak to Richard, who still had her flash drive. She was anxious about its safety now that Carla reminded her.

"Did you tell the detective about Piet?" Carla nodded as she called Connie over to ask where Richard was. She seems to be running the Pannekoek all by herself.

Connie told her that Richard was booking a lecture in Utrecht for the following Monday and would be back around four. When they arrived back at the office, Ula at the reception desk told her that André, her fiancé, would soon contact Ingrid in connection with Piet. His superior officer called him back just as they came back from lunch. The water feature's message of love in the foyer worked like a tonic amongst all the dramas.

She had Richard on the line after four, but his speculations on the crop-circle symbol didn't give her any clue. He told her that the ancient hieroglyphic translations of the eye of the eternal library stated that the symbol of the eye mirrors the highest level of perfection, encompassing all the qualities of omnipotence and omnipresence. Many speculations passed through her ever since Toon had talked about the Pleasure Park complex in France becoming the first hologram park, and she remembered that Excerpt six had mentioned a modern temple at a resort.

"The eye of Horus could mean a dimensional gateway, or what is now called a portal. Ingrid, are there any large light beams inside the dome structure?" Richard asked.

"Yes, they all have them, especially over the pool area, laser beams, which make colour patterns in the water, combined with sound. Why do you ask?"

"According to the Sumerian clay tablets, some purification ceremony was practised. They also mentioned that the gods offered gold during the ceremonies."

"Really! Why was the gold important, do you think?" She recalled the radio message the day before. Gold seemed to be a link.

"I haven't been able to find out why... It has something to do with atomic gold, which contains unbelievable healing properties that allow the cells to carry phenomenal amounts of light energy."

"You've lost me, but said you wrote it all down."

"Yes, the symbol means that when the seventh light beam intelligence repaired the spectrums of limited colour and membrane radiations. The lower forms of intelligence and limitations would be free. That is the literal translation." Ingrid was thinking about the underground tunnels, but why would anyone want to jeopardise the construction of the large dome?

"Ingrid, it does not make much sense, but after what you've told me, I feel that we might be getting nearer to an answer, thinking about Annelies' decoding workshops and the tonal frequencies she and Tieneke call the 'Language of Light.'"

"Mmm, Richard, there might be something on that external hard drive the burglars were looking for on Monday at Mr. Brinks's house. The original aerial photos are missing, but thank goodness you have the flash drive. Can I fetch it from the coffee shop after work?"

Richard asked if he could keep the photo on his computer for later study, and Ingrid had no objection. Mr. Brinks, who looked very depressed and tired on Monday, had declared that this would be the last holiday resort he would build. When she was about to phone Mr. Brinks, her screen brightened.

<Kitty, the title 'Eye of the Observer' reflects the four platforms within your resort. They mirror the four "elements" or "frequencies" that are the basic building blocks of your planet. These elements are Earth, Air, Fire, and Water. Within these elements are many corresponding cycles, like wood and metal, through which energy flows in the physical body.>

Has that already been happening last year? It appeared as if it was on fire with a blinding light, she typed. Ingrid trembled in awe, wondering, was this all for real? The text flashed back in reply:

<Your transformation has already been sped up and will be sped up more, as you will soon be moving further into an electromagnetic null zone. The planetary mind will soon fully enter your spiritual dimensional space and time zone through rotational circumvention, creating artificial time warps.>

Again, this made absolutely no sense to her, but when POWAH mentioned the four platforms, the architectural design of the resort in France included wood, which was part of the outside walkway with the steel structures that supported the four bridges over the tropical gardens and the wave pool, with its centre platform. Where the fire element would come in, she couldn't imagine, unless... the gold...

POWAH, is the island in the Pleasure Park in France a hologram temple?

She still could not understand how that would come about. Oh, she needed Toon. He could explain it to her.

<Yes, Kitty, as above, so below. You live on a planet of energy; you are energy, and your physical body is a pulsation of life becoming life. Humans receive the multispectral frequencies or energies through what you call 'spin points'– mini vortices>

What did their chakras have to do with all this? POWAH took her intellect for granted; she had no idea what he was talking about.

<From these 'spin points' arise axial lines which radiate in a fine grid network, transmitting energy to every cell of your physical form. When the time has arrived, and your participants are earnest in their awakening process, we of the Galactic Council of Light know the time is ready to challenge the unconscious mind of man by channelling more information that has been inaccessible due to fear-based belief systems.> The recent events have left her feeling bewildered. The atmosphere in the office outside her glass partition was tense due to the ongoing investigations. She was sure everyone would panic if they discovered what she had witnessed. Meanwhile, the screen kept on displaying more text...

<The human mind is constrained by the manipulator, an electrical matrix that controls the collective consciousness on Earth. To ascend to higher dimensions, one must expand one's self-awareness and process many releases through the grid pattern of the human aura in this lower-dimensional realm.>

She needed to phone Mr. Brinks, but time seemed to stand still when she was communicating with POWAH. Lately, she had been trying to understand human perceptions. Their physical matter was all she knew, or did she? Her office and computer felt real, as did the people she could see through her glass partition. When it came to energy, she wondered how she could get her head around it all. Did she have to understand it to ascend?

<Kitty, the universe is not filled with matter; that is a human concept.>

You mean we humans are just energy waveforms?

She typed, trying to envision herself as the core; physical matter is simply an energy form that resonates.

<You appear to be real, but it is just a "stage" for your human Souls to experience themselves, make choices to evolve into higher resonance and states of consciousness, and journey back to their source.> Why was it so difficult to get beyond everything that was very physical to her? Had physical matter no value at all? Intellectually, she could imagine that energy waves formed her desk and keyboard without any life force.

<Kitty, the evolution of human consciousness is influenced by the choices people make and the values they uphold. These factors determine the path everyone takes towards higher states of consciousness. Each individual has a unique DNA blueprint, which has a crystalline structure and constantly communicates with the universal wave fields automatically and instantly.>

Oh, now she got it. Matter doesn't matter; it's what is behind the matter that matters...When excerpt number fourteen appeared on her screen, she wondered if she would receive the next one through the post box now that she had taken the next week off.

Excerpt Fourteen[1]

Program Planet Earth

The Imbalance of Narcissism

Rule four *of the Ascension Decoding Card Game*

In absolute awe, she was reading the following text after clicking on the link.

---

1. https://allrealityshifters.wordpress.com/powah/the-reality-shifters-excerpt-14/

<Kitty, your visit to the causal plane was partly to show you the power of thought. Now you see how important it is to release many negative thinking patterns. This causal plane, as it is now, which is indeed about five to six years ahead of time, will look a lot worse if the human population does not change its destructive and harmful thought patterns.> Wow! Reading about the causal plane as it is now, which is years ahead, is that how POWAH knew about her weird experience in the coffee shop?

Her concentration for the rest of the day was nil. The text responded again on her screen to her thoughts.

<Kitty, the outer-directed extrovert, suffers from the loss of self-identity in continuously being drawn into the dramas of others. They generally find themselves in partnership with inner-directed introverts to find a balance.> It still amazed her that time seemed to stand still while her screen bewitched her. She knew she was an introvert, so what was her drama?

POWAH, does that mean that Toon and I would help each other to find that balance?

As she typed her question, her body was trembling from pure amazement. Was she chatting with her own higher self? The screen stayed blank, so her thoughts drifted back to her experience in the coffee bar with Liesbeth. Had she glimpsed into the future and seen Yolanda on horseback? How did Liesbeth do that to her? She was now keen to play this card game with her cards. Then, the screen responded again.

<Kitty, at no time are we ever to interfere in each individual's choices because of the free will of any co-creator. You can experience incredible transformations when you practice just being in the present, in your body! It came as a great shock to realise the level of ignorance that many fragmented souls have about their power of thought. Kitty, think about the four rules you need to embrace.>

Was she ever able to think logically again?

"Oh, Toon, where are you?" she beamed. The whole week had been hectic, and it was already late afternoon. Carla had just left.

She didn't want to go anywhere as she sat at her desk, staring at her screen with one leg stretched across her drawing stool. There would be no class, and four weeks had passed since Toon had left, and it felt like forever.

"Oh, Toon, I miss you; I can feel you are near, but where are you?" Toon had no experience of marriage or any long relationship. She wondered if he could enter a relationship with her without expectations, conditions, or attachments. What about herself? Could she love him unconditionally?

She knew nothing about him, and what about girlfriends? He was surely not a man who would have withheld himself from sex all those years! The screen suddenly caught her attention again.

<Kitty, pure love is to be found in the higher spiritual realms, where the creative forces of soul-love, the erotic emotional force, and the biological sex force are experienced simultaneously, creating the feeling of unity. That is the real orgasm. Physical orgasm is nothing compared to that blissful experience.>

That must be something; she grinned at herself, interacting with who knows who. The idea that it was her own higher self that was still difficult to grasp, and who then would send her the excerpts? Why was she so stuck in her physical reality? Trapped was the word that POWAH used. Would Toon know all this? She couldn't wait for him to read her journal.

<Kitty, there can never be a point when you know the other Soul entirely, nor when you are known entirely. Every human soul has a unique style, which is reflected in every thought, act, and wish of that person. However, two developed souls can fulfil each other by revealing themselves on a soul level. Are you

ready for such a union?> She just sat there, knowing that at that moment, all she wanted was to be with Toon, listen to him speaking, look into those grey-blue eyes, and be swept up by his passion for life and his enthusiastic humour that emanated from him as a solid fresh breeze over the horizon.

Yes, I am. She typed in bold away at the keyboard.

<Kitty, only when you meet love, life, and the other being in such readiness can you bestow the greatest gift on your beloved, namely, your true self. Then, you will inevitably receive the same gift from your beloved. You and Toon have the spiritual maturity to have chosen each other. You intuitively waited for each other and longed in your unconscious for each other.>

POWAH, why am I still fearful?

<Kitty, you will never have to be afraid of losing the love of your beloved; use your relationship as a tool to discover your creative, authentic self. By honouring your feelings, you honour yourself.>

POWAH, certain people believe that they can cut out sex and the desire for a partner and live completely for the love of humanity. Is that valid?

<Kitty, is such a life possible for you? Is that what you want? It is possible for some, but certainly not healthy or honest for most. The real reason some people renounce relationships is fear of the life experience of this love. The fearful renunciation is rationalised as a sacrifice; unless it's a friendship between two people, then that is brotherly love.> POWAH signing off.

She had no idea how long she had been sitting at her desk. She understood the power within and around her for the first time. Almost as if time were no more. A new life was about to start; it felt like...a new life...While it lasted a few moments, she wanted to forget everything, permit herself to feel nothing, and surrender completely. She gently stroked the brooch...as if she knew he was already with her. Then she became aware of a presence that filled her whole being...

When she looked up, she saw Toon standing in the doorway. ...she had no idea how long he had been watching her, but as she got up she almost glided towards him. For the first time, looking into those eyes, instead of feeling the fluttering of her nerves, she felt a power rising within her, a soul connection that wanted to be in total union with him. Her smile matched his while his eyes electrified her whole being.

"Kitty, I have been dreaming about this moment, and all I want to do is hold you, kiss you."

"What is stopping you?" He laughed and took her in his arms, holding her body pressed to his as he kissed her passionately. They stood in the middle of her office, knowing in their souls that their desire for each other would endure for eternity. He slowly let go of her.

"Kitty, I've never been so in love before," She looked at him, placed her hands behind his head, pulled him towards her, and kissed his face gently, softly and caressingly. It was a face she had known before.

Toon helped her close up the office, and at the last minute, she saved part of the new drawing on a USB stick in her bag, already knowing she wouldn't find time to work on the drawing. As they ran through the rain, she looked up into his eyes, where laughter greeted her with such force that she felt like a schoolgirl going on her first date. He drove behind her so she could pack her bag wherever he took her.

Toon followed her everywhere in the house. When she started to pack her overnight bag in her bedroom and took her evening dress off its hanger, he took it from her with one arm while encircling her.

"Kitty, please, will you wear it for me?"

'What, now?" Knowing very well where that would lead.

"Do you know what I went through when I saw you in this dress?"

"What do you mean, saw me?" Toon dropped the dress on the bed and started to kiss her neck and her shoulder down inside her blouse...then he gave her a big wide grin. "You don't know, do you?" She had difficulty not buckling from his penetrating stare.

"I had your whole opening ceremony videotaped since I could not be there physically; I would be with you from Cyberspace. I could not stand imagining what you would look like while others would see you in the flesh! That was inconceivable, so I organised a direct line, which took some doing."

"You mean the video camera, were you? I knew it!... A part of me knew it...and was it worth it?" Her eyes are brilliant with expectation.

"How did you know it was the biggest punishment I could give myself?" He uttered these words with such torment that she laughed.

"Toon Haardens, that served you right! Sneaking up on me!" Somehow, she must have picked up the frustration he was experiencing, looking at her and not being there.

"Kitty, you have no idea what I've been going through, especially with Ed...The thought of losing you again...but I'm forever grateful to Annelies for arranging Ed's welcome dinner that I asked for, I would have given anything to have been there. Did you remember the music?" His whispering as he was nibbling on her ear while pressing her firmly against him aroused her so she had difficulty staying calm.

"Oh, love...how clever of you to play that music at Ed's dinner! You knew I would want you to be there with me!" she said, trembling while removing his shirt.

"Oh, Kitty, I want you; I have been imagining this moment for I don't know how long. *To make love to you.*"... she could feel his longing for her had become close to a point of no return.

"Kitty, when is Jeroen coming home?" She quivered as he looked silently at her, waiting for an answer. She knew they had the whole evening to themselves. Jeroen was gone for the entire weekend, and there were no classes. His eyes told her that he had read her mind.

"I can't stop now. I want you, and I can feel you want me as well," he moaned while his hands were under her blouse. While he was undressing her and removing her blouse, she sagged in his arms. When he carried her to the bed, she heard him gasp when he re-moved all her clothes, feeling his hands moving over her breasts as if he were learning for the first time the intimacy of her body. His lips were on her nipples, and then he travelled all over her, explor-ing every detail.

She heard herself whimpering from ecstasy. What he was doing to her felt acutely intimate, and she was totally in harmony with who she was while moving with a rhythm that revealed all her sexual passions.

She felt the weight of his body pressing onto the length of hers, caressing her with purposeful insistence. He acted as if he needed no consent from her. She responded to him with every fibre of her being, and her arousal reached a point of total bliss. When their climaxes came simultaneously, she heard Toon gasping out of pure joy, and it gave her intense pleasure, knowing it was her body that made him feel so satisfied.

Ingrid felt a new spiritual sense that had been unconscious before suddenly sprang open from deep within. A reunion took place that was meant to be...She reached out in an embrace of wonder, know-ing she had never experienced lovemaking this way.

"Is it not wonderful that our bodies can give us so much joy?" he whispered after they both returned from a place where they had been completely one... She could hear his thoughts, "Kitty, you were well worth waiting for." How he looked at her told her everything about herself, and what he saw in her eyes was a reflection of himself.

"Snooks, I love you." ...her breathing was still unsteady after being swept into a different octave. They were lying next to each other, staring into each other's eyes, never to feel alone again. This reunion made them know with absolute certainty that they were twin souls. Their separation of aeons was over, and their new journey had just started.

Both were utterly independent individuals who had found their mirror image. Each knew that before, there had always been a lack of fulfilment in the many relationships they had both experienced, which they had not wholly realised until they came into each other's lives.

"Gosh, you are so deliciously perfect. When I saw you for the first time, I felt adoration for you so overwhelming that...I wanted to sweep you up and take you away with me there and then."

Ingrid snuggled up in contentment so that each with their thoughts slowly drifted away on a wave of pleasure....

After they had slept for at least three hours, Ingrid awoke and wondered when he had arrived in Holland. Toon was still sleeping, and she observed his face, nose, mouth, and whole body.

As she was reaching over, trying to look at the clock radio, he woke up and grabbed her by her waist, and while holding her on top of him, he admired her breasts that still retained their youthful firmness.

"Snooks, are you hungry?" While squirming away, feeling very exposed.

"And how! For you, yes!" Oh, how she loved this man, and he aroused her so much that she wanted to make love again! She could not resist doing to him what he had done to her, hearing him moaning, which made her even more excited. Toon suddenly rolled her on her back and entered her so fast that she gasped with pleasure. Ingrid felt a massive sense of relief, having found someone who could bring her so completely to this height of ecstasy.

"Kitty, this is almost a whole new way of experiencing sexual pleasure. When I entered you, such rapture came over me that it struck me like a shaft of lightning," he whispered while caressing her.

"Love, I'm very starved after making love to you. Please wear that silky dress, and let's go and have dinner. After that, I'll take you away for the whole weekend." The joy in his eyes matched hers as she stepped into the shower.

As the water cascaded over her body, she heard Toon asking Fred to book a table. While he took a shower, she dressed in Yolanda's creation, pinned the brooch on her shoulder, and dried her hair when he walked in. She could see that he was watching her in her mirror while she was observing his naked body. She turned around and stood in front of him, smiling at his face, and for the first time, she saw that he could be shy.

"Snooks, you have a magnificent body."

"Have you any idea what you look like through my eyes?" Toon's admiration as his hand travelled intimately over the deep-blue, silky fabric excited her.

"Snooks, you'd better stop that; otherwise, we'll never get away, and it's already eight o'clock!" Ingrid giggled in response to his fondling.

She fed Fluffball and left a note for Jeroen, telling him she went with Toon for the weekend. Suddenly, she spotted a blue envelope on the floor in the hallway that was not there before. She put it in her shoulder bag to read later.

When they arrived, Fred waited for them in the hotel's foyer. Ingrid wondered if he would know that they had made love.

"You have no idea how brilliant your auras look" Fred whispered so that nobody would hear.

"Toon, I ordered your taxi in two hours. In case Ingrid wants to change before you both leave, I have a table for you ready in the family dining room. Both Annelies and I will join you later for a late-night snack if that's all right?" Fred's eyes travelled appraisingly over her dress.

"Where are we going?" Ingrid whispered to Toon.

"You wait and see." The family dining room had an impressive decor.

"Snooks, I'm curious about this place. Will you tell me who the artist is?" Toon's eyes travelled over the artwork. Unusual paintings of worlds within worlds told a story only an image can achieve.

"Kitty, this dining room still holds memories of glorious and sorrowful times for me! I will tell you all its secrets and surprises one of these days. Leo Jaarsma, Ben's twin, is the artist."

The waiter arrived with their starter; they ate so quickly that Ingrid laughed. Toon's eyes shone with absolute glee, knowing how hungry lovemaking had made them.

"Well, if it is not the arch-manipulator who swept my sister-in-law away from me," Ed's voice broadcast. Ingrid saw Toon's face fleetingly express a hearty surprise; then he laughed while greeting his friend with a slap on the shoulder.

"What have you been up to?"

"I have a date with Yolanda. When Fred told me that you two were having a cosy, private late dinner, I thought I would join you while waiting for the others. When I wanted privacy with this lady, I did not get it, and we all knew why. Ingrid, you look breath-taking! Is that one of Yolanda's creations?"

"Are you remarking on the dress or the contents?' Toon teasingly remarked while pouring Ed's wine. Ingrid noticed how at ease and relaxed Ed was.

"My friend, when Yolanda arrives, you say nothing, do you hear? I've not revealed my telepathic skills yet, while I'm enjoying her response to my thoughts, but she is outstanding."

"Ed, that's not fair!"

"My dear, I can relate to him! You gave yourself away over the phone. I was unaware that you were telepathic because Ed never told me."

"When did you know then?" Thinking about how she had been aware of his mental probing.

"When I saw you for the first time, I heard every thought and sensed every detail of your emotions." Ingrid could feel herself blushing, and Ed smiled because he had heard it all.

"I'm not sure if I can or will keep quiet!" Ingrid beamed just as Annelies, Yolanda, and Fred joined them.

"Ingrid, your dress looks stunning! How are your drawings going, and what can you not keep quiet about?" The look Ed gave Yolanda triggered an idea of how to help her friend without giving anything away.

"Thanks, I can see you smite my brother-in-law. Do you know that?" As she felt Toon's hand sliding intimately over her thigh, she had to stifle a giggle. Her delight with the whole set-up was interrupted when Annelies' inquisitive mind projected:

"Ingrid, what is going on? Have I missed something?" she flirted with Toon, who tried to stare her down.

"How much did Annelies tell you about the Jaarsma Orphanage, Kitty?" Toon gleamed, steering the attention away from the mental dialogue.

"We were all asked to investigate our family history. Annelies, I've not told you this, but I spoke to my sister, Quincy, when we reviewed the family photos. We discovered that our grandmother Kitty Jaarsma had a twin sister."

"Is your sister younger or older, and is she telepathic like you?" Fred interrupted.

"She's a clairvoyant like you, but two years younger, blonde with blue eyes." Ingrid wondered why Fred was single.

"Is she married?" Yolanda asked.

"She's getting a divorce as her husband found someone else a few years ago," Ingrid's voice carried a tone of sadness for her favourite sister.

"I didn't know that! Oliver was her husband's name, I remember. A lawyer, I believe?" Ed commented while filling their drinks.

"Ingrid, did your grandmother awaken you and your sister's psychic skills? That would again confirm our research into the Jaarsma orphanage's history."

"Yes, my Gran died when I was nine, but my mother wanted nothing to do with any esoteric teaching, so she banned it from our home. Quincy pursued it more than I did; that's probably one of the reasons why she had problems with Oliver. He could not come to terms with it."

"How did you repress your telepathic skills, Ingrid, with Jan?"

"Ed, I wasn't aware that I was telepathic. I thought everyone could read others the way I did, and I learned that I had to stop making judgments about not being able to communicate with Jan in that way. When did..." Ingrid stopped. Covering her mouth with her hands when she suddenly realised what she was about to ask him. Instead, she stifled a giggle.

"Toon, did you teach Ed telepathy?" Yolanda looked at Toon, and her eyes widened.

"Ingrid, you must tell me, I, oh...Ed Barendse, if you do not reply to me mentally, I'll get up and leave this minute," Yolanda beamed so strongly that Ed practically choked on his wine. Ingrid saw Ed looking at her in a way that would make any woman quiver.

"I adore you even more when you are angry, but I know you are not angry, are you? I did so enjoy knowing and reading your feelings..." Ed projected on an open channel. Ingrid saw that Yolanda's blue eyes enlarged slightly, and Fred laughed.

"I might not verbally hear all your telepathic dialogue, but boy, the sparks flying in this dining room are truly a spectacle. What do you think, sister? Are we intruding on the two couples?"

"Toon, please tell Ingrid about your philanthropic passion for establishing communities," Annelies said, ignoring Fred's leaving intentions. Ingrid knew that Annelies was enjoying herself far too much to go now and wondered about Ben, her husband and how the private sessions with the others had been.

"What do you mean by a philanthropist, Annie? I work very hard for my living," Ingrid knew they greatly admired each other.

"Toon, what made you aware of what you had to do in your life?"

"Yolanda, as you know, I've lived in many countries where I've seen great wealth and incredible poverty. I can be very addicted to good living, but I could not enjoy it if it deprived anyone else."

"But what made you think about communities?"

"People are gifted in various ways, and humans must learn to pool their gifts and talents to survive, especially financially. I realised that I had found my opportunity by establishing community living environments for them since I have the means to do so, so I had to start exploring my passion."

"Finding you added meaning to my life, love."

Toon's sincerity and devotion to his purpose made her love him even more, and his love for her filled her with humility. She could see that Toon is a powerful, influential, and energetic person who attracts many people to him. She felt so grateful to have manifested this amazing soul in her life. His hand stroked her under the table.

"I feel that about you, too!"

"Toon, what is your vision of these communities?" Ingrid knew that Yolanda wanted to know this because of Ed's partnership in a settlement in Australia.

"When transformation occurs globally, within each human Soul, a working knowledge of what the individual wishes to contribute will awaken."

"Annelies, did you do the workshop with Toon?"

"Yes, Yolanda, I have been used as a guinea pig up to where you are now. When transformation happens, many people who fully immerse themselves in their higher selves' soul energy will express various talents, gifts, and skills they need to share." Toon replied as he watched the time.

"My love, because of the massive global physical transformations, the survival of our species will depend on the calibration level of consciousness from which each person operates." Ingrid could see how happy Yolanda was when Ed joined Toon's explanation.

"Kitty, I see our communities as light centres where everyone will contribute equally, and a new civilisation will flourish. For the last few hundred years, our world economic system has robbed people blindly. Our communities will operate under a new paradigm where people exchange their talents, skills, or gifts for daily commodities. I want to establish places where people will be free to do this, hoping they will stop selling themselves out for money or money-related privileges. Money is very much a biological trigger within most people's genetics. The fear of a lack of money keeps most people in tow and, therefore, susceptible to manipulation. "

"Oh, love, I'm so glad you said that."

"Ben would probably agree; his passion lies with exposing the dark forces that unconsciously have embodied many people on the planet who cannot access compassion because of their lack of feeling." All of a sudden, Toon looked gravely at Annelies.

"Toon, this new world order, as you called it over the phone once, are they aliens? Are they looking like humans, but they are not?" She still could not come to terms with it as it sounded like a science fiction script where people were being subjected to a controlling technique like brainwashing, shape-shifting and all that.

"Ingrid, remember that we discussed the dynamics of creating our reality when we project a magnetic thought vibration, like a radio that is broadcasting?" Annelies clarified.

"Yes, you mean that our thoughts attract people with similar ideologies and beliefs, meaning we broadcast on a similar wave band."

"Kitty, this new world order is represented by fallen angels who became demonic, fragmented Soul personalities that are addicted to being in control. They are NOT aliens, what they want you to believe. They do this by stealing energy. We see this reflected through the usury tactics called interest rates, to mention one. We are all, in a way, genetically brokered when we trace it back to our ancestral lineages."

"You mean, like politicians or businessmen who are unscrupulous?"

"Kitty, most people conform to behaviour that they think is acceptable to others rather than expressing who they are themselves. Do you agree?" The waiter served various mouth-watering snacks with their coffees and liqueur. She observed that Toon declined any alcohol and drank juice instead. She wondered about that.

"You will see."

"Yes, I see what you mean," she replied but tried to read Toon's mind. His grin made deep creases on his cheeks.

"Today, money has not only become the main controlling device. Electronic technology, such as cell phones, laptops, tablets, and other gadgets, is what our teenagers are brought up with. Hans worries they have more elaborate plans to put us back to sleep." Annelies added.

"Really, how?" Yolanda asked while looking at Hans

"Like doling out lots of money, they create out of thin air so that millions can buy stuff and put themselves back to sleep. Or by conducting a literal false-flag operation," He gravely replied

"They can control our external reality, but not our inner reality. We have to wake as many up as possible to what is happening inside of them that reflects what's happening outside them." Liesbeth added as a reminder.

Gosh, I know that most people can be bought, and dogmas, religious beliefs, and traditions do the rest, but how can anyone control 15 billion people?" The music from Amadeus enhanced the cosy family atmosphere. She looked up at Hans and Liesbeth, wondering.

"Who are they?" She asked out loud, wondering about POWAH, who was he?

"Ingrid, when we are outside the matrix, we can see things objectively, even going to hell and speaking with the demons there. They don't look very nice. They are conflicted beings and as devious as hell itself. Hell is not a place in the universe. It is just a space for accommodating those who disagree with the truth that we are all particles of god source." Hans explained

Looking through the window at people having coffee on the terrace outside, she wondered...

"Surely many people would not...I see...we are all wearing masks! Our personalities could very well be under the influence of some form of control." Ingrid suddenly realised how easy it would be.

"That's right, Kitty, and the moment you say 'I'm a unique aspect of all that exists, I am that I am,' you will be confronted with ridicule." Toon placed his hand protectively over hers on the table.

"The fear of facing this condemnation gets most people to behave like sheep, and fear, being the most powerful weapon, is then applied to ensure total control," Ed added, looking pensively at Annelies.

"Now I understand where you all are coming from. You mean that
if we want to live our lives from our awakened state, instead of still
being trapped in the matrix by the economic and physical snares,
your communities would be a sanctuary for awakened people to
hold on to their newfound freedom." Ingrid glanced at Toon with
understanding.

"Yes, quite right, but I have an ulterior motive. I love the activities
of building and creating beautiful environments, and this seemed
to be the way to go about it, especially the idea of a community on
water. In our small and densely populated country, meters below
sea level, we are most at risk from climate change and rising sea levels." She remembered Jeroen's enthusiasm as she peered at Ed.

"Already, a row of amphibious houses lines the waterfront at Maasbommel, all panelled in blue, yellow and green. They have a hollow
concrete cube at the base to give them buoyancy." Ed added.

"My love, we are trying to develop new types of more sustainable
buildings which have no adverse impacts on the environment. I'm
still a building engineer at heart. But you expressed it very well," his
arms slid around her waist while kissing her neck, "With you as a
partner, it'll be even more pleasurable."

"How did the two of you meet?"

Toon watched her... "You tell them, love." Yolanda's face turned into a worried frown as she listened. "I never knew that you worked
for that firm, Ingrid. How did I miss that?"

"But...I've talked to you about my work! You've asked me a few
times, remember?"

"It's the name Pleasure Parks that escaped me. I'm sorry" ...

"Toon, something is going on. Interpol investigated the firm." Ingrid
knew Ed was projecting to Toon, but there was a mental

screen...then she saw Annelies was showing one of her wavering expressions as if something had come to light.

"Toon, why did you buy that landscaping business? Was it to get closer to Harry Brinks or Ingrid?" Toon raised his eyebrows.

"Annie, is Ben still undercover?" Ingrid was surprised by Toon wanting to get to Harry Brinks. What was Annelies getting at, and where was her husband?

"Yes, he is" she sighed. "But I know that Interpol has greatly harassed Harry Brinks. He told me so, and you know Ben, I wouldn't be surprised that he knows much more about what is happening. Toon, do you know where Trevor is?" Both Fred and Annelies expressed unease.

"Toon, what are they after, do you know?"

"I don't know, Annie, "Leo has asked me about the site where the tunnels are, but I don't know why." Ingrid knew that Toon had responded to Annelies telepathically, but he was almost screening the rest. Why?

"I'll tell you all about that soon, love. Please, will you go and change into something warm and comfortable... *Yolanda, you did a terrific job, but. Ed, the content is for my enjoyment, thanks to you."*

Ingrid pushed him playfully for that last mental remark. The atmosphere in the dining room lightened up.

"Ed, can you explain why Toon is thanking you?" Yolanda asked Ed directly. Ed was throwing his head back, laughing and wrapping his arms around her.

"Often when Toon and I were having a drink together in Australia, we used to brag about the women in Holland to the other Australian guys. I often used Ingrid as an example, and Toon mentioned his cousin occasionally, as I recall."

She could see that most at the dinner table had followed Ed's telepathic communication. "Both Otto, your uncle, and Toon taught me telepathy, and Ingrid and the Barendse family are also related to the Jaarsma orphanage," Ed said more for Fred's benefit.

"I didn't know that," Ingrid voiced when she was on the point of leaving. Ed looked up at her, and in the silence of his stare, he projected something she knew only she could hear.

"I'll always have a special love for you, you know. Goodbye, Ingrid."
She knew this was Ed's way of closing a chapter in their lives. Toon got up as well to get her overnight bag from his car...

Chapter 15
Emotional and Mental Addictions

Buttercup Valley

The taxi driver, who seemed to know Toon, took their bags. Ingrid decided to relax and see what surprise Toon had for her. It was now completely dark outside, and they both longed to be alone.

"You've made me the happiest man by just being here with me," he gazed as he held her close in the back seat. She was again the young girl in her dream, beautiful and desirable.

"What do you remember, Kitty?" Her dream lingered like a movie she had been watching somewhere in Canada.

"Everything, I think, and you went away!" she beamed.

"I'll never do that again. It still haunts me, you know, that I went away to find greener pastures, leaving you behind." The silence created a timeless cocoon.

"Where are we?" She mumbled when the taxi came to a stop. From the car window, she saw the outlines of small aeroplanes. She vaguely recalled reading the name Soesterberg. She could feel a slight breeze blowing when she got out, while Toon took their bags.

"Have a good flight, sir."

"Are we flying?"

"Are you frightened of flying?"

"Are you kidding? I love it!" She looked around, somehow expecting to see more people.

"Toon, who's flying the aeroplane?" Toon did not reply, but he took her bag and opened the plane's back door, parked in front of a hangar.

He went in first, then took her hand and guided her into her seat up in the front. She was sitting next to the pilot, that much she knew. Then, the next moment, Toon climbed into the pilot seat! He teased her with his eyes, settled her in and placed a pair of head-phones on them.

She listened intently to the radio, giving out a burst of tower talk that sounded like the static sound of another world. She felt exhil-arated at the prospect of flying. Toon talked to the control tower people who all knew him! Lights were glowing on the panel in the front, and Toon was taking the small eight-seater plane to the start of the runway. Then, with a forward thrust accompanied by a long, perilous run, gathering power and going faster and faster, the plane went up while her stomach jumped into her throat.

Looking outside, she could still see the ground under them and the tops of trees slipping past. There was enough light to see that everything became smaller, and the exhilaration of being free of the ground made her wonder again who this man she would spend her life with.

"Kitty, please love, can you reach behind you on the seat in the back for my laptop and take it on your lap? I need some information from it." When she positioned it and switched it on, Toon instruct-ed her, and a map appeared. Oh, dear, she was not the best map reader! What now? She was out of her depth.

"Kitty, look at the lever on your right in front of you, next to your control button; now punch that number in on the left-hand corner of your screen."

Suddenly, the map changed, enlarging a portion of it. Toon turned the laptop to face him and looked at it, then started speaking to the control tower through the microphone attached to his headphones...

After that, they both sat silently, enjoying each other's company. It was getting jet black outside, and the lights below twinkled. She wondered how long they were going to fly and where. Toon was talking to someone down below, somewhere in the outer world.

"Oh, Kitty, I've dreamed of this moment all my life; I've searched for you in many women and never found what I was looking for. Then, at my lowest depth of despair, when I had let it all go, I released my searching for good, knowing I had to look for my fulfilment within myself when I heard this voice: I would never give you the idea, the desire, and the wish, without also giving you the power to make it true. Kitty, after hearing that voice, knowing they were not my thoughts, I knew that one day I would find you again."

The awesomeness of almost hearing his thoughts took her back, reminding her of the scenery from another place, knowing they were the same Souls, living out a lifetime on this planet. What she had learned from her opportunity card helped her to gain some perspective. Annelies had told them to be aware and become observers, and that tests would come up for each during the two weeks before they would have an inner circle together.

Looking outside, flying through the clouds had an almost hypnotising effect. So much had happened since she had started the decoding workshops. Her reality was truly changing, but how had that happened? The laptop on her lap suddenly transferred into the familiar background and text, switching her attention back to the present.

<Dear Kitty, there are many energy cords connecting Souls. You have made a strong Soul connection with your beloved in many different time zones.>

Good grief, how was that possible? Was she imagining POWAH's text? How could her higher self connect to the laptop and communicate by producing text for her to read?

<Kitty, you are not separated from your energetic consciousness, I Am. That feeling of separation from everything else is just an illusion. In any reality, there is no separation.>

She sensed the hurt in her dream for the loss of Mc. Nealy was what POWAH was referring to. How was it that even high up, flying in a small plane, POWAH managed to link up with her? Was she mentally such an open book? Could it be that their physical world was becoming less dense? Is communicating telepathically with other dimensions a sign of their time? How could someone or somebody know what was in her mind? What field or energy separates people's thoughts, creating an illusion that thoughts are private?

<Your intentions, desires and secrets are well-known to your higher self. That is why a past life memory is now surfacing. The relational cords between the two of you from the second chakra were prematurely damaged, owing to the choices you made at that time.>

Toon showed his surprise when she started to type, but she had to ask.

POWAH, what energy makes me quiver every time he looks at me? How could we feel so connected again if we had damaged each other's relational cords?

Then Toon beamed. *"With whom are you conversing? Not me!"*

<You have both chosen to reconnect in this lifetime. You both need to heal this relational cord to experience the union of life's fruitfulness in both your sensual and sexual activities. Your core stars in your solar plexus were activated when you came into physical contact.>

Wow, did it ever! She still revelled at the instant attraction she felt for Toon, like a spark of lightning, but the replaying text kept bewildering her

<Kitty, your life force in the front and back of your sacral chakras made contact, connecting you both with your heart chakras so that you both mature to an awakened consciousness of compassion and unconditional love in this life. You will help each other to awaken and express the full I AM you are in this lifetime.>

Toon tried to see what she was doing and freed his hand from the controls. Before she could stop him, he turned the laptop towards him, studying the question that she'd asked POWAH. She now wondered if he could also read POWAH's text. After reading it all, he looked into her eyes, and its effect on her was almost too much to bear.

"Kitty, you've been playing with me from the first moment you saw me. When I saw you the first time, I wanted to make love to you on the spot in your office! You were wearing a soft green silk blouse that revealed a pair of beautiful, sensual breasts that reacted immediately to me. Still, it was so contradictory to your actions that you made me believe it was in my imagination. Even when I could read your thoughts, I was not sure! How did you manage that?"

She had difficulty not giggling.

"It was pure self-control. You do not own me," Toon laughed out loud. *"Are you kidding yourself? We are at one with each other,"* He beamed while stroking her thigh.

<Kitty, when you both respect the uniqueness of your mate, you will activate a deep, holy, natural urge to mate on the physical level and the deep spiritual yearnings to unite with Divinity. This reunion represents the marriage of both the spiritual and physical aspects of two human beings.
Love to both of you.>

POWAH.

The silence between them took her back just after Jim had passed. Now, she recalled that she had sincerely asked to be in connection with her higher-soul self. If only to fully understand the reasons for living.

July in the Alps

Ingrid woke up with a jolt...when she heard Toon's voice speaking to the control tower below. Far down in a valley, she saw a sweep of trees with snow-capped mountains in the distance. They had been flying for a long time. Switzerland, Germany! Where were they? Vaguely, she remembered that they had landed before, but Toon hadn't woken her. The sun was coming up through the clouds. Toon flew southeast towards the highest mountains that obstructed the sun's path. Some houses with steeply pitched roofs appeared when the sunlight reached the snow in the crevices. Had she been sleeping while missing all this fantastic scenery before her? And Toon! Her love for him had turned into a concern, thinking he must be tired, for he'd been behind the controls for at least five hours!

"Are you awake?"

"Snooks, I never realised, but I must have slept for hours," The clock on the panel in front of her said 5.05.

"Good grief! You must be tired and stiff. Have you not moved from your seat all this time?" She was feeling stiff all over. They circled downward as she saw the rocky ground approaching and the ring of mountains rising higher, with the peaks drawing closer together in the sky. Then she felt a thump. One moment, they were free, and the next moment, they were touching the ground. The aeroplane landed on a small concrete strip, and someone ran toward their plane.

Toon took his headset off and looked at her like a true lover looks at his beloved.

"Welcome to Buttercup Valley."

"You're kidding. Is there such a place? Snooks, where are we?"

Suddenly, the door at the back swung open, and a man in his sixties came inside.

"Hi, folks; I expected you earlier. Were you held up?"

"I rested for an hour at Luxembourg airstrip before take-off. I'm delighted to see you so well," Toon replied, shaking the man's hand.

"Toon!" Thinking this man had been without proper sleep for far too long. Toon introduced her to OTTO as they moved out of the plane. Otto's windswept hair matched his beard, both of which were white with a dark brown undertone.

Otto climbed down first, grabbed her hand, and stood shaking on a small concrete runway, cushioned on both sides with a thick cushion of sloping grass sprinkled with wildflowers. She was transported by the profound stillness in the early morning as the light streamed down from behind the mountains. At that moment, a profound sense of being in the presence of sacredness transformed her entire being. But where was she? In the distance, she saw yellow Buttercups, almost laughing at her, all happily growing as if planted just for fun, to express creation in all its glory.

"My dear lady, did you have a good trip?" The older man with dark, penetrating eyes asked. She felt in a short moment, while he observed her, that she was being evaluated on the spot like a prize piece of real estate! The man suddenly produced a great loud sound that came from far. His face was full of joy but, at the same time, emanating wisdom and compassion.

"Toon, she's all you said she would be! Congratulations." Toon glowed like a young schoolboy who had just received a medal.

They strolled toward a row of small log cabin cottages set deep into the woods with beautiful flower boxes and ornate windows. When they walked past a sign, she stopped and read what it said: **By your choice, you dwell now in the world you created. What you hold**

in your heart will be true, and what you most admire, that you will become.

A woman about the same age as Otto sat on a wooden veranda in front of a charming traditional wooden chalet. She had one of those faces that showed no age at all.

"I have no idea where I am, but for all it's worth, your place is one of the most breathtaking properties I've ever seen."

Toon introduced Jill, and as they shook hands, her firm grip suggested that Jill was one of those women from the sixties who remained idealists, loving the land and being very independent. Ingrid looked at Toon and felt it suddenly her duty to take some control.

"Toon, before you show me around, I insist you nap now! You look tired. Jill, just now, I realised that he hadn't had any proper sleep since returning from South Africa!"

Grinning from ear to ear, Toon held her tightly as they followed Jill, who agreed with her. They followed her on a path that took them past several log cabins with ornate wooden railings that enclose the porch areas.

The crisp air and silence were invigorating. She was mesmerised when they stopped at a more extensive, secluded, traditional, handmade timber mountain cabin.

Their charming log-cabin style mountain chalet had lovely timber furnishings inside that complemented the setting of the Alps. The living area displayed a love of wood, with captivating and original furnishings leading into the large bedroom with a private dry-heat sauna and Jacuzzi.

The bedroom had a veranda with panoramic mountain views overlooking the valley below.

"Now I know what you meant by good living. What a magical setting!" Toon opened the sliding doors wide and, from behind, encircled her as she leaned on the wooden railing, admiring the view.

"Kitty, I've waited for aeons to take the woman of my desire to a sanctuary like this and to share with her the joy of being alive," he whispered. Toon's jawline reminded her of the first time she had seen him in her office, a face of rare serenity and unflinching perceptiveness without pain, fear, or guilt.

"Please, Toon, take a nap; I'm going to look around," firmly removing herself from his embrace.

She strolled around outside the cottage while Toon reluctantly obeyed. She revelled at the fragrance of pure air and the view down through the treetops to where the concrete rectangle of the airfield marked the bottom of the valley. Where could he have taken her after almost four hours of flying? He must be an experienced pilot. She knew this place to be high up because there was a crispness in the atmosphere that was free of any pollution. Looking down the valley gave her a feeling of belonging. Birds made summer sounds, busy with their existence, and nature made its music...she felt like resting and sat down admiring the peacefulness...

Gradually, she became aware of the sound of an animal grazing nearby. Her watch indicated it was still reasonably early, but she must have dozed off. She climbed toward the cottage from the other side of the slope when Otto and Jill's cottage came into view. Jill waved to her.

"Come and join me for some tea and warm strudels with fruit if you are hungry. I saw you walking around and lying down near Bambi's grazing pad. I knew he would look after you! Have you rested?"

"Yes, thank you." The aroma of warm apples made her hungry as she sat down. More Buttercups and cornflowers of all colours decorated the surroundings.

"Since when is this valley called Buttercup Valley?"

"As far as I can remember, it was always called Buttercup Valley because of the many varieties of Buttercups that grow here."

"Jill, what is this place? Do people come here for holidays? Does this valley belong to you?"

"Good grief, no! It all belongs to Toon. We're just the caretakers for as long as needed, and then we move on."

"Move on to where?" Otto joined them, helping himself to the most mouth-watering apfelstrudels she had ever tasted.

"So, we finally meet Ingrid! Toon never stopped talking about you the last time he was here," he looked to his wife for confirmation. *"She's stunning! Toon has good taste,"* she heard, but pretended she didn't.

"Ingrid wants to know where we move on when leaving here. I think she is one of us; what do you..."

"That'll take some time before we move on. Toon purchased this valley six months ago, and the building plans have not yet been approved."

"Is this becoming one of the communities that Toon says he's building worldwide?" How many communities did this man build around the globe all at the same time?

"Yes, this is the first one in Europe. It is magnificent. Toon has a special nose for these faraway places." Otto replied proudly.

"Have you always planned this together, the communities, I mean? You're his half-brother, aren't you?" As Jill poured more tea, she suddenly remembered where she'd heard the name Otto before.

"Yes, we go back a long way. Let me think: Toon was taken in as a foster child by my father in his second marriage when he was four or five. They brought him up as their own. I'd left home already by then, so we only really got to know Toon when he took over the running of his family's many enterprises when he turned twenty-one."

"He seems to be very busy with lots of interests."

"Toon's grandfather was a self-made millionaire, and Toon's parents, Steven and Siska, died in a car crash when he was only seven months old." Otto was munching away at the pastries filled with fruit.

"His grandparents took him in, but they were killed in a tramway accident in Amsterdam a year later when they were visiting Toon's mother's family in Holland. He was left behind at the Jaarsma orphanage until foster parents could be found.

"Really... Toon as well?"

"Yep, we all belong to the Jaarsma Clan."

"So, it seems. How extraordinary."

My family prepared him to run his grandfather's business enterprises under the supervision of the chairman of the Technology Committee of the World Enterprise Union Legislature. His grandfather made many stipulations in his will. Previously, his only son, Toon's uncle, Steven Haardens, was managing his companies."

"Otto, have you been talking her head off?" Jill teased when she came back with a new pot of tea.

"Jill, she knows nothing about Toon."

"We only really got to know him when he was a young bloke then, full of crazy ideas and thrown in a world where his outlook on life was rarely accepted."

"Are you a Civil or Building Engineer too?"

"We both are," Otto said with pride. The sparkle in their eyes and how they observed each other made her realise how strong a bond was between them.

"There you all are, having a treat, I see!" Toon joined them, grabbing a chair. Jill poured the tea while Toon helped himself to the delights on the sideboard.

"Did you have a good rest?"

"Yes, I did." As he stretched his long body, his eyes studied her with an intensity that triggered a flutter in her belly.

"What have you been doing while I was asleep? I missed you when I woke up," Ingrid heard, but she would not react.

"She's been sleeping too, right in Bambi's paddock."

"What, did he allow that?" Toon remarked in surprise. "At that moment, the sound of a truck filled the valley; it stopped in front of their cottage, and their quiet, intimate breakfast party was over. In big letters, Buttercup Construction and Landscaping Co were written on the side of the lorry.

"Who's Mr. Haardens?" a man asked when he jumped from the cabin.

"I am." Toon inspected the docket, signed it and handed it to Otto while checking the lorry's contents.

Ingrid felt suddenly out of place in her creased clothes. She wanted to refresh herself and change into something more casual, seeing that Toon had changed into jeans and a casual shirt.

"Toon, I'm going to take a shower. I'll see you later. I can't wait to see your plans for this place."

While climbing the path to their cottage, she could feel that the two men were following her with their eyes, as evidenced by the sound of Otto saying something and Toon laughing in response. Ingrid would have loved to know what they were laughing at because she had not received it mentally.

Toon's clothes were hanging over the chair, and the laptop was on the bed. It felt wonderfully intimate to walk into the bedroom they would share. The sauna was already turned on. She stood in the shower for as long as she could, shedding the sensation of stiffness and feeling her body return to new life. All the cells, atoms and molecules were revitalised with each moment.

Big white terry towels were in the bathroom when she remembered the cream she had thrown into her shoulder bag. She was about to retrieve the tube when she looked at the screen of Toon's laptop, which was still on. With one touch, the screen changed, and a bright, familiar background with large text appeared. It was a conversation with POWAH! She could not stop herself from reading.

<Hello, Toon, this is POWAH. It took synchronistic manipulations from the realms of illuminated truth to unite both of you in this final chapter of your planet's history. Are you pleased?>

Who are you? Toon had typed.

<I have been given the job (I believe you call it) of guiding both of you. I AM the love, the light and the life of creation. I AM YOU. Are you pleased?>

Are you also communicating with Ingrid in this way, through both our minds?

<Yes, I'm the primal sun group Soul that speaks. Toon, you are one of the few awakened Souls that belong to the top environmental group spirit, and together with Kitty, you are committed to reinstating the elemental true energies of the global planetary spirit. We salute you. I have chosen this form of communication by using both your sixth and seventh chakra energy vortices. You both have an affinity with symbols. Words are symbols in the written text. I asked you a question: are you pleased?>

That was the first time POWAH identified himself as a primal sun group Soul, whatever that is.

Yes, I'm delighted! POWAH, is there a higher purpose to our union?

I remember that we lived together in other lifetimes. Did I hurt her so deeply that it took me almost a lifetime to find her? Are Ingrid and I together to prepare each other for the birth of the new earth to which the ancient scripts refer? I seem to have lived in similar communities. Are they visions of the future or the past or what?

YES, to your question. You can theoretically remember every life that was lived on this planet and others as if you were the one who lived it.>

Why did it take so long to find her?

<The I AM seed within needs to be re-awakened first, and some experiences must be re-lived to bring back the memory of the Soul's purpose. Toon, remember that time is not real. You live many lives simultaneously and on interplanetary planes. You are synchronistically attuned to community living because you created many communities of light at other timeline periods. They are still around! There is also some inner work that needs to be done between the two of you, and your chakra systems must be realigned to achieve true rejuvenation. >

<Some healing and internal forgiveness must be experienced by both of you. At a later stage, you must share the latest news so that the people who are ready to hear have access to this new way of living and together, you will accomplish a lot.>

POWAH, what is my Soul's purpose?

<To acknowledge the I AM presence within you. Then, the I AM will amplify your effectiveness a thousand-fold. You are one of the awakened ones who have returned and chosen to re-main fully incarnated during the awakening of your planet.>

Do you mean that I can physically ascend, even at fifty?

<Yes, if that would be your Soul's choice. If the speed of energy in the atoms of an awakening physical body were to accelerate beyond the speed of light, that person would vanish from your world and appear on another plane of quantum reality. You will physically ascend when you have fulfilled your Soul's purpose. You will stop your ageing process when your cellular restruc-turing returns again to a crystalline cell that will rejuvenate it-self. Your etheric Light body, you can inter-space travel, which makes a reversal of ageing possible. The awakened ones are the healthy cells in my planetary organ of intelligence. The teach-ers, healers, builders, and visionaries teach the laws of love. POWAH signing off.>

The screen went back to its screen saver. Ingrid sat on the bed thinking that if POWAH were communicating on the same mind wave as theirs, would people automatically attract similar mind waves toward themselves? She speculated why she had only started remembering things that so obviously belonged to another time, when suddenly the screen responded to her thoughts. Usually, she never spies on someone else's laptop, but somehow, she felt she was meant to read their conversation.

<At the beginning of Earth's physical formation, an organic DNA coding was created to divide human civilisations into seven distinct periods for the Soul's initiations. Humanity evolved through ensouling seven great successive root races. Do your research about the origin of humanity, but always stay in your present awareness. Only awareness and energy exist. When attention has the power to "do" something, that energy forms in the shape of light called photons; look it up.> She stared in awe at the screen. How was her mind putting words on the screen? But it can't be...she...would she dare type and ask a question?

POWAH, have Toon and I been incarnated in different lifetimes many times?

She always wondered who answered the questions when she felt a loving energy engulfing her.

<Reincarnation under the great impulses of time affects solar systems, planets, man, animals, plants, and all forms of life. It is one vast, continuous process of repeatedly strengthening, individualising and refining. The law of rebirth holds the secret of the present crisis. Groups of souls come together to work out karma created simultaneously.> She wondered what present crisis POWAH was referring to.

<During each lifetime, the Soul must merge more with the physical form to dominate the physical situation and assert its authority.>

Ingrid understood that an aspect of her Soul connected or channelled through her higher self. But why and how could she suddenly be in two different time zones all at the same time?

<Kitty, sometimes emotional factors bring people back together, life after life. Your I AM is choosing many lifetimes to experience different aspects of itself. When it reaches a specific goal, it again makes a choice, either to leave the physical body to be born into a different incarnation or, during these transformative times, it can add another lifetime to this one.> Was it adding another lifetime? Did he mean she would not leave this body ever? Somehow that didn't...

<Before birth, your IAM chooses the genetic ancestral blueprint most suited to your spiritual growth. These DNA grid formations build a body. In a sense, you separate a portion of your greater being, and the fragmented consciousness part creates a body. If you complete that purpose in this lifetime and reach a specific goal, you can add another lifetime if you choose to do so. You interweave previous I AMs instead of seeding a new I AM aspect that would incarnate into the next incarnation. Both you and Toon have made that choice; have you not?>

Somehow, it made sense to her, and she even felt that her body was different already, as if she were in a new cycle. Was that why she remembered experiences from other lifetimes?

<Kitty, your body template is a tool you have created to focus on specific points within the self that you wish to transform most efficiently. The biggest problem at this moment in Earth time is to obtain this broader perception that is necessary to produce a healing effect on higher levels.> She now wondered if all the conspiracies about alien hybrids that were in control of humanity were true. The chirping of birds outside and her interaction with POWAH felt so...unreal. As if she were already on a different

plane, but were they? It was as if the text kept appearing when she thought of a question.

<The individual human mind is restricted by the narrow perceptions that the brain is programmed to receive. Your awareness is one face of the trillions of awareness in the Deity Planes. And, just as "god" can create anything, so can you. You are also from the god-source awareness field. There is no such thing as another "type" of god of alien other than all the awareness levels sharing awareness.>

Ingrid's whole body tingled out of awe, wondering if her interaction with POWAH was unique.

<Kitty, all human beings are capable of travelling and experiencing the many multi-dimensional aspects of creation if only they desire to learn and develop the skills. Instead, they concern themselves entirely with mastering the outer visible material world. When your mind begins to drift along the consciousness spectrum away from time-space perception, and this happens during your dream state, or while contemplating, meditating, or while being so engrossed in a creative art form that you become less aware of the immediate physical world, you will become conscious in another you: your IAM, your guardian angel. The problem lies in perception and the translations of it. Many are misguided by using current space analysis and measurement systems.>

Considering her two life cards from Annelies' workshop, she understood it better. She did wonder what her obstacles were and if she could overcome them.

<Kitty, do you want to find out?> The question practically jumped at her.

Did she have the courage to find out? She wanted to live out this lifetime, fulfilling her Soul's full potential. If that included discovering if she could overcome her obstacles, she would...or hoped she hadn't asked for something she would regret later!

< Kitty mastery means to eliminate victim consciousness. It means to be free of physical death as a necessity. It means integrating your Soul, mind, and spirit with your body. >

Then, the screen changed, and a familiar page showing excerpt sixteen appeared with rule number six. Something was not right. Where was rule five? Or excerpt fifteen? She was sure one was missing.

Excerpt Sixteen[1]
Program Planet Earth
Becoming Aware of Emotional and Mental Addictions
Rule Six *of the Ascending Decoding card game.*

< This is one of the man's most difficult addictions to let go of. When under the control of the ego during great duress and stress, the power of the mind will activate the mental self-programming of the illusion. > POWAH's message made her think of all the conspiracy theories on social media. That humanity is being lied to and controlled by a group of beings from their physical world and other dimensions. How much was true? How was it possible that what she was physically observing around her was an illusion?

< Man escapes into his fantasy world to not feel separated from the source and Soul. Nothing ever comes to you that is beyond your conscious, available mind. What is in your mind will make its appearance in your physical world. Kitty, only when you no longer accept anger, hatred, guilt, and conflict as being real or having value will there be no reason for them to be in your thoughts. Above all, choose love and peace above anything else in any situation.
Love POWAH >

---

1. https://allrealityshifters.wordpress.com/powah/the-reality-shifters-excerpt-16/

She must ask Toon to print this out for her journal, which she will give to Annelies the following week before the group's reunion. Ingrid wondered if she could adopt love and peace in any situation. Piet came into her vision, and she was troubled by her intolerance towards him. At least it said that you had to be aware of the addictive behaviour within yourself.

She started to shiver, for she had been contemplating the excerpt, and it was still not warm this morning.

The sauna's heat welcomed her, and the smell of the herbs invigorated the confined space. As she poured water on the hot coals, a lot of steam arose, and she revelled in the luxury of it all. Toon had been very open-minded about POWAH. Would another man have been? She'd always wondered what sharing metaphysical subjects with a partner would be like.

Suddenly, she felt cold air coming in. Toon's eyes travelled slowly over her body as he closed the door. *"Kitty, you are beautiful; you are made for making love, too."* She held her breath instantly, knowing that she had betrayed how much she wanted him. She gasped when his hands caressed her all over. The steam had gone, and they saw each other. Her smile told him she had permitted him long ago...so long ago. He took her simply in the quivering act of her total surrender to him, merging with her.

"Oh, Snooks, I...never realised how much I missed this sexual pleasure."

"I've been an absolute saint to have waited so long. The first moment I saw you in your office. You were on the phone. I went almost dizzy for a moment when your silky sleeve slid away to reveal a beautiful, round, soft"...his finger travelled slowly over the contours of her breast.

"That's what I must have felt then; you mentally were already making love to me." She nibbled his ear as they heard the phone ringing in the bedroom.

"That must be Otto." Toon carried her out of the sauna onto the bed, where they admired each other's nakedness in full sunlight.

Toon answered his cell phone and, after a few minutes, told Ingrid that Otto had invited them for lunch.

"We'd better get dressed then," Ingrid giggled when his eyes turned hopeful. "Hey, Toon!" she said, jumping away.

"Snooks, I saw you had a communication with POWAH on your laptop. How do you think it happens, the interaction?"

"I have no idea, but Leo and Trevor will know, and the more I experience, the more I realise how little I know." The joy in his eyes mirrored her feelings as they got dressed, switching her off from trying to remember who Leo was.

"You look stunning as always," Toon took her hand as they walked past several empty cottages. Happiness bubbled up like she had not known for so long that she had to squeeze his hand to confirm it was real.

"Toon, thank goodness, you've finally come back to us. Ingrid, when Toon met you, he slowed us down with this project for at least six weeks. The last time he came flying in was only to cut Buttercups from the valley," Otto mocked, wanting to get back at Toon for his neglect.

Toon's piercing look at Otto made her smile.

"Don't give everything away all at once," Ingrid remembered the Buttercups he'd brought in that first day he walked into her office. Now she realized they were the same flowers growing all over here! She adored him for that particular gesture.

"Come and join us on the veranda, you two. Jill, come and sit down and let Greta take over. We need you here now." Otto was ordering them around a makeshift drawing table with a big map with lots of loose paper, drawings and sketches.

"Before all of you explain anything to me, first, I want to know exactly where we are!"

"Toon, didn't you tell her?"

"Jill, there was no time! You can imagine the Inquisition I would have had if I had told her I intended to fly to the Alps in Austria!"

"You're kidding me?" Otto took her by the arm and brought her to a big aerial map on the wall inside the cottage. This valley is a part of the Rhaetian Alps!

During lunch, which Greta, a local girl from a nearby village, had served on a sideboard, Jill told her a bit about how they'd all worked together in the past on many big construction sites all over the world and how they'd practically adopted Toon, whose only dreams were to do the impossible. Otto and Toon were earnestly debating engineering problems. She turned to the drawing table to see if she could determine what they had in mind.

"Snooks, where are your proposal plans? I see lots of papers with ideas, but" ...Toon came over and explained on a clean sheet the vision he had in mind for the community. She listened to his schemes and wanted to add some ideas and suggestions.

"Oh, love, how I wish I had my office on my back! I'm eager to make you a proposal plan so that you can show your contractors what you have in mind. Nobody will make head or tail of these scribbles,"

Ingrid's frustrations blew while Toon snuggled up from behind and whispered, "What do you need, Kitty?" Leaning back against him, she replied.

A desktop computer with a professional 3D drawing tool and pencil sketching programs. Symmetry tools ... paper and a photocopier to expand them to A3 size for my overlay keyboard...Photoshop, a scanner...She was thinking about what she used in her office...Oh, and a wide 3D screen if possible, to display any 3D content on it; the lot. I'll have to do it at the office after hours."

"Ingrid, I'm sure that Toon has all that equipment at his added office attached to your cottage. Come, put that girl to work. We've earned it after all your temporary diversions."

"Hey, she's here to relax, and she hasn't seen anything of the valley, not to mention the lake! Stop ordering us all about," Toon complained to Otto, but with a grin on his face as deep down he began to enjoy getting to know Ingrid.

"Snooks, take me to your office. I can see the property later. Jill, thank you for that lovely lunch, but I'd better get to work, and I'm too excited to go sightseeing now."

"*Toon, you could not have picked a better partner! You'll go far, mark my words.*" Otto approved. When Toon took her to the back of their chalet, where wooden steps brought them to the enclosed porch showing her his office, she had to be firm with him as she could not do any work if he hung around staring at her with spaniel's eyes.

"Snooks, go away! I cannot concentrate! Go and do what you must, and come back later."

"This isn't what I had in mind; I want to do other things," he sighed while looking at her shapely bottom that was showing up from the stretch of the pantsuit she was wearing.

"*I just can't get enough of you; I've been starving all those years! I have to make up for it, don't you see?*" Toon fondled her all over. "

Snooks, I heard that! Go away and come back at, say...four o'clock. I want to see the valley and everything around here before it gets dark," she beamed while she pushed him out of the office....

Chapter 16
The 'Lower will' and the Higher Self

Community living

Ingrid was in her element with Toon's multi-monitor and program hardware that supported a wide range of graphics cards that could create the 3D effect. A part of her that needed to play came to the surface. During those moments of absence from the mundane world around her, the unresolved obstacles she'd carried into this life came up. As if something in her mind was triggered, freeing her to remember.

While doing her work, her mind drifted off...into a different plane of reality.

Ingrid felt herself standing in a different room, also at a drawing table, but the drawings were very different, almost...as if she had experienced this before! It was just a vision...But the graphics were more of the planets? The universe? the galaxies? Her tools were old-fashioned, and she wondered what period it was...

She returned to her 3D layouts of the community centre and was so engrossed in her work that she didn't hear Toon coming in until he encircled her waist and kissed her neck amorously. " *Kitty, I missed you.*"

"Toon, how many lives do you remember?" She was thinking about her flashbacks.

"I remembered that I lost you," he murmured, burying his head in her neck and clutching her so hard that it almost hurt, but she didn't stop him, and for a long time, they just stood there...

"Kitty, I...words that say it are inadequate," he muttered while she turned, holding him tightly.

"Kitty, this will only end up one way." She knew what he meant, but then he gasped, staring over her shoulder at her work, and let go of her.

"Kitty, that's it, you've got it!"

"Talk about rejection," she laughed while he was studying her drawings.

"Love, a large part of me has only one thing in mind, and you feed it constantly. "He got hold of the significant printer that could copy her Artist impressions and pressed the button for an A1 poster-size print.

He took the poster, rolled it up and guided her on the path past the empty log cabins. The whole valley looked like it was once a holiday resort of sorts.

"Otto, come here! Look at this," he exclaimed excitedly, "I told you she reads my mind! She's drawn it exactly how I've seen it with my mind's eye. Including the Healing Domes. Isn't she a marvel?" His pride in her while displaying the drawings on the table was captivating.

"Yes, amazing. Ingrid has drawn several healing domes where people's stress and pain are reduced through harmonic resonance. Otto, you have always said that we will use vibrational medicine with Quantum Sounds and real sunlight technology in the future." I'm impressed. Jill remarked.

Both Otto and Jill studied her proof layout and loved it. They discussed their implications, and Toon took her for a stroll. She fell in love with Buttercup Valley.

***

When they walked through a gorge where a field full of yellow Buttercups greeted them, her eyes widened in absolute amazement.

The profound stillness was broken when she heard how water can create a melody when it breaks up in waves against the shore. A large lake that mountains had hidden suddenly dominated the scenery.

"Snooks, who is going to live here? Who decides that?"

"That seems to happen without me having anything to do with it. Otto and Jill joined me in this venture, and there are many others you haven't met yet. We already have seven communities almost running: one in South Africa, one in New Zealand, one in Australia, one in the UK and three in the United States. This is Europe's eighth and first one, apart from the community that will be built on water." Ed is a partner in the one in Australia, as you know, and in the floating project in Holland."

"Yes, he told me something about it. I was amazed at how he has changed, or we probably both have!"

"When did you see him last, I mean before now?"

"When we had Jan's funeral, I was not the best company. I was so tired emotionally and physically that I had no energy left for him and just wanted to close that chapter in my life. He needed some comfort that I could not give him. Something happened between us long ago that I misunderstood at the time, and I think I must have hurt him deeply." Her feelings of guilt erupted, and her voice dipped as Toon looked behind the pain.

"Kitty, Ed had a deep affection for you?" Ingrid was silent as she had difficulty looking into herself and how she had felt about Ed all these years. At the time, in the seventies, Ed had smoked pot, whereas Jan never did, which made up her mind. She wanted children, and Ed would not have been the right man as the father, which was the deciding factor at the time. She knew she longed for Ed differently, almost like she now felt again for Toon. In the previous years, when the symptoms of Jan's illness appeared, she thought she was being punished.

She was a good partner for him, but somehow, she never experienced the spark with Toon now. Something told her that she could have had a similar relationship with Ed. Ed got married once, which had a painful effect on her. His marriage didn't last, and there weren't any children.

"I never want to lose you, Kitty!" Toon's agony revealed his insecurity.

"You never will." They stood very close in the middle of a gorge, with giant cliffs of craggy majesty, hiding them from any civilisation.

The lake gave her a sense of longing. An inexpressible rapture that was usually guarded as one's deepest desire, as if they had seen each other naked in that moment, provoked the following action. He kissed her so ravenously that neither could have stopped what happened next. He lay her down on a soft patch of grass among the buttercups and slowly removed all her clothing. Her body came alive as she mentally screamed, "Please take me."

Both were almost as exhausted as if they'd climbed a high mountain, but simultaneously, the energy of their climax that had burst through them had somehow healed a far deeper wound from a different, more etheric level of their being.

"Kitty, I'm going to need an early night."

"What! To recuperate? You are a beast, you know." Knowing very well how she enjoyed making love.

***

After they came back from their tour around the valley, it became overcast. Otto was waiting for them at their cottage.

"Toon, your cell phone has been ringing. You left it behind at our house, so I answered it. It was Harry Brinks. Can you please contact him as soon as possible?" He invited Ingrid to join them for a drink. Jill had prepared dinner and joined her in a glass of wine outside on their overhanging wooden veranda.

"That's my boss! I wonder what can be so urgent." She told them about her work and Harry Brinks and the problems with the new complex in France.

"And what do you think of this place?"

"Jill, what can I say? It's perfect. Is Toon finding these places by flying over them, and are they all like this, high up in the mountains?"

"Toon follows a grid pattern shown in his mind. At least, that's how we understand it works. He gets a sudden notion, and off he goes. In the early days, Otto and I couldn't know how he did it, but everything always seemed to work; the money was always there, and he still works.

"Yes, he seems to travel a lot. I have no idea what businesses he has worldwide, apart from a community he is building in South Africa." She still knew very little about Toon's background. Jill made her feel very accepted the way she fussed over her only grandmother types. Her clothing was very manly: an apron over her rolled-up shirt sleeves and boots with rolled-up blue jeans that could belong to Otto.

"Toon is an unusual character. Take the landscaping business he purchased a couple of weeks ago and your connection: that's how things fall into place for him. Mind you, he has always been searching for you, and sometimes we were worried when he used to sit for hours talking about you but never really knew if you existed. At least, we never thought so! We just took it for a fantasy he held on to."

"I know so little about him apart from the fact that he never married. I shouldn't ask those questions, but things happened so fast."

"Well, mind you, twice he considered marriage, but somehow he always walked out at the last moment. He broke many a heart that we can tell you," Jill's earnest face reminded her of Mc.Nealy...she suddenly laughed.

"You know, I don't even know how old he is. When is his birthday?"

"The 15th of April. He turned fifty this year," Otto informed her, joining the woman on the veranda.

She pondered the affinity the two astrological fire signs, Leo and Aries, might have. While Otto fetched a jumper for Jill, she asked: "Jill, how is Otto? I've been meaning to ask you; I know he had a mild heart attack because he told me when both Annelies and Toon visited him."

"Do you know Annelies?"

"Yes, I've joined her decoding classes; I'm writing a journal on the first level of what Annelies calls: The Ascension Decoding Body Codes of Light workshops." They both looked at her in amazement. Ingrid realised she had created a stir in their world for some reason and was dying to know why when Toon joined them.

"Well, love. There's a change of plans. Something happened at the site. Remember the hologram park? Well, things are crumbling." Ingrid could see that he was worried.

"Snooks, are there opposing parties involved? Are there people who have objections, and are the rumours about underground tunnels valid? If you know anything, then please tell me. I've been plagued with many questions about the whole project from the start." Ingrid frowned while her whole energy turned into frustration. Both Otto and Jill looked at Toon.

"You'll have to tell her about some of the dangers, Toon; she's quite capable of deciding what is right and what is not in the interests of humanity," she heard Otto beaming at him.

"Snooks, what is he implying?" Knowing they would hear. Otto looked startled.

"Ingrid, we must teach you how to direct your thoughts to one person. You're mentally beaming at the whole universe."

"You mean you two can mentally have a private conversation? I'm still new at this! I still can't believe there are so many people using telepathy."

"There are not that many, but we're very happy for Toon's sake that you can. How did we miss that?"

"That's me, I think. I can screen her off mentally from others, *"Kitty, this is for your mind only: I adore you. I want to play with you. I want to..."*

"You both didn't ...what he just...beamed?"

"Well, not all that clearly as when he projects it to us or in the open, but we know it was intimate, as the feelings are all there," Jill guessed with a wide grin.

"All right, love, let me explain something about my part in the confusing affair of Pleasure Parks. Ben, Leo, and Trevor approached me last year about purchasing the Harry Brinks property in France.

"According to our investigations, he was the estate owner except for the small section where the old mine entrance is. This old building that used to belong to the chateau belongs to Nick du Toit." Otto added.

"So, this Nick du Toit and Mr. Brinks are in partnership?"

"Oh, no! Ben discovered Nick had illegally forged the documents and divided the property. There's even a suspicion that he murdered the old English archaeologist who lived there. Interpol is investigating this."

"You mean Annelies' husband, Ben?" Both Jill and Otto looked at each other...

"Kitty, when Harry Brinks purchased the estate, he was unaware that it did not include the chateau, and he's been trying to buy it from Nick du Toit through a broker, but with no luck. Last year, Nick du Toit was arrested for having heavy gambling debts, and so I managed to purchase the illegal document from him through my legal broker, Hans." Toon was helping himself with freshly baked Croissants.

"Ben got Nick on probation through Interpol connections. That was their deal. But we now realise that all of us have been used for a far more sinister purpose."

"But, Toon, if he illegally acquired it, why buy it from him, and what do you mean by sinister?"

"To buy time, Leo and Trevor have their headquarters at the chateau. They have found things in the old mine shaft that the English archaeologist left behind."

She now wondered about a nearby chateau she had not seen on any plan.

"So, Toon, was it correct that your interest in a landscaping and construction firm was more than you led us to believe?" "Why did you not share the conspiracy with us?"

"Otto, I was not all that aware of treachery then; none of us were, and when we 'woke up' Ben, like me, wanted to keep Annelies out of the whole sinister business. He went undercover, as you know."

Ingrid stood up to help herself to drink more wine when Toon pulled her onto his lap; she knew Toon liked to express his affection openly.

"Jill, can you fill her in?"

"Ingrid, Nick du Toit was my first husband. It's a long story, and I was very young. Nick lived at the chateau that was turned into an orphanage during the war."

"You mean like the one in Apeldoorn?"

"Yes, it belonged to the same family. The children that were born there were all named Jaarsma. I knew Nick's fascination for the old, eccentric English gentleman was only because he thought a treasure was buried there that was only assessable from the property under the chateau. He wanted to be in on it. ,Nick had always been a gambler; even I was acquired through a gambling debt, but that is another story I will tell you one day." Jill's lower lip shoved out, and her voice trembled.

"What is happening in France, Toon? You haven't told us what Harry Brinks wanted," Otto interrupted. "Or is that also a secret!"

"No, not really. Both Leo and Hans told me one evening about how the gods of human mythology have ruled the galaxy for thousands of years, and the image that looks like the all-seeing eye on the dollar bill could indeed be an energetic DNA activation portal. Still, there might be a spoke in the wheel."

They were all looking at Toon to go on, except for Jill. She had no idea what Toon was suddenly referring to, but Jill nodded. What was she thinking about? She didn't pick up any mental dialogue.

"What do you mean?" Otto suddenly leaned forward, putting his arthritic hands on the armrest of his chair to get up.

"I've been told that there might be a negative agenda to do with CERN going on," Toon replied, waving his hands as if he was unsure.

"Who told you that?" Otto's voice sounded stern, almost disbelieving.

"Both Ben and Leo are looking into it. Hans is also involved. The dome covering the Centre Portal of the building project is preventing CERN's agenda."

"Really? Mmm, conspiracy theorists warned that CERN's Large Hadron Collider was being used to revive the Egyptian deity Osiris or open a portal to hell, but it all sounds to..." Otto seemed to have more of a clue, but both Jill and she were floored at Toon's suspicions about CERN.

"OK, so far as I have grasped, it is the following. The underworld, Armand, and Lucifer control CERN. who wants to create a particle reverse spin pattern that will disconnect people from the Primal Light Fields, the source of eternal organic life energy." She could hear in his voice that Toon had difficulty sharing a far-out conspiracy theory.

They were all silently absorbing what had been discussed. Jill had placed a hand on Otto's shoulder. His posture was like a statue contemplating.

"Oh wow, you mean that keeps anyone who wants to go through this portal from ever ascending any higher within this Time Matrix?" Otto replied in awe.

"Something like that, yes."

"I'm so not understanding all this. In his journal, I hope Richard will go deeper into these complicated energy grid systems." Ingrid commented.

"Harry Brinks is being blackmailed to deliver a map that reveals the underground tunnels."

"Toon, do you mean they know there is a map?"

"Yes, love, they do now; when you spotted the symbol, I realised the tunnels are the lines that form the symbol in the photo."

"What is so special about these tunnels?" Otto asked. "And does that explosion at CERN last year have anything to do with it? Did they not close down?

"The hadron collider is encased in an underground bunker at a secret place. CERN has been tapping into dark matter, so who knows what has truly happened."

"They want the map to find the gold. That's it; they are after what is hidden inside them, or what they suspect is there." Toon speculated.

Ingrid suddenly knew that was why Piet was so nasty; she had chanced upon the drawings! Toon explained all he knew about the hologram deck to Otto and Jill. Otto knew that Ben was troubled by Interpol.

"But...is he not an agent?" Her mind leapt.

"That's the sinister part, he is, and he uncovered something they were hiding!"

"What Interpol?"

"Kitty, people are subconsciously manipulated but are unaware of it and probably feel they are doing some good. They are now boycotting the whole project. Harry Brinks wants us to join him on the site on Monday."

"Who are they?"

"That I have to find out." Toon was reluctant to break up their short getaway stay at Buttercup Valley.

"Snooks, why did you purchase a whole construction firm? To become one of the subcontractors?"

"Yes, love, but there is a lot more at stake. I'll tell you all about it in due course, but I do no know what is going on now." He shook his head and sighed. Ingrid thought that she only knew the one subcontractor, Roelof de Beer. Her in-laws had many dealings with him, but she now wondered. She didn't know the other two subcontractors, as Piet had handled their contract.

"Snooks, is Mr. Brinks aware that I'm with you?"

"He knows. I was just as surprised at that as well." Toon flirted.

"Is that a problem with you?" His expression showed pure adoration and mischief.

"Take that smirk off your face! I'm just surprised. That's all." Sliding off his lap while ruffling his hair. Ingrid's stomach ached from all the delicious food Greta, a cook from a nearby village, had prepared. She stretched while leaning against the wooden rail, admiring the view.

"Mmm ... I'm sure the connection must be Annelies or Yolanda. Who knows?" Unless Ed ...

"What about Ed? What's going on?" Toon laughed, and Ingrid realised that her thoughts were open to them. She needed to learn

the skill of screening soon. Then Ingrid told them a small part of the conspiracy she and Liesbeth had schemed; she made them all promise never to tell, realising that Otto and Jill knew Ed very well. "I'm glad for Yolanda. That first husband of hers was no good, and he's heavily involved with the same crowd Nick hangs around with. Thank goodness I'm free of them," Jill exploded when Otto grabbed her hand.

"*Remember, love. It is a subconscious manipulation.*" *Jai, Jai, Jai*"

"*Toon, please do go slow with that one. She has no idea what she's in for, but at least she has Annelies on her side. Tell us how you managed that!*"

"*Jill, Annelies was never aware of the connection; she's slipping up,*" Toon laughed. "Mind you, it took all my mental powers to block her probing mind, I can tell you."

"*Wow, but you must be getting stronger than.*"

"Yes, but when Ingrid joined us telepathically, I had more difficulty screening her projections and pretending I didn't know her thoughts," he continued, slapping his knee.

"Ingrid, you didn't know?"

"Well, yes and no. I was being very discreet in general," *Except to you, of course,*" She tried to beam that thought directly.

"*What do you mean? You are not discreet with me?*" Toon beamed while flirting.

"*I haven't even started with you yet!*" Both were enchanted with each other in the silent mental beam of delight that Jill and Otto heaved from laughter.

"*Toon, she's outstanding!*" Ingrid felt as if she had found her long-lost family. Never had she connected with others in this way. She had always thought it was just her imagination and tried to block it out when she felt people were lying to her. Now she understood why she felt so comfortable with them. They were crystal clear because their words at least matched their thinking!

"Welcome home," They beamed in unison, which brought on tears. A massive release from years of repressing other people's thoughts because the subconscious betrayal was over. Toon stood up to hug her.

"Toon, take her to bed! She looks tired, and you both have a busy day ahead of you." Jill projected.

"Kitty, are you worn out by me?" Toon teased when they strolled back to their cottage.

"Snooks, don't kid yourself; I don't tire that easily, but do you know what I feel like doing!"

"What?"

"Soaking in the Jacuzzi with lots of bubbles!" They ran gaily towards their cottage, elated by each other's company.

Halfway House

Ingrid was woken up the following day by the probing beams of sunlight that filtered through the wooden windows. She felt Toon's eyes on her. He was lying on his side with his arm supporting his head, high enough to observe her.

"Did you sleep well?" he whispered.

"Mmm!... Yes, stretching herself out like a cat, releasing all the stiffness in her muscles.

"Did you?" she reached out to touch his cheek.

"Oh...yes."...He stroked her face. "You are...so...lovely!"

"I think you are terrific too!" She looked at him with a relaxed expression, thinking she could not have invented a better bed partner, lover, business partner, or whatever they would be to each other. She observed Toon fluffing some pillows, settling himself so that he could see her clearly, then he pulled the duvet away slowly, his eyes travelling over her naked body. She needed to move because of his gaze.

"Please stay still, Kitty" he choked.

"I have to get up, but when you move, something happens to me that I cannot control." They flirted to see who would be the first to break the foreplay both were engaged in. Toon made a sound at the back of his throat like a deep animalistic call, and she couldn't help but burst the bubble by responding, "You are an animal!"

That was plenty of reason for Toon to make love, as she knew he would.

***

Toon was working out their flight plan on his laptop to the Pleasure Park site near Paris, where they had arranged to meet Mr. Brinks. She used Toon's cell phone to inform Jeroen that she would not be home before Monday night.

It was Sunday morning at 8:30 when Jeroen answered with a sleepy voice. She chatted to him about Buttercup Valley while sending him some pictures of the valley over the phone.

"Mom, Mr. Brinks phoned here and was very determined to get hold of you or Toon. I phoned the lady where you go for your classes to find out if they knew where the two of you went. Should I not have given him Toon's number?"

"Oh, now we know. We both wondered how he knew I was with Toon."

"Mom..... are you....you know?"

"Jeroen!" She scolded, looking up at Toon, who gestured for the cell phone.

"Jeroen, what would you like to know that your mother might not tell you?" He made a comical face when listening, and she tried to read his mind. Jeroen seemed to suggest some arrangement.

"That'll be splendid! I'm looking forward to meeting all of you. We'll keep you informed when we are back, and, Jeroen, I'll look after her very well." Laughter was spreading all over his face.

"Well, your son has just informed me that his sisters were shocked that he never told them about me. They all insisted on an informal introduction."

"I hope you are up to this. My children can be very insistent when it comes to family matters!" She hugged him with all the strength in her arms.

"Kitty, I'll be very proud to meet them. I never had any children, and I would love to be a good friend to them." His sincerity was apparent.

"Snooks, nobody, not even my children, has any say about whom I sleep with or am in love with, but I'll be just as proud to show you off." Her kiss demonstrated how much.

"Kitty, I have to talk to Otto before we leave, so let's have breakfast with them." He took their bags, and they walked past the empty cabins on the narrow path towards their cottage.

***

"Good morning! Do tell us your plans." Jill greeted them, having laid out breakfast on the patio. The sun revitalised the whole valley with its radiance.

"Jill, I've contacted Peter and Helen. We have to be on the Pleasure Park site by Monday afternoon, so I've booked us into their B&B. It's only one hour by car, so I'll use that opportunity to introduce Ingrid." Toon pulled out a chair for her.

"Ingrid, you'll adore their three children. They are our pride and joy. Peter is our adopted son. Our family is complicated, but you'll know our clan one day. Leave it to Annelies and give them our love."

Otto joined them and started discussing the large crew coming soon with Toon.

"Ingrid, do you know if the name Jaarsma is in your family?" Ingrid looked at Jill in amazement.

"Gee, this fascination about the Jaarsma name!"

Her mind returned to...a sudden vision of a massive building and children's laughter in the background. What was her connection with this image all of a sudden? Ingrid realised that she had been drifting off in a split second into another time, just like in the coffee shop! Then she responded to Jill's question.

"Yes, my grandmother, whose name was Kitty Jaarsma, died when I was nine years old. I remember her very well as visiting us when we lived in Amsterdam." Otto stopped his conversation with Toon.

"Jill, do you think it's the same Kitty I think it is?"

"Oh, yes, that explains a lot, and I bet Annelies is aware of it as well."

"What are you two on about?"

"Toon, did Annelies never talk about the conversations she had as a child with a nun called Dienie?"

"Otto, I wasn't even aware that you knew about it. What brought that up?" Toon looked perplexed.

"Something Annelies told me years ago, before I met Jill, I never really thought about it until now because the name 'Kitty Jaarsma' came up."

"Are you going to tell us what Annelies told you?" Toon asked more for Ingrid's sake.

"Ingrid, we're a large family but very scattered. Annelies and Fred are half-brothers and sisters to my sister Margaret and me. I was visiting our home in Leersum when Margaret moved out to start her nursing career. Toon, was that the time you came to live with them Let me think. It must have been in when you were about five. Annelies must have been fifteen when she told me the story one evening. I remember it well. Fred, who must have been around five as well, got very ill, so I was asked to look after you while our father took him to the hospital."

"Annelies always talked about Dienie, the nun who started the Jaarsma orphanage with the two Jaarsma sisters. Annelies always saw this nun in the gardens of our home in Leersum. It was a big joke in our family as nobody except Annelies had ever seen this nun. One day, Dienie told her that she, Annelies, was responsible for gathering the Jaarsma Clan together because they were going to play a huge role in the transformation that was to come. That's why we thought that Annelies had a role to play in getting the two of you together. Toon, do you remember anything about the orphanage?"

"No, not really. Something about nuns, yes, but I think I remember more things from what Annelies told me."

"You're all talking about the Prinsengracht hotel or the one in France?" Ingrid butted in, looking at Jill with large eyes.

"The one in Apeldoorn, but it didn't look anything like what it is today; it was very run down when Annelies and Fred bought it. Did Annelies show you the star painting?"

"Yes, she did."

"We are all connected in one way or another. It captured Leo's fascination because of the etheric and genetic bloodline that runs through us all." Otto added. Ingrid recalled that he had given a talk at the United World Congress in Zurich.

"Otto, my grandmother's name was Katrina Jaarsma, not so?" Toon asked.

"I know you and Annelies have the same grandmother, but we're confused about how Ingrid relates."

"Annelies tried to decode the Jaarsma orphanage's tree. I know that Mien Jaarsma was the second wife of my first husband. Her father was also a John Jaarsma," Jill said with laughter when she saw Ingrid's face.

"Otto, you've still not told us about the story Annelies told you about the nun," Toon reminded him. Ingrid was drawn into herself, recalling what Liesbeth had shared a few weeks ago that she had incarnated on Earth before and lived to be a nun."

"No, but Toon, hey, you two must leave. It'll take you about three hours to fly. It'll have to wait for another time. Tell Peter to prepare to move up here in six months, will you?" Otto's regret in his voice was very apparent. He liked Toon's company, and now that Ingrid had joined their circle, it seemed unfair to break up their discussion.

When Ingrid looked around her, she felt how all the building materials being offloaded from the big lorries made the place suddenly different from the previous day. They said goodbye to Otto and Jill, hoping for another meeting soon. She still had much to ask them, especially things about Toon.

"*What do you want to know?*" he beamed after he had talked with the control tower.

"*Lots of things. For a start, explain to me again how you are related to Annelies.*"

"*Annelies' mother was my mom's sister. My parents died together in an accident when I was seven months old.*" The noise in the cockpit made no difference to them.

"*Toon, when did you become aware that you could project thoughts like you do?*"

Mmm... Toon fiddled with some settings, "*Annelies used to practice on me, saying it was the nun Dienie that told her to teach others to communicate properly.*" He took her hand and brought it to his lips. "*Kitty, you're improving all the time, you know.*"

Ingrid was admiring the beautiful scenery down below and revelling in the freedom of being up in the sky. They were still flying at a high altitude. Toon was in contact with people in the control towers whom he knew by their first names.

"*My grandmother must have been very telepathic. She used to talk to me as we are now. ...My mother tried to stop her once. I think she was aware of our thought projections. Quincy always talked to my Gran about the colours she saw around people when my mother was not around. I never saw colours, but I could hear voices. Toon, tell me about Dienie."*

"Before I go into that discussion, Kitty, can you get me the laptop connected to my CPS system and bring the air map on the screen? I need to do some calculations." He spoke into the microphone because the noise was deafening if they took off their well-padded headphones. She remembered the program and turned the screen to Toon. He changed the control panel and talked again to someone below. She turned around at the back, where there was a flask of coffee and some strudels Jill had packed for them.

"Toon, you were going to tell me about Dienie?" she said, handing him his coffee.

"Kitty, Annelies is ten years older, and to me, she is both a sister, a teacher, a friend, and even a counsellor in her later years. I owe a lot to her as she was there for me when I was very depressed. She told me a story that was so fantastic that I did not take it all that seriously until many years later, when I was searching for answers." She glanced at him sideways, wondering how much Ed had told him about her.

"A lot, Kitty, so much so that I fell in love with you before I even met you. When Ed and I used to go to a bar after a big job, we used to offload on each other. At those moments, he always talked about you." Ingrid felt a stab of pain for Ed's unhappiness.

"I was getting so familiar with you that I used to look forward to hearing about you. He loved his brother, and when he got ill, he had to restrain himself from running back home to be with you." That must have been when she felt so guilty, thinking Jan's illness was a punishment.

"I know his father tried many times to offer him the directorship of the firm in the past, but he kept declining it. Kitty, I can feel your hurt; what are your feelings now?" She could feel his reluctance, perhaps

his fear of hearing the truth. What were her feelings? Now, she regarded Ed as a brother, but it had been different in the past.

*"Snooks, when Jan and I were courting, Ed was always with us. I
knew we had a connection on a different level, a bit like we have now,
but now I know it would never have been like what we have. I hope
for his sake that >he will find happiness with Yolanda."*
Toon kissed her fingers, arm, and elbow, *"heeey, watch out!"* He
dived down! And up! The crackling noise from the station below
was buzzing in her ear. Was he doing something he shouldn't? Toon
started giving instructions to the mike while giving her a big grin.
*"I wanted to jump for joy, that's all." You have no idea what agony it
has been, thinking that I've stolen the love of his life. Kitty, I want to
be married to you. I want you to be my wife, my partner, my lover,
and my best friend. Above all, I want to awaken next to you physically
and spiritually. Kitty, don't answer yet if I'm too fast for you."* Did she
hear all that? A telepathic marriage proposal? She knew she loved
him deeply. She wanted to be with him, but marriage? Would it be
the same?
*"Toon, I want to live with you first. I'll be your lover, friend, and com-
panion, and I will want to wake up with you, physically and spiritually."* Toon suddenly held her by her blouse and pulled her towards
him. She could feel and hear his thoughts, which were very visual
at the same time.
*"Meaning I will move in with you? And you'll come with me when I
need to go away?"* She planted a kiss on his nose.
*"Let me hold on to my job for now, at least until the project in Paris
is finished. I'll make up my mind about the marriage part after the
opening of the Paris complex in September."* He was laughing while
still holding her tightly.
*"You'll make sure you have the last word, lady, but that's because I'm
occupied."* He was being called on the radio, so their thought projections were not possible anymore. Toon needed all his attention for

his flying. She knew he was a powerful and persuasive man, and she needed to keep her wits about her to maintain her independence. They landed at Liechtenstein to refuel and continued. Occasionally, he asked her to look up something on the computer screen from her laptop. They flew lower, and she could make out villages, motorways, mountains and green hills. Our planet is beautiful; why could it not always be like this? Suddenly, the laptop screen brightened.

<Hello, Kitty, let's talk about joy. First, you feel happy, which is an emotional and personal reaction. Then, you feel an inner joy, which is the quality of the soul that is activated in the mind when alignment takes place.>

"Is that POWAH?"

"Yes, it amazes me every time." She turned the laptop for him to read.

POWAH, that accelerated happy feeling. Is that mostly my personality? she typed

<Yes, Kitty, but by bringing joy to others, you will always have joy, and by bringing about conditions which help others express themselves freely, your joy in the living-ness is a service. Ponder on joy, happiness, delight, and bliss. These release the channels of the inner life and extend to a wide circle of people of many kinds. Kitty, joy heals the physical body and helps you do your work effortlessly. Learn to feel joy. You are both standing in the doorway of significant changes in your personal and community lives.>

"Kitty, ask about these changes." But before Ingrid could touch the keyboard, the screen reacted instantaneously.

<The best for both of you is to be fully present. The joy you and Toon feel is the key you must cultivate together. This relaxed flow that feeds you both is an ecstasy of inner bliss, the eternal presence within, which has always been there! Such a state of

consciousness will allow you both to enjoy the sped-up energy currents and heighten your awareness. This frequency of higher currents will sweep through the earth during the expansion of the non-time interval.>

POWAH, how will these higher currents be manifested on our planet? Will they interfere with our energy resources?
Toon asked this after he read POWAH's message.

<Yes, Toon, it will, but long before the moment of collective awakening happens. Around the planet, sufficient groups of people have already received this inner calling. Some individuals must live in communities where they can operate at higher frequencies of awareness to counteract the influences of those who may react with fear.>

You say some people, but you mean that not all have to live in those communities? she beamed, facing the laptop to see if that worked. Ingrid's mind was working overtime.

<That's correct. Some are light workers, like you two, who will independently travel and display this inner truth. When this joy and love radiate from you both into your surroundings, healing will occur where needed. It will come to pass that you will need to visit these light centres to reconnect, just as you now require a break from your work. The chaos brought about by fear-trapped, fragmented Souls and the physical damage expressed through war can deplete all of you.>

POWAH, I get the feeling that we don't have all that much time left. Is that so? Toon beamed while flying. Again, her amazement at the direct response to his thoughts created some proof that everything is just waves or frequencies manifesting as text. Their interaction shifted her outlook on life.

<Toon, in specific places on earth, chaos and destruction is already in the process of erupting at any moment. The hurricanes from years back were the beginnings. The centre you started on

in the Rhaetian Alps is needed there to create a powerhouse, just as you now have power stations on your planet for your energy resources. When your natural energy resources start to collapse, this and many other light centres will take over the function of your present energy supply. Your small family unit will become a beam of light soon. You both will discover your soul's purpose and how it is for the good of all.>

"POWAH, you seem to know our future. Can you see what is happening before we know it?"

<Toon, the I AM within you knows there is no 'here' and no 'there' but only omnipresence. It's your Soul's potential to enjoy perfect spiritual freedom from time and space. Your free will and how you use it will create your manifestations. That which is created returns to its creator. But you both know that, so why ask?>

"I know that I still have some fears that make me anxious about making mistakes, and I also know that I will be more determined to live my soul's full potential with Kitty at my side. I know she has some fears of losing her freedom."

She heard Toon's thought and wondered what her Soul's purpose is that POWAH says she'll soon know.

<Humans are perfect reflections of each other, especially when they are as close as you are. Toon, you are reflecting on your fears about commitment. Kitty has proved beyond any doubt the ability to commit fully to a relationship, but have you?>

Gosh, typing wasn't even necessary. POWAH directly answered their thoughts. "Ingrid was almost sorry for him having to get such a straight answer." She looked sideways and saw that Toon was grinning.

"Wow, that was very direct! Or is my mind giving me a taste of my pitfall?" They were descending, and Ingrid could see a runway in the far distance.

<Your mind and mine are the same. You'd better land your plane before you run out of fuel. Your love for each other is a joy to behold. Contemplate the following excerpt.

Love POWAH>

"POWAH sends his love and tells you to land the plane soon, Snooks," she beamed before reading excerpt seventeen. She was still sure that excerpt fifteen with rule five was missing.

Excerpt Seventeen[1]

Program Planet Earth

Handing over the Lower will and Surrendering to the Higher Self

Rule Seven *of the Ascension Decoding Card Game.*

<Mastery over the three lower chakras will expand the size of your auric field as more significant segments of Soul descend. <

When Ingrid saw Toon looking at his fuel gauge and swearing to himself, she knew from his mind that he'd been so preoccupied with her and POWAH that he'd not been paying full attention to his control panel.

The control tower was directing him for landing, and she was amazed at how the time had just flown by. Her legs were stiff, and she looked forward to feeling the ground under her again. She still wondered what had happened to excerpt fifteen...

---

1. https://allrealityshifters.wordpress.com/powah/the-reality-shifters-excerpt-17/

Chapter 17
Beliefs and Judgments

France

When Toon had completed the landing procedures, a short, stocky, jolly man greeted them.

"Hello, Toon. I am glad to see you! We expected you sooner, and your people have waited at least an hour. What happened?" Toon shook his hand with his arm, hugging Ingrid's shoulders.

"Ingrid, this is DIRK. We learned to fly together; he runs his airbase, and I'm forever grateful to him because he looks after my plane as if it were his own, something I'd entrust only to him."

Toon's pilot's brown, vast, round eyes melted away into a look of confusion while staring at her face. His black hair fell across his forehead, but his weathered appearance expressed confidence.

"I'm pleased to meet you, and thank you for looking after Toon's safety." Shaking the man's fleshy but warm and dry hand seemed to have given him time to pose.

"Your partner? Toon, have you finally found her? Wait until I tell Christine." Toon held her close, whispering. "He and his lovely wife tried many times to hook me up with a date. Thank goodness I don't have to go through that again." Suddenly, Ingrid heard a commotion of little feet running.

"Uncle Toon...Oh, you've come, you've come!" Two children, a boy of about seven and a younger girl, came dashing from around the corner of the hangar and were hanging on to his legs the moment he put his bags down. He picked them both up, expressing his joy at seeing them. It charmed Ingrid's heart to witness his love for those children. A young, smart-looking couple, the woman carrying a toddler, greeted them.

"Well, we're glad you've arrived! We were getting worried. Did you have bad weather?" The man shook Toon's hand and simultaneously disengaged the children from Toon with difficulty.

"TIMMY, please give Uncle Toon a chance to introduce us to his lady friend," the mother told him.

"Hi, I'm HELEN, and my husband is PETER." Helen's dashing shoulder-length sandy blond curls complemented her light-blue eyes, giving her an artistic, free, caring look. Peter's piercing observation of her told a lot. She was sure that both Jill and Otto had been talking about her. Ingrid felt at ease with their warm welcome.

"We've already heard much about you from Mom and Dad, and we're thrilled by your visit. Come, the car is waiting to take you home."

To her surprise, she felt a little hand sliding into hers; glancing down, she looked into a pair of big blue eyes that held such openness only a child could display, accepting her as if she knew her well.

"Hi, and what may I call you?" The little girl's light blond curls bounced while chatting.

"My name is KARIN, my brother Timmy, and my baby sister is JENNY. What's your name?" Ingrid smiled.

"You may call me Ingrid."

"When are you going to get married?" Timmy, a duplicate of his dad in miniature, asked with a severe frown when they arrived at a Landover. Toon roared, his eyes challenged her.

"Kitty, I adore you. Marrying you is a commitment I'll gladly undertake."

They were all standing next to a Land Rover, waiting for her reply. She was thinking fast because they were not letting her get away with any answer! She remembered from Otto that these were the people who would move to the community at Buttercup Valley.

"Let's see...when the summer's over...and you have to start school soon...before you move to your new home...in the mountains.

Toon and I will invite you to our wedding party. Satisfied?" She was suddenly picked up from the ground by Toon with such adoration. She felt very exposed.

"Oh, Kitty, I love you, I love you, I'll always love you." He kissed her as if he was never going to let go. Helen laughed, "I have to phone Mom and Dad! I know they want to hear this news."

They all climbed into the Land Rover. Both children squeezed themselves between her and Toon. Helen was still holding her chubby toddler while turning her head, "Please, Ingrid, will you take baby Jenny from me since I'm in the front?"

"But of course." "I'd love to."...she took Jenny in her lap. To feel her soft, cute body resting in complete confidence against her was a surprise. Usually, small children were not eager to be handed out to strangers.

"Mom, she has clear ears as well!" Timmy beamed at his mother as Toon ruffled the boy's spiky hair.

"Peter. You'll have to start teaching him to stop eavesdropping."

"Toon, you try. I've explained the rules, but he has not noticed them yet."

It had been a long time since Ingrid had a small child in her arms. What a joy to follow Jenny's questioning blue eyes! Both girls had curly, light golden blonde hair, like their mother, but Karin's hair was long, and many a teenager would 'die' to have their hair do what Karin's did.

Toon told Helen and Peter he'd followed a longer flying route to show Ingrid some scenery when she beamed teasingly.

"You never did such a thing! We were having a conversation with POWAH while you were circling!"

"Who's POWAH?" Peter asked out loud. Both Toon and Ingrid looked at Peter in his rearview mirror.

"Sorry, I seem to have broken my own rules." From behind, Peter's average height looked tiny next to Toon's tall, large frame, but he manoeuvred the landcover with the skill of a racing driver. While cruising through breathtaking scenery, Ingrid thought she could easily live here.

"I'm so glad you like it here, Kitty. Look around, as we'll be coming back here."

Peter stopped in front of an imposing gate opened by a remote control. Ingrid grinned at the traditional gates that operated by modern high-tech electronic devices. They drove up a winding lane lined with rows of trees, creating an atmosphere of tranquillity. They arrived at a beautiful chateau with a sign:

The Cup of Gold Halfway House B&B.

By your choice, you dwell now in the world you created. What you hold in your heart will be true, and what you most admire, that you will become.

"Toon, that's the same sign you displayed at Buttercup Valley, named after the flower!" Helen laughed at Ingrid's surprise. "Didn't you know that you have a very wealthy man who's madly in love with you?"

"Meaning what? Toon? Does this also belong to you?"

"Kitty, it will belong to people who live here. Nobody has to own it, use it."

After a short drive on a twisting gravel lane, Peter stopped in front of a wide stone staircase that led to a massive front door. Giant trees and shrubs hid the view of the building.

"This chateau will be a 'doorway 'to the community in the Alps," Helen explained. "What do you mean by a doorway?"

"Toon's vision is that people who want to live in a community have to release most of their attachments to material possessions, meaning that they will retain their privacy and lifestyle in their cottages, but on paper, little will belong to them personally."

"You mean people must be willing to leave their material possessions behind?" There was a great sense of peace in the air. The sound of birds and running water revealed a nature sanctuary not far away as they entered a foyer filled with plants. A water feature next to a staircase reminded her of the arrangement Toon had delivered at work.

"Ingrid the normal personal items and mementoes that establish our taste, which is still important to us, we keep, and any tools or other equipment that come along with the skills each person brings in, yes, that stays one's personal property, but for the rest, our daily commodities, like outbuildings, sports activities, recreations and any equipment that a community needs to be prosperous, will belong to the whole group," Helen explained as she leaned out of the window pressed an intercom button to announce their arrival.

"Most people are not ready for a changeover, even if they think they are" Peter added. He came across as a man who had found his purpose in life. His slim, lean, athletic appearance suggested he might be a health freak. They arrived at the chateau's entrance when Peter asked Timmy to call Heidi, their nanny.

"Kitty, this property is like a stopover where selected people get introduced to a new way of sharing before they take up community living. We are also training people for emergencies. None of us knows when the first signs of the rising waters will affect the great masses of our population. All over the world, many people are already moving to higher ground, especially after the hurricanes in America two years back and the horrible wildfires that destroyed a great part of California. As you know, much of Holland is well below sea level."

"How can we possibly be prepared for such a catastrophic event? Especially the bartering system that you said still has to be improved as time passes." On his laptop, Toon showed visitors they could sign up for their Talents bank account. "Snooks, what do you mean by selected people?"

They were all out of the Landover, and someone took their luggage. She realised that they were running a guest house. The chateau was certainly large enough.

"Kitty, anyone who has seriously arrived at a point where they would rather choose an alternative lifestyle that will support their Soul's passion instead of staying in the old paradigm and has already gone through major changes in their lives, don't you agree?"

"Snooks, yes, I do agree. Gosh, this place is gorgeous. How old is it?"

This newly restored 19-bedroom chateau, dating back to the 17th century, is accompanied by 27 hectares of land and numerous outbuildings. Peter proudly beamed.

She had never stayed in a place like this, and learning that Toon purchased this was a surprise. After a quick tour, they arrived at Peter and Helen's private section, where Toon opened massive glass sliding doors onto a wooden terrace overlooking a vineyard.

Karin released her hand and ran to a tricycle in the corner. Jenny began to feel a weight in her arms. Ingrid was impressed by the abundance of it all. She imagined that many people would gladly walk away from their mundane lives to partake in a new lifestyle; however, seeing all this is challenging.

"Ingrid, you are right", Peter beamed. "People are staying here who have explored many options for new economics." He added as he handed Toon some letters.

"Ingrid, the Halfway Houses worldwide are used for trial stopover places, as Helen mentioned. The focus on individuality versus the whole group approach, in terms of living conditions, is earned through the skills each person is willing to contribute. We also have to make this enterprise work for itself. Nobody gets any handouts. That's why we run a guest house, a vineyard, a plant nursery, and a small publishing house. Soon, we hope to open an art gallery with a tea room where people can meet and display their talents." Peter's eyes glittered, showing his passion for the Halfway House project. "Your future husband is a good businessman." Helen smiled at Toon as she spread her arms wide, admiring the view. On the wall, she read on a large scroll banner with handwritten modern calligraphy.

In the 21st century, illiteracy no longer means being unable to read or write, but instead being unable to let go of false beliefs.

"Wow, that is so true," she remarked.

The children's nanny appeared, and a wriggling golden cocker spaniel called 'Snoopy 'immediately adopted her.

"Ingrid, will you come up to help me change?" Karin asked. The five-year-old was a real charmer. She thought she'd better give Helen a hand, thinking about the many tasks that were probably waiting for her. She was still holding Jenny in her arms when she saw that Toon was staring at her hypnotically, and at that moment, she longed to be alone with him. Jenny broke the spell when she indicated she wanted to walk alone.

Ingrid came downstairs after the nanny had bathed the children and given them their supper. She was surprised that the parents did not eat with their children. They were waiting for her in the lounge, having cocktails. Snoopy jumped up to say 'hello' but was pushed back by Helen.

"Ingrid, my apologies, but Snoopy likes you." Toon patted at a space next to him on the couch.

"Is Heidi managing upstairs? I've promised them that if they eat their meal in the playroom tonight with Heidi, they may be allowed to go with us tomorrow morning to the aeroplane and look inside. Toon, I probably bribed them, but it's sometimes so nice to be free for an evening." Helen was peering at Toon for approval.

"That's a deal. Ingrid, I've told Peter and Helen why we came here. They're going to drive us to the building site tomorrow after lunch. I've just spoken to Harry Brinks, who, by the way, knows both Peter and Helen very well."

"Really?"

"Harry Brinks is a brother of my grandfather," Helen explained.

Ingrid was no longer surprised, thinking about the family tree. Ingrid and Toon relaxed in their company. Her eyes roved over the beautiful Turkish carpet on the lustrous brick floor.

"Love, I'd like to invite your uncle Harry to our guesthouse tomorrow evening, if that's all right with both of you? I think he's on his own a lot since his wife died about five years ago."

Both Ingrid and Toon were impressed by Peter's hospitality. Toon would offer him a lift back to Holland on the plane.

After dinner, Peter and Toon spoke about the building plans for Buttercup Valley while Ingrid listened to Helen's idea of starting a particular school when they moved to the mountains. Helen was a school teacher who'd always wanted to teach on her own, based on the educational philosophies of Rudolf Steiner and the awakening material.

Ingrid got excited and soon began making sketches on a sheet of paper at their dining room table for a school building on the main street of the property. They were both so involved that Ingrid never noticed that Toon stood behind her, looking over her shoulder at the drawings on the table.

"Kitty, that's great! I'll have to scan this drawing for Otto and send it so he can prepare the site for the school immediately."

Helen talked to her about how they got involved a year before when Toon needed a couple who could run the Halfway House. She and Peter had been to Damanhur in Italy for six months before that to learn as much as possible about community living and the new economic systems on trial there.

"Peter is very interested in Permaculture, so together, we have run this Halfway House as best we can. The publishing business was here already, and Toon has asked if Liesbeth would be interested in running that section after we moved to Buttercup Valley."

"She never told me that!" Writing and editing were Liesbeth's skills, but was it her passion?

"Ingrid, this came for you through e-mail, so I printed it out." She was speechless when Peter handed her excerpt eighteen. Toon explained about POWAH.

Excerpt Eighteen[1]
Program Planet Earth
Mastery over Beliefs and Judgments about Them
Rule eight *of the Ascension Decoding Card Game.*
<**Radiating love to all under all circumstances is the most difficult of all. This is necessary to maintain your connection to your higher self and the divine.**> Ingrid wondered why POWAH had written that she could do it. Under what conditions would she not love? Ingrid felt a wave of sadness that she shook off quickly. They all wanted to read the excerpt online from the cell phone, and Helen asked about the other transmissions. She was distracted by Toon's arms that he wrapped around her from behind.

"I want to go to bed, what about you?" he shot on a private beam as it felt more...intimate.

Helen showed them to their suite, and although they were tired, they both looked forward to their lovemaking, which formed such an essential part of their growing familiarity with each other. Looking at the shower, both were having the same thoughts. Toon undressed her slowly while she unbuttoned his shirt, "Kitty, is it always going to be like this?" His breath gasped at her nakedness.

---

1. https://allrealityshifters.wordpress.com/powah/the-reality-shifters-excerpt-18/

"I hope so! Are you complaining?" She always reacted to Toon's intense observation of her body, and when he pulled her head back, his eyes conveyed the full meaning of his longing.

"We have made love five times, but not yet in the shower. It's about time." His mouth seized her lips with desire as the water washed over them. His body's motion and driving hunger continued, searching endlessly, as if she were only a sensation of endless joy. When the excellent release that united her body with his into a single shock of pleasure happened, just for one split-second, she knew that something was different, "Oh, Kitty, I never knew anything like this!"

Toon turned off the tap while holding her close and slowly lifted her as if she were his most valued part. Ingrid had, without a doubt, experienced a sudden awareness that something had joined them in their union. Was that possible? She was already forty-five. Could she still conceive? She hadn't taken any precautions, and neither had Toon.

"Kitty, I felt it too. Can you still have children?" She never for one moment thought she would be confronted with that option! A kind of disbelief overcame her. Nothing had prepared her for this. She glanced at him, "What are your feelings about that possibility?"

"Oh, Kitty, it's not fair on you! You had children, but when I looked at you standing with Jenny in your arms, I suddenly knew what I would still love to experience!" She remembered the look he had given her on the terrace. Was that what he'd felt? Did Toon want a child? Could it be that carrying his child was her Soul's purpose? It would be meaningful, but was she not too old for this?

"Remember, love. You will never be too old."

"Toon...promise me one thing."

"What?" Anything! What?"

"Snooks, to no one, not a single soul, mentally or verbally, do you reveal this possibility, this intuitive feeling we seem to share before I've some medical proof that I'm pregnant," Ingrid said with such conviction that his eyes started to dance. He roared with laughter at her serious face. How well she already knew him! This would be the hardest thing ever. No shouting from the rooftops what he wanted everyone to hear!

"Toon?" ...she knew that holding him to a promise would challenge him. She needed time to get used to the idea if they were right.

Toon got up, pulled something out of the bedside table drawer and brought it back to the bed. He placed his hand on the book on her lap, his face beaming with a smile, which made her laugh at the comical situation. With a straight face, he said:

"I solemnly promise not to say or even project a thought about our possible miracle, that I made you pregnant, that you might carry my child, that we are having a baby, that..."

"That's more than enough! Please come to bed; I'm getting cold and want to snuggle up."

***

As the tiredness hit her, she curled up, asleep at his side. While sleeping, the unconscious part of her knew that the inevitable would happen; she would simultaneously experience a subconscious existence that would take her into a reality that belonged on the subconscious astral plane, where any remaining genetically related. Karma that hadn't been released was waiting for her, the initiate, to transcend this unresolved issue during her dream...

***

Laura (Ingrid) found herself on a high plateau.

She was about to cross the narrow ledge – some distance out, she froze, unable to move forward or go back. Waves of vertigo swept over her, and she began to tremble violently. She battled to stand on the edge of the massive slab that protruded far into nothingness. Was she going to jump? Then it would be over, her baby would go with her, and nobody would ever know.

She knew deep in her heart that the penalty for taking one's own life was not as fearful as the priests made it out to be. She had lost her brother years before when she was only ten. The evening of the day of his death, alone in her bedroom when her grief had become intense, she had sensed a presence that made her look up; standing in the room, silhouetted against the moonlight, was her beloved brother.

"Eddie, can't I go with you?" she had pleaded. He had grasped her hand, and she had felt herself going up.

"Eddie...I...I'm not a bird; I can't fly!" she had called to him.

Gently, he pulled her up and slowly rose to the room's high ceiling. She remembered when looking down that she had seen herself lying outstretched, seemingly fast asleep.

"Am I dead too?"

"No, you are not. Look." He pointed to a thin glowing thread linking her to her sleeping body. When she moved further away, the cord stretched...

Eddie told her that the place where people go to after death looked at first just like the place one had left. He took her to many places where they played. There, she met Annie, a woman who had taken her own life. She remembered asking Eddie why she was not in hell.

"Laura, these are the lower astral planes where everybody goes after death. She's here as long as she wants to be until she's ready for a new life. The only thing is that in this new life, she'll have to confront the same hurt and pain that made her take her last life.

"Really, why?"

"Annie left many others behind who cared about her. Others suffered when she committed suicide." When she grew up, he told her it was not her time to go....

Standing at the edge, she wondered whom she would hurt deeply if she were to jump. Her father would be very disappointed, especially if she had to tell him that she was pregnant.

She shuddered at what his reaction would be. He was a very important astronomer, and their family was well respected. Girls in their social circle were not supposed to work, but her father allowed her to draw the charts and illustrations for the book he was writing. She loved the work, but leaving her home to be married was unacceptable. She had been given away in marriage a year before, and her soul was screaming out at the very thought of it. Her family still practised that tradition, and although she argued about it relentlessly, she could not win. She had met her future husband only once. He was already old, so the wedding would occur the following month. Laura wondered what they would do if she told them she was pregnant.

Her mother would be devastated, more for the shame of it. The prospect of confronting them was unthinkable. They'd never really gotten over Eddie's loss when he was only twelve. Oh, if only Eddie were with her!

Looking ahead, she heard the church bells ringing in the distance. Then she felt someone was watching, and as she turned, a man's eyes held her in such adoration that deep in her heart, she knew he was a part of her.

He was wearing a kind of dark robe like priest's wear. His eyes as he studied her were full of love, and she felt that he was preparing her for some ritual. Her mind and his were joined! She could hear his thoughts!

"Kitty, don't ever let go of life; don't ever lose faith in the power of real love, the energy that transforms all things." Then he disappeared, and she was alone again.

Who was he? Laura felt she had connected with a part of her that she'd always looked for but never found. She knew in her heart what to do, so she fixed her eye on the narrow area in front of her, avoided looking down and crept slowly up and out of danger away from the cliff.

Laura suddenly had a purpose for living. She would take clothes, money, and drawing tools from her home and go to a convent that took in young girls in her condition. Only the previous week, her mother had discussed with Snobbery the convent that a nun and two other women ran.

Her nanny would help her find this convent; she was sure of that, especially if she threatened Inge with the exposure of all her lovers! Laura did not need to experience married life; she could become a nun if necessary, and she would have the baby.

She did not know what would happen after that, but meeting this priest, whoever he was, had made up her mind. She'd become pregnant by John, who worked for her father. She knew in her heart that she could have stopped him, but her curiosity got the better. She did not love the man, and he was already married. When he started to flirt with her in her father's office, she knew she was responding to it. She was always curious about what happened when a man and woman came together.

Her mother never wanted to talk about it. Inge had explained to her in detail the pleasures of it, leaving out the possibility of falling pregnant. When she remembered again that her period had not appeared that morning, Inge asked her why she did not need sanitary bandages. Her face! It was almost comical, then Inge had slapped her. "Who is the father?" she raged.

Laura had never even considered the possibility of becoming pregnant. She had sex with John twice, after which she'd had enough. It wasn't worth the effort.

Whatever Inge, her nanny, had been raving about, she'd found it an overrated pastime. It also hurt, so how could there be any joy in that? To think she would have to endure that experience every night when married! The thought of that option was unbearable, and being a nun became far more attractive. She only regretted giving up her drawings and studies. Somehow, she didn't think that was what one did in a convent.

She would not mind working with children and would offer her services for free board and lodging. The more she thought about her plan, the more she looked forward to it. At least she would not be marrying an older man. "Where have you been?" her mother's whining voice made her cringe when she entered the dining room. She had been gone for two hours, and the whole family was in an uproar.

"I needed some fresh air, but Nanny knew where I was. Why didn't you ask her?" Laura replied in a tone that always made her father recoil. When he came out of his study, he joined his research library. "Laura, that's not the way to speak to your mother! Go to your room and stay there until I call you." That was no problem for her. There was little love between her parents, and they never considered that she had any feelings.

Eddie had been the only one who had taught her what it was like to feel loved. She wanted to speak to Inge, wondering where she was when she went to her room. While packing her bag, she looked at everything she had to leave behind.>Her drawing of the planets in the Milky Way was her pride and joy.

Her father had complimented her on her precise detail, which was the only acknowledgement Laura had ever received from him. He was a well-respected astronomer, but this project she was to do was kept a big secret. Why, she had no idea. She decided to take the drawings with her when her door flew open.

"What have you been telling your mother?" Inge shouted.

"Nothing. All I said was that you knew where I was. I told you I was going for a walk," Laura said calmly. "But I need your help,"

"What makes you think I'll help you?" Inge had been with the family since after Eddie died because her mother was bedridden for months after the accident, and Inge became her Nanny and took care of her. That was nine years ago.

Laura would turn twenty this year, and her parents had decided it would be a good year for her to get married.

"Inge, I overheard my mother talk about a convent or orphanage last week. I want to go there, have the baby and become a nun if possible, and you will help me." Her voice was calm but determined. Inge's face changed from utter disbelief into a rage. Laura could hardly avoid laughing because of the in-between thoughts that Inge juggled in her mind about her position.

"I know you're worried about your job, but that's your problem. If you don't help me, I'll tell my parents some stories that will make them discharge you so fast you won't have time to pack." Her determined face must have convinced Inge, but inside, she felt the fear interfering with her decision.

"Well, I can see that you've decided, but can't go tonight. I have to find out about the convent in the morning. But how do you know they let you in?"

"I don't, but you'll make that happen, won't you?" Laura had a bout of biliousness, which galvanised Nanny into action.

The next day, her father called her. He had just finished a chapter in his book, and her drawings had to be changed. His calculations conflicted with a colleague from the university. There was quite a debate over the disagreement. Looking at the date 1888, she thought, This is the year I give birth to a baby.

"Laura, pay attention. What is the matter with you?" Her father was a proud but stubborn intellectual whose impatient outbursts could snare you to bits.

Laura wondered what had happened to John as she stood at her drawing table, adjusting the star measurements' placement and making notes. She realised that she would miss this work...but...she mentally visualised the priest's eyes. Where did she know him from?

"Your decision will change the direction of many things and affect many people." What a strange thought!

Outside in the street, she heard children's voices and... Ingrid heard children's laughter when she woke up. Toon was awake next to her, watching her.

"Kitty, have I been dreaming that something happened last evening in the shower?" His wondering tone as he bent over her and kissed her navel reminded her...Could she be?

"What do you think? Can you know something like that immediately?" Ingrid thought back to when she had fallen pregnant the last time. Debbie was already nine, and the twins were twelve. She didn't want another child then and never told Jan what had happened.

She had a painful miscarriage after Jan had gone to work. The pain was so bad that she almost passed out. Sascia came looking for her after she had shouted to them through the bathroom door to make their breakfast for once. Sascia knew something was wrong and asked through the door why she did not come out. She didn't want them to see what had happened, so she asked her to wake Quincy, who was visiting them at the time. Thank goodness Quincy was there. She did not want to tell Jan about it later because the steel business was in jeopardy. She knew Jan was very hurt when she withdrew from him, and she became aloof. Would this be the same Soul that knew then the time was not right?

"Kitty, don't do that," she heard Toon's plea.

"What? What did I do?" He cuddled her like a small child.

"Kitty, now you must promise me something," he said gently, placing her hand on the same book.

"Promise never to keep me out of your innermost pain, no matter what. I don't want you ever to feel that you must keep anything from me, no matter how bad, for any reason. I want to share everything with you and live with you for the rest of my earthly life and beyond!"

Ingrid returned his gaze, knowing he meant every word he said, so she placed her hand on the book.

"I promise always to confront you with things when I recognise that I become aloof and withdrawn." Then she drew his head down on her stomach.

"Toon, if I'm pregnant, we'll not know that for at least four weeks. I'll ensure you know every move, every kick, and squeal this little girl makes."

"How do you...know it's a girl?" Toon gasped.

"I've no idea, but let's get out of bed. I want to join the children downstairs, so you'd better get some training just in case."

"Kitty, what about having sex? Could you lose it?"

"Toon Haardens, I heard that. If you for one moment think I would want to quit having sex with you for whatever reason, you must be mad. Don't you know by now that I love making out with you?"

"That's what I like most about you."

"What? Having sex, or that I like it?" She threw a pillow at him.

"Kitty, how far would it be in those few hours?" Toon appealed, showing how important it was for her to have the baby.

"I remember from reading about it that this new individual spends the first few days gradually moving through the fallopian tube, but is not yet implanted. Snooks, having sex would do absolutely nothing, that is, if I'm pregnant. We could be making this all up, you know," she uttered softly, knowing already that he would be disappointed.

"Mmm, thanks for telling me. I would go crazy with frustration looking at you if I could not have you," Toon affirmed as he caressed her.

"Toon, I had a strange dream. It was genuine. I think it was a different life this time, and you were, I think, a priest!"

"Kitty, that must have been a nightmare. Me, a priest? Did I have to save you from something?" he teased, relieved that it was just a dream.

"Yes, you prevented me from throwing myself off a cliff!" She regarded him carefully, remembering the vivid dream but withholding that she had been pregnant in the vision.

"Mmm, that makes sense, and you are now my reward for doing that," Toon said with total conviction.

"You think so?" Ingrid loved the way he laughed. His whole face was an open book. He was candid and sharp, yet he seemed to have a knack for optimistically observing the world. Then they heard a knock on the door.

"Uncle Toon, Daddy asked if you want to have breakfast before we go," Timmy's voice muffled through the door. Toon grabbed his pants and looked back to see if Ingrid was covered up before he opened the door.

***

What a glorious Monday morning! After Peter and Helen showed her around the estate after breakfast, she met quite a few people who all knew Toon. Timmy kept reminding his mother of their outing. Both children were excited to see Toon's plane, and Timmy told Ingrid he wanted to be a pilot. Dirk, Toon's air-technician friend, talked to Toon about changes around a new ILS instrument-landing system he wanted to install before they flew home, while Karin tried on a pair of headphones inside the cockpit.

Ingrid felt so happy she could burst. She knew everything had changed; her life had taken a different direction. She knew she would be confronted with challenges, also, but from now on, she would take POWAH's advice and live just for the moment. Holding onto that inner joy felt so exhilarating, as if this was what was normal. All the colours outside were brighter, and she felt generous towards everybody and everything. Would she ever lose it? No, whatever direction or experience she encountered from now on, she knew what it was like to feel inner bliss, and in bad moments, that would give her strength.

***

Peter dropped Helen and the children off at a friend's home after Toon treated them to lunch at the airbase. He drove them to the Pleasure Park site to meet with Harry Brinks. Something was going on, but neither could determine the cause of the problems. Toon's discussion with Otto and Jill about underground tunnels and the insinuations that CERN was somehow connected started to feel somewhat far-fetched. Conspiracy theories could sometimes be misleading. Ingrid wondered how they could be of assistance.

Peter had stopped the Land Rover on the side of the road so they could look at the whole construction from a higher viewpoint. It was the first time that she saw the large building project lower down in the distance.

"They did make a start. I can see the woven strings and tubes Ready to be assembled." Toon was pointing at a heap of materials surrounded by giant bulldozers.

"Some scientists believe that these microtubules in this fabric of neuronal cells carry consciousness," Peter remarked.

"Really?" She was impressed by Peter's comment.

"Yes, first, a form of a tent is dropped over a geodesic dome frame constructed out of pipes. Then, a layer of inflatable air form, steel-reinforced concrete and polyurethane foam insulation is added. A Swiss eco-resort inspired me." Toon explained.

"So the largest centre dome construction is what is giving all the trouble, not so?" Peter asked

"It seems so. Look, there are the office containers." Toon pointed to the right outside, away from the cranes and bulldozers. Let's find out why they have stopped the construction of the enormous geodesic dome."

Thinking back to the last drawing plans for the new proposal, which she had drawn up only a few days before Piet left, Ingrid remembered Piet's reaction to the latest drawings. He'd shouted at her for her interference. She was so shocked at his outburst that she belittled him.

Could the problems have anything to do with the foundations of the enormous dome?

She hoped they wouldn't stay for long at the site, because this morning, she had to wear the same pantsuit she'd worn when they made love in the valley. Ingrid wondered if she was strong enough to project the image of their love spot as a pure thought–– impulse. Only Toon would know what it meant, so she visualised the grass bedding. Toon turned to her, and his eyes sparkled. *I saw that! That suit you're wearing will always bring back memories.*" His look warmed her. Nobody else reacted.

Peter parked his Land Rover next to a Volkswagen van that had no windows. Funny, but she felt as if they were being spied on. What a weird feeling! Getting out of the car, Ingrid spotted three of Toon's Toon's lorries with the Buttercup landscaping logo. One was parked at a strange angle, and police cars were everywhere. What was going on?

There were lots of people about. Toon put his arms protectively around her shoulders, as he must have felt the same. Something was wrong, and Ingrid was engulfed with dread that made her shiver.

"Kitty, we won't stay here long; I feel it too. This is a place where lots of energy has been tampered with. Now I'm beginning to understand your drawing problems with this place."

Suddenly, Harry Brinks appeared from a crowd of people, looking haggard and distracted.

"Thank goodness you're here!" He shook hands with the men while holding Ingrid's hand.

"Toon, you're stealing away my best planner on the drawing board, I believe. Ingrid, you look lovely! Whatever you both are up to, it seems to agree with you. Sorry for disturbing you both this weekend. I still hope it was a good one?" Harry glanced at Toon while Ingrid blushed as if everyone could see what had happened between them.

"You look glowing, that's why."

"Now, I need all your help to sort out this mess. Come, let's go into my trailer office where we can talk. Peter, please join us. Maybe some outside perception might throw some light on this whole business." The air was stale inside the trailer with cigarette smoke and unwashed dishes. Harry Brinks turned to Toon when he closed the door.

"Before I start, Ingrid, have you got a flash drive with you where you stored the last changes of the drawing plans?" Ingrid was startled and, for a moment, had to think, what had she done with it? Then, she recalled that it was stored on three separate USB ports. The image files were huge and did not fit on just one. That was when Toon came to her office; she focused on him, concentrating.

"Toon, you were with me. ...I can't...We were otherwise occupied, remember? Kitty, I've no idea. All I remember from Friday in your of-

fice is seeing you, wanting you." Taking her eyes away from his, she started to think aloud.

"Maybe I threw it in my bag? Everyone had already gone that afternoon, and I would not have left it there. I remember now I was going to work on one drawing. Carla had already locked the safe. I've got the same bag, so it's still in the Landover. Is it important?"

"Yes, very much so. I got an anonymous phone call yesterday, asking me what had happened to the newly drawn-up plans. It took me a while to register what they were asking, and when I asked who was calling. I received a lot of verbal abuse. I was about to hang up when I was threatened. The man mentioned my granddaughter's name, informing me that I would not recognise her when he was finished with her." Harry's whole body was shaking.

Ingrid flinched as the image of Tieneke's face flashed across her mind.

"Did you tell the police?" The pain and fear for her only daughter, Hennie, made her recoil.

"The whole project would be hijacked if I did not produce these plans immediately. I called André the detective, but apart from the insinuated threats, he has nothing to go on."

"Could it have something to do with your burglary?"

"Peter, the police also think so, but I've no idea. I now wish I had never even purchased the property; I know I did it to spite someone. All I can think is, what could have been on that drawing that was so important?

"Could the arrest of one of its contributing physicists on suspicion of terrorist activity at CERN have anything to do with it?" Peter suggested.

"I have been following some articles about what it is like to live near CERN. The dangers associated with an accelerator only occur when a human is in the tunnel. As you know, Leo has found several old tunnels, but those are still a lot further away..."

Ingrid recalled that Leo was Annelies' brother-in-law. They were all studying an aerial map of the landscape, pinning where the Pleasure Park site was in relation to the chateau, CERN and where Leo had discovered many tunnels.

"People could run out of oxygen before returning to the ground level. If a big magnet quenches while you're down there, you could get hit by heavy equipment or a high-voltage spark. Strong magnets can turn nails into bullets. That is what I read in an article." Toon remarked.

"But accelerators are not nuclear reactors; there are no chain reactions to go critical, or any beams that could get out of the tunnel 100 meters underground, or anything else I can think of," Peter remarked.

"Toon, I realise now that I have been in denial, not wanting to take note when things start to go wrong. Apart from the rumours about deposits of gold, there is far more going on. The Interpol involvement makes me almost believe in the rumours. My daughter Tieneke always talks about the Lower astral world reptilian invasion." Both Peter's and Toon's expressions altered in shock. " Toon, Trevor also has some weird theories. One evening, when he stayed over one night, he talked about an anti-Christ takeover. He calls it the psychic wars in the heavens. Helen and I found his theories far too far-fetched, and the name reptilian triggered some unease."

Ingrid was so uncomfortable with what was discussed due to knowing far too little about it all, and the shouting outside made the stuffy air inside the trailer even more oppressive.

"Harry, why do you think Interpol might be part of the conspiracies?"

"Peter, I have to get hold of Ben. Do you know where he is?" Peter's eyes lifted as she heard the mental question.

"Interpol also wanted to see the aerial photo showing the eye symbol. That's when I thought of you, Ingrid; I hoped you'd have the flash drive with the last drawings with you. Do you?" Ingrid responded by leaving the trailer straight away.

It started to rain softly, so she sprinted to the parked Land Rover. Again, she felt this unpleasant atmosphere emanating from the Volkswagen! She opened the side door quickly and took her bag from under her seat.

What occurred next was so sudden that she never really knew what happened. Someone grabbed her from behind in a violent manner. She felt herself being dragged into the side door that had opened from the Volkswagen van. Someone pressed a cloth to her face. She almost gagged from the pungent odour, and the last thing she remembered was Toon running towards the Volkswagen as they reversed, hitting a parked car and speeding off. Then she heard a gunshot and saw Toon staggering in her mind's eye as she passed out...

Chapter 18
The Higher and Lower Aspects of Intuition

Abducted!

Ingrid ached all over when she regained consciousness. She sat upright, squashed between boxes on the seat of a rapidly moving vehicle, and she was tied up. Her head swayed a tiny pattern of instability. It took her a while to regain all her senses as her eyes would not focus. Sounds of police sirens and screaming voices became louder, but the ambulance siren in the distance jerked her fully awake. Where was she? Toon! She remembered shots being fired. Who had been shot?

By whom? Oh, no, this could not be happening! All she saw was Toon running and then the sound of a shot.

"Oh, snooks!" Overwhelming grief hit her stomach, and an instant panic that erupted into fear overtook all her senses. She was thrown about by the speeding vehicle. All she could make out in the dark was technical equipment and two men up front. One was fast-driving and shouting at a man next to him. They were being chased, but the sound of the police sirens was getting fainter. She then clearly heard the man's familiar voice beside the driver, swearing angrily. As he turned and leered in her direction, she recognised him. It was Piet! The look he gave her was so full of hatred that she clutched her breath.

"You bitch, see what you've got yourself into now. It's your stupid fault!" he yelled over the noises from the speeding engine and the police sirens outside.

"Piet, keep your trap shut. Get useful for a change. Knock her out and wind a rag around her eyes. I don't want her to see where we're going." Ingrid saw in horror that Piet got up from his seat and moved to the back, where she was. The look on his face was positively demonic.

She tried to struggle to free her hands behind her back when he slapped her hard and pushed a rag into her injured face. The pain on her cheek was nothing like the shock she felt at being beaten like that. She felt nauseous. She came to her senses when she realised that it would harm the baby if she didn't calm down...then she passed out...

***

She regained consciousness when the van came to a stop; they grabbed her roughly by her arms that were tied behind her back and dragged her out of the Van. She felt her ankle snap and screamed out in pain.

"For heaven's sake, man, what's wrong with you? Give her to me and lock up the Volkswagen. You're getting us into more trouble than she's worth," a throaty voice snarled as she was lifted and carried into an enclosure. Her ankle was so painful that she almost blacked out when she heard a woman shouting.

"What did you bring her here for?"

"Shut your face! We need her. Piet's too stupid to change the drawings himself. Get a chair. She hurt her ankle, which is starting to swell, damn!"

Need her for what? What was Piet supposed to change? What was going on? The pain in her ankle was spreading to her whole leg. Had she broken it? She felt herself being dumped into a chair, and the rag was removed from her eyes. A heavy, thick-set man with a cruel face leered at her.

"Piet, you never said she was pretty. Are you losing your touch?" his sneering voice gave her the shivers. An anorexic-looking woman with thin, greasy, mousy hair placed her foot on a stool, and she had difficulty not screaming out loud.

"Please, can you get some ice? It will help with the swelling," Ingrid begged the woman as politely as she could muster.

"Bloody hell, what am I supposed to do with her? She could have broken her ankle. This wasn't in the deal. All you were supposed to do was to get her cooperation, no funny stuff. Piet, if this is the dame you worked with, you handle her," the gaunt, youngish woman snapped.

"Shut your face! She deserves anything she gets. I've tried to ask the arrogant woman to cooperate before," Piet's insulting manner astounded her as he swallowed the last word. The woman's grave grey eyes revealed she was on drugs, vacant and haunted as if she had not slept in days. Piet also appeared very scruffy. She let herself sink into the chair. Her heart still pounded in her chest, but she tried to calm down and closed her eyes...

***

When she opened them again, being stiff and highly uncomfortable, she was on her own but still tied to the chair with her arms pulled back.

She could hear a debate going on somewhere above her. The room stank of dampness, like a dark basement; the chair with a faded pansy pattern material was dirty, and her foot resting on the stool was rickety. The walls were covered with technical drawings, but she hadn't a clue what they were. There were three computers, but only one was like the one she used at work. Something far more sinister than she ever imagined was going on.

Why had they kidnapped her? She started to shiver from the cold or, more likely, the reaction from the adrenaline that had been racing through her body. The same slender woman, shouting at the large, heavy man, came down the open metal staircase bolted to one wall, carrying a tray with food.

"Piet, bring a blanket. It's freezing in this basement." So she was in a basement, and it must have been getting dark outside. Not that she could spot any windows; she just knew. The woman placed the tray onto a box next to her chair. Many boxes were lying about.

"Look, I was against bringing you here from the start, but you'd better do what they order you to do. Bruce is a dangerous man to mess around with; he has no Soul, I'm telling you," she hissed as she untied Ingrid's arms. She felt the pain as her blood ran through them again.

"I have no idea what I'm supposed to be doing."

"Oh, you'll know soon enough. I hear that you're one of the people responsible for the changes with the other guy who got shot."

"Toon! Is he hurt? Please tell me!" Ingrid's heart leapt when her mind started considering dreadful, unacceptable possibilities.

"Is that his name? I don't know. I witnessed chaos when the drawings were altered and the excavation was relocated to a different site, where blasting commenced. I have already revealed more than I should have. I do not support kidnapping, and please don't let anyone know about what I have shared with you."

"What are you blabbering about? Iris, get your butt in gear! I want some grub," the bulky man shouted as he descended the metal stairs. He pulled her blanket away and sat down heavily on a metal box next to her.

"Now, let's get down to business. I know you must be pissed off for being dragged the way you did, but we had no choice. As Piet said, you brought it on yourself." Ingrid wondered what on earth they were accusing her of. His breath had a fishy smell.

"What happened to the man you shot?" Her rage was hard to contain in her voice, but tears threatened to well up.

"What was he to you?" he asked her directly. His eyes were gleaming with an exhilaration from feeling the power he seemed to think he had over her.

She closed her eyes, concentrating not to strike at him. All she wanted to do was to kick him in his fat stomach. He gave her the shivers ...

"Ingrid, stay calm; stay centred. Be still; don't fight it. Can you hear me? It's Liesbeth." Could it be? All she could think of was Toon. Why did she not hear his thoughts? Was it possible that Liesbeth was projecting onto her? Was her mind playing tricks with her? Feelings of despair welled up; she kept her eyes closed tightly, projecting rapidly while visualising a beam of white light and Liesbeth's face.

"Please, tell me what happened to Toon? I saw him fall as I heard a shot! What's happening? I'm so scared, Liesbeth! Piet is involved." She wondered if her vision and thoughts were strong enough to reach her.

Would Liesbeth have picked up Piet's name? She kept her eyes closed, hoping not to give away that she was communicating with someone. If only they knew! ...

"Ingrid, Annelies here, stay calm. Focus on your solar plexus by visualising light in your uterus, protecting it with love. You and the baby will be all right. Take care of yourself first." While trying to listen to Annelies, she pushed the coarse blanket with her foot off the floor and, with her tied hands, pulled it onto her lap, partly as protection from the brutish creep referring to Toon in the past tense... *"Ingrid, anger is not a bad emotion, but don't direct it at a person. Try to stay aware that you see an illusion! I know it must not be easy, love, but do try. We are all directing our thoughts to you to give you strength in this ordeal. I'm glad you feel*

angry, which means you're fighting, but try to rise above your person-
ality. Let your higher self take charge. It is far more capable of deal-
ing with this kind of situation." Hans's face, which came as a flash of
comfort, comforted her.

Ingrid felt vastly relieved for Liesbeth, Hans and Annelies reaching
her telepathically. When she opened her eyes, the scary man was
still waiting for her answer when he jerked her blanket off and undressed her with leering eyes! She'd seen him before!

"Well, do I get some answers?"

"What is the time?" Her mind reeled when the market scene
jumped into focus, ignoring his threatening question. Was Toon in
any danger? Was he still alive? That thought brought on more tears,
and she started to shiver, partly because of his offensive stare. Those
eyes! ... Oranges!

"I thought so. He's your lover! Well, all I can say is that I did shoot
him, but he got up into the Landover and started to chase us. He
didn't get very far." He grinned maliciously.

"We're going to have some fun, you and I."

"Bruce, the boss is on the line. He's pissed off, so you'd better get up
fast," Piet shouted from the top of the metal staircase while she still
shuddered at his insinuations. Bruce cursed as he got up and pointed at her food.

"You'd better eat. We have work to do, and it's already after eleven."
He stomped up the staircase, and she was left alone again. That's
late already!

She'd been tied down for so long; no wonder that her arms were
numb. She must have lost her watch in the struggle. They had met
Mr. Brinks just after lunch, so it must have been just after two
o'clock. Where had the almost nine hours gone? Why hadn't Toon
contacted her? Why only. How did Annelies know about her...?
She understood that Toon must have reached out to Annelies, im-
ploring her to help Ingrid. Oh, Toon!

"Annelies, can you hear me? What's wrong with Toon? Oh, please.... Please let him be all right!" She tried to project, but she knew that her acute anxiety for him hampered her focus. Nothing had prepared her for the unacceptable possibility that he could have been fatally shot!

She couldn't eat and wept helplessly. She needed to know the truth about Toon. She tried to project mentally, but she was too played out. With difficulty, her foot dragged the scruffy blanket near behind her chair, and slowly, her tight hands dragged the blanket up so she could somehow drape the blanket around herself. It felt like hours, but somehow, she fell into an anguished sleep.

***

Eventually, she awakened in darkness, in considerable pain from her ankle and from her restricted position.

"Kitty! ... I can... You are in pain! ... she heard or sensed! Oh, Snooks, is that you.... What have they done to you? My love, I'm going crazy with worry! Are you hurt?" Ingrid started to cry, sensing his thoughts, and a vast relief washed over her. Toon was alive!

"Kitty, I'm so worried. Are you in danger?" ... she could also sense pain coming from him. He must have been injured! She felt a resurgence of strength now that she knew Toon was taken care of. He must be beside himself, being so helpless since nobody knew where she was.

"Snooks, I'm much better now, knowing you are all right. Where are you?" Her mind was racing when suddenly he was gone, and she did not feel him anymore!

"Ingrid, we're all together! Don't worry, love; Toon has lost consciousness but will be fine. He had an emergency operation on his shoulder in Paris. After he came around, he refused any painkillers. He wanted to contact you first and needed us to boost his mental powers." Ingrid

cringed, sensing his injury. Where was Toon now, with Liesbeth? She was...

"Ingrid, they flew him down to our hospital in Utrecht. He's been given a blood transfusion because he lost a lot of blood. Your three children were here this evening. Harry Brinks has taken them to his house. Ed, your brother-in-law, has just arrived, giving me a mental boost. He's powerful." She sensed Annelies' fear, but why?

"My dear, we have to know where you are. Do you have any idea?" She knew that it was Ed asking her. Ingrid felt some calmness flowing over her. She was not alone, so why had she lost faith so quickly? Toon must have been badly hurt. She wondered how her children were coping with all this. Toon was in physical danger but in a different kind of danger.

"Ed, Annie, I'm so glad you are with Toon. Tell my children that I'm all right. I do not know where I am, but it could be only a few kilometres from the site. I'm in some basement. I can't believe we drove for so long, but I lost count of time. Tell Mr. Brinks that Piet's involved, and it's something to do with the changes in the last drawing...They're coming back again...I'd better stop beaming. Otherwise, they'll know what I'm doing. I'm scared! Oh, Annie, Ed, I'm afraid! Keep talking; it makes me feel better...

Annie, how did you know about the baby?... Oh, dear, I'm so cold......" her mental focus blurred, and she felt her head spin from the effort of trying to visualise...

Piet de Wit

She must have slept for quite a while because they were shaking her to wake her up. She was still shivering, and her ankle was extremely painful. She had tried to put her foot down next to the chair before, but the pain was too bad. She could not have felt happier and more secure that morning in the Land Rover. She never believed she could be catapulted to the opposite emotion from that state. Her personality mainly reacted through fear, a legitimate survival instinct, but unfortunately, man's worst enemy, and she had to keep it under control.

Ingrid tried to take deep breaths as they shook her, keeping her mind empty of fear-based thoughts. When she opened her eyes, all three were standing around.

"Thank goodness she's all right," Iris remarked, relieved. "I tell you now, when the Boss is here, she'd better be cooperative if only for both your sakes, and you don't achieve this by force!" Iris hissed at both men.

"Ingrid, your life is not worth much if you don't cooperate. Our boss is coming soon and needs you to change something on your drawing; if you don't, you're finished," Iris told her bluntly. Bruce was holding the USB stick that came from her bag.

"What's this?" He glared at her while Piet took the flash drive and loaded it. Then he swore.

"I can't get in; it's write-protected!"

"For starters, I need your access code! Quick, we haven't got much time left. It's already midnight, and we've been stupid to let you sleep this long. Bruce yelled, but Ingrid knew that not everything was on that flash drive. She remembered that she had split the file in three and stored it the old-fashioned way. She knows where the other two flash drives were. Usually, she was very efficient when storing away her work, but she had been distracted by Toon at the time. The access codes on all three files on the flash drive were different but easy to unravel because they were her three children's names. Piet was not the brightest man around. Otherwise, he could have discovered a tiny slider switch that needed to be moved to the unlock position. She had to think quickly: if she told them that there were other flash drives involved, that they were in her office, Piet would have to get them.

She was dragged, with the chair and all, in front of a different computer next to him. How did Iris ever get herself involved with this lot, she thought when Iris left her with the two men.

They untied her hands. She needed to rub them to get the blood flowing, but they pushed her to get started. After unlocking the small slider and plugging the flash drive back on the side, Ingrid punched in 'Jeroen' to show them she intended to cooperate. Bruce looked over her shoulder at her files; she tried to move sideways away from his fishy breath.

"Those are not all the drawings. They are not all there? Where are the others?" Piet shouted. He was leering over to her from his seat in front of the computer he was looking at.

"In my drawer at the office, I wanted to work on only one file on this flash drive." She was hoping to avoid his angry, threatening temper.

Bruce swore and jerked her chair around.

"You bitch, you'd better be telling me the truth." Then he grabbed her by her blouse and pulled her up. She tried not to lean on her ankle in any way, but Piet pulled the chair away from under her.

She screamed in pain, bringing Iris running down the stairs to see Bruce clutching her blouse that was torn open.

"You fools, what are you doing?"

"You shut up. The bitch is making idiots out of us. She tells us now that her office has two more flash drives." Bruce was glaring at her while his eyes fixed greedily on her exposed bra.

"Piet, this is all your stupidity. You were around when they made the changes. Why did you not swipe the old ones, then? I wonder what it will take for her to cooperate?" Bruce sneered.

"Yes, why didn't you, Piet! It would have saved us all this hassle, and Bruce, you'd better cool it," Iris said sharply with disgust when she became aware of Bruce's hungry stare...

"Bitch, watch out who you are speaking to!" but he let go of her. The tension was so electric that Ingrid needed to say something. "If you would only explain why and what you need from me, I would not be so in the dark." At the same time, she was massaging her ankle and holding onto her ripped blouse. Attacking Piet would not help her situation at all.

"Yes, you'd like to know, wouldn't you?"

"Piet, it makes sense. Why not tell her? She's not going anywhere. ever." Bruce grabbed Iris's arm and pulled her into a corner. Iris was getting fed up with them, and they argued while Piet glared at her, dragging the chair back." See what trouble you caused us! Why could you and your lover not have shut up about the changes?"

"Piet, what are you talking about? Tell me, why are my new drawings so important to you lot? I can draw the same plan again." Ingrid was sick of being in the dark and of Piet's offensive manner.

"Hey, you two, what if she does the whole drawing again?" Piet shouted at them in the corner where Iris and Bruce were arguing.

"Would that take long?" Bruce replied while glaring. She gave him a look of disgust when he jerked her arm away from her blouse while getting hold of her bra at the front at the same time, violently tearing it off. Ingrid struck him hard, and he was stunned.

"I like that, some spirit!" He threw her torn bra in the corner.

"You'd better start drawing, so I won't be tempted." His drooling face made her nauseous. Her skin was shaved from the torn bra straps.

She clutched at her torn blouse, shaking with anger. They were more ignorant than she'd thought if they believed she could quickly redo a drawing that had taken her at least a week to create.

"If I have to start from scratch, it would take at least a week, but if I had the previous drawings, it would help. I also need the right drawing program and a scanner, unless you can get the two other flash drives out of my drawer at work," she said while covering herself in the blanket for protection—anything to prolong what they want from her.

"A week!" Bruce shouted. He was about to grab her again out of frustration when Iris called from upstairs, telling them to come up fast. Her voice screamed with fear, which made her even more afraid.

They left her alone in the dark basement. She let herself hang over the keyboard, crying when she became aware of a strong feeling of Toon!

It was a mixture of confusion, dread and....

"Oh, no, Kitty, love! What have they done to you? I'm with you. I can see you. Oh, love, what are they wanting from you?" The feeling of him around her was so strong that she suddenly wondered.

"Snooks, are you all right? Why do I feel as if you are near me? Oh, Toon, please, don't let me think you are...dead. Toon, I love you! Please come back." In her despair, she let the blanket slide off her. Why did she suddenly think Toon was gone? Died! Was it because she had felt his whole essence near her? Her grief took hold of her.

"Please, POWAH, my higher self, my Soul, the source of all that is, I don't want to.... please, give me the strength to deal with this pain. Give me a reason to live!"

Then, a third man appeared from upstairs with Bruce and Piet in tow. This must be the Boss! Ingrid had difficulty not breaking out in a sweat of panic.

Piet and Bruce were talking to him, and his face showed an inner rage, but he stayed very calm. His eyes, of a usual pale blue, were icy. His shiny skin was stretched taut upon his acne-white, bony face. He wore a striped, well-pressed suit. Nothing like the other three scruffy individuals. She knew straight away that he was the most dangerous of them all.

"Well, well, so this is Toon Haardens' fiancée. I wonder how much you are worth to him?" His cold, pale eyes were staring at her breasts while giving a hand sign to Bruce.

He pulled the blanket off her lap while Bruce pulled her up, kicked the chair, and grabbed her arms behind her, ripping her shirt and pants off while pushing his knee between her legs from behind. She shuddered in humiliation as both men's animalistic glow was mentally raping her naked body.

"Mmm, I know where your lover is. We have someone outside his hospital room. One word from me, and he's a goner. Ingrid had difficulty not showing any reaction, but the fear for Toon's life was intense.

"Give me the cell phone," the Boss ordered while glowingly travelling over her nakedness with small, calculating eyes. He dialled a number... Ingrid held her breath, closed her eyes, and tried to contact Annelies. She could feel the tears gushing down her cheeks, partly out of the physical humiliation and partly out of her fear for Toon . *"Annelies, please hear me; someone outside Toon's room is in contact with these people. Please, he's in great danger!"*...

"Mr. Brinks, listen to what I have to say to you. I'll only say this once. You have little time to save your employee and Toon Haardens." Ingrid looked again at the man, who kept his glare on her while listening; then he gave instructions in a resolute voice into the cell phone, and then he turned it so she was now facing the camera, when suddenly she recalled his unpleasant squeaky voice!

"If you fail to do so or draw any attention to yourself, Mr Haardens will be the first to die, and at this moment, we are all looking at your employee's lovely breasts that are very. ...

" Ingrid could almost hear Mr. Brinks shouting, as he must've seen the image of her being naked from his cell phone's screen. She saw the man's glaring expression change as he clicked away pictures with his cell phone. He made a sign at Bruce, who grabbed her with his big, dirty hands, travelling from her breast down to around her waist over her navel while she clawed and screamed at him. The cell phone was clicking away. Then the boss man made Bruce push her back into the chair.

He disconnected his phone and gave Bruce a sign to stop...which Bruce did reluctantly, gleaning at her nakedness.

"Now, I want some cooperation from you, lady. You get your pre-view drawings, and you'd better start working, or I'll order Bruce here to release his frustration on you!"

"Boss, that will be a pleasure!" His eyes were drooling. Piet grabbed her torn clothes and threw them back. She clutched at her ripped blouse while pulling on her pants. The hatred of glaring eyes ripped her of any privacy. Iris helped her and draped the blanket over her shoulders.

They retrieved her old drawings on the screen so she knew what to do for the first part. She still needed an architectural drawing pro-gram to revise the alterations. She asked Iris for the program she had used and looked at Piet, who suddenly got into gear and down-loaded the 3D program into the very sophisticated desktop com-puter. They left her alone for at least an hour when Iris brought cof-fee. Ingrid looked up and managed to thank her.

"*Ingrid, two policemen are outside Toon's room. Girl, keep your fear level down; you must be exhausted! What are they doing to you? ... Love, please, can you concentrate and project to me?*" Ed was men-tally with her, acutely aware of her ordeal. Ingrid looked up to see what they were doing. Somehow, she now had to work and project simultaneously!

"*Ed, I must redo the whole drawing of the site near Paris. I have no idea why. They have threatened Harry Brinks. They got him on his cell phone.*" Suddenly, the boss man stood behind her. She had never heard him coming down the metal steps. She hoped he was frantically unaware that she had been playing with the keyboard while projecting.

"Why was the plan changed?" he asked abruptly. The Egyptian eye flashed across her mind. She hoped that Ed could read her thoughts while thinking and speaking simultaneously.

"The blasting was causing problems because of something to do with what was under the soil, so a decision was made to move the large dome to a different side of the property and relocate some of the smaller Geodesic domes. She had made that all up because she had no idea why.

He grabbed the mouse from her, retrieved some other drawings from the C drive, and projected them over hers. Some parts were the same, but some were in a different place. What was that drawing? It looked familiar but was not a building, more like an electronic plate.

"Ed, it looks like... a sound card! Why would a computer or electronic plate have to match my drawing plans?" It made no sense at all.

As the bossman deleted it and looked at her drawing, she saw that he was thinking, and she tried to read his mind. All she picked up was... *why it worked before...*the rest was technical. He looked at his watch, started swearing, and walked to the others, leaving her alone.

Ingrid was so tired. She wanted to make her mind completely blank with no thoughts, nothing. She didn't immediately react to her screen when it suddenly turned bright, and there was POWAH! The warmth and love she associated with the bold text made her fully alert while quickly looking around, but they were all upstairs.

<Kitty, it cannot be transcended in contemplation when the mind is stunned into inaction by intense fear or persistent repetitions of meaningless thoughts, such as threats. You lose your mental telepathic connection. Focus. Focus. Focus. You can do this.>

That's easy to say! You are not me! She thought in a panic. How are they ever going to find me?

<Kitty, all thoughts have to manifest at some time. Take this as an opportunity to release any thoughts of violence. If one holds on to an idea of violence, one shall experience violence.> What was he implying? Those words hit her solar plexus. Has she manifested this herself? That was all too much; maybe this awakening way of life was not for her. How could she ever believe that she was good enough? Her whole body sank into a dark pit. Tears streamed down her cheeks. Images of unimaginable violence flashed past, clutching her in terror. Why did horrific thought forms suddenly surround her?

Even POWAH's bold text looked frightening. It gave no hope. The images still coming up in droves created turmoil in her stomach. She knew the screen had changed. She hardly wanted to read more disturbing ideas, but her curiosity got the better of her.

<Kitty, there are no real victims; some live from an earlier incarnation or their ancestry's thought form, fantasies or beliefs. Just let them go. Embrace the feeling and quality of forgiveness. That energy alone will free you. Now more than ever, you must direct your attention to the good of all and control your mind so that your brain becomes a sensitive receiver of the thoughts and desires of your higher mind. Then, you'll reconnect with your I AM.>

After choking on heaps of air from her shallow breathing, which made her whole body shudder, she suddenly felt an inner core, like a fire burning inside. She allowed it to spread all over until she became numb. She had reached a place of indifference. Her shaking had stopped when the screen flared up again.

<Kitty, you and I are one, but if you want to clear your mind correctly, you must focus with total concentration so that all other thoughts stay clear. Kitty, when you telepathically send a

message, you have to be able to concentrate in a one-pointed way. You can do that already; that is how they will find you.>

"POWAH, I'm so tired, I'm cold, I'm in pain, and all I want to do is sleep. I don't care anymore," she mentally projected.

She knew the moment she had thought it was not true; she wanted to draw the correct energies toward herself, Toon's love, those of her children, Liesbeth, Ed, Annelies and all her dear friends.

<Kitty, concentration involves bringing your personality to a one-pointed vision of a selected subject or object. It then creates a condition of quietness and calmness fused with stillness. Your mind is your sixth sense, and your brain is your receiving plate. It becomes a reflector of whatever you have your focus on!>

"POWAH, is that what true meditation is? When I'm focused, I'm meditating. I thought you had to be still and listen!" she beamed at the screen.

<Kitty, true meditation is an attitude of mind that grows out of a concentration philosophy, and most important, LOVE. Continue at your own pace, and your Divine Self will guide you from within. You will create a channel for more life force energy to enter your field. Fixing your mind upon a particular object or a chosen topic of thoughts means reorganising your mind, withdrawing from the sense perceptions and drawing yourself into the brain. Kitty, use your third eye centre. The stillness will come. Then, the trust that all is good will become your reality. That is genuinely praying.> She sat staring at the screen, shivering and mulling over what POWAH seemed to project to her; she wondered if her logical mind questioned how she could see the text... She saw the text. Was it her holistic mind that just allowed it to be? Was that all that was needed to wake up?

The excerpts had made her aware of how difficult it was to release and master any of the virtues and qualities of the Language of Light in moments of despair. She was never going to keep her intent. It was too hard. All she wanted was to be with Toon. Her life was not going to be worth living without him. Sad but true...

The screen suddenly changed, and a file was downloaded. To her utter amazement, the following excerpt, nineteen appeared... Did someone know where she was? ... But how. ...

Excerpt Nineteen[1]

Program Planet Earth

Mastery over the Higher and Lower Aspects of Intuition

Rule nine *of the Ascension Decoding Card Game:* How was this at all possible? Was it just her who was seeing the text on the screen? The gift of life is mastering the 1st red root chakra at the base of the spine. The 2nd orange energy vortex chakra gives structure to life, and the 3rd yellow energy vortex chakra gives wisdom to your life. Gaining Mastery over the three lower chakras will expand the size of your auric field as more significant segments of the soul descend into the human experience.

<Kitty The primary nature of the mentor or your guide is to ob-serve; it plays no part in your lower physical realm.>

For a split second, she let her fear come up in case someone would come down.

<Any mentor energy is your feedback system to the Jaarsma clan group soul. The frequency fence does not hinder it because it is neutral and cannot be polarised.>

POWAH calls himself a mentor, or a guide. Was that why they all connected or experienced the same mentor? For the first time, she started to comprehend who POWAH was. More like a guardian angel helping us all to protect, guide and guard ourselves.

The familiar flash on the screen showed up, followed by POWAH's text.

---

1. https://allrealityshifters.wordpress.com/powah/the-reality-shifters-excerpt-19/

<When the higher intuition is activated by telepathy and other psychic abilities, your subconscious mind becomes active, and you can receive impressions from other people, the group mind, and the collective consciousness. Remember that I AM the Keeper of the Game! LOVE POWAH>

After reading POWAH's text off her screen, she took a screenshot and saved it on the flash drive. Why had she not done that before? It had never occurred to her to do so.

The excerpt had given her strength, but she felt more alone than ever, and she shouldn't. Her ability to communicate telepathically and experience having a guide who knows her every move, why did that not give her inner strength?

POWAH wrote in Excerpt Nineteen that she was always in the right place, but what would she do if she were in the correct location? She felt as if all her good intentions had gone overboard with the first real crisis when her personality took over. Would she ever learn not to react?

Annelies in Utrecht

Fear is our greatest obstacle, and releasing it is the test. Annelies knew this while trying to relax. She felt exhausted by the feelings Ingrid mentally projected because they were horrific. What were they doing to her? Liesbeth and Hans had left. Thank goodness for their telepathic powers that far overshadowed hers. She was curled up in a chair next to Toon's bed, eyes closed, glad Harry Brinks was still with her.

Harry Brinks had been so traumatised by the pictures he had received on his cell phone that he had sent them to Ed, who went ballistic while both Liesbeth and Hans stared in horror. Her body had been shaking from pure hatred. They all agreed. Toon was never going to see them. Harry had then deleted them all.

The last time they had seen each other was when they both were bidding for the hotel six years before. So much has happened since then. When she glanced around the hospital room, Ingrid's children were all crammed next to Toon's bed on the other side, trying very hard to be brave. Toon had been given something in his drip to make him sleep. The noise from the life-supporting equipment was depressing.

By now, Annelies knew what Ingrid and Toon meant to each other. Toon had risked his life trying to follow her, and then, before he would let them do anything to him or give him any medication, he got her attention telepathically. Annelies knew it must have taken all his energy to manage that, but luckily, Peter was there to help give him the extra mental boost he needed. It was Liesbeth who had suddenly burst through, telling them to focus on Ingrid.

The last four hours of Toon had been bad. They almost lost him because he was determined to follow that Volkswagen. He lost a dangerous amount of blood from the bullet wound in his shoulder, just a fraction away from some major arteries.

Annelies heard what happened from Peter and Harry Brinks. Peter and Harry saw Toon fall as they listened to the shot; he got up again, got into Peter's Land Rover, and followed the van while shouting at Peter to get to the plane. Peter knew Toon was injured, but not how badly. Peter took Harry's Mercedes and followed Toon instead while Harry got to the plane. Peter could see that Toon was in trouble when his driving became unstable, and the van he was chasing gained speed.

By then, the police tried to bypass Toon, who was blocking the road as he was heading directly for a ravine; Peter managed to ram into him just before he would have gone over the cliff.

When he reached the side door, Toon was still conscious and tried to get her telepathically, asking for Peter's mental assistance. Peter then knew he was in bad shape. The ambulance was quickly on the scene, thanks to Harry Brinks. Toon had lost so much blood that he passed out in the ambulance. She heard it all from Peter first;

then Harry filled her in on the phone while he stayed with Toon in the ambulance to the nearest hospital.

Toon's friend, Dirk, his pilot, took the plane up in the air, hoping to find some clue as to where they had taken Ingrid, but by then, the police had lost the van.

The police were still outside the hospital room, and Annelies' worst fear was if it leaked out, they could continue to communicate! If the newspaper had learned of that, Ingrid would be in grave danger. Toon's Pilot had picked up her and Ingrid's children by plane. They all insisted on being with Toon.

"Harry. It's already after midnight. Ingrid's children must have a rest, however hard it must be for them," she whispered. Harry nodded.

"I'll stay with Toon, just in case he wakes up. Please, can you drive them to Peter's home?" Harry looked haggard, having not slept since the incident. He blamed himself for getting them involved in some sinister plot. Annelies had mentally picked up from Harry's inner dialogue that Ingrid had been furious at someone, but she had difficulty reaching her to find out why.

"Harry, call my brother Fred for me; I need to get in touch with Ed, Ingrid's brother-in-law."

"Annelies, Uncle Ed is already on his way to the hospital," Sascia, Ingrid's twin daughter, replied instead.

"Harry, Liesbeth told me that Ingrid had mentioned the name Piet. Does it mean anything to you?" She looked into his sad, dark brown eyes full of worry that turned into rage when she mentioned Piet's name. She had managed to project to Ingrid, telling her about Toon, so Ingrid knew he was looked after. When Toon told her about the baby, she knew he would not want to live without her.

"Harry, please keep it to yourself. They must not know how I found out from Toon... please," knowing Harry himself was not aware of how she could communicate with Ingrid. Harry grasped her shoulder, needing her strength for a moment.

Debbie was crying. Jeroen was consoling her while Annelies saw Sascia sitting, staring into space. She was the only one of Ingrid's children who seemed to have some telepathic skills, but they needed to be activated.

Sascia announced that she was staying! Annelies knew that Sascia knew she was in contact with her mother. The other two could not comprehend it. They knew something was going on between them, but it was too much for them to grasp the possibility of telepathy.

"Jeroen and Debbie, please don't say a word to anyone about our telepathic skills. If that leaks out, I don't have to spell it out, do I?" They were both looking at her with big eyes, full of fear for their mother.

"Annelies, can we phone Quincy? She's very close to Mom and must have heard something over the news or in the paper by now." Jeroen needed someone close to be with them, and she hugged them both.

"Look, yes, get your aunt to be with you, but say nothing that happened until I've spoken to and seen her. Understand. I mean this very seriously." They both nodded and were about to leave when they all heard Toon making a sound, trying to get the tubes out of his nose. Annelies rushed to him.

"Please, Toon, leave it in. It'll help you get stronger. You're no help to us if you get weaker." His eyes were full of emotional pain as he made a gesture to Jeroen, and all three rushed to his bed. His eyes rested on Sascia.

"You're the photographer?" he mumbled weakly, taking her hand.

"You look so like your mom. Harry, take her with you when my pilot, Dirk, flies over the area tomorrow. Sascia, you must take lots of photos. Your mom is somewhere not far from the site where it all happened. I want to see all the photos tomorrow evening," He pressed her hand, then lay back, unable to talk more. Sascia's tear-streaked face acknowledged for the first time that this man would not leave anything to chance. If anybody got her mother back, he would. She nodded, and all four prepared to go when Toon made another attempt to speak.

"Harry, Dirk must phone me on his cell phone, please. Don't leave me trapped here, knowing nothing," Toon pleaded, showing signs of profound exhaustion.

"It's a promise! You get some rest and get better fast," Harry's voice broke; they all looked tearfully at Annelies, who whispered, "Go."

Outside, a policeman was sitting in the hospital hallway. They were taking no risks. Annelies went back to the room when Toon was sleeping. She would try again to contact Ingrid but fell into a light sleep at the side of the bed.

Toon's stroking hand awakened her. He looked relatively peaceful, and she saw Ed on the other side of the bed. How he managed to get to the hospital from Apeldoorn that quickly was a mystery. When Toon opened his eyes again, he knew Ed was there, so they must have talked while she was asleep. "Annie, is she back with us again?" Annelies suddenly let go of her own emotions, needing to cry, and Toon held her against him with one arm.

"Annie, I've learned more in this one long day and night than in my life. I now truly understand what fear can do, and for the first time, I've experienced how to project myself beyond my body. I didn't get far, not even out of this room, but what a sense of freedom! Annie, I know everything will be all right if I keep my focus."

She had been focusing on Ingrid for hours, with no response, and she knew Ingrid was not sleeping. They had both been aware of Ingrid's fear.

Toon woke up twice to join her mentally, after which he almost lost all hope of being connected to her again. Liesbeth made all the difference, and they knew Ingrid could mentally hear them.

"Let's try again, shall we, together. *"Ingrid, we'll all join our focus on this wave band. Toon is looking a lot better. Hold your attention; create a force-field of light around you so strong that we will find you by it.....don't ever let go. We need your help to find you. Look after yourself. Be still and listen to us when we are near and try to get some sleep,"* They were all quiet for a long time, and then they mentally heard her.

*"Ed, Annie, I'm so glad... Toon. Tell my child. ... I'm all right now. I've no idea where I am, sort of a basement. I can't believe... all that long. Tell Mr Brinks ... Piet is involved ... something to do .... drawing changes,...Oh, they are coming back again ...Just now they'll know what I'm doing. I'm scared. Annelies or Ed, keep talking to me. It makes me feel better...Annie, how did you know about the baby?... I'm so cold...*Annelies glanced at Toon and saw that he was asleep again. She turned to Ed. *"Did you hear what I heard?"* Ed was crying.

"Yes, I'd give anything to be with her. What drawings is she talking about? Can you fill me in as to what has happened so far?" Ed asked in a broken whisper so as not to alarm Toon. She told him about the shooting, the chase, and Toon's operation, and that Harry would fly the next day, with Sascia taking photos, when they were both mentally interrupted.

"Annie, my love, I'm breaking our agreement. I heard what happened. Look after Toon, dearest; we'll get her back soon." Annelies' head was pressed into the sheets, and her shoulders heaved; she broke down and cried.

"Ben, oh, how I've longed for your connection!" Ed read Toon's chart to try to block himself off mentally to give them privacy.

"Ed, how much did Toon share about the Jaarsma estate in France?" Annelies whispered, appreciating his discretion.

"I've no idea what you are talking about. I know Harry Brinks because our steel company has dealings with them, and we are aware of the legal battles that are going on. We've employed our investigator, but that's for financial reasons. My dad has great regard for Mr. Brinks and has not subscribed to rumours filtering through to his office," Ed whispered.

Suddenly, the heart machine made a different noise, and Annelies went stone cold. She looked up at Ed with absolute horror, only to see the same expression of despair and anguish on his face, not wanting to believe that Toon's heart had stopped!

The door burst open, and the trauma unit went into full action, shoving Ed and Annelies out of the room...

Chapter 19
The Heart Chakra

Toon Haardens – Intensive care

Toon drifted into his inner mental world, where the past and future became the present, as he remembered the first time he saw her... She had bewitched him on the spot, leaning against the wall with one hand holding the phone to her ear. Her feminine beauty instantly captivated him, and her posture activated his imagination. He knew he had found his beloved.

So, this was the Ingrid Ed was always raving about. Many a night after a long, hard day's work, he and Ed Barendse would visit the local bar in Darwin, and inevitably, Ed drifted into his pet topic: Ingrid, his brother's wife that he could never get out of his mind...

When he was five, Toon was put in foster care with Dennis and Hetty Zwiegelaar, who already had two children. Fred was his age, and his sister Annelies was a strong-willed teenager. Dennis Zwiegelaar had two more children from a previous marriage, Otto and Margaret. Toon was well-loved by his active foster family in the hotel business.

When he grew up, Toon became one of those men who never wanted to place any limits on himself, so he denied himself anything. He was productive at whatever he did and had the gift of an unusually happy disposition because he truly assimilated his experiences. When he was approached by the board of directors of his deceased father's estate when he turned twenty-one, he had no idea of the accumulated wealth that came with it.

Otto Zwiegelaar took his role as the half-brother to young Toon very seriously and influenced him to study building and civil engineering.

Later, Toon travelled with Otto and worked on many large construction sites around the world that partly belonged to the estate he would gradually inherit over the years, according to the will's stipulations. Toon was good company because of his enthusiastic outlook on life.

Whatever he did, he did with enthusiasm. He would never dream of doing anything because someone else has said it was necessary. He only did it if he felt like it.

The only thing in Toon's first fifty years of life that had been hard on him was the lonely feeling of missing someone he knew, but he'd never met his Soulmate. He searched for her in many places and thought he'd found her on many occasions, only to discover that it was not her.

Caught in the snares of wealth and success, disaster and betrayal, he abandoned his search, and the walls he created for his emotional protection became his prison for many years.

Dylan Haardens, Toon's grandfather, a self-made millionaire, started life as a simple coal miner in Liverpool. He hated banks, labour unions, and evangelists. Besides his oil business in Alaska, he owned a publishing company and a steel pipe manufacturing plant that supplied many oil rigs around the world. When he decided that he wanted a wife, he looked for her in the same manner as he approached his many enterprises.

When he met a young Dutch girl, Vera Jaarsma, who was running a boarding house in London where he stayed on one of his visits, he proposed to her after observing her for six days. He had made up his mind. That was the first time something else became meaningful to him besides making money. Vera, his wife, started a restaurant in London where he had his head office. On the birth of his only son, Steven, he lost interest in making money. By now, the vast accumulated fortune of his holdings was of such magnitude that he wisely looked for the right people to run it. He was a good judge of character and established a board of capable directors from an office in New York to manage his affairs. Even during the war years, his investments had been handled profitably. Later, his son became the managing director of his father's companies.

Toon's parents, Steven Haardens and Siska de Jong, died in 1969 in Rotterdam under suspicious circumstances when he was only seven months old. The investigations got nowhere, so their murders became a cold case. Toon was looked after by his grandparents on their estate in England. They were killed a year later in a tramway accident in Amsterdam when they were visiting Siska's family in Holland. He was left behind at the Jaarsma orphanage until appropriate foster parents who would prepare him for running his grandfather's many business enterprises were found.

When Toon turned twenty-one, he was the only heir to a colossal fortune. He was introduced to the responsibilities of the position of managing director. He took to it with the same enthusiasm as he did to anything else. By then, his passion for community living was slowly unfolding through powerful visions he had in his dreams, which he shared with a close friend, Ed Barendse, and Otto, his adopted half-brother.

Then, only after his fiftieth birthday, when Toon met Ingrid Barendse, did he know that his life had finally started to have more meaning. The discovery of love and joy... and... would he experience what it was like to have a child of his own?... Toon's mind drifted to the surface as the throbbing pain in his shoulder woke him.

***

He was attached to a drip, and he felt stiff all over. He vaguely re-membered nurses being with him. He recalled that Annie had been there, and together, they managed to reach Ingrid telepathically when he was too weak. Toon felt a heartrending sorrow sweeping over him again when he thought about Ingrid. What gruesome or-deal was she facing? Never in all his life had he experienced such love for a woman; the thought of living without her was unbear-able. Surely life could not be so cruel.... that possibility made his heart stop.

"Kitty, please love, I'm coming. I want to be.".... the heart monitor to which he was strapped made an odd noise, and nurses came rushing in. Toon felt himself slipping away. The pain in his chest became unbearable; all he wanted was to be with Ingrid...

The pain...he wanted to leave...away from...Then he saw his own body, lying very still; the heart monitor made a sound that prompt-ed everyone into action. There was a lot of commotion, but nobody noticed him! He felt a hand pulling him away.

"Leave it to them, you wanted to be with Ingrid, come," a voice in his head said. Toon vaguely saw a person standing next to him. He felt a hand guiding him. The voice had said 'Ingrid' when suddenly he felt a floating sensation...a sense of warmth.

He was free of physical sensations...free of pain.... Was he dead?

"No, you're not. Your consciousness is detached from physical reality for the moment because your physical body is having a heart attack. Still, it's operating autonomously, and your alarm and alert system will call you back when needed. Come," he was aware of someone nearby, but there was no detail...was it someone he knew? ... For a moment, he thought he saw...then different shapes became visible, like a metal staircase; the place looked run-down, with mildew on the walls.

The man! Richard was his name. Now he remembered. It was In-grid's friend from that coffee shop! He was about to ask him what he did there when he saw her! A dark, dirty blanket was draped around her as she was working on the computer and to his horror, he saw her ankle and... a piece of her clothing... Her bra.

"Oh, no, Kitty, love! What are they doing to you? I'm with you. I can see you. Oh, love, what are they wanting from you?" He tried to touch her, but he went right through, which shook him more than he cared to admit.

"Snooks, are you all right? Why do I feel as if you are near me? Oh, "Toon, please, don't let me think you are...dead. Toon, I love you! Please come back," Toon saw and felt her despair. Ingrid was crying, and the blanket slithered off, revealing her torn blouse. Her ankle rested on a box and looked swollen. He could do nothing! He felt so helpless! Why would Ingrid think he was dead? The voice said he had a heart attack!

Toon felt a great need to return; he didn't want to be dead and leave his Soulmate on her own again! His intent to fully awaken in this life became an even stronger desire now that he found his twin flame. His goal was to transition into a new world, as promised, but he did not want to shift to a higher frequency without her. He would have to rescue her fast, but he needed to recover first...

***

His whole body felt as if a steamroller had tried to flatten him. Where was he? He vaguely remembered being flown some-where...was it Dirk, his pilot? No, he was in a hospital room sur-rounded by medical equipment.

When he opened his eyes, he saw Annelies, Ed, and Ben standing beside his bed.

"We cannot do anything more for him. He is stable, but his heart is fragile." The doctor explained. Toon's chest felt as if he had been run over. Had he been asleep? He remembered something, but what?

"Annie, have you" ...

"Oh, Toon, you scared us! Please stay with us!" Annelies implored. She was stroking his face while Ed grasped his hand.

"Toon, you scared the daylights out of us. You had a heart attack," Ed's shocked voice was full of pain. Then, when he saw Ben, Leo's twin brother, who was one of the most honourable men he knew, standing next to Annelies. Ben was the same height as Annie, but his stocky Dutch physique made him look taller. He recognised how serious his condition must have been.

"Where am I?" Their emotions triggered his frustrations.

"Toon, they flew you in an air ambulance helicopter to the University Medical Centre in Utrecht, where they implanted a pacemaker using the latest three-dimensional imaging equipment," Ben replied. Was that why he felt so weak? He had a pacemaker! "Ingrid, have they..."

"Toon, Harry Brinks has been in contact with someone holding Ingrid hostage, but everything is being done to find her love. Ben has decided to quit his assignment." Annelies quivered with relief.

"Oh, Annie, you must be so pleased. Ben! Can you still carry on with your work? I'm so glad for you both, but please, all of you, help me with the project for Ingrid. She needs to know I'm alive! she...I think...she thinks I'm...dead? I don't know why I think that?" He felt an urgency...but why?

"Kitty, I'm all right! Please, love, hold on, we'll find you. I know we'll be together for a long time. Both Ed, Ben, and Annie are here with me." The others beamed their message.

"Ingrid, Toon's all right. Just do what they ask of you and focus on love," Annelies knew from Harry Brinks how serious the danger Ingrid was. Ed had just arrived. They were all relieved that Toon was now treated in the very sophisticated life-saving heart treatment unit nearer where they all lived.

Ed's eyes were closed, beaming. *"Ingrid, all you need to do is look after yourself. There are lots of people out looking, and we have a few tricks up our sleeve,"* Ben squeezed Annelies' hand.

"Ingrid, I'm Ben. Please look in your bag and read my letter, then destroy it and follow the instructions. Hold on to your thoughts of love." All four were silent for a long while, each trying to focus on Ingrid. Toon had a vision of her in a damp place with a metal staircase....his tears were creating a slippery mess as his powerlessness overwhelmed him.

They all looked up at Ben, who had closed his eyes, wondering what instructions he was referring to.

"Oh, Snooks, now I know that you are still alive! Oh, love, be careful; a new man has threatened Harry Brinks. Snooks, be careful, this Boss man has been talking to ...What letter, what must I do?... I must look in my bag... Toon, I love you. ...Get better...I can't...stay"...

"Did you all receive that?" Toon's trembling voice was nevertheless getting stronger.

"Ed, I must speak to Richard about the aerial photo, but I can't remember why", Toon mumbled weakly. His throat was sore, and the tube in his nose made it impossible to talk. He wanted to eliminate all the contraptions in his nose because they were not helping him. He pressed the alarm button. He wanted some freedom and felt stronger already for knowing that Annelies's husband, Ben, was back.

Both Ed and Annelies were staring at Ben. As a detective, he had been undercover for a long time and had only been in telepathic contact with Hans and Annelies.

"Do you know what is happening with the drawings Ingrid is talking about?" Ed's trembling voice whispered. His sharp tone was full of rage. Ben silently directed Ed to follow him outside. He did not reveal any information inside the hospital room.

Iris van Hattum

Iris woke her up with black coffee and stale bread, as apparently, they'd run out of supplies. Ingrid had been working a full day and had seen nobody the whole time. Her ankle felt better, and she should try walking on it. She needed to go to the bathroom again and hoped she could convince Iris to take her to a proper toilet, not to the disgusting long drop where she had almost passed out.

"Iris, is there a proper bathroom?" The temperature in the basement had risen considerably, so the weather outside must be hot because Iris had changed and was wearing shorts and a skimpy top. Her arms were full of bruises.

"Upstairs, come, I'll take you before those men return."

Ingrid almost passed out when she put her weight on her foot; the tears smudged her cheeks, and she was running a temperature.

"Iris, can you get me something to wrap around my ankle?" She hid her miserable state, knowing she could be stretching her luck.

"Anything will do, like a towel. I can cut it into strips," knowing that Iris was not the most intelligent woman, but even simple people could grasp ideas if one presented them with logical steps.

Iris came back with a rag, similar to the one they'd used to gag her with. Ingrid tore it into strips and bandaged it tightly around her foot and ankle. At least it would give some support. Then she grabbed her bra from the filthy floor, and her revulsion for the man welled up.

Iris helped her up the metal staircase. She tried to see if she could see any windows or anything upstairs that gave anything away from the surroundings. The building was in bad shape, like an abandoned factory. The bathroom was appalling, too, and Ingrid started to feel dirty from the urine smell. She could have done with a nice hot bath, but thinking about it brought on depression. When she saw the face of a battered woman with a bruised cheek in the cracked mirror, tears of misery erupted. The buttons on her blouse were gone, so she fastened it tightly in the front with a knot to hide the fact that she was braless.

Her pants' zip was broken, but Iris shouted for her to hurry, so her ripped bra strap became useful. Going down the stairs again into the basement was much easier than going up.

"You have lots of work to do, so shout if you need anything; I'll be upstairs."

"Iris, what am I doing all this for? What is so important about the drawings?" She was still not any the wiser about what was going on.

"I only know that something went missing in your drawing. You did something when you used that drawing program, and it interfered with the information in the background. I've no idea why, and I wouldn't want to know. I'm only telling you this because these people are dangerous, and I want to get out of this mess. Remember, the more you know, the more you are a threat to them, so don't ask any questions, do you hear!"

Iris helped her settle in front of the computer. The two other flash drives that Piet had given her during the early morning reminded her of his sneering remark: "Witch, I warned you about the treatment you gave me when I asked you about the aerial photos."

Ingrid remembered very well that she was angry and irritated just before she picked up the phone, and Toon was on the line phoning her back about the Buttercups. Oh, so much had happened! It felt like ages, and yet it was only twelve weeks! Thinking about Toon plunged her back into heartache.

Had he been near her during the night? She didn't even want to believe that...the inklings of loneliness were emotions she'd known very well, especially after her miscarriage and the years after.

When she opened the file on the one flash drive, she wondered who had found it in her office. Would anybody at work already know about her kidnapping ordeal? Ingrid became rigid. They were not duplicate files! Someone had made copies! But who, Mr. Brinks?

When she opened the one with the password 'Sascia', she expected to see five files with her listing, but something was different. Ingrid opened one of the files, and the background was back! How? She scanned with her mouse over her drawing and suddenly spotted some typing she knew was not hers. It looked as if someone was pretending it belonged to the drawing. It said: A proposed site is to be projected from an aerial view in connection with the noise pollution. Two light (laser) beams launched to the primary source will join the three proposed entertainment areas. Then, enter the Lasers and Photocathodes section at CERN... Ion sources and targets, fixed targets for experimental regions.

It made no sense at all. What was someone trying to tell her? She had a feeling she had to alter something, but what? Where did the noise fit in? What would they do with her when... then she remembered the sound card?

"Your mind is your sixth sense, and your brain is your receiving plate. It becomes a reflector of whatever you have your focus on!"

Who? Why did she suddenly think...the foundations? She copied the three drawings and her new proposal on one screen. There were not all that many changes, but someone had tried to tell her something. But who?

"Kitty, I'm all right! Please, love, hold on, we'll find you. I know we'll be together for a long time. Both Ed and Ben and Annie are here with me." Her heart filled with relief; Toon was alive! She knew Toon's thoughts were getting stronger.

"Ingrid, Toon's all right. Just do what they ask of you and focus on love," she telepathically heard, sensing Annelies' anguish.

"Ingrid, all you need to do is look after yourself. There are many people out looking, and we have a few tricks up our sleeve," Ed's love for her beamed across. She had no idea what time it was, but the need for the bathroom was back. If only her ankle were not so painful! She

was getting thirsty, and her throat was feeling raw. Oh, please, let me not get the flu!

"Ingrid, I'm Ben. Please look in your bag if possible and read my letter, then destroy it and follow the instructions. Hold on to your thoughts of love,"

Oh, if only... she wanted her pregnancy to be real; she wanted a child from Toon, and she was determined to prevent anything that could jeopardize having his baby.

"Oh, Snooks, now I know that you are still alive! Oh, love, be careful, a man threatened Harry Brinks. Snooks, be careful, this Boss-man has been talking to... What letter, what must I do? I must look in my bag...Toon, I love you...Get better...I can't...stay"...

They were arguing upstairs, so she removed the two typed text lines from the drawing on her clipboard just in case. As she peered into her bag to see if there was anything in there to suck on, she spotted the blue envelope that, as an afterthought, she had dropped in her bag from the hallway on Friday before they had dinner at the Prinsengracht. Ben had projected to her something about a letter!

Nobody was around, but she still heard angry voices. She looked inside the envelope when she noticed the missing Excerpt 15, and a letter was stuck facing inward to the back of POWAH's note. It was a letter addressed to Toon and her.

Dear Ingrid and Toon

I would give almost anything to see your face when you read this, Toon, but I'll have to wait until you return next week. Ingrid, let me introduce myself.

I'm Ben, Annelies' husband.

When I found out that Toon was going to take you to Buttercup Valley, I took the chance to enclose this letter, knowing you would read it far away from Apeldoorn. Ingrid, the drawing that has led to many complications has to do with the symbol of the eye you rightly spotted, but there is more than meets the Eye.

Toon, when I approached you about acquiring the company with the landscaping division, I had no idea what complications it would bring. Some of them have been a blessing, I believe. I cannot explain all the scientific details in this letter, but Ingrid and Toon will know if I asked you to draw the dome's position according to the following plan. You would help us activate a vibration that will release certain stored tablets Leo needs for further research from the underground tunnels.

The dome's correct position will release tremendous energy levels, thereby shifting a planetary portal – required to revoke the other planetary vortex portals around the planet. These holographic portals have been held within the control of the dark forces.

Leo thinks that the dome position will accelerate the collapse of the 3D hologram template due to what they do at CERN. Our world has been trapped in a frequency wave. Opposing forces want you to prevent that by changing the dome position. They want to keep complete control of our planet. Keeping our physical illusory reality intact.

I know that Toon has the drawing equipment at Buttercup Valley, and I have sent the correct information to his email address. I will not go into detail about the conspiracies, but believe me, if you manage that, Ingrid, you will significantly serve us all. Toon, I look forward to seeing you next week and meeting Ingrid in person. Say hello to Otto and Jill for me.

Ben

Ingrid was riddled with confusion. She couldn't believe that Ben would have known she would be kidnapped, suddenly recognising the danger if they found this letter. She had never looked into her bag again after Toon took her away, so she had to dispose of it somehow. What a relief that they had never opened the letter with Excerpt 15 handwritten.

After reading it three times, she tore it up into small pieces and scattered it around the dirty basement. She started to read POWAH's excerpt fifteen, which was missing!

Excerpt Fifteen[1]

Program Planet Earth

Mastery over the Compassionate Gateway, the Heart Chakra.

Rule Five *of the Ascension Decoding Card Game*

When she read **<Kitty, each individual must desire personal awakening from their heart centre through a lifetime of service. By keeping your thoughts on love and having compassion for all life, the magnetism you create around you will bring you the freedom you desire.>**

She now knew this was coming from...her higher Soul-self, her mentor, which they all seemed to share.

She would keep it, hoping they would not look into her bag. Ben's reason for using her drawing skills was beyond her; the rest of rule five she would read later, but reading POWAH's message reminded her once more of her power.

She focused on Toon and their love for each other, the union they experienced, which she would always be grateful for and sustain for the rest of her life. She concentrated on her love for him, feeling it spreading over everything around her; she felt again the joy of living, being in the moment. She drew this energy into her solar plexus and up, through her heart, up her throat and head. She experienced a diffused light somewhere far away, and then she felt the stillness coming over her...then the computer brightened up again.

<Kitty, losing your life can help you find it. Through Love and the Christ force, you learn to surrender everything, even the spiritual joy of closeness. In moments of abandonment and despair, you must be willing to let go of all joys. This is often the final period of testing.>

---

1. https://allrealityshifters.wordpress.com/powah/the-reality-shifters-excerpt-15/

"But I failed! I did everything wrong!" I...her thoughts were stifled by emotions of guilt.

< Kitty, I understand the message you are trying to convey. It is true that many people around the world have suffered and continue to suffer in horrific ways. It is essential to learn from these experiences and work towards creating a better future for all. Breaking free from negative programming and striving for personal growth can be a positive step in this direction.>

Gosh, was her kidnapping supposed to be a good thing?

< Kitty, if you believe that by simply projecting a world around yourself that holds no bloodshed and destruction, you think you are creating a new reality, not so?>

She had to admit, yes, that is what she believed. Her thoughts and feelings do create her reality.

<So, what happens in the basement where you are kept against your will? Why are you allowing it to continue?>

That wasn't very clear. How come it is her fault that she has been kidnapped? She was keen to type what was in her mind if only they would peek from upstairs and believe she was working.

"Yes, they kidnapped me, so, for now, I'm in their reality, so how do I change my situation? Please tell me." She mentally beamed

Surely, her own human experience was still different. No matter how horrible her predicament was now, she could still telepathically communicate with her friends and lover, for starters. They were all awakening and intended to leave this reality, so they must do something right. She was wondering if they were able to fluctuate between different realities.

While communicating this way, she knew from experience that time stood still, as if she were momentarily away from her body.

< Kitty, what will shock you is when you consider yourself awakened. By refusing to accept the reality around your real-life world out there, by believing that if you project your world

around you where there is only love and happiness, that doesn't
work. Do you know why?> She had no idea. So far, it had worked.
She had attracted everything so far, even when she had not been
aware of it.

"Please enlighten me as to why it does not work."

<Because you are sharing one consciousness field. There is only
one mind field, one collective human Consciousness.>

*"How are we then individually able to heal the united field of human
consciousness?"* her thoughts replied

<You will have to collect all the pieces of your collective mind
back to wholeness so it can work in cooperation.>

Gosh, how can anyone do that unless there are many people who
all understand how? Like when hundreds of people meditate united on one topic...

<Yes, you got it. By understanding that, let's say you are one
facet of a kaleidoscope. Suppose you avoid the reality of what
is happening halfway around the world as if it doesn't exist. In
that case, all the other particles of the total kaleidoscope reality
field will continue to act as if there is nothing to do to correct
it. Your awareness commands you to stop certain things, or it
doesn't. The kaleidoscope is not here to impose its own will on
you; it is here to impose your will on the reality of your world.>

Wow. Now, some of Annelie's images of a kaleidoscope design on
her wall in her workshop began to take on a deeper meaning.

*"OK, I get that. No matter how horrible I find it to read or hear about
what goes on around the world, I need to do a mental and emotional
cleansing and let it go. Is that it?"* she beamed.

The noises upstairs were slowly disappearing as if she were alone.

Yes, your human body has a sending and receiving antenna, and
your auric field is powered by electromagnetic energy.

<Millions of years ago, telepathy was erased from your Human
hive genome during a genetic massacre, and your cellular lan-

guage was disconnected. That left every human being born on the planet separated from one another in their awareness for millions of years. At one time, the Angelic Human Soul was aware that it was part of a united I Am expression, and if one knew something, they all knew that same thing.>

Oh, now the bible story of the town of Baal made a lot of sense.

"You mean humanity was originally one hive mind, interacting and communicating with each other, so whatever happens in the world is happening to me as well?" typing her reply, pretending she was working.

< Yes, as you know, most of the souls who belong to the Jaarsma Clan group have been activated, like many other group souls on the planet, during these end times. >

So, they lived during an end period, but in what way, physically, or their human civilisation? It took a while to contemplate what POWAH was trying to tell her.

"You are implying that I'm trapped by people who are not awake?" she typed, if only to pretend to be working.

<Yes, if the awakening community wants to create a world where there is no suffering, then people MUST NOT continue to act like they are alone here and allow all the rest of humanity to suffer and die as if "it's their problem, not theirs.">

"How can we do that?" she mentally asked.

<Through LOVE, compassion, and understanding for all life, regardless of what is happening, because you share one awareness.>

"Even with evil people? She was now so confused. Here, she was shivering and in pain, and her higher voice was trying to tell her that she needed to love them upstairs. Ye sure!

<Kitty, in a way, yes. Everybody can reconnect again, but if individuals refuse to think that an unaware neighbour is not part

of their reality because it is uncomfortable for them, the broadcast antenna isn't sending the signal to the whole group.>

That was altogether too much for her. Why now, when she was genuinely feeling like a victim?

<Do you know that all species, including many human beings, are still joined by a hive mind that enables that species to survive against all odds? And without it, they will all perish?>

"I suppose so, especially with the animal kingdom."

She replied as if she were working in case somebody would look from the top.

<Your captors share a terrifying low-frequency hive mind. You are now awakening to your individuality. Your 'I AM' can lead to isolation in your thinking, but that does not exempt you from responsibility. If you want to create a world where there is no suffering, then I repeat, you MUST NOT continue to act like you are separate from others who are unaware.>

"But...is that not the idea? Separating ourselves from the hive mind that believes they do not need to change?" she typed

<If you feel that is true, you will continue not to feel their pain. That makes their situation "their problem, not yours, but...you will never elevate your frequency to tune into the channel that the rest of your body could operate on.>;

Somehow, that reply made her even more depressed and sad. If only she could find a way...Now she understood why creating the ascension cards with their Language of Light Soul qualities would work! These soul qualities would help clear away all the distorted karmic beliefs.

<Kitty, tell your life story so that everything that happened to you was potentially good but often obscured. Feel your life, explore it, and know that you will reshape your future as you align your thoughts with the many mansions of God's universe. You have passed your first initiation already by participating. Your

way is through the inner reaches of the latent powers of your mind, knowing that it exists. Kitty, welcome home to one family, one Soul, one Spirit of I am that I am.>

The tears welled up, but this time from relief. Suddenly, the eye symbol spoke to her from a great distance as intuitive insights flashed across her mind. Then she understood that the scheme of the universe was good; only man was out of harmony with it. In a single, beautiful moment, she gained insight into the timeless reality of consciousness that was limitless. Now, she understood her part of the plan. She would write her story as POWAH had asked her to do initially.

Thinking about the drawing, she could redraw the dome's angle, which was wrong! She opened her pictures again, thinking about the placement of the two light beams because they would not pierce simultaneously at the right angle! The insight that she had to change the dome's angle came from somewhere. She had to accommodate the two enormous constructions that regulated the intense light beams that would illuminate the whole dome. It reminded her of the laser beam used to operate on the human eye! That was it! Of course, it would be a laser beam used when the hologram ran! Only then would the planet respond to the changes, thereby experiencing the opening of the planetary third eye. It would give the platform on the island a passage to the many different dimensions. Where did that idea come from? Were they her thoughts?

Her ankle was throbbing painfully, but it took second place now that she understood the magnitude of her opportunity. She was in the right place at the right time! As her screen brightened again, it was as if the screen, the message, and her receptive mind were one.

<Kitty, in ancient times, communities worshipped the mother goddess collectively. They manifested the law of spirit and did not matter like the races of people today do. Your deep memory

of how to create and peacefully live on planet Earth is now acti-vated by those ancient intuitive recollections.>

Ingrid knew that she needed to recall every emotion, hurt, and pain that triggered her to release it. Now she clicked. She had started to recollect her I AM's of the many lifetimes into the one law of the spirit.

<Yes, holding onto dark thoughts will create an incomplete awakening, for it is in the gaps of missing DNA strands that the dark forces can work through one's field. Humans had highly developed 'right brain' minds before the hemispheric thinking mode was separated. It was an exquisite period of non-separa-tive, erotic, and yet peaceful living.> She wondered if it was true about the rumours around aliens, wanting to prevent them from evolving.

<Kitty In the lower dimensions and heavenly realms, Souls are divided into many aspects, and various dark thought forms have been dumped into the sub-realms surrounding planet Earth from fallen creations. These distorted energies resulted in a series of cataclysms, such as the Ice Age, and caused a decline in consciousness. Accessing records and artefacts from this sig-nificant period is most easily done in your dreams.> Ingrid was mesmerised by POWAH's response to ancient cultures.

So it was true! In his letter, Ben referred to them as opposing forces. Did he mean that dark, evil forces were in control? Through people who unconsciously invited them in, but why had she attracted this violence?

<Kitty, the subconscious harmful thought patterns are not pleasant; some act like an inward abuse, and some react to an outside abuse. They are the same.>

Gosh, had she attracted outside abuse? Was that a pattern within herself? She hated that idea. She speculated what this hologram island at Toon's resort would be used for, and how she suddenly knew what to do with the drawing, and that it connected with sound. The screen jumped at her again.

<Kitty, close your eyes for a moment.>

Wow! What was this? She closed her eyes and let her body sink deep into herself...she started to hear a sound, like a kind of high-pitched singing...

<As you are now one with my spirit, the sound you hear pulsating in your brain is a high-pitched resonance that is not audible in the third dimension of your visible world; it is only recognisable if you find the bridge.> Then she saw a ball of red light on her right side while a green light appeared on her left.

<Kitty, the two complementary colours cannot exist without each other; the same applies to what you manifest in the world around you. The rule of duality states that complementary colours and manifestations cannot exist independently. Both good and evil have arisen only through separation from unity, which is neither good nor evil but divine. When you unite in your consciousness two halves of yourself, you've found your way back into the infinite.>

A beam of light entered through the roof and floated gently down, submerging her. Within this brilliant white cloud, she saw colours whirling, and she felt warm and glowing with a radiance of love ...then Toon's face flashed upon her mind, her complementary half, with whom she could experience this Soul love....

<As a co-light-worker in the great divine plan, Kitty learn to love the divine within each person. Then, you will experience the unity within the self. As you awaken to who you are, you will experience different states of consciousness as dream pictures without being conscious of either time or space.>

The text disappeared from her screen when she heard a different noise. It came from far away, but it had not been there before... Police!

There was a lot of shouting going on upstairs; Piet, Bruce and Iris ran down the metal staircase, and Ingrid was drawn back into the basement. What had happened? What were they going to do with her?

"Quick, she's done it. download it all onto the flash drive!" Bruce yelled.

"Why can't we just leave her and go?" Iris screamed as she pulled the flash drive out while Piet ripped at all the wiring. The drawings were torn off the walls, and Bruce shot the computers to bits. Ingrid's whole body became cold and stiff.

"Do as you are told", Bruce shouted at Iris. She heard a car speeding away, and Bruce swore while grabbing her by the thick knot in her blouse and pressing a rag in her mouth. The foul taste made her heave, and his fishy, repulsive breath close up made her...then she lost consciousness...

***

At a mystery resort

Ingrid was outside, resting on a large recliner. She had been given a steam bath and a massage, but she had no idea where she was or how long she had been there. Had she been drugged? The last words from POWAH, asking her to close her eyes, made her mentally see her drawings, then the upheaval. Thank goodness she'd destroyed the letter from Ben...then his foul breath... She was blindfolded to the place where she was now.

Bruce had carried her the whole way, that much she knew. She heard noises from people at a distance. She was aware of Bruce's face all the time; it made her go rigid all over, and his breath was even more repulsive. "It's a real shame that I didn't get a chance with you", he had leered at her. "The boss told us to treat you like royalty. Why this is suddenly the case is totally beyond me, but you are in luck. You'll get the treatment of a movie star if you keep quiet. Are you listening?"

He had pushed her down into a big chair while holding her blouse. She couldn't bear his coarse hand on her bare skin and had managed to kick him away. When he ripped off her blindfold, she was in some entrance hall. Iris was talking to someone at the counter, and Bruce hissed at her, telling her not to say a thing. Where was she? It all looked very luxurious. Then her eyes were drawn to a picture that hung on the wall facing the entrance; she inhaled sharply; it was the same star painting Annelies had! How was that possible? Bruce's sneer brought her thoughts back.

"This is where the very rich go when they need a makeover. We've been told that you must keep quiet for at least two days if you want to see that lover of yours. There's still someone outside his hospital room," Bruce threatened in fury.

"Hello, darling, your daughter told me all about you. We'll put you in a wheelchair, and you can have a long, hot bath," the woman behind the counter had squealed to her in Flemish.

She wanted to comment, but seeing Iris's petrified expression, she sensed how crucial it was to keep quiet. She would go along with them, but had already spotted a phone in the corner.

They wheeled her through a narrow passage. Iris went into room 22 to inspect the windows. It was a very posh place, but the room had no warmth.

"Ingrid, I don't know what's happening, but I want to escape this mess. I'm glad they've dumped you here, and I'll inform the police of your whereabouts. Yes. I promise that if you lie low for at least two days. I know the Boss was not bluffing. I've never seen such rage when he was told why he had to let you go. Ingrid, don't say anything until two days have passed." Iris was dead serious, her face crumpled with fear; she almost felt sorry for her.

"Where am I?"

"Believe me, you don't want to know, say nothing, you hear!"

"I hope you get out of the company you're keeping?" All she wanted was a bath and some fresh clothes. The tub was there, what about clothes?

"Well, since I'm to be treated like royalty, get me something else to wear. I don't want to get into these again after my bath!" Her need to pamper herself after her ordeal made her abrupt.

"I'll see what I can do, but don't talk to anyone, do you hear?"

"You'd better take your life a bit seriously and start afresh somewhere.

I'll pretend, for now, that I have not seen you." Iris's deplorable state made her almost want to hug her. At least she had been some help. Iris had never been a threat. Piet was entirely different, and the big boss had triggered raw fear!

But Bruce was the most revolting of the lot; he had shot Toon, and his insinuations gave her gooseflesh. Iris had walked out of the room, locking her in!

After she managed to have a bath and hopped back to the bedroom, she found a nightgown, underwear and a tracksuit on her bed. All are very neat and smart. This must be a place for the very affluent. I'm wondering who was paying for it. She had tried to project to Toon but could not do it while they were racing her away, knowing it was almost impossible when she was nervous or emotionally stressed. Thinking of Toon, she activated her psychic senses.

"Kitty, where are you? We're all trying to reach you. What's happening to you?" Toon's overanxious state of mind shocked her...

"Snooks, I'm fine, a lot better. They've moved me. I've been ordered not to speak to anyone for two days, but I long to be with you! Are you in a lot of pain? Toon, someone is outside your room that would 'deal' with you if I...Oh, I wish this nightmare were over, but I'm far more worried about you.". Ingrid was so exhausted after that projection that

it made her head spin. What day was it? Wednesday, Thursday ?...*"I love you! Go to sleep. I'm fine. Tomorrow, I'll find you"*...

When she awoke, her ankle was feeling much better; she could almost rest on it without wincing. This place reminded her of a health retreat, except for the missing energy of peace and wholesomeness. It was more of a scientific centre. Somebody had brought her breakfast, but as most staff spoke French, she could not communicate adequately.

She had asked for a phone, but nobody noticed her request.

She got a massage, and her ankle was seen by an older woman, who prodded it. When she drew back in pain, she bandaged it in robust and stiff support, making it feel much better.

Later, after she'd slept for some hours again, she wondered if they had put anything in her coffee or dinner; she felt so drowsy! How would that affect the baby? Sometimes, her mind drifted again to the possibility of pregnancy since she had lots of time to think about it...

They had her resting outside again because it was a very mild evening, and a small plane that flew over the area brought her back from her thoughts. When she looked up, there it was; could it be...no. Toon was in the hospital! But somehow, she felt a connection with that plane. Then it went away. It was probably wishful thinking, and perhaps they had drugged her because she kept feeling drowsy. ...

When she woke up again, it was getting darker. She remembered the little plane and seeing Sascia's face in her mind. A staff member collected her in a wheelchair because she still could not walk very well.

Where was everybody? This place must be very isolated, but there were other people about.

A man in a white coat she'd never seen before took her inside and pushed her through the foyer. If only she could get to the phone!

The woman behind the counter took her to her room, locking her in! Ingrid felt fury welling up. Why was she being locked up? Nobody said a word. Were those people robots? They all had a numb, flat look about them. Revulsion came over her; those people had no thoughts!

No feelings! Something was wrong with them, almost as if they were not human! She must have drifted off again because a lot of noise woke her up...

Chapter 20
The Rules of the Fourth Dimension

Half-way House

Mom, where are you?... Mom, it's Jeroen...Mommy, can you hear me? Are you there?"...

Ingrid was stunned...Could it really be Jeroen?... As she jumped out of bed, the stabbing from her ankle made her flinch,... but...nevertheless, she managed to stumble to the door...

"Jeroen...It that really you?..." Her voice broke as she heard the sound of running feet.

"Mommy, are you all right?" Sascia exploded into sobs of relief. A man's voice argued. Who were they? They were fiddling with a key and then...her door flew open...Jeroen grabbed her so suddenly she almost fell.

"Mom! Are you okay? Are you hurt? Oh, your face!" Sascia called out as the tears of worry poured down both her twins' faces. She held their shaking bodies close to her. Oh, it felt so good, feeling them, touching them, keeping them. Then she looked up into the taut expressions of Hans and Richard.

"Well, I've got a whole party rescuing me, I see," she embraced both men cheerfully, but felt false. Her ordeal, and now that it might be over, had not quite sunk in. Jeroen and Richard took turns carrying her, even though she had tried to convince them she could walk. Hans seemed to have the establishment under his mental control.

Peter was at the wheel of a sedan. He came running up and took her from Jeroen after a big hug. He settled her gently in the back seat and handed her his cell phone.

"Hello," she knew who was on the other side. There was no sound, just breathing,.. "Toon...are you there?" she whispered breathlessly, her whole being almost rigid with expectation.

"Ingrid, it's Annelies, Toon is a "...

"Kitty, oh, love, they found you!" His weak voice gave her quite a shock.

"Toon...thank you".... she started to cry again.... "for my children, it was such a surprise. Is Debbie..."

"Mom, are you okay? Toon called me as I just walked in." Debbie broke into a whimper.

"Debbie, I'm fine, really, but how is Toon? Please, Debbie, is it bad? He sounds so weak!"

"Mom, Toon is fine now that you've been found." Debbie was crying, and Ingrid knew that she had been lying!

"Kitty, I'll be fine. Come back soon. Dirk will fly you all back to-morrow morning. It's too late now." His voice sounded better, but she knew he was in great pain. Ingrid looked at the clock on the dashboard as the car drove down a familiar road. It was nine-thirty. That was not late!

"Peter, can't Dirk fly us back tonight?"

"You'll arrive after midnight, Ingrid, and you cannot visit him then. They won't let you near him!"

"Snooks, please go to sleep; I'll be there as soon as possible," she uttered softly through the cell phone. *"I love you, remember. We both love you."* Ingrid smiled when she knew that he got the message. She fell back into her seat, and Sascia kissed her softly on her bruised cheek.

"He's a wonderful guy, Mom! Where did you find him?" They were all four in the back seat of a sedan. Sascia was squashed on Richard's lap while Jeroen sat beside the window.

"What makes you think Mom found him? I think he found her!" Jeroen's tone expressed relief, and they all started to laugh. The desperation of the previous four days evaporated, the air was clear, and for one moment, it almost felt as if nothing had happened.

After some time, when everyone had been silent during the drive, Jeroen whispered in her ear if it was alright to ask questions. They all wanted to know where she had been locked up and how she got to where they found her. Describing the dark, dirty, broken-down building was almost impossible. After some briefing, they allowed her to doze off.

Helen awaited them on their front porch when they drove into the familiar driveway. Peter helped her out of the car, holding her like a fragile doll, and Snoopy came running, greeting her with lots of licking and wriggling. Helen's voice broke as she hugged her; the tears dripped.

"Oh, Ingrid, your face! They hurt you, your ankle! Ingrid, we've had four of the worst days ever. Even the children picked up that something terrible had happened, and they've been impossible!"

"Are they already asleep?"

"Not Timmy! You know that he's very telepathic. We had great difficulty keeping stuff from him. He's troubled about Toon being shot.

He still can't come to terms with it."

Helen's distress made Ingrid aware of how many people were affected by aggressive behaviour. She introduced Sascia, Jeroen, and Richard. Hans organised with Dirk a time in the morning to fly back.

"Ingrid, your daughter looks so like you, only taller, and Richard, is that her boyfriend?" Helen asked while re-bandaging her ankle.

They were all in the dining room where a late supper was spread out.

Nobody had eaten yet. Ingrid had to smile, watching Jeroen gulp down his dinner. He'd always been one for food, whereas Sascia was more restrained, and Richard was conversing with Peter while eating at the same time.

"He's my other daughter's boyfriend." She mentally explained to Helen that Debbie was with Toon, the nurse on duty near his ward.

"Mmm, are you sure?" Hans interrupted them, carrying Timmy in his arms and told Ingrid that Timmy had insisted on seeing her for himself. The six-year-old ran to her as if she were someone he'd known all his life.

She took him on her lap and hugged him. Timmy was quietly staring at her. His earnest look, spiky wet hair from the bath, and mental silence made Ingrid wonder what happened in this child's mind. "Timmy, Toon is okay; I promise we will both come back soon when he's out of the hospital." Timmy's puzzled expression slowly changed into a small smile; he put his head on her shoulder, cuddled up and drifted off to sleep on her lap while Snoopy curled at her feet.

Ingrid's emotions had been put through a shredding machine; she needed to close her eyes and let the bottled-up feelings of fear, humility, and anger wash away to be replaced by relief and gratitude. Peter gently took Timmy from her.

"That is the first time he's fallen asleep by himself since Monday," Helen remarked when Peter returned after taking Timmy to bed.

"Ingrid, this came over the email for you just now. It resembles the letter you received the last time you were here. Who sends them?" Peter handed her a printout of excerpt twenty. Her mind tumbled as an idea started to surface about how someone could always trace her...

But how?

Excerpt Twenty[1]
Program Planet Earth
Awakening to the Rules of the Fourth Dimension
Rule Ten *of the Ascension Decoding Card Game*

Wow, this is another one of POWAH's puzzling letters. Very thought-provoking when reading: Many Soul families like the Jaarsma Clan decided a long time ago to incarnate during these times when the Earth's frequencies are moving into a harmonic resonance, enabling you all to move into higher planes of the visual spectrum. This is called ascension into 5D, which is long overdue.

She would have to start seeing all the excerpts together and playing the card game. She looked forward to returning to normality and her friends in the group again! A noise came from Snoopy, who was lying at her feet. Her tail moved as she looked up at Ingrid, tapping the floor as if she telepathically heard her think! What did Snoopy know and sense? She would have to pay more attention to animals from now on.

"I've no idea who is responsible for sending the excerpt to me, Peter, but I'm beginning to suspect that Ben might know more about it. I think that is how they found me. I'll have to ask him. Whoever is sending them knows where I am and is determined that I include them in my journal." She was thinking that the letter from him in her bag was in the same blue envelope.

After telling them a bit about her ordeal, she decided not to disclose the intriguing part of the drawings related to the park. Peter seemed to think that Toon had been the target for some unknown reason, which made her somewhat uneasy, thinking of the threat that the boss had made.

"Ingrid, watch your thoughts on fear, as they can still keep you from becoming free. Hold them in the light," Hans projected. She felt his genuine affection and received a wink.

"Thank you for reminding me." Hans knew far more but was probably under some form of oath not to get involved up to a point. It must take some incredible self-discipline not to interfere. Ingrid wanted to know how they had found her at the mysterious resort, and for some reason, they all looked at Richard.

"Ingrid, you look exhausted. For now, you need your sleep," Hans got up. Helen directed them to their bedrooms, and Sascia insisted on sharing a double room with her.

"Mom, are they going to become family?" Sascia asked her when they had both climbed into bed. She felt so heavy with sleep that she had difficulty even uttering a reply.

"How would you feel about that?" She glanced at Sascia in the other single bed next to hers.

"I just wondered. It is a lovely place to visit! I wish I had all my camera equipment with me. I'd love to do some photo shoots here, especially of the children. Could I ask them if I could return in a few weeks?"

Ingrid smiled. "I'm positive that Helen would love to have you here. Do you want me to mention it?"

"Mom...I've quit my job," Sascia shared with her that she wanted to go freelance and asked if she could stay home until she was on her feet. She had to remind herself that there would always be a home for her.

When Sascia asked where Toon would live when he came out of the hospital, she realised she had to share more with her children.

"Sascia, I'm carrying Toon's baby. I love him very much and want to spend the rest of my life with him. Is that a problem with you?" Sascia looked stunned. She sat up, leaning over.

"You're pregnant? Oh, Mom, I never knew! Now I understand Toon's reactions, the devastation, the pain! It was like seeing a man mourn for...of course...Now I understand. Mom, I just never visualised you with someone else. Please forgive me, I didn't know.

Jeroen never told me." She fell back into her pillow, her arms behind her head.

"Jeroen doesn't know. All he knows is that Toon has the hots for me." Ingrid giggled, thinking about that day when he'd said it. "But nobody knows about the baby. It's too soon to know anyway, but it seemed appropriate to tell you. Was it?"

"Oh, Mom, yes, I'm glad that I know, and I'm happy for you, but I've still got to get used to the idea of you having a baby. Mom, are you not....too old?" Sascia's frown made her smile.

"No, I don't think so, but don't worry, I'll take every precaution. Otherwise, I'm sure Toon will!"

"How does Toon like that idea? Becoming a father at his age?" Ingrid grinned at this age part. He would never be too old for her in any way.

"He likes the idea so much that he had to swear to me on the scriptures not to tell a soul, but I think he broke that promise after a couple of hours. He must have told Annelies, but they're very close, and he was apprehensive about me. I forgive him for that indiscretion, but Sascia, please; I don't want this to go any further."

"Not even to Jeroen and Debbie?"

"No, not yet; I don't think announcing something like this is right too early. Toon wants to get married right away, I told him sometime in September, not sooner, but now we'll see." Sascia was having difficulty taking it all in.

"Sascia, I loved your father very much, but with Toon it's different; he's part of me. I don't know how seriously he's been injured, but I don't want him to be a day longer in that hospital than is necessary. I hope he will come home soon, and your room is there, too. Sascia, what about that boyfriend of yours? Vinny? He lives in Amsterdam. Is he aware of your plans to come home to stay for a while? You mean you're giving up your flat?"

"I don't know, Mom. I'm confused."

"About what?" Ingrid looked at her lovely face, wondering about all that had gone on that she had missed. All she picked up were her scattered thoughts, all trying to come into focus. She could relate; she'd felt the same the first time Toon had taken her to dinner at the Prinsengracht.

"Mom, how do you know that you love a person and that a person is the right one?" She had asked that before, hadn't she?

"Darling, you will feel it. You will know that you want to be with that person always. I did feel like that about your father when I was 18, and then, when you grow older, your feelings move onto different levels. What I feel for Toon differs from what I felt for your father. But in its way, it was good. But I wouldn't want to go back." Ingrid was dreamily thinking of Toon and her lovemaking.

"But Mom, I liked Vinny, and I still do. But..."

"Let me guess, he does not make your heart flutter every time he touches you, he doesn't make you quiver when he's flirting or looking into your eyes. He's not making you feel you are the only woman he has eyes for." Ingrid's voice animated the rest.

"No, he's a good friend, but oh no, not that ...other, definitely not." Ingrid glanced up at her. Sascia sat up in bed, hugging her shoulders. The bliss of chatting like this made the kidnapping ordeal almost unreal.

Sascia was far away, pondering. Then, she made herself comfortable.

"I want all that you describe, Mom, and also the friendship, the lot, yes. Now I know! Thanks, Mom; now I know what I want for myself." Sascia leaned over, touched her face slightly and switched off the lamp.

"Oh, Mom, I'm so glad you're okay", she mumbled under the blankets.

"Good, let's go to sleep. I can't wait for tomorrow. I know Toon is miserable.". ...

"Mom?"

"Yes, what?"

"Is that what Toon does to you?" Sascia asked her softly, and Ingrid smiled. Suddenly, she had an awakening with that question.

"More, a whole lot and more. I learned that I can be my true self with Toon, or at least find it. With Toon, I started to love myself because there's no obligation in our relationship, only a glorious opportunity to express my Soul's desire! Sascia, we communicate with telepathy, making it even more special."

"Yes, I know! Richard told me. Wow, can you connect with him now?"

"If you keep quiet and go to sleep, I might." She had missed their conversations, and they had never been so intimate. Now, she was sorry for the times she'd seemed distant from her children. She now knew that she needed to be more open and trusting to speak her thoughts aloud and share them with others. When she looked sideways, Sascia seemed to be asleep.

"Kitty, are you finally free? I've been trying to get your attention. I'm already sick of lying here. Please, love, now you must rescue me. Sleep well, see you soon."... Ingrid was not too tired to send him a loving beam.

"Snooks, I've already been refurbishing the house in my head so that you can be at home with us. I'll take care of you. You go to sleep. The doctors must give you the go-ahead to come home. So be very good."

Peter & Helen – Karin & Timmy

Ingrid had been awake for two hours, only seven o'clock. She would have wanted to leave long ago if it had been just her, but Sascia was still fast asleep. Oh, how she longed to be with Toon! Then she heard a soft knock.

"Yes, come in," she whispered, smiling...knowing it was Karin and Timmy...They strolled towards her bed.

"Come, climb in," she whispered, opening the bedcovers. Karin sat up, looking at Sascia in the other bed, and she asked with a child's curiosity who that was. The cute five-year-old made her broody, hoping they would have a little girl with dancing light blond curls like Karin.

In a dramatic whisper, she told them stories about her children.

"When are you coming back with Uncle Toon?" Ingrid fluffed up Timmy's spiked hair that was all scrunched up; his mind was still in turmoil, and she could feel it.

"You've been very worried, haven't you?" Timmy nodded.

"I heard Mommy saying to Daddy that Uncle Toon would die. Is that true?"

"No love. He will be with us for a long, long time. He'll see you both grow up."

"Really? So, he was not shot?"

"Yes, he was, but you don't always die when you get shot, Timmy."

"People do in the movies I've seen; they always do." Timmy rocked on the bed.

"Timmy, it's not always good to look at movies; they make you believe in things that are not always true. Darling, did you hear Mommy and Daddy do mind talk?" His eyes became rounder.

"You heard them having a mind talk when they said Uncle Toon would die?" Timmy's hands made a fist. Poor children, the little boy knew that mind talk was always more accurate than loud talk. She cuddled him while Karin was still peeping at Sascia.

"Timmy, sometimes we hear thoughts that people think are going to happen, but when they don't, we see that people have been mistaken."

Timmy was pulling at his ears, pondering.

"But Daddy said that people with bad thoughts hurt Uncle Toon."

"Yes, well, we all make mistakes. You will as well when you grow up. When you hear upsetting things, remember that not all thoughts are real. Many people, especially grown-ups, especially Mommy and Daddy, are not always aware of what they are thinking! And some thoughts are different from talking. You know that, don't you?"

"Yes, when grownups say 'yes', they think 'no,'" Timmy stated wisely, which made her want to squeeze him to her; he reminded her of herself when she was little.

"There you both are. Ingrid, have they been bothering you?" Helen asked when she brought tea on a tray into the room. Sascia woke up and asked what the time was. Jeroen peeped around the door, and the children saw a playmate in him. Jeroen took them downstairs so she and Sascia could be ready in ten minutes. They all tried to leave for Holland, knowing she was anxious to get to the hospital.

***

For Ingrid, the flight and the drive took forever. It was already eleven in the morning when they finally drove towards the medical centre.

The closer they came to Toon, the more impatient she became, and her heart started to pound. She almost wanted to jump out of the car when they drove into the hospital grounds. She insisted on walking, which was slow going, but she was not arriving in a wheel-chair!

When they were getting out of the lift on the floor where Toon's room was, she spotted Harry Brinks, and then, from nowhere, Ed appeared. He had tied his sun-bleached hair into a ponytail. The joy on his face that changed when he noticed her bruise was almost too much. She was shocked at the way Harry looked. He had aged overnight, and she had never seen him in a casual tracksuit!

"Thank goodness you are safe," Ed hugged her.

"Ed, how is he?" Then suddenly, from everywhere, more people were asking her all kinds of questions.

The press?...Oh no!..."Mrs. Barendse, why were you freed? Who were the kidnappers?"... Annelies came marching through them; her black and white long caftan looked like a woman you do not mess with. She looked at Ingrid, holding her arm's length while Ed and Harry pushed people away...

"Are you ready...Toon is still on life support and a heart machine."

"Oh, has it been that bad? Did he have a heart attack, Annelies? Oh, no!" Annelies nodded. "They gave him a pacemaker. I just wanted you to be prepared. Now go in. We'll be outside, and I'll make sure you two are alone for a while." Many people wanted to ask questions, but Ingrid only wanted to be with Toon.

As she opened his door, her heart pounded at what she would find. The machine noises and disinfectant smell for a second took her back. The hospital smells almost choked her. A screen was in front of the bed, and she saw aerial photos everywhere.

Toon was sitting straight up, supported by big pillows; his shoulder was bandaged, some wires were attached to his chest, and he had a drip in his arm. There was no air pipe through his nose, thank goodness.

Annelies must have been mistaken because she cringed, almost fainted, remembering Jan's last moments when she saw Toon's pale, worried frown when he saw her, his eyes filled with tears. She ran to the bed, ignoring the nasty twinge of pain in her ankle.

"Oh, Kitty, are you in pain?" His arm encircled her, and the strength was still there! He pulled her onto the bed and kissed her neck, her hand and her ear, but Ingrid, being more mobile, took hold of his head and very gently kissed his mouth, which was so dry and hot.

"Oh, Snooks.... oh, love," she repeated. She lay down very carefully next to him. Toon took the blanket to cover her, and she could see that he was in pain as his eyes gave it away. Their tears dripped over each other's faces, and they cried for joy but could not speak. She just lay there, saying nothing, holding his hand, stroking his face, his neck, very gently pressing her body against his......

"Kitty, I would not have wanted to live if you were not sharing this life with me. What do you think POWAH would have said to that?"

"He would say that we would never be apart, love."

"Oh, Snooks, I don't know, I felt the same. One day, we will ask him, but we are together now. You will not get rid of me easily now that there might be two of me." ... they stared into each other's eyes, melting their love. He softly touched her bruise; for a fleeting moment, his eyes flickered, and then he whispered,

"At least our baby will have a chance to settle as I won't yet..."

"Toon, where are your thoughts!" His glint was back in his eyes.

"Kitty, you are the sexiest, most desirable, loving, beautiful, warm-blooded woman I've ever known." She kissed him on his nose.

"You are the most persistent, seductive, sexy, charming, gorgeous hunk of a man I've ever encountered in my whole life. You'd better get your health back in shape, as you'll soon have to make an honest woman of me."

"When?" he asked, his arm pulling her against him tightly. He leaned his head against her breasts.

"Kitty, when I'm with you, I almost get a glimpse of who I am. I want, purely for myself, to enter into a sacred marriage with you for the glorious opportunity it gives me to live my life to my fullest potential." It felt so good to touch, hold, and hear him mentally say that.

"Oh, Toon, you are so good with words, even when you just think them. I want the same for myself," she whispered into his ear. She had to be careful of the draining tubes that were attached to his chest on his right side. When somebody knocked, she looked at the heart monitor, which seemed very stable to her.

"Snooks, I must get off this bed. Otherwise, they'll think I've come for only one thing."

"They would not be far off the mark." Toon chuckled. She flinched when she had to take a few careful steps to get her ankle used to her body weight again.

"Kitty, you were hurt!" He got up to reach out for her while the heart machine was changing its tune simultaneously. The door flew open, and the doctor rushed in to see what was happening.

"Well, well, you must be Ingrid! I'm glad to see you. Toon, has she been exciting you? I can see your heart is getting stronger!" A tall man in a long white doctor's coat with dark brown eyes and a warm, friendly face observed the scene on the bed, not fooling him that Ingrid had just left.

"Really? I got a fright. It changed its tune; it did, didn't it?" Ingrid interrupted his reading, worrying while shaking his hand. Doctor Don van Houten glanced at Toon's chart, took out his stethoscope and listened to his chest.

"Good, it has a much stronger beat now. We'll remove the machine this afternoon."

"Really? Great! Oh, I'm so glad. How long will it take before he can go home?"

"We'll talk next week, after the weekend. What did you have in mind?" his eyebrows lifted while his eyes bore into hers with a serious frown. He seemed like a nice man in his forties.

"I'll be at home the whole day. I'll be nursing him, and Debbie, my daughter, can show me what to do with the bandages." He pondered seriously, taking her chin and looking at her bruise.

"Oh, yes, Debbie, that's right! Well, Toon, it looks like we will get rid of you soon to this lady of yours. I can see why you were so worried."

He observed Ingrid again. "How are you?"

"Don, can you ensure they take an x–ray? I'm sure she has a badly injured ankle?" Toon's insistent tone faded when he talked.

"That we will, Ingrid. I'll make an appointment downstairs. I think we'll keep you overnight, just in case. Your ordeal needs to be considered, Ingrid; you were very fortunate to have escaped from the hands of people who are so brutal." While he talked, his professional observation did the rest.

"Yes, but I'm fine now that I'm back."

"Don, can she not stay here with me? I don't want her in another room." Toon asked in all seriousness.

"Toon, you are asking a woman to share your hospital room?" A laugh spread over his face, indicating his relief about his patient.

"I'll see what I can arrange, but, Toon, you need your rest. Do take it slowly. I can see that you are a lot better, but don't fool yourself. It was a warning, so take it seriously!" Toon looked up with a weak smile, admitting that he was tired.

The doctor left, and she sat on the edge of the bed next to him while he dozed off. He looked so pale that it was difficult not to feel a strong aversion to the man responsible for this. She had great difficulty accepting that Toon had attracted all this to himself: the heart attack he might have had because his travelling could not have been that healthy.

The door burst open, and the room was suddenly full of people. Annelies, Ed, and a man with very short, almost bold grey-dark hair looked at her, which made her guess he was the undercover detective. Annelies's husband, whom she had not seen before, came in. Toon was awake again, and he held her close to him.

"Toon, I deserve a medal; I've kept them all out as long as possible. Crumps! You already look a lot better!" Toon's grateful gesture as he brought Annelies' hand to his lips without letting go of Ingrid spoke for itself. When Debbie rushed in past all the visitors and saw the bruise that started to look more horrific by the moment, she hugged her mother, crying. Ingrid knew she had a great deal to be thankful for. Toon squeezed her

"I know we are blessed, aren't we, love?"

"Mom, they are organising a bed for you in Toon's room so you can stay the night, and I've to take you down to the X-ray department for your ankle." Debbie's surprised tone expressed astonishment; she told them that Toon seemed to have twisted the doctor's arm because she knew Dr. van Houten had been very persistent when the head nurse protested. Her bed was rolled in as the man she had not seen before held out his hand to her and shook Toon's simultaneously.

"Ingrid, I'm so glad to meet you, but very sad about the circumstances.

We don't always understand why things happen, but my resources told me that your last drawing had the right effect. We have to thank you for that." Ben's voice was dynamic and direct, with a hint of humour as if life was one big adventure. She reckoned he was the same age as Annelies. His eyes were of a dark blue that openly looked at life without inhibitions, like children do. The sincerity in his face reflected a deep thinker who had learned his lessons well through some harrowing experiences. He was almost the same height as Annelies, but he gave the impression of being a large man.

"Ben, I want to discuss a lot with you. I know that Ingrid needs to know much more about the part you have played in all this, but for now, I want her for myself," Toon's voice became stronger by the moment.

Ed placed the wheelchair next to Toon's bed, and before she knew it, he had picked her up and gently settled her in. Debbie took her down in the lift to have X-rays taken. In the passage, two people, obviously reporters, approached her suddenly, asking her questions. They were from the Utrecht Dispatch newspaper.

"Can you tell us who kidnapped you and why?" The reporters probed, following them into the lift while Debbie manoeuvred her wheelchair.

"Was any ransom paid for your release?" they persisted. Ed must have seen what was happening as he was suddenly in the lift with them and asked both reporters to give her some time to get over the shock from the whole abduction ordeal. He promised them both a full report in the morning. They finally left her alone.

"Thanks, Ed! They took me totally by surprise. I would not have known what to say anyway." Debbie left them together to organise her X-ray appointment.

"Ingrid, I must ask you things about this Piet you projected to us. *What did he do to you?*"

"Oh, he was dreadful. He slapped and threatened me all the time. I'd worked with him for many months; that came as the biggest shock. I still can't get over the fact that he hated me that much." Ed just sat with his arms around her, and the silence made her look at him.

"How are you and Yolanda? Where is she?"

"Oh, my dearest, I must thank you, you know, for introducing her to me. I always thought you were the only one for me, and for years, I was miserable thinking about you, yet the moment I saw her, it was as if a thunderbolt struck me. I would not have believed it if someone had told me this was possible." Ed's face and eyes were glowing when he mentioned Yolanda.

"Oh, Ed, I'm so glad. I do love you, but now you know it's different. But where is Yolanda? I thought that somehow she would be here?"

"Ingrid is so miserable that she does not want to see anyone. I communicate telepathically with her, but even I haven't been able to get near her since the kidnapping. When I discussed with Ben that Wednesday evening and told him about Piet, Yolanda went all pale and shaky."

"What has Piet got to do with her? Piet de Wit, don't tell me, oh no!.... was that her ex-husband?" Ingrid felt shattered. She remembered Yolanda's expression when she had reacted to her working for Pleasure Parks. So that was it! She knew Piet, her ex-husband, worked there as well.

"Ed, what about Connie? Does she know about her father?"

"No, Yolanda is determined to keep her out of it for as long as possible. She feels so bad about what he did to you; he gave you that bruise, didn't he?"

"But, Ed, she is not responsible for his actions!"

"I know that, and deep down, she knows that too, but she somehow seems to blame herself for not being more intuitive about him and thinks that she could have prevented all this. By the way, Ingrid, who shot Toon, do you know?"

"Not Piet! The man's name is Bruce; he is far more." ... Ingrid was shivering, thinking about him, the humiliation and his insinuation.

"Oh, love, I'm so sorry...I mentally eavesdropped...Did he...to ask you this now so soon? You must be so shaken, and all I'm thinking about is myself. I'm sorry." Ed choked while stroking her face. His warm embrace made her shudder, thinking back at how those creeps mentally raped her. Ed's shaking body made her take note since he could read her thoughts.

"Ed, nothing happened. It was just... very humiliating. Gee, I even became violent and slapped him, as I recall, but Ed, can you contact her, I mean, telepathically?"

"You mean now?"

"Yes, now at this moment, together with me," *"Yolanda, Ed is with me. I now know why you are not with him. Please come. I need you as a friend; you must come." "Please, my love, are you listening? Ingrid is fine. Come and look for yourself."* It always amazed her that they could do this, and she wondered how many more people worldwide were starting to communicate this way.

When Debbie returned and took her to the X-ray room, she looked at Ed and said, "Don't worry. Yolanda will get over it. Take her away; she needs you." Ed kissed her on her forehead.

"Take care of your mother, Debbie." He walked away.

"Mom, was there something between you and Uncle Ed?"

"That was a long time ago, love. He has now found the love of his life, but what about you, Debbie?" Ingrid suddenly remembered her and Richard and wondered.

"Oh, Mom, life is so...unpredictable! One moment, you think you are in heaven, and the next time, you are thrown into hell again." Debbie's light blue eyes were troubled.

"That, my dear, I can relate to that," she said with conviction, realising that it was an inner cry from Debbie herself. They all created their physical experience, POWAH had said, and each individual could only change it for themselves.

"Mrs. Barendse, may I ask you a few questions? I'm Detective André Jaarsma and have been assigned to your case at the request of Mr. Haardens." A charming, familiar-looking man held out his hand.

When she shook it, she knew. This must be Ula's fiancé and or Niels's brother. They could almost be twins.

"My mother must first have some rest. She's just had a lot of X-rays taken. Can't you come back later?" Debbie was determined that her mother was not going to be unnecessarily harassed.

"It's all right, love; I might as well get it over. May I call you André? I would first like to settle in. Can you come back, say, in thirty minutes?"

All she was interested in at the moment was Toon. She had been away for at least three hours!

The heart monitor had been removed; she was so glad. It had brought back sad memories; she realised how much the atmosphere of hospitals still affected her.

"Debbie, what took them so long?" Toon's voice was a lot stronger.

She was helped from her chair onto her bed next to Toons's with just a bedside trolley in between. He tried to pull back the curtain that separated them.

"I'm so glad they took your heart monitor away."

"Love, I hope this drip will soon go as well. Debbie, how long do you think? Must I stay here? I would hate to be here when your mom goes home, and I feel a lot better now that she is safe."

"Toon! You had a heart attack only three days ago! Then they operated on you, giving you a pacemaker. Dr. van Houten will not keep you here one day too long. Mom, I overheard that he booked you in for the whole weekend. He calls you 'Toon's medicine.' He's never known a patient to recover as fast as Toon has since you were freed and returned."

"Kitty, what's the verdict on your ankle, do you know?"

"Mom's ankle is very swollen, so they wanted to ensure nothing was broken inside. It's just very badly sprained. Mom, Sascia will come tonight to bring you some clothing. She thought you would hate our hospital gowns. Ingrid looked into her daughter's face to see if she read anything Sascia might have said about the baby.

"Kitty, don't even try to find out. They'll soon know anyway,"

Toon glinted at her; she felt all glowing at their mental intimacy.

"Snooks, how do you know what I wanted to learn from Debbie?"
While grabbing the curtain, she peeked.

"Woman, I know you! You've told Sascia about the baby."

"The whole weekend. Mmm, yes, then I need some different clothes. Debbie, when are you off duty?" *"Snooks, there is a detective, André, wanting to speak to me. I told him to be back in thirty minutes. How much do I tell him?"* She beamed

"I'm already off duty and will see if Richard is back with Sascia. I'm meeting them and will have supper downstairs at the restaurant later." Debbie kissed her mother and went readily to Toon's side as well, receiving a kiss on her hand as he held her.

"*Kitty, he is investigating the possibility that I might have been the target, but for different reasons. Ben wants to engage a security firm around the clock to ensure. Thirty minutes! I want some time alone with you!*"

"Debbie, I'd better stay in your good books! You can come in quite handy. ... please, Debbie, tell Richard I want to see him."

Ingrid could see Toon was getting better by the minute as he was using all his charm on her...She was genuinely shocked at the possibility that Toon was a target, but how come? "*Snooks, do you have any idea why? Does Hans know?*"

They were alone in the room, but she had to leave to speak to the detective as promised. Now that Toon admitted to something she knew nothing about, she didn't want to leave him.

"Kitty, we will come through this. I don't want you to worry. Surely, that is not good for the baby." his hands gently stroked her tummy. "*Hans will let me know if it was serious love. I've closed a lot of holdings related to oil in Alaska. That was when the treats started. Nothing to do with the pleasure park site. I'm truly not worried.*"

"Love to and come back soon," he whispered, but his eyes spoke a different language. "

Chapter 21
Becoming Aware of Being Unaware

A Proposal

"Kitty, can't we move that trolley away and push our beds together? You're too far away," Toon blurted in frustration after Debbie had gone.

"After the visitors and the nurses don't have to come back, I'll make a plan. Snooks, what do I say to this detective?"

"He's all right, love. Tell him whatever you know, but I want you next to me, come!" Toon held out his arm, and she moved from her bed into his under the bedspread.

"Snooks, people will talk!"

"Let them! I don't care. Do you?"

A knock announced André, the detective. He acted as if seeing two people up close in one hospital bed was normal, but she did detect a humorous glint in his Indonesian features.

"Snooks, his name is also Jaarsma! Is that a coincidence?"

"It's a common name, but you never know. I wonder if he has already spoken to Annelies?"

Ingrid gave a complete description of what she remembered, especially the two creeps who were the most vicious. They knew of Piet. Toon had some difficulty not reacting out in anger, and he practically smothered her by his overwhelming feelings at the distress she had endured.

"André, do you think I'm hysterical thinking Toon could still be in danger?'

"Mrs. Barendse, I would never call you paranoid. Many people who have had your experiences would have cracked under the sheer terror of it all. We'll keep someone from our police force observing the door of Mr. Haarden's room to monitor everyone who comes and goes."

"André, please, Toon and Ingrid will do. Have they heard anything more about Piet de Wit? I only heard yesterday that he is my niece's ex-husband. That came as quite a shock." His last words formed in his head for only her to hear. *"Kitty, I know Ed told you because I asked him to."*

"No, we haven't found any trace of them yet, but the French police found the deserted warehouse two miles away from the Pleasure Park building site. We were all surprised that the local population hadn't noticed anything suspicious. Every trace of them is gone, and the smashed-up technical equipment in the basement has been removed for investigation."

"But that was all shot to pieces; what do you hope to find in them?"

"Ingrid, you would be surprised; we are trying to link the burglary at Mr. Brinks's home with the intrigues the Pleasure Parks project brought to light and what they wanted from you."

"André, what about the security firm that's been patrolling on the site because so much equipment is lying around?" Ingrid was amazed at Toon's strength, which had returned quickly. André shared what he knew, some of it they knew, and she was relieved to hear that Hennie, Tieneke's daughter and Mr Brinks's granddaughter, seemed all right.

André seemed to be entirely on the ball, and she wanted to get past the inquiries fast now that they were together again. When André left, they were by themselves for a while. Toon's hand softly stroked her belly button.

"What an ordeal it must have been for our baby," he said, resting his head on her shoulders. She felt peaceful again among the many well-wishing cards, flowers, and plant arrangements that started to dominate the room.

"Snooks, go to sleep. I can feel you are tired, and your soft stroking is very soothing, very comforting, very thought-provoking, and"... She peeked at him and seeing his eyes were closed already, she relaxed against him, his head near hers.

Her mind was focused on the foetus, which might be a little girl and whether it was confirmed that she was pregnant. She was almost sure, even though a medical test was required to prove her intuition. Ingrid was contemplating the Soul that had chosen them as parents when she became strangely dizzy, as if she were spinning slightly, and things went out of focus...

A weird feeling came over her... *Then she saw ... what looked like big yellow flowers, many almost growing like a creeper into a tree, called cups of gold. She heard delightful laughter coming from a little girl. She was holding hands with a much older Timmy!*

Her light blonde mop of curls tumbled around her expressive, shining face, and her great blue eyes were mesmerised by the golden cocker spaniel puppies.

"Timmy, why can't we keep them all? Snoopy won't want to give them away. They are her babies! People don't give their babies away, do they?"

"Sandra, it's different with dogs. They like to be special to people; they want to be close to people to help them wake up. Remember when we asked Snoopy?"

Timmy's wisdom, while he stroked her hair, revealed that he loved this little girl; it almost reminded Ingrid of herself long before...she had had a brother...but Timmy was not the little girl's brother...

***

"Kitty, are you awake?" Suddenly, everything became focused again, and Toon beamed, *"We have visitors, love."*

"Hi, I'm sorry, I must have dozed off...gee, hi, Liesbeth! It's wonderful to see you! Gosh, I had the same experience as I had before, in the coffee shop, remember?" Liesbeth was standing next to her with a gigantic smile. Hans was on Toon's side with a laptop and some papers for Toon to sign.

"Toon, what do you intend to do with that laptop?" she suspiciously asked when he moved to sit up higher. She could see that he winced in pain.

"Hans, can't you take it away? The pain, I mean. Don't you have some special healing powers?"

"No more than you have, Ingrid, but I'll give it a go, Toon," Hans shovelled him gently. He held his hand over Toon's shoulder where the bullet had entered. Ingrid watched as a blue glow suddenly appeared between Hans's hand and Toon's shoulder. Toon's eyes were closed, but the indulgent smile on his face reminded her of a hot iron that took creases away. Wow! Most people would call this a miracle. "Don will be surprised that my wound is healing this fast." Hans's hand looked pale when the blue light seemed to enter the skin. She could feel the heat, being that close. She could feel that her eyes were on stalks while holding her breath, watching as Hans gently pulled out the draining tubes! Toon moved his shoulder around, and Ingrid peeped up close. All she could see were some markings on his skin from the bullet. There was no longer an open wound! This form of healing was miraculous. Toon massaged his shoulder in absolute disbelief.

"Toon! What are we going to tell the doctor?"

"I'll tell them that it was you who was doing. You, next to me, made me heal fast because you are my medicine!" Toon was ecstatic. The blue light had given him a new boost of energy. Hans had beamed his healing thoughts to one specific point, which she knew from Quincy, but...

"Hans, can you do that for her ankle?"

"Toon, I'll do it for now because both your auric fields are still trembling from the trauma, but remember, whatever I do, you can both also do. Hans removed the compress as she relaxed on her bed, and slowly, she saw the same blue light appearing, a tremendous heat that simultaneously made her feel very loved penetrated her whole feet.

That was the description! The feeling of that 'love' emotion came from the heat! They were the same! If only Debbie could see this now! As a nurse, surely this kind of healing would interest her.

"It is better when Debbie and others see this type of healing when they fully understand that it is no miracle, no special power." Ingrid was acutely aware that Hans had read her thoughts.

"Ingrid, if people see this type of healing, they immediately classify it as separate from themselves, which serves no purpose.

Your body healed you because it responded to Hans' energy field that communicated with both your auric fields to realign the vibrations around each cell," Liesbeth explained earnestly.

"It all sounds so easy," she sighed. "I know my body is an energy substance like yours, so what you say is that consciousness expresses itself through molecules and atoms. If I'm consciously thinking about it, I can heal or realign them according to my will."

"Yes, you can explain it that way, and you must be able to project love that comes from the heart chakra into the energy around you and focus on a specific part; then, it will start to glow and generate light. It forms a light, for love is light." Ingrid tentatively put her weight on her foot and found that the pain was gone! She walked around to test it further and was amazed to experience a feeling of total well-being in her whole foot. Both Hans and Liesbeth were delighted at their recovery.

"Kitty, you'd better come back into bed. I don't want them to think you can suddenly go home sooner. They promised you to me at least until Monday."

Both Liesbeth and Hans laughed at his natural deviousness, but sensed that he was apprehensive simultaneously. At that moment, their supper arrived, and the visitors departed, apparently to join all the others, including Debbie, at Mr. Brinks' house for dinner. Mr. Brinks had a live-in cook who loved entertaining.

It was wonderful to be alone with Toon while enjoying the flowers' perfume that started crowding their room. While inspecting their supper, Toon complained to the nurses, who had not seen that the draining tubes were out, that he preferred a juicy hamburger. They responded with laughter. Toon certainly had a way with women.

"Toon, I've so many questions, I don't know where to start."

"Kitty, ask me anything. I've no secrets from you, but join me in bed. I hate you being so far away." Toon was getting fidgety with being immobile because of the drip that Hans had left for the nurses to remove. Ingrid snuggled next to him again.

"Kitty, it feels as if today has been like a whole week, yet this morning you were still in France with Helen and Peter, and now you are close next to me. Did it all happen?" When Toon began nibbling on her ear, a shiver returned. His physical grounding, powerful masculine energy, and highly evolved spirituality created a large field where their soul-love for each other would flourish.

"Snooks, was this all meant to happen?"

"Kitty, when we are linked by a common purpose, who knows, we move together through the external mental creations we all still have to deal with. I've also been contemplating that, and Ben summed it up by saying that we all experience the divine mind directly through our inner intuitions. We create coincidences because we are in a flow with each other, and each has a part to play. I only hope you did not have to suffer because of any of my karma still floating around," he said, resting his chin on her head.

"So, I was in the right place at the right time? I mean, I had to alter the drawing?"

"Kitty, we all belong to or are part of a group, Soul. Annelies has been guided to give it a family name, as you know – the Jaarsma Clan. I understand our ancestors were born into the same period to work together during ongoing incarnations. You and I have been particularly blessed by finding each other to support each other through this resurrection process." She could feel the rhythm of Toon's heart as they kissed...the nurses had taken the dishes away, and she enjoyed their privacy.

"How do you see Piet's role? Could he not also be part of the same group, Soul?"

"Yes, he is. From what I've heard from Yolanda, Piet tends to be aggressive when dealing with women. There must be karmic energies he is being influenced by. He's trapped in a control drama of his own making, and I believe he's a gambler too." She wondered if Piet's childhood could have made him react so brutally.

It was hard to believe, sitting in a hospital bed together, that she was in a very different space not so long ago, with all the flower arrangements around them. Which one was real? Was this how they would experience being in two dimensions all at the same time? Would the third and the fifth earthly reality intermittently overlap according to the frequencies they were vibration on at any given time? That idea was very troublesome, especially when her mind returned to the moment...

"Watch your thoughts at all times, Ingrid." Hans beamed.

She did wonder how he was so aware of their mental level. She could only pick up telepathic messages when they were purposely directed at her or when she projected her thoughts to someone.

"Oh, love, seeing through Piet's violent behaviour, especially towards you, is not easy. I've never met him, but Annelies told me a few things. She suspects that Nick duToit forced him to get involved or that there is some connection between them through their gambling addictions."

"Snooks, POWAH said that Piet was living out the effects of his creation. I can see what a trap that can be. As you say, he is controlled by fear, but we all are. I know I was." She shivered as she thought back, especially Bruce, who had made her recoil, and how terrified they were when 'the boss' took over! Toon cuddled her, sensing her reaction to the trauma and the humiliation.

"Kitty, I've experienced that sheer fear made me lose control. I fell right into its clutches when I saw that you were forced against your will in that van." *"Oh, love the pain of losing you!"*

"Oh, Snooks, you paid a heavy price, almost too big! Let's never take our physical bodies for granted. Please, stop travelling so much without proper breaks in between," she firmly pressed against him. Toon's hand was slowly sliding under her clothes over her abdomen, stroking her belly button.

"What did you say was the feeling when I do this, very soothing, very comforting, very...what?"

"You were asleep!"

"Oh...stop doing that...not here...it's too delicious...Oh, I'll get you for this," her voice trembled with arousal when they both heard a knock. Toon took his hand away and pretended to look at his laptop, which he quickly placed on his knees. Ingrid looked at him with a glint of mischief, *"I'll test you soon. Watch out, mate!"*

"What have you in mind?"

"What, already working! Ingrid, this man has changed from a very ill patient to a far stronger man within hours! What is your secret? I could use some of that?" Dr. van Houten exclaimed in blank amazement.

When his eyes travelled over Toon's shoulder and prodded him all over, they could see that he was puzzled now that the draining tubes were out. They both grinned at his disbelief and confusion. *"Kitty, don't say anything about your ankle! Let the man recover first."* Her eyebrows are high, she beamed.

"That's not your reason....!"

"Toon, what happened? Please, I've heard some rumours.... but this...I need to understand this. What kind of healing took place here? This is not normal." Toon explained that he had been healed by a friend under the understanding that no publicity would result from this. Don asked many questions, and they both realised he had an open mind and was genuinely interested in learning more. He would contact Annelies.

After he wrote something on the chart that would protect them from curious people, he made sure to have Annelies' address.

"Does that mean I can go home with her on Monday?' Toon asked eagerly.

"Toon, let's not overdo it. You were almost gone from us for a good three days. We will first monitor your pacemaker. I must be convinced of your miraculous recovery by Monday to make any decisions. I'll tell the nurses to remove the drip. I came to wish you both a good weekend. Toon, you can leave bed slowly tomorrow to get your circulation going. I'll see you both on Monday."

He left them alone again. Ingrid looked amorously at him and slowly moved her hand under the covers.

"Kitty, don't you dare; I'll rip the needle out of my arm if you." Toon took a deep breath that suddenly made her come to her senses.

"I just wanted to see how well you had recovered," she giggled, looking worried and wondering about his heart. Toon pretended to be totally oblivious when there was another knock on the door, and Sascia and Richard came in.

"Hi, Mom! Gee, you both look better, Toon? Is he sleeping? I brought you some clothes. I hope I chose the right ones," Sascia chatted.

"What is this daughter of yours implying? Are you going to seduce me while you think I'm incapable of any decent action?" She ignored him with a smile and took the overnight bag from Sascia, peeking inside. As she winked at Sascia's flushed face, she jokingly asked why she was glowing like a ripe warm plum while touching her cheeks. Toon suddenly awoke, wanting Richard's attention.

"Mom! Please," Richard seemed captivated entirely by Sascia the way he watched her as he handed Toon a letter. Toon seemed to know what was in the letter because he suddenly became suspicious and secretive.

"What are you hiding from me? What's in that letter?" Toon opened it slowly, reading it while Ingrid tried to read his thoughts. Both Sascia and Richard looked flushed. Richard was trembling. What was going on? Then Toon looked at her with so much love she almost melted.

Ingrid knew something was brewing when he kissed her hand and looked deep into her eyes.

"Will you marry me?" Passing the letter. Oh, yes, she would marry this man whenever. She opened the paper, and all it said was: We can organise, by special request, a wedding ceremony in the hospital chapel on Sunday in the late afternoon. Leo.

"What, here? In the hospital?"....

"Oh, Snooks, yes, I will," she beamed and kissed his serious face gently *in front of Sascia and Richard, who were* observing them with great delight.

"Mom, Toon, I'm so...I don't know...happy for both of you, I guess. What a surprise! Toon, how did you arrange that from your hospital bed?' Sascia asked in astonishment while she hugged both her mother and Toon. She could see that Toon had stolen her daughter's heart.

"Yes, tell me, how did you? And Richard, what have you got to say for yourself? I sense that you know more about this scheme," Ingrid demanded. Sascia was equally as curious by her expression of bewilderment. Richard became shy from both women's probing. He was indeed a very handsome man. Was there anything between those two?

"I'm only the messenger boy. Toon, I did as you told me to do, and Ben gave these letters on instructions from Leo, I believe, to get co-operation from the legal people."

Richard handed him more papers. All Ingrid could think of now was what she was going to wear. For obvious reasons, Toon loved her blue-linen suit, so she whispered to Sascia, explaining what to organise from her side for this mind-shaking event that still felt unreal. She knew that their private room was not restricted by visiting ours, but when there was a knock on the door again, Richard and Sascia bid farewell.

The nurse removed his drip, and the relief of having both hands free made a great difference.

While she cuddled up against him, Toon was working on his laptop. The numerous commitments he was still responsible for now required his attention. Then the screen suddenly changed without any warning.

"What's this?" But they both knew it was POWAH when the text appeared.

<If the time has arrived for both of you to announce your feelings for each other through a special demonstration or ceremony, make your declaration to each other a claim that you will both live your truth. Do not make your love for each other an obligation.>

What! I want Kitty to be my partner, lover, wife, everything. That is, for me, living in truth! Toon typed in reply.

"POWAH is suggesting that we should not make a promise to each other?" Toon responded with great disappointment and confusion. "Snooks, I think I know what he means," and she reached over to type her question."

POWAH, you mean that when you give a person total freedom, you also provide yourself with space, so they don't need to promise anything.

"But, Kitty, I would never want to take your freedom from you!"

<Toon, many changes are taking place in your commitments to each other, but viewed from a higher level of consciousness, in your world, you use pieces of paper to ensure agreements are being kept. Would you not give and share automatically, regardless? You are already living by that principle with the building of your communities.>

"I know what he is implying, Kitty, but what is the point of a marriage between two people? I want to marry you, have you always next to me, have people call....and he typed.

POWAH, I would love it if Ingrid would carry my name. Is that so egotistical?

<Why?>

Ingrid giggled at Toon's expression of total frustration; she had begun to love that look so much that she only wanted to hug him.

I want to tell the world that my relationship with Ingrid is very special and that I hold this relationship above anything else, and make that a promise. What's wrong with that? Toon typed feverishly.

"Snooks, you don't have to make any promises to me; we'll always live in love for and with each other. You are denying your freedom when you need to make that promise."

<Toon, it's not a question of right or wrong but of what would serve you both. Can you predict your future?>

"I suppose not since I can change how I think and feel, but I cannot, " he declared while kissing her nose.

"Snooks, I'll always want to love you because I want to, not because I have to, because I made a promise to do so," kissing the tip of his nose. Toon encircled her and from within the embrace, he typed:

"I'm beginning to see what you two are on about. Most people seem to perceive a marriage as some form of institution. I've seen plenty of couples that treat it that way. You are implying that when people go into an agreement with each other, it should be with complete freedom, even as far as acknowledging that one person is not more special than another. Still, I've not yet reached that kind of unconditional love."

Ingrid wanted to ask more about her feelings and being called Mrs. Haardens. Correction: she would like to sign her name, Mrs. I K B Haardens, for she would keep the B for Barendse, but all these things were trivial and unimportant; she knew how human they were.

POWAH, are you against marriage? She knew that typing their questions made it somehow more...

"Kitty, whatever the text replies, I want to marry you only if you want. We can write our marriage vows. My love for you has no stipulations, but I would like our child to be brought up in an atmosphere of family life, and I love the sound of Mrs Haardens," Toon softly stroked over her tummy.

<I have no judgment about anything. I'm an observer, but real love does not require an exchange of vows, yet you seem to need them. The limits you place on your love for each other will reflect the values you hold about what love is.>

"Snooks, what if our marriage vows have no limits at all? Why don't we write our marriage vows? Would they allow us to do that? Who's doing the service anyway?"

"Oh, yes, Kitty, Leo is performing the wedding ceremony. You will meet him tomorrow. He is the head of the family clan and was ordained as a Buddhist priest years ago. That's another story; I'll promise to tell you soon," he winked and started to type;

'I, Toon Haardens, now declare publicly my love for Mrs Ingrid Barendse, whom I call Kitty, and that it is my choice to live and grow in enrichment with her.

Ingrid had an urge to type her statement after his.

I, Ingrid Katrine Barendse, agree with the above statement and want to add that our bonding ritual is a reminder and a rededication of a firm commitment to the truth we already are.

Toon glowed, and his fingers hit the keypad.

I, Toon Haardens, hereby declare that I view this physical structure called marriage as a symbol of sharing my life with Ingrid Katrine Barendse, without obligations, but rather to create opportunities for my full self-expression, so that my life may be lived to my highest potential.

Ingrid loved the way he stated everything. After a cuddle, she followed up with her own added version.

I, Ingrid Katrine Barendse, agree to the above statement and add that we uphold each other truthfully through this sacred ceremony. We will never limit, control, hinder, or restrict each other. I, Ingrid, ask Toon, whom I call Snooks, to be my partner, lover, friend, and husband; I intend to be with him forever.

Toon reluctantly had to take his hand from under the covers to type his answer.

I, Toon Haardens, through this holy communion, promise to love Kitty as an equal partner, sharing equally both the authority and the responsibilities of a genuinely loving partnership, bearing together what burdens we may need to carry, and equally rejoicing in the glories. I intend to give Kitty my most profound friendship and love in suffering and joy. I further announce that I will always seek to see the divinity within her and to share with the god within me, especially in the moments of tribulation that may come, and that we together do the work our Souls were destined to do and share all that is good within us.

While Toon had been busy typing, she had been tickling him until he trembled with an ecstasy he needed to respond to.

"For someone who had a heart attack, you are very active, my love. I know they took the drip away, but are you sure you are up to your very high standards of..." *Snooks, not here; anyone can come in!*"

Toon had pinned her in such a way that she could only wriggle away to prevent him from caressing her in a way she would completely forget herself.

"You are genuinely asking for this, madam! Remember, I'm getting stronger by the minute and won't spend any more nights without you.

On Monday, I'm coming home with you to finish this activity properly; you can be sure of that," Toon said with relish.

< To both of you, in universal communities, cosmic couples are united in a degree of union that you two have experienced now. You two will climb high together, my dearly beloved. Those who are practising co-creative couplehood are paving the way for humanity. I salute you both.

LOVE POWAH>

They both had to laugh; this was uncanny as if someone was watching them! Oh, she needed to understand how it was possible that they could have a chat like you can have over the Internet with POWAH.

"A galactic communications network might be possible, according to Leo," Toon explained, sharing some computer possibilities with her and suspecting that Trevor, Leo, and Ben would know much more.

"Oh, Snooks, it's eleven o'clock; I know that's still early for you, but love, please, you need to sleep." Ingrid suddenly could not keep her eyes open. She climbed out of Toon's bed just before the night sister came in to check on Toon's progress. Before her head touched her pillow, she drifted off...

Leo & Ben

The following day, Toon was up and about for the first time since the shooting. Ingrid's ankle was completely healed, but Toon pretended it was still necessary for her to have her feet rest on his lap after breakfast.

They sat in two comfortable chairs opposite each other in the luxurious hospital room that started to look like an indoor nursery.

"How is your shoulder?"

"But, love, you know I have no pain anymore! Only my arm is stiff, and I have to start moving about. Incredibly, one can so quickly become like jelly. Even this little exercise is almost as strenuous as walking a marathon," Toon massaged her feet and ankle with a firm hand.

"Snooks, tell me a bit about Leo. He's Ben's twin brother, but they are not alike?"

"You're right. They're not. Leo has always been the quieter of the two. He's a man who can sit for hours without moving as much as a muscle in meditation, and at the same time, he can produce a work schedule that makes most people run away."

"You said he was the head of the family clan. What do you mean exactly?"

"I was referring to the Jaarsma star map he painted right after he came home from India. He had some amazing revelations while in retreat, slowly revealing some of his awakening experiences. Kitty, you have beautiful legs, you know." Toon was by now stroking her whole leg from her feet up.

"And you are an amazing masseur. It's good to feel your hands. Toon, I'm sure they also have a healing quality about them. Oh, Snooks, I forgot to tell you, but I saw the same star painting at the entrance of that weird resort! When I saw it, I was stunned." His thoughts momentarily distracted Toon from concentrating on her legs.

"Snooks, do you think Leo or Ben is behind the excerpts I've received?"

"What makes you say that?"

"I don't know. What does Leo do for a living? He sounds like a very knowledgeable man."

"He is, and he never expects from others anything he cannot do himself. He has the mind of a scientist and studied genealogy; he's a mathematician and has discovered a hidden code throughout many ancient scripts and texts through spiritual, esoteric Christianity and even the Bible. He is also well-versed in mythology and can write creative stories about them."

The noises outside Utrecht's academic hospital's parking bays announced that visiting hours would soon start. Toon's room was a private suite with a bathroom. He was moved from intensive care the morning she came back. What a difference this all was compared to when she visited Jan. He was in intensive care a week before he passed over. For the first time, she could think back without getting all depressed.

"Kitty, your other leg, I need to be useful." When Toon made an intensive study of her feet after dabbing a blob of hand cream on them, she needed to do the same.

"Hey! Give me yours, and we both are useful to each other." Toon's comical sounds of ecstasy as she was kneading his toes brought her to tears while asking more about the intriguing twins.

"Both Ben and Leo are researchers but in different fields. When I was eighteen, they took me through India and Tibet. I'll never forget those times I spent with them. Leo stayed behind for an extra few years while Ben pursued a career in criminology."

"Really? Do you mean the police force?"

"He's a former criminology professor, and while studying law, psychology, and criminology, he discovered or uncovered various sinister plots related to interbreeding. This was done in the past and continues to be done today. It's to create bloodlines of people who can expand their control and power worldwide. Ben's theories are that it's to enslave the population of our planet to prevent people from awakening," they were interrupted by a knock on the door.

"Well, good morning to you both! Toon, seeing you up and giving each other a foot massage is so good!" Annelies chuckled. Ben followed behind her.

"Toon, I can't believe that your auric field was ready to integrate with the astral world only a few days ago, and now it is playing a symphony!" Annelies' eyes wandered over all the arrangements.

"Gee, Ingrid, you need a truck to move them all."

"I believe we have a rather joyful event tomorrow, and Leo is arriving from his retreat, especially for it. You two should be honoured! Ben's humorous voice boomed out. He was holding a blue envelope, which he handed to Ingrid.

"Are you responsible for sending me the excerpts?" As she peered inside, she saw two letters.

"Ingrid, that's rather a complicated affair. Trevor is the computer genius, so to speak; the one who made it possible that text seemed to appear on your screen for you and Toon in a way that telepathically answered your questions through the medium of POWAH."

"So at least POWAH is real?" Ingrid asked with some relief.

"Very real, my dear. That is in a more etheric sense."

"Ben...but how...did I receive an excerpt in that ghastly place?"

"My dear, the symbol that appeared in the background of your drawing is a sort of tracking device. It would be best if you asked Trevor. We'll come tomorrow with the rest of the family, Toon. I'm now grabbing this woman of mine to go to Richard's lecture in Amsterdam. I want to test his knowledge of the hieroglyphic text Trevor has prepared for him," Ben grinned.

"Really? What is his lecture about? Do you know?" She asked. It was uncanny that an Interpol detective and a criminal professor talked about hieroglyphic codes and the ancient mysterious monument in Egypt. Her mind was jumping from Egypt to the underground tunnels in France and CERN. It seems that all the secrets that have been hidden for centuries are now coming to light.

"His lecture is on what might be under the Sphinx in Egypt." She had to get used to the mental synchronicity between these Jaarsma people.

"Be kind to Richard, will you? What has Trevor in mind for him?" Toon asked

"Nothing he cannot handle, I'm sure. Theo tutored him very well. Annie, what do you think?" Ben turned to Annelies.

"He's here, you know," Ingrid heard mentally. What was Annelies implying?

"*Oh, he's checking up on you, is he? My love, you know I'll never compete with him, so let's be off.*" Ben and Annelies were the most dynamic, flamboyant people she'd seen in a long time.

"Toon, what was that all about? Who's Theo?" she asked when they left. Toon had moved the chair next to her and took her hands in his.

"My dear, there is a great deal to this family of ours. I'll gradually explain it all, I promise. I can't wait to leave this hospital, take you with me, and show you places. May I?" He took the envelope from her, and they both started to read.

"Wow, Ingrid, this is almost like an unfolding plot! Can you remember what excerpt seven was all about?"

"It was all about the sound frequency that creates the illusion of time and a mental hologram. I know that POWAH talks a lot about the Language of Light."

Excerpt Twenty-One[1]

Program Planet Earth

Becoming Aware of Being Unaware

Rule Eleven *of the Ascension Decoding Card Game*

"Snooks, I'm not so sure I understand all of this. The image I saw when that creepy boss man was looking at my screen in that horrible place looked like a sound card. Was that idea planted in me, you think?"

Toon was still rereading POWAH's message as if he needed to ponder over every sentence. "What are fire crystals?" She asked, looking up at Toon. "I'm baffled. I have no idea what an Oversoul means."

"I'm intrigued that he mentions using a sound beam that will act as a tuning fork in the Pleasure Park temple. I'm sure we will understand it all in good time, love," he said, pulling her close to him.

There was a knock on the door, and when they both simultaneously called out, André walked in, followed by Harry Brinks and Carla.

"Good grief! Annie told me about your recovery, but this!" Harry Brinks was so overwhelmed by Toon's miraculous improvement that he was completely off guard for a moment. André stayed in the background, observing the scene, while Carla gave Ingrid a long, warm embrace.

"André, have they found Piet and the other kidnappers yet? Toon asked as he pointed at some chairs in the corner for them to use.

"No, we haven't. Carla told me all about the harassment that Ingrid endured during the last weeks from this Piet, and we were hoping

---

1. https://allrealityshifters.wordpress.com/powah/the-reality-shifters-excerpt-21-2/

that you might be able to remember something that would help us with the investigations?"

"Ingrid, why did you never tell me about Piet's conduct? He only got the job because Tieneke's husband, Roelof, bugged me. I would never have employed him, and did so against my judgment. Now I see how important it is to follow one's gut feelings, especially when they are screaming at one."

Roelof de Beer was quite ill, and the kidnapping affair had pushed him over the edge. Roelof had been beneficial with their investigation, and Ingrid suddenly remembered that she had seen Bruce at the market in Beekbergen. She recalled the truck with oranges that had turned over one morning on the way to work. She told André as much as she thought was helpful.

"Ingrid, that is a break; if the police were involved in that accident, we've got him. If you both feel up to it next week, we would like to review some photos we have on file." They were only allowed to stay for a short while. Andre told them that the nurses at the front desk were strictly instructed to check every person who claimed to know both Toon and Ingrid. The security was still in place. When they left, both were somewhat depleted from the complexity of events.

Ed's voice boomed in the hallway, and Yolanda and Ed walked hand in hand. Ed's eyes almost popped, looking at them both.

"Yolanda, I'm so glad to see you! Come here and sit next to me." Ingrid pulled the chair close to her. Yolanda still looked somewhat troubled, and the tears, mostly from relief, were running down her cheeks when she hugged Toon.

"Ed, you said Toon was very frail, but there's nothing frail about him!"

"Ingrid, I heard from Harry just now in the hallway about the....what has she done to you, Toon? Believe me, love, Toon looked pale, thin, and pathetically weak two days ago."

"Toon, did Hans have anything to do with it?" Yolanda seemed to recall something as her hands drummed frantically on her armrest.

Yolanda's fascinating outfit complemented her long blonde hair. Ed was besotted with her.

"Yolanda, have you seen him using his healing powers before?"

"I think so, on Joris! Toon, when you were in Australia, Joris was hit by a guest's car in the hotel's parking bay. Hans and Liesbeth had just arrived. Hans picked him up, and Joris was all limp, and still, he took him inside, and he stroked his whole body. I thought he was feeling for broken bones when I saw a blue light that seemed to ooze out of his hands."

"Blimey, did he do that trick on you, Toon?" Ed asked. Toon explained why Hans didn't want anyone to know about his healing powers for apparent reasons. Ingrid wondered if they all knew about it.

"Toon, Ingrid, tomorrow is your wedding! Ingrid, I'm so pleased but sorry that I suddenly lost my faith in myself and the people I so dearly love," Yolanda interrupted her thoughts while gazing at Ed in absolute rapture.

"Hi, Mom!" Debbie's voice interrupted their conversation. She had never heard her knock. Ingrid looked proudly at her petite blonde, blue-eyed daughter in her uniform. Ingrid introduced Yolanda, explaining their clothing enterprise together to Debbie. Ed had always been Debbie's favourite uncle, but Ingrid knew why. Looking at them now made her see how much of a resemblance between them.

Kitty, you were right! That means you are also right about being pregnant with my child this time! Ingrid tried not to blush at Toon's mental comment, but now she knew he had known all along. Ed must have told him.

Ingrid, what is Toon implying? Is Debbie mine? Ed butted in with a strong mental reaction. Yolanda stared at her in absolute wonder, and then she looked at Debbie, who was unaware of what was happening.

"Mom, I went past the chapel just now, and they are busy deco-rating; congratulations!" Debbie was acting as a nurse at the same time. When she placed her hand on Toon's now healed but still in-flamed-looking shoulder, she suddenly closed her eyes and looked in utter surprise when she opened them again. Both sensed her confusion.

"Debbie, what is it?"

"Mom, I've never told you, but...lately, I've been getting powerful mental pictures when I touch objects, and I know when people have been injured in an accident. When Toon came in a few days ago, I saw the shooting scene before my eyes when I placed my hand on him! The shooting, the lot!"

"But it's gone now. How come?" Everyone was silent. Good grief, Debbie was becoming clairvoyant through the sense of touch. How appropriate!

"Debbie, you have an amazing gift! You must tune up your psycho-metric senses, and I will explain to you soon why your mental vi-sion of the shooting is gone, but do something for me, will you?" Toon placed her hand on Ingrid's ankle, asking her what she saw.

"Nothing! Mom, when I bandaged your ankle, I received from you the image of being dragged out of a vehicle, and now it's gone!

"Love, isn't that disturbing? I mean, to see some of the traumas people go through when they arrive?" she asked.

"Yes, sometimes, but it's still very new to me. I've been reading up on psychic power lately, knowing that I'm not telepathic as you both seem to be, and I'd never taken much interest in it before now. But you know it can also be fun. I told a friend battling to fall preg-nant that she is expecting a baby." Toon grabbed Debbie's hand and placed it on her abdomen in such a hurry that she heard laughter coming from both Ed and Yolanda.

While Debbie's eyes were closed, she saw a vision, and all of them could read her mind when she converted her image into words.

Toon glowed with such joy that Ingrid had to laugh. Yolanda's mouth hung open, and Ed just smiled since he already knew.

"Mom! You are pregnant! Did you know?"

"Well, Mmm, yes, but please, all of you, this is somewhat embarrassing. It's also too early in its development, and I still don't want this to be publicly announced. Toon, take that smirk off your face," while grabbing his shin. Toon took her hand and gently kissed it with such theatrical panache that they all laughed at his boyish joy. *"Ed, we have to talk about Debbie! I'm puzzled!"* Yolanda projected openly to Ed, who was staring at Debbie.

Chapter 22
The Eye of the Observer

The Jaarsma clan

"Toon, should I have told Debbie about Ed being her biological father?" Toon had walked around, but it still tired him more than he would admit.

"Kitty, you were never sure about that, but if she needs to know, you must tell her. I would not be surprised if she had awakened to that fact now that she has discovered her psychic talents."

Before they could say anything more, children's voices rose outside their door. Timmy and Karin burst into the room, each with a bunch of buttercups. During official visiting hours, the wards started to become busy with visitors.

"Uncle Toon, are you okay?" They were both planted on the bed with no room to spare. Both Helen and Peter sat on Ingrid's bed, while Debbie must have seen them arriving because she joined them and took the flowers after she had been introduced to the visitors. Timmy and Karin had never been to a hospital, so Debbie took them on an inspection tour.

"What a charming girl, but she looks so different from Sascia and Jeroen! So, Richard is her boyfriend?" Helen conjectured.

"I think so... but now I'm not so sure ...Thanks for the flowers! They bring back wonderful memories." She said, winking at Toon.

"Tell me about it! At least we have earned a free weekend at your Tilburg complex because of the buttercups," Helen sighed when Peter suddenly placed his hand over her mouth.

"Toon, I'm sorry, but this woman cannot keep secrets well. It runs in the family, I believe?

"What do you mean? Why a free weekend because of Buttercups?" The silence in the room brought the hospital noises to the foreground.

"Helen, when did you make a booking at our new complex in Tilburg? I can't remember,"...

Ingrid suddenly heard a playback of Marijke's voice: "Sorry, Ingrid, but what shall I do with this booking? I have a client on the line, and before booking her holiday bungalow in Tilburg for July, she wants to know if there are any buttercups or cups of gold creepers growing at the new complex in Tilburg. This woman is persistent because she had read somewhere that those flowers are poisonous, and she is worried about her small children."

Toon's arm glided around her waist while he dug his face into her neck.

"Toon Haardens, I seem to remember that less than four months ago, I phoned your firm to ask about Buttercups, all because of a difficult client Marijke had to deal with. Explain to me in minute detail about this incredible coincidence," Ingrid fixed a stare while simultaneously getting hold of him under the covers in a way that took him by surprise.

"Kitty! Well, it all started... *Stop that or else!*... All right, I asked Helen to phone Pleasure Park after I had heard your voice. I knew I wanted to meet you, and I couldn't think of any reason for you to go out with me.

"Kitty, stop!" "I knew you were very private, so, yes, it was a set-up. Now you know my secret. "Please have some mercy on your future husband; you are making me all shaky, and I'm supposed to

stay cool." Both Helen and Peter were laughing at her confrontation strategy.

"How did you know I would phone your firm?" Ingrid's interrogation, while ignoring his plea, made his whole body shake from both laughter and enjoyment.

"I didn't know; I was beaming thoughts at you the whole day, hoping you'd phone me back." *"Lady, you are playing with fire!"*

"Have you both been to Buttercup Valley recently?" Toon asked to divert her attention.

"Yes, Dirk flew us all here after fetching Mom and Dad for the wedding. We are all staying with Uncle Harry. I believe Leo is arriving tomorrow morning."

"Where has he been for the last six months?" Peter beamed.

"Toon, how many more secrets are you hiding from me?" she joined in, hoping they might learn about that before Debbie returned with the children, but it was too late. Karin and Timmy joined them on the bed.

"Where is your baby sister Jenny?"

"Connie is looking after her and sending her love," Helen replied as she lifted Karin off the bed. She suddenly wondered about Quincy, whom she had not seen in a long time.

"Ingrid, Quincy's helping Annelies with the preparations for your wedding. She'll be here soon," Helen had responded to her thoughts.

Ingrid felt incredibly privileged to have the love and support of so many friends and relatives. They were taking their children for a treat to Pleasure Park's tropical jungle resort near Bilthoven, so they said their goodbyes.

Ingrid was still mulling over Toon's scheming: so he'd been waiting for her to phone back the whole day when his voice had enchanted her, or...was it his mind?... Toon took her hands and observed her with the utmost seriousness.

"I didn't know if you would phone back; I just followed my intuition because your voice gave my memory such a jolt that I had to find out and remember the name 'Ingrid' was not altogether unfamiliar."

"You then knew already who I was? From Ed, I mean."

"No, not really, there are so many Ingrid's. I don't even think that Ed knew you were working. At least, I didn't, but when you confirmed it by telling me about your children, then I knew." She then knew they had met twice, once at the Pannekoek and in the pouring rain.

"I know. I was on the way to the radio station in Apeldoorn!" Toon was still trying to be very earnest, but she knew he had been snooping, asking Richard about her.

"But you didn't know about my being in Annelies' class, did you?" She held back her laughter while holding firmly onto his hands so that he could not copy her intimate strategy.

"Oh, no, not at all; that was the absolute proof the universe gave me. All my uncertainties vanished, all my longings were fulfilled, and I knew I had found you. I have called you to mind many times, you know! I'm so happy...I wish we were not so publicly exposed, the things I want to do..." Toon's voice was drowning in his own need to love her. Ingrid felt the same. Would this always be like this between them?

"Yes, I think so because you are a part of me." Toon demonstrated physically.

"Snooks, some would blame it on hormones...but"...

"My love, it's our Souls that control our hormones." Toon's hands were sensually stroking her belly.

"Snooks, in what way are you saying our Souls are one?" She was mentally seeing her light body first being separate...but vibrating on the same wavelength...very compatible...then...their blending and a wave of ecstasy entered her solar plexus. This was so different, almost...

"We share the one divine expression; you are the female, and I'm the male expression of the one divine full circle; my light body is now joining yours." ....they both felt much more alive, and the enjoyment of just being in each other's presence in the silence, made them more in tune with their selves than Ingrid had ever felt previously. Ingrid knew that healing took place on many different levels.

After the fine weather that day, they were sitting close together on a bench out on the roof terrace of Holland's largest hospital, where the sun continued their healing. She loved the temperatures in August, being the sunniest of the three summer months. Many tourists would have already booked their holidays in one of the Pleasure Park resorts. Today was a mild sunny day with a promise of rain in the evening. Lately, the weather has been unpredictable, but there was a clear forecast predicted for tomorrow, their wedding day. Ingrid was still bursting with questions.

"Snooks, why did you purchase the building construction that included the landscape division? I know Ben and Leo asked you, but why?" Both blended into the scene through the dressing gowns the hospital had provided.

"Let me explain what went on before I came back to live temporarily with Annelies. She had planned a birthday party for me that I hated, but she bribed me by reminding me that her vision of long ago was soon going to happen, and I had to be at her home." Toon played with her fingers, tracing her palm lines which made her ticklish.

"What vision was she talking about?"

"Annelies told me when I was around sixteen that I would meet my complementary half and that she, Annelies, had to prepare me for this reunion so that her work and mine could start. At the time, I had no idea what she meant. I don't think she did, either. Then she told me the same story again in January of this year."

Ingrid wondered if that was why he had always been looking for her. Annelies had had a precognition, like she had with Ed and Yolanda.

"And where were you when she told you all this the second time?"

"Oh, I was in Sydney." He sighed. "Annelies and Ben had come over because they'd been going through a difficult time, and Ben thought that a trip and a cruise would help their relationship."

"Did it?" Knowing how much Toon loved them both.

"I think so. The love for each other is real, but they don't have what we have experienced so instantly. I think their relationship is now very passionate, make no mistake, but I think Annelies knows the difference, and she has had to come to terms with the fact that in this lifetime...well,...I don't know. I think they're happy enough now." He hugged her while his other hand traced the lines inside her palm.

"Who had told Annelies about your meeting your twin soul?" She now knew that her marriage to Jan paled compared to the rapture she felt for him. She started to study his palm. Annelies told them that during the second level of her workshop, they would learn about their individual lives through their journey map, which was already in their hands. Toon started to squirm from the sensation.

"Oh, Annelies must have been around fifteen when she started talking about Dienie the nun."

"That was what Otto asked you?" So that was the story he was going to tell her! There was much more to come, and who was this Dienie?

"You have a good memory, don't you love?" Toon squeezed her tightly to him.

"There you both are! I've been looking all over for you!" Quincy suddenly appeared.

"Toon, meet my adorable sister," Ingrid jumped up to hug Quincy. Toon stood up, and shyness came over him. Quincy looked stunning in her stylish pantsuit. It reflected her personality as being both practical and innovative. She didn't encourage familiarity, but when her wavy, long blond hair was not tied up, she was relaxed, almost as if she had come straight from home.

"Who is looking after your health shop?"

"I started working as a part-time sales lady two weeks ago to give me some spare time at home." Ingrid noticed that she was summing up Toon's aura in a big way. Toon knew it, too.

"What is she seeing, Kitty? She makes me feel naked."

"You are to her, believe me," ngrid beamed when Quincy smiled at Toon in a way that would melt any man's ego.

"Toon, you are so tall! I'm so glad to meet you. I've been very well informed by your wonderful half-sister, Annelies, who took me into her home on Thursday when Ingrid was still missing," Quincy said heartily, embracing them both enthusiastically.

"Quincy, I'm so glad she did. I hope you didn't have to hear it over the news?" She observed that Toon felt somewhat guilty.

"Oh no, Jeroen contacted me, and I've been staying with the twins in Apeldoorn since Thursday. We heard from Ben on Friday that you requested marriage at the hospital. Sascia told us yesterday that Ingrid had consented, so Annelies leapt immediately into gear, as you can imagine. We have some surprises in store for you both," Quincy added mischievously. She would not tell them what and knew how to conceal her thoughts!

Toon was considerably impressed with Quincy, who had an air of sophistication that reminded them both of somebody... Their eyes met for a fleeting second. *"Kitty, I know what you are scheming,"*

They had a wonderful chat and would see more of Quincy the next day. She took her leave after a short while, as she still had a great deal to do before the wedding.

"Kitty, do you think your sister has met Fred already?" Ingrid laughed at their synchronicity.

"I don't know, but I can imagine the two are made for each other. Why did Fred never marry, do you know?"

"For the same reason that I didn't! Annelies said that Dienie had predicted that he would meet up with his twin soul later in life. Gosh!

Kitty, what do you think? I would give anything to see Fred's expression when they see each other for the first time. I know they will recognise each other as we did! I can feel it." The glint in his eyes reminded her of the tidal wave he gave her.

"My love, at that same moment, I suddenly got all warm, you know where?"

"Really? Where?" She glanced around to see if they were private as she demonstrated where.

"I want to get back to our room, lady. I need some privacy with you." The air in their room started to smell like a florist; the head nurse who came on night duty had already complained that it took them at least ten minutes longer to remove all the arrangements from their room to clear the air before the night.

"Well, matchmaker, we'll all be together tomorrow." Ingrid placed her feet on his lap for a massage while looking in the blue envelope, recalling it had two letters inside. She read POWAH's excerpt twenty-two out loud that was addressed to them both.

Excerpt Twenty-Two[1]

Program Planet Earth

Having the Motivation and the Desire to look into 'The Eye of the Observer'

Rule Twelve *of the Ascension Decoding Card Game*

< My mission to Planet Earth, which is a living library, was initiated at the request of the planet herself. Gaia wanted to make an

---

1. https://allrealityshifters.wordpress.com/powah/the-reality-shifters-excerpt-22/

inter-dimensional evolutionary leap but felt a great responsibility towards her inhabitants, realising that many would not survive such a journey without some travel preparations. We, the collective cosmic counsel from the sixth spiritual realm, have been observing your evolutionary process for many aeons and have realised that you like to play GAMES! >

The key codes of the excerpts:

Ingrid was profoundly impressed at the contents and the coincidence of their discussions. Toon was very quiet; his hands trembled when he took hold of the letter.

"Oh Kitty, I feel so privileged, so...now more than ever, I want to follow this ascension path, as Annelies calls it. No matter what it takes, we have been granted the honour of receiving these messages." The joy of finding a partner who felt like she did made all the difference, but even without a soul mate, this ascension journey would still be worth travelling."

"Toon, is this all due to the relocation of our solar system into the photon belt?"

"The theory on the photon belt is years old, but it grabbed my attention when I needed to shift my awareness levels. Leo, Trevor, and Annelies work on the fact that our divine Blueprint is connected with the Great Pyramid. This pyramid is a physical tetrahedron with an inverted twin that forms the planet's star tetrahedron. We are trying to activate a similar star-gate in the Valley of the Gods resort underneath the dome. I'm so glad I've found you, my twin Soul." Toon embraced her, kissing her, and as always, she melted in his arms.

"But what of others who do not experience this kind of union?"

Thinking back to her first marriage, there had been moments of great happiness which she would not have missed either, and some people would never know the difference anyway. One cannot miss what one never had, but what if one knew? Was that Annelies' experience? And telling Toon was why he'd suffered the longing, even knowing that searching for it was not the answer? But she hadn't. Oh, she always had so many questions!

"Not everyone has this passion that we share, Kitty. That has good reasons, too, I'm sure. It has been prophesied that many soul memories would return when the frequencies are raised. This is for your journal, not so?" Toon rolled both letters up and tied them with a ribbon from the arrangements.

"Annelies was told that on every awakening level of her decoding workshops, a journal had to be kept by one participant. Richard has taken on the second level of the awakening initiation game. I'm looking forward to playing that card game and reading about his experiences after Liesbeth re-edited his journal into a novel."

"I'm curious how she changes our story into a novel. I take it she does change our names?" Toon remarked.

"I feel that it's written so readers can relate to what is happening during the end times without just being our story."

"Yes, you are right. Hans told me that the journals are projected as a visual slide during the presentation to their elders and that the written text becomes animated. How? I have no idea."

"Gosh. What kind of technology is that? Did Hans tell you how?" Toon shook his head, saying, "Different spiritual dimensions have ways that we cannot yet grasp, but I'm sure we will."

"Toon, that reminds me of something. That it has been done before."

"What do you mean, how?"

"I'm trying to recall where I read it. It was shown to travellers into Tibet a long time ago."

Toon mentally recalled his time in Tibet as a youngster. "I know! Now I remember who you are talking about. The author's name is T Spalding. Life and Teaching of the Masters of the Far East."

"Yes! In one chapter, he describes how a future projection was shown on a rock wall inside a cave. Not so?"

"I have to look it up. I'm sure we can find it on the Internet these days. So, the first card game with your cards will happen next Friday?"

"Yes, possibly, I hope so. Will you join us?" Having Toon there would indeed be an experience.

"I hoped you would ask! I have to dig up my spacing. When Annie used me as a guinea pig, I never dreamed it was to prepare me for all this. I'm curious how this card game will prepare us to enter the hologram platform in the centre at Pleasure Park Resort." The head nurse interrupted their privacy, asking if it was all right to make any more arrangements in some rooms that had nothing.

They both insisted that they took some from their room as well. Toon made a note on his laptop for a regular delivery to the trauma unit as a token of his appreciation.

"Snooks, have you always been attracted to plants and flowers?"

She noticed that he had a fondness for plants. She had noticed that he automatically cleaned and pruned the arrangements subconsciously.

"I suppose I have. At the beginning, I thought that was why I needed to get involved in the construction and landscaping of the parks."

"You mean the one in France?"

"Yes, and Ben told me it was to protect Harry Brinks from losing the property because Leo had encoded a grid pattern that ran under that site. Only when I spotted the symbol did I realise there was far more to it. Then I got side-tracked by my other responsibilities and by you!"

Toon had been walking around and stood behind her chair, ruffling her hair. She washed it in the shower at Halfway House, removing the filthy grime from that rundown warehouse.

There was a knock, and André, the detective, came in, followed by Mr. Brinks. Toon and Ingrid exchanged glances.

"Talk about thought technology, Kitty."

"We won't stay long. Annelies and your sister have prepared a family dinner, so they will fetch you both shortly. André has just come back from Tieneke. Roelof made a full confession. He's very ill, but he wanted to come clean. His doctor thinks that he has little time left." Mr. Brinks looked a lot better wearing a summer suit.

"Ingrid, Roelof was shocked when he heard what had happened to you both and told André stories you would not believe! I have to come to terms with some of it."

"What about Hennie? Was she ever in danger?" Harry Brinks's eyes looked troubled when she mentioned his granddaughter.

"We think she might have been fascinated by some of Roelof's gambling mates. André wanted to ask Ingrid questions before he went off duty." Harry glanced at Toon for his approval.

"Mrs. B...Ingrid, Roelof said that you knew he was blackmailed because he told you," André commented. He still had difficulty calling her Ingrid.

"Yes, he was very short-tempered and said a conspiracy was happening. I heard rumours about his separation, but you know how gossip influences one's judgment. That's why I didn't take his panic seriously. I wish now that I had."

"Ingrid, where was Piet at that time? Can you remember?" She knew Piet had already gone home.

"André, you must ask Carla because I recall that she argued with him and told me that Piet had been bothering her after hours, but she must have told you all that?" Ingrid remembered that day very well.

That whole Monday had been a nightmare, but just before closing, she had Roelof on the line when Toon appeared, holding a bunch of yellow Buttercups! Toon winked.

"That day when Roelof made that insinuation, I was with Ingrid. I spoke to him over the phone when he was shocked about the truck accident. Thinking back, I realise I wasn't concentrating as I should have, so I'm also guilty of not taking him seriously."

"Well, Toon, both Roelof and Hennie managed to keep their un-savoury associations from Tieneke, and that says something be-cause she is very intuitive, so don't feel guilty. I'm sure you two had better things to do than." Harry Brinks commented.

"That's an understatement if I ever heard one, love."

"Ingrid, we have found the address of Bruce, who lived with a woman called Iris. They have skipped Holland, but Interpol has a search out for them; they won't get far. Regarding the third man you called the Boss, we have a suspect in custody on other serious charges.

Could you come to the station next week for a line-up? We think it is the same man." Ingrid shivered, and Toon, while embracing her, asked how important it was.

André reassured them both that it would not take more than three minutes. He would contact them again on Monday, thanking them for their cooperation and congratulating them on their wedding the following day. Harry walked him out as Debbie arrived, asking if they both felt like dressing up. She would take them to the dining room, where people were waiting.

"Are you going to be there? I hope so, or are you on duty?"

"Mom, I'll join you all later as I'm free after seven. I have to submit my report on both of your conditions. A lot of wheeling and deal-ing has happened around this wedding! I believe our hospital poli-cies have been tested, and apparently, a large donation made all the difference."

Debbie's face beamed knowingly at Toon, who only slightly raised his eyebrows. When they both arrived at the room hired for the occasion, they joined up with Fred, who had just come. He embraced them both with great tenderness.

"Fred, have you been involved in organising this family dinner?"

"No, Ingrid, I have left that to Annelies and your sister Quincy. I'm looking forward to meeting her. Annelies has been bragging about her talents." He winked at her while his eyes gleamed with mischief. Toon squeezed her hand when they both walked in.

"Let's watch what it looks like when twin souls meet!"

"But Snooks, we don't know that for sure!'

The dining room was decorated with yellow buttercups and a cup of gold creepers. Everyone was there: Sascia, Richard, Jeroen, Liesbeth and Hans, Harry and Tieneke, Ben and Annelies, Ed and Yolanda, Helen and Peter, Otto and Jill, but where was her sister?

"She's probably with the kitchen staff. I'll get her as I'm also curious," Annelies projected. Ingrid realised that most of them could mentally hear thoughts. This was going to be very interesting. What a pity she could not see their auras, but she knew that Liesbeth, Hans, Annelies, and Fred did so that she would read their minds.

The table plan told her that her sister would be sitting on one side of her. Fred had already found his seat, which was next to Quincy. When Quincy appeared with a radiant smile, her eyes rested on Fred. Ingrid knew because she could see a recognition of something. Fred greeted her in front of everyone in a tender embrace that astonished them all.

Quincy was shaking when they laughed as they both turned their attention to them. Fred escorted her sister to her seat and revealed to them with relish what happened when, after hearing from Ingrid about a sister in Delft, he had investigated Quincy by paying a visit. While eating their dinner, Fred flirted outrageously with Quincy, sharing how they recognised each other.

"Whoever was in Quincy's health shop must have had a feast."

Toon and Ben roared with laughter.

"When did you meet Fred for the first time?" Ingrid whispered.

"Directly after you had dinner with Yolanda that evening, he phoned me, and later, when Ed was introduced to Yolanda, Fred asked Ed about me. Then he visited me in the shop, well, the rest... we've been out a few times. It's not that long ago, only"...

"Hey sister, he kissed you as if you two had known each other much longer! Now I know why you took on a shop assistant."

"I know, that was not in the plan! He took total advantage that I tell you, but Ingrid, I'm so...what's the right word?" Quincy whispered so Fred would not hear.

"In love, trembling with ecstasy"...she whispered back

"Well, yes, yes, do go on," Quincy said, embarrassed, while Ingrid saw that Fred was listening with a big grin, which warmed her heart. The dinner was a great success. Liesbeth winked at her.

"I can see your love for each other is becoming more stable; you are more synchronised, both your energies are very connected, and it's a joy to see. We feel very proud to be with this family."

The Wedding

The water was cascading on them. Toon insisted on having a shower as his bandages were gone. Ingrid could see that the bullet hole left a scar, but his strength was improving each moment. His longing for Ingrid was getting stronger as well.

"How can you expect me to stay calm when I can feel your whole voluptuous body rubbing against mine?" Toon was still resting on a high chair while he was pressing her against him, soaping her everywhere while she did the same for him. Oh, she wanted to make love to him, but what about his heart?

"Kitty, my heart will burst if I don't! My mind will become a wreck. I"

This was the most private place they would have before getting married that afternoon. She mentally overheard that Ben and Annelies had something schemed for after the wedding. She could no longer control her own needs when he started to use his mouth in all the right places. She became as accommodating as possible, and Toon took advantage of every opportunity.

"Oh, Kitty, this is the one addiction I hope I'll never have to give up."

"Do you think you have to?" She was enjoying again the physical sensation of lovemaking.

"Kitty, I feel that we experience spirit in matter for a split second at our moment of ecstasy. I don't care what others say, this is. This feeling of oneness expresses that I love you with my whole being." She snuggled up close to him, leaning her head on his wet shoulders.

"Snooks, what do you think mystical marriage is?" He looked up at her and turned off the water.

"Kitty, I suppose the union with a higher power only occurs in consciousness. If we both awaken more in consciousness after having experienced this bliss, maybe we are ready to let go. I'm content with your magnificent capsule that activates all my physical senses for now." His face expressed both seriousness and joy at the same time.

When they were both dressed, the sparkle in their eyes would give away what they had been up to. They were so engrossed in each other that they didn't hear a knock at their door when Leo appeared in their room to discuss the marriage service.

Toon embraced him with a respectful gesture. Ingrid was quiet for a moment regarding the ageless countenance of this man who had that same stocky Dutch build as his twin brother Ben, but his boldness and dress code made him appear as if he could be from an eastern genetic background. His eyes were dark blue, and he observed them with a wise, loving expression.

"Toon, I'm so glad you have found each other for both. We have little time left, but I have seen and read your marriage vows, which you both typed so well to each other, and I'd like to go over them."

"Leo, how is POWAH communicating with me?" Ingrid butted in, determined to get to the bottom of this still unanswered puzzle.

The smile in his eyes deepened as they travelled in astonishment past all the flower arrangements.

"Ingrid science has an uncomfortable way of pushing human beings from centre stage. That is why we all, from the Jaarsma clan, chose to become aware of the computational nature of the universe as a whole; POWAH represents cosmic intelligence. He communicates with us all on a Soul level. We were not designed to be "cut off" from the universal lattice. That has been imposed on humanity by the fallen ones and the rulers of this world.

Ingrid wondered who these fallen once were. Would she recognise them? She saw that Leo had read her thoughts.

"Many people will become aware of their inner guides during the following years, but some of these guides take over our identity and give us a new one, a name, and we are entered into their control system."

"That sounds so scary."

"Yes, indeed, Ingrid, that is why many Soul groups join online, especially on social media pages. They are all trying to mitigate the negative effects the lies still have on many fragmented Souls who are misled. Many more people must wake up and be aware of the dangers."

"You mean the people who kidnapped Ingrid? Does an anti-human agenda control them? Does it have anything to do with CERN and what goes on inside our planet?" Toon asked in a severe tone.

Yes, Toon. Dark energy, a repulsive force responsible for the accelerating expansion of our universe, is the energy of space." Leo was silent for a moment, thinking.

"The fundamental forces that bind atoms together would be powerless against this repulsive dark force. Nothing could ever form galaxies, stars, planets, and life as we know it. Without it, we would not exist."

"That sounds alarming, but I'm not a scientist, so I cannot understand the connection with my project?"

Leo paused, and the silence was almost palatable.

"Toon Trevor and I feel that we may be entering a new era in physics. An era where we have hints that we live in a multiverse that lies frustratingly beyond our reach."

Leo rested on the bed and took Ingrid's hand in his.

"Ingrid, your journal will become the first of a set of volumes written in a way so readers can be the observers and begin to understand the 'bigger picture."

"Toon, we have been discussing how the novel would come about just now."

Leo smiled knowingly.

The hospital noises reminded her of what Annelies had told them, that the following years would bring different changes for many people.

Some would leave the planet, while others would receive a wake-up call to participate in the incredible transformation that would affect everyone. Some, like them, would simultaneously live in both the old and the new worlds.

"Yes, we live in 'times' where the word evolution is taking on a different meaning for us all," Leo replied to her thoughts, nodding his head.

"Already there is evidence that more and more people's 'neocortex', part of the human brain, is rapidly developing so that thought-activated visions are instantly perceived and manifested."

Leo must have seen her frown as she tried to grasp what he was implying.

"Ingrid's spiritual science has an uncomfortable way of pushing human beings out of their comfort zone. Every human being today will be challenged by recognising that what they believed to be true was all lies, told to control the masses."

Lately, there have been so many contradictory rumours about in-credibly violent happenings streaming through the internet, on TV and in the newspapers. Ingrid was ready to remove all these com-munication gadgets altogether. She was thinking of the baby that was growing inside her. What kind of world was it being born in?

"You will both know and be guided when the time comes.

POWAH knows us all intimately, as you know yourself; he knows all our thoughts, fears, and feelings and is within all of us, Ingrid. I'm just a channel for Trevor, who intuitively knew how to connect to a wavelength through the microchip inside the motherboard. There is no easy way to explain how text that shows up on your computer screen, so that you can validate your own experience, is linked to your thoughts.

But it was necessary with you, wasn't it?" Leo's musical voice was both humorous and warm.

"So, we are multi-dimensionally communicating all the time?" She could still not grasp how they blended an intuitive message on a computer screen that answered her thoughts!

"Ingrid, you have the same heightened sensitivity with POWAH as you have with each other. You communicate with him through your Soul senses, meaning that all your psychic channels are simul-taneously experienced. It feeds and sustains you, and it was respon-sible for the two of you meeting so that you could begin to live the unlimited potential that you both have on a higher Soul level."

"POWAH does communicate directly through Annelies as well, doesn't he?"

"He communicates through all of us, but only as individuals do we experience it differently, depending on our individual Souls' expe-riences and the talents of the personality aspects we have attracted in this embodiment."

"Which part of us is real then?"

"The I AM presence you both experience when you feel an unconditional love for each other, that feeling is from your real Soul essence. This spirit spark, your life force, can trigger radiation, which is the animating principle of the physical body. When this activity occurs, as it has with both of you, shafts of light spread through the upper part of your body, not so?"

Ingrid saw Toon smiling at Leo's question.

"Each of our Soul is the totality of the consciousness of all our re-embodiments, but as with most of us, this Soul consciousness is fragmented as your workshops have already revealed." The quietness with which he answered her questions impressed Ingrid no end.

"So, you are saying that Soulmates are people who lived together before but don't necessarily share the I AM presence as we do?"

"Ingrid, in this life experience, your complementary half is Toon. Throughout time, choice brought you together again to make you each consciously aware of yourselves. Only in this divine identity can you reach the cosmic consciousness that will prepare you both to begin your journey of cosmic couplehood."

"Leo, you mean we can awaken how we might physically ascend?"

"Yes, Toon, with the overlay now removed, we can re-access our original blueprints contained in the Akashic records that contain everything we have ever done or experienced. Even that incredible possibility can become a real experience if you are so intent."

"I still don't grasp it. I can accept that this reality is not real, but..."

"Toon, the nature of a morphogenetic field is such that when one individual or a group begin to resonate at a certain level of energy and frequency, it permeates through the rest of the matrix, lifting all up in the process. Reaching full consciousness while having a physical experience means different things to different people, so let's say that we have to awaken to our unity consciousness state as a group Soul first." Toon was trying to read Leo's mind. She could see it from his expression.

"What are morphogenetic fields?" she asked, knowing that Leo waited for a sign from both of them to reveal an understanding.

"Morphogenetic fields are non-physical blueprint codes that give birth to forms. They are centred at the gateway of our hearts, awaiting us to release the illusions that bind us before passing through the pillars and entering a higher realm." Leo replied, smiling.

For the first time, she started to grasp POWAH's role in the scheme of things. Somehow, for her, he represented both her guide, her Higher Self and also the energy that Leo called a group Soul. It always felt as if someone or a force was overseeing them. For now, she would settle for the idea that her Higher Self was connected to a group of Soul energy.

"Let's join the others for your sacred ceremony, shall we? Ingrid, this last letter from POWAY is for your journal. From now on, you will experience your expansion of consciousness together into the twenty-first century. We are all connected in this manner and through our ever-expanding nature, while in this physical form, we activate and unite with Gaia's divine blueprint and beyond."

Thanks, Leo, I needed some form of explanation, even if I can't yet fathom it all." Leo's smile made her feel good.

Leo escorted them to a car to drive to a different building on Utrecht's extensive hospital grounds. Ingrid nervously grabbed Toon's hands in the back seat. She took out the letter, and they both stared at the title.

Dear Kitty and Toon

The Awareness of the Power of Words

• Words like numbers and letters are energy pockets when they are combined.

• Words represent the substance of pure energy.

• Words have a vibrational essence which transcends and goes beyond the interpreted meaning.

• Words can bring into focus certain feelings and perceptions.

• Words cannot only be isolated and created to define the immediate perception from the human perspective.

• Words are much more than they can help, assist, guide, and move our consciousness towards the limitless Wordless.

• Words can only go so far, for words are used only to interpret, label and define.

• Words must flow, so don't contain them.

• Words must be what they are.

• Words point the way but can also get in the way.

Move beyond Words and feel the wordless meaning of being presented.

• Words are only stepping stones to the truth.

• Words can only serve as arrows pointing toward the Inner Truth, the Divine Self, the Real Self, the Higher Self, and the Real You.

All of these concepts are simply words that attempt, from the human perspective, to describe that which is indescribable, which is infinite, which has no boundaries, which has no limits.

Words can only be a medium of exchange between souls that recognise the love and the light of Creation.

Both my beloveds, your awakening journey has started. Practice surrendering the lower will and embracing the higher self. Recognise yourselves as being in a state of grace, and remember that you are always at the right place at the right time and that the I AM of you and the IAM of me are the keepers of the Game.

LOVE POWAH

"The Power of Words. That is the name of Fred and Yolanda's bookshop!" Ingrid whispered.

They both looked at each other in rapture, wordless.

Timmy and Karin were dressed in cute light blue outfits when they arrived. Liesbeth and Hans were their witnesses. The whole chapel was decorated with so many flowers. The fragrance was overwhelming.

The music was the Celtic mood tune that Toon had played the first time in his car. She squeezed Toon's hand tightly, tingling, knowing Toon felt the same.

They stood next to each other, holding two lighted candles, and as Leo began the ceremony, all Ingrid heard were the words they had spoken to each other before in the hospital room, and her mind went back to the dreams she'd had of Toon dancing with her and Toon as a priest...Leo brought her back to the present with the words...

"These two candles symbolise your spiritual nature and your spiritual truth, which shines upon you now and always. Toon and Ingrid, are you both fully committed to the marriage vows you have written for yourselves?"

"Yes, I am," Toon removed the ring next to the candle and gave it to Leo.

"Yes, I am," Ingrid swallowed a lump in her throat before replying to the same question and doing the same with her ring.

Leo held up both rings.

"These two rings symbolise the divine circle of the immortal original, each ring representing both the masculine and feminine polarities that join as one."

"Toon, please repeat after me."

"I, Toon Haardens, ask you, Ingrid Barendse, to be my life partner, wife, lover, friend, supporter, and above all, my twin soul in discovering who I am. At this moment, I declare my intention to treat you with the deepest tenderness, love, and compassion...her mind jumped ahead as if many lifetimes flew past...like a movie...Then Toon's words drew her back "so that we may share all that is good within us and live our full potential for the good of all." Toon kissed her hand tenderly after ending his commitment.

Leo turned to her and asked her, "Ingrid Barendse, do you choose to grant Toon's request for you to become his wife?"

"I do," she said, and she made the same vow; a part of her remembered Toon's words, which he expressed so well. She then took his hand and kissed it. That brought some laughter from the congregation because Toon had difficulty withholding his need to kiss her more profusely. While their eyes locked, she was aware of a sensation of absolute bliss as if they were making love, but this was an experience that transcended the physical union entirely. Leo's voice brought them both back to the chapel with the words;

"Toon and Ingrid, please take these rings and repeat after me:" Toon held her hand, repeating in his low, powerful voice:

"With this ring, my beloved, I take you as my wife so that all may see and know my love for you." *"Kitty, I'm so honoured, so incredibly blessed to have found you to share this momentous occasion with."*

"Oh, my love, I'm so grateful to our creator for having granted me such an incredible person to share my life with," she took his ring and repeated: "I take you as my husband so that all may see and know my love for you."

Toon's gentle expression made her feel so loved and cherished that, again, only Leo's voice brought her attention to what he said.

"I give you each a candle to symbolise your understanding of this sacred ceremony called marriage. I ask you each to light the large candle with your own to symbolise the union of two Souls."

They both approached the enormous beacon, and she saw Toon's grey-blue eyes laughing at her through the large flame they had ignited.

"I pronounce that in the presence of the one living spirit in which we all reside that you are now husband and wife," Leo called out in his musical voice. Ingrid was somewhat shaky when she had to step back and wondered how Toon was doing.

"Love, I feel fine! I think my happiness is holding me up."

"Toon and Ingrid, may your home, wherever that may be, always be a place of happiness for all who enter it; a place for sharing, love, music, and above all, a place for laughter. Toon, you may now kiss your bride," The audience roared at Toon's enthusiastic response.

When they had to sign the register with Liesbeth and Hans, she officially wrote Mrs Ingrid K B Haardens for the first time. She sensed Toon was very exhausted, and Hans took him aside to boost him with his healing energy. The many hugs from everyone were overwhelming, and she rejoiced at seeing each one individually, including friends from work and Annelies' class.

Her now-former father-in-law, Dennis Barendse, congratulated Toon; he had come to terms with the fact that Ed would marry someone else.

When she held Toon's hand again, he looked a lot better. Helen's children were throwing the buttercups around their feet, and Sascia was taking many photos while Debbie had Jenny in her arms.

When they both walked hand in hand out into the glorious sunshine, she heard the music "Are you awake?" in the background. Toon's laughing blue-grey eyes sparkled when she listened to a mental voice very clearly beaming...

"My love, we are the Reality Shifters going home."...

The Jaarsma Tree - The Prinsegracht Hotel

Hetty Jaarsma   Vera Jaarsma   John Jaarsma   Lizzy Jaarsma   Laura&Kitty Jaarsma   Corrie Jaarsma

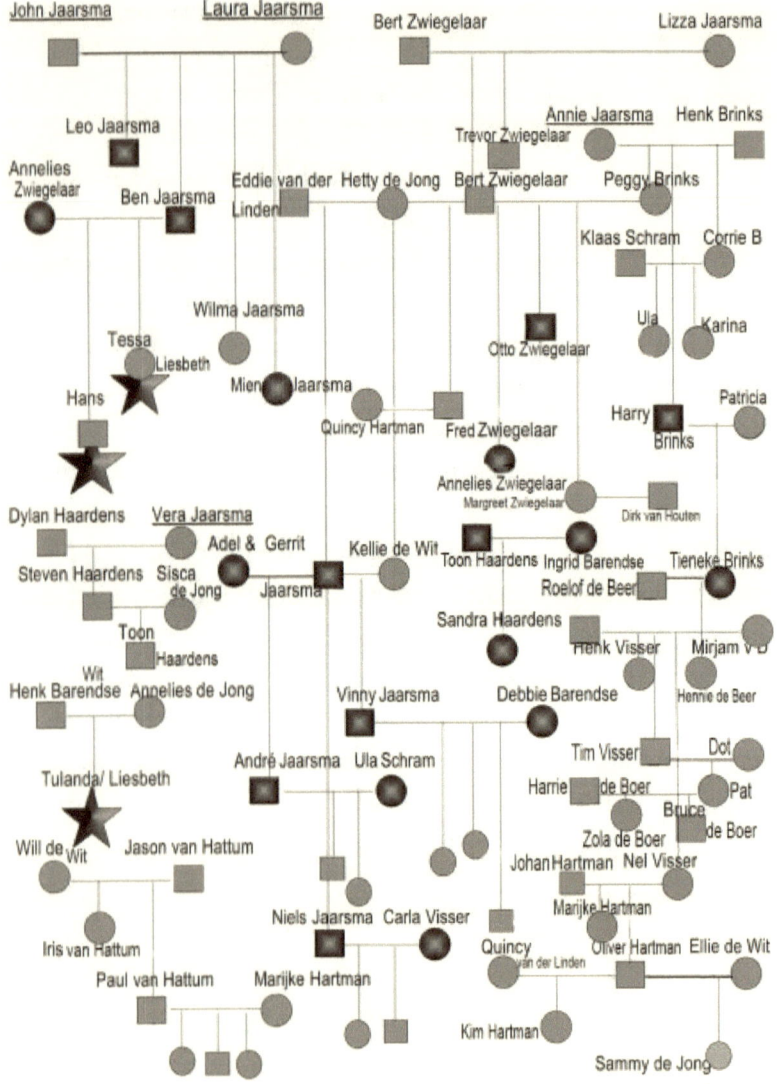

The Jaarsma Tree - Chateau / Half-way House

Hetty Jaarsma   Mien Jaarsma   Anna jaarsma   Corry Jaarsma   Quincy Jaarsma   Wilma Jaarsma

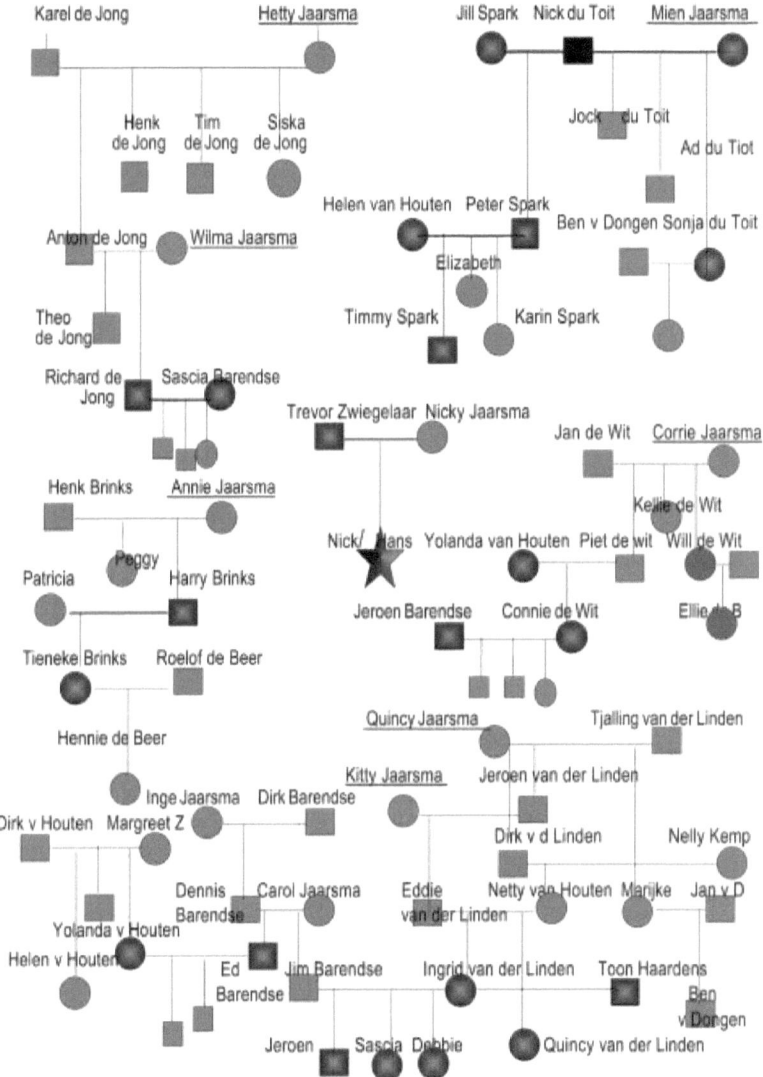

About the Author

The Ascension Journals

I was told during the mid-eighties that there would be a great AWAKENING happening and that people would become highly evolved, wonderful human beings when our reality on Earth would be in great chaos.

My five ascension novels were inspired by dreams I had over the course of twenty-plus years about the five levels of awakening (*as written about in my Language of Light workbook*). I had no idea about the 'timelines' when I started to write the first Level One Ingrid's journal as a visionary fiction novel: The Desire to Become Aware.

Don't miss out!

Visit the website below and you can sign up to receive emails whenever Nadine May publishes a new book. There's no charge and no obligation.

https://books2read.com/r/B-A-NGXEB-KNLZC

BOOKS 2 READ

Connecting independent readers to independent writers.

About the Publisher

In 2001, I published my first novel with Kima Global Publishers. Over the years, I published 12 more titles with the same publisher, who eventually became my husband. Sadly, he passed away in 2023. After much consideration and weighing my options, I have published my two-book series, "The *Self*-Employed Housewife," and the five-book visionary fiction series, "Awakening to our Ascension," under the name 'The Power of Words' through Draft2Digital.I plan to include my Art Therapy books at a later stage. For now, they are still only available locally in SA.

Read more at https://nadinemay.company.site/.

www.ingramcontent.com/pod-product-compliance
Lightning Source LLC
Chambersburg PA
CBHW032255020726
47495CB00001B/118